Raves for the novels of Marshall Ryan Maresca:

"Superb characters living in a phenomenal fantasy world, with a detective story that just sucks you right into the storyline. Marshall Ryan Maresca impressed me with *The Thorn of Dentonhill*, but *A Murder of Mages* has secured me as a fan." —*Fresh Fiction*

"Veranix is Batman, if Batman were a teenager and magically talented. . . . Action, adventure, and magic in a school setting will appeal to those who love Harry Potter and Patrick Rothfuss' *The Name of the Wind*." —*Library Journal* (starred)

"Books like this are just fun to read." —The Tenacious Reader

"The perfect combination of urban fantasy, magic, and mystery." —Kings River Life Magazine

"Marshall Ryan Maresca is some kind of mad genius. . . . Not since Terry Pratchett's Ankh Morpork have we enjoyed exploring every angle of an invented locale quite this much." —B&N Sci-fi & Fantasy Blog

"Maresca's debut is smart, fast, and engaging fantasy crime in the mold of Brent Weeks and Harry Harrison. Just perfect." —Kat Richardson, national bestselling author of *Revenant*

"Fantasy adventure readers, especially fans of spell-wielding students, will enjoy these lively characters and their high-energy story." —*Publishers Weekly*

MARSHALL RYAN MARESCA

THE WAY OF THE SHIELD

A novel of the *Maradaine Elite*

DAW BOOKS, INC.

DONALD A. WOLLHEIM, FOUNDER

375 Hudson Street, New York, NY 10014

ELIZABETH R. WOLLHEIM
SHEILA E. GILBERT
PUBLISHERS

www.dawbooks.com

Published by DAW Books, Inc.
375 Hudson Street, New York, NY 10014.

First Printing, October 2018
1 2 3 4 5 6 7 8 9

Acknowledgments

Several years ago, I had a vision for an interconnected series of books, following four sets of characters, who each have discrete, individual stories, but a larger story brews beneath the surface, each series bringing its own pieces of the puzzle.

Back then, when it was still just ideas and outlines, I laid it all out to my dear old friend, Daniel J. Fawcett. And he said, "That's fantastic, but for it to work, for you to be able to do what you want to do, you're going to need the right editor and the right publisher."

Fortunately for me, Sheila Gilbert and DAW Books were *very much* the right editor and the right publisher. Were it not for Sheila and her astounding faith in this work and my big plan, we wouldn't be here with *The Way of the Shield*, launching the fourth Maradaine-set series, and laying down the foundation for the last pieces of the grander puzzle.

Much thanks also to another old friend, Brendan Gibbs, who helped lay the initial seeds behind Dayne, a hero who fights with his heart, who risks everything to keep people alive.

Of course, there were also my two amazing beta readers, who saw this particular manuscript through a few revisions: Kevin Jewell and Miriam Robinson Gould. They have been there to help me make each book as strong as I can make it. My agent, Mike Kabongo, has been instrumental in making this big, mad plan happen.

And finally, I would not have possibly done this without my family. My parents, Louis and Nancy Maresca, my mother-in-law Kateri Aragon, and most important my wife and son, Deidre and Nicholas. They've made all of this possible.

THE
WAY OF THE
SHIELD

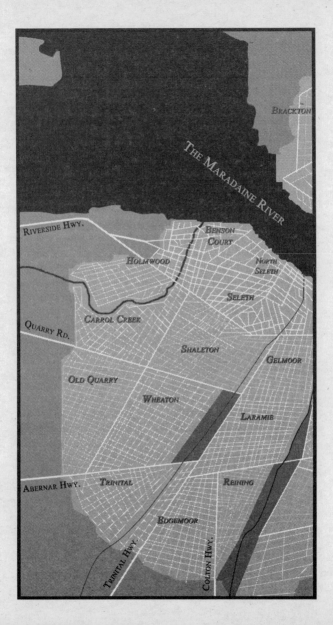

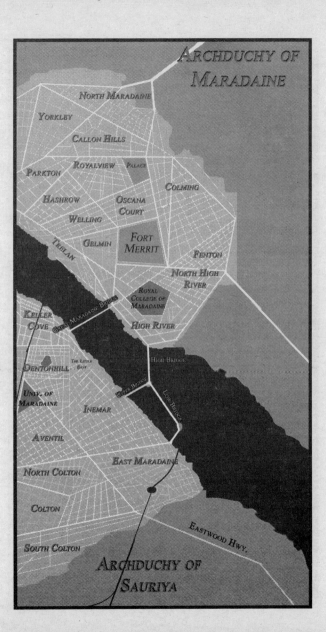

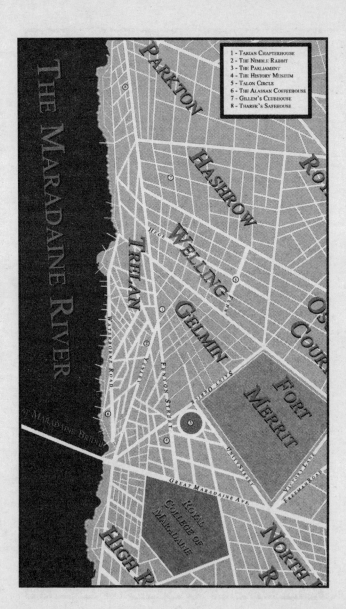

Chapter 1

FROM THE TRELAN DOCKS, on the northern bank of the great Maradaine River, the city of Maradaine smelled of tar, horses, burning oil, and sweat. The scent hit Dayne Heldrin like a wet sack, but he was amazed at how much he missed it, how immediately he recognized it. This wasn't home, but it was very close to it. It was far more home than Lacanja had been for the past two years.

A small crowd gathered right at the foot of the gangplank, demanding the attention of the ship's recent passengers. They shouted and waved, ready to sell trinkets or sweets. Several old men were waiting with rolling carts, anxious to help people with their trunks. Dayne had let most of his fellow passengers leave the ship first, partly from politeness, but mostly in the hope it would thin out this crowd.

"You, you!" one old man called out to him. "You need help, yes?"

Dayne was carrying his trunk over his shoulder. Heavy,

but nothing he couldn't handle. If this man tried to carry it, Dayne feared it would break his spine.

"No, thank you," Dayne said and continued to walk by.

The man pulled his cart along as Dayne walked. "No, sir, please. Allow me."

"I've got it." Dayne knew this aggressive helpfulness was simply this man's way of making of living. The old man's arms were bare, wearing short sleeves in the warm spring sun. A faded tattoo of a ship's helm and hash marks showed he had given twenty years to the Druth Navy. Given the man's age, that had to have been during the war years.

"Then maybe you need a carriage? Or a room to rent?"

"No to both," Dayne said. "I know where I'm staying, and it isn't far."

"Where'd you come from?"

"Lacanja."

"Oh, lovely city," the old man said. "Tell you what, I should have gone there when my tour ended. Could have gone to any city on the coast, and I chose here. Stupid mistake."

"I didn't care for it," Dayne said. That was an understatement. Enough misery and failure had befallen him in his two years in Lacanja to last a lifetime.

A pair of newsboys came up to Dayne as well, holding out newssheets from rival presses.

"Where'd you come from, mister?"

"Why you got a shield, mister?"

"You want to know what's going on, mister?"

"That a real sword, mister?"

"Off, scads," the old man said. "The man's a Tarian Knight. Don't you know anything?" He then snarled, and the boys ran off.

"Tarian Knight" was not the proper term, even if he had been an Adept or Master in the Order. It was a common mistake that Dayne wasn't going to bother to correct. Instead he handed a half-tick coin to the old sailor, and pointed to the small group of men standing on a low crate holding up a crude wooden placard. "The True Line Lives" was painted in blue letters. "I want to know what that's about."

"Foolishness," the old man said, taking the coin. "How long 've you been gone?"

"Two years."

"This doesn't make it down south?"

"First I've seen it."

The old man chuckled. "That's comforting. The stupid hasn't infected the rest of the country."

"Is it dissent against the throne?"

"Against the king, not the throne, to hear those folk. Their whole point—I'm just telling you what they say, I think it's bilge." There was something in his tone that was a bit too apologetic, like he was telling Dayne what he thought Dayne would want to hear.

"I understand," Dayne said. He noticed a few men— dockworkers, oystermen, something of that nature— moving over to the men on the crate, walking with the predatory swagger that comes with a few beers. Men who had the intention to start things. Keeping an eye on them, he nodded for the old sailor to go on.

"It's popped up since the old king died," the sailor said. Dayne had already left for Lacanja before King Maradaine XVII died, and his son took the throne as Maradaine XVIII. Some major news of the royal house had reached him: he knew the new king had married, and then the queen had died in childbirth. He had heard some talk about the Parliament wanting to force the king to remarry to produce an heir. "This sort of thing was even around when Seventeen first took the throne back in the day, but I think you're a bit young for that."

"Yes, but I read about it," Dayne said. The dockworkers were moving in. Dayne got a count of them—eight men, all stout of arm and back. One of the drunken dockworkers had picked up a rock from the ground. Dayne put down his trunk. "One moment."

The dockworker had wound back his arm and hurled the rock at the men on the crate. Dayne dashed across the distance, bringing up his shield. The rock clanged against it and dropped to the ground.

"Step away, gentlemen," Dayne said. "No need for this to escalate."

"Who are you to say what?" the main dockworker asked. He came up, puffing up his shoulders in his approach. This was a man who was clearly used to intimidating people with his height and muscles. With most people, he'd probably succeed.

With Dayne, he had to crane his neck. Dayne was at least a head taller.

"I'm the one who said 'step away.' "

"Ayuh, what's with this fool?" another dockworker said. "Who carries a rutting shield anymore?"

"He's got a sword, too," the third said. That one looked a bit nervous. "And he's in uniform."

"Ain't a constable or river patrol."

"He's a Tarian, you dunces!" the old sailor shouted.

"Look," the lead dockworker said, still trying to stare Dayne down. "We're going to show these traitors we don't like their kind on our docks."

"They have a right," Dayne said.

"You're going to stand up for their disloyal sewage?" He glanced around Dayne to look at the three men on the crate. "You've got a thrashing coming, you do."

"I'm going to defend their right," Dayne said. "Even if they're wrong."

"Wrong to want an unsullied bloodline on the throne?" the center man on the crate snarled back. Dayne sighed a bit. He feared that was what this was about. Some people never move on.

"Shut it," the lead dockworker said.

"Make us!"

"You aren't helping," Dayne muttered.

"Come on, boys," the lead dockworker shouted to his mates. "We've still got numbers here."

"No," Dayne said firmly. "You will leave these men unmolested."

"You're going to stop us?" The rest of them found their courage and took a few steps forward.

"I'm a Tarian," Dayne said. "And I will stand between them and harm."

Dayne wasn't being completely honest with them, but he doubted any of them were familiar enough to read the pips on his uniform collar. To truly call himself a Tarian, he'd have to have reached the rank of Adept. He was just nearing the end of the second year of his Candidacy. He might be promoted to Adept in a few days, but . . .

But that was definitely *not* why he had been recalled to Maradaine.

"You'll get a thrashing, too, Tarian," the dockworker scoffed. "We'll knock you back a whole century, where you belong."

Dayne knew he had to disable the leader in a way that would dissuade the rest from fighting. He knew he could hold off all eight of them, but not without hurting them. And that would hardly be fitting for a Tarian, especially a second-year Candidate hoping to make Adept.

As the dockworker took a swing at Dayne, Dayne crouched down, bringing his shield into the man's chest. Rather than knocking him to the ground, Dayne went up, raising his shield high with the man on top of it.

The man flailed about uselessly while Dayne held him nine feet off the ground.

"Stand down and disperse," Dayne said firmly to the rest. "Before anyone gets hurt."

The dockworkers scattered.

Dayne smirked. Feats of strength usually let him avoid an actual fight. He looked up at the leader. "I'm going to put you down, and you're going to walk away, yes?"

"Yeah, yeah!"

Dayne tilted his shield and let the man slide to the ground in a crumpled heap, and then he scrambled away.

"Thank you—" the leader of the True Line started.

"It's what I'd do for anyone," Dayne said. "No matter how distasteful I find their views."

He went back over to the trunk, which the old sailor was diligently guarding. "So you see what that's about," the old man said.

"I thought it had gone away," Dayne said.

"Yeah, well," the old man said. "New king, he . . . he's not who his father was, you hear? Doesn't inspire the same adulation."

"There is a proper line of succession!" a man on the crate yelled. "You should know, Tarian, of Romaine's Gift."

"Shut your blight hole!" the old man shot back. Dayne had had enough of this encounter. It was well past time to make his way to the Tarian Chapterhouse.

"Thanks, sir," Dayne said, giving him another coin. "You'll excuse me, but I think I see a friend here for me." The man let him go, not arguing with getting two ticks for little effort. And, indeed, on the far side of the dock, standing up on a tall crate, there appeared to be a Tarian Initiate, searching the crowds.

Grandmaster Orren had sent someone to escort him. Even if it was just an Initiate, that could not be a good sign. This was not to be a joyous homecoming.

Jerinne Fendall hated running errands for Grandmaster Orren. Especially when the errands were clearly pointless. Escort an arriving Tarian Candidate from the Trelan docks. Jerinne failed to see why she was needed for that. This Candidate—Dayne Heldrin—was more than capable of getting to the chapterhouse on his own. He would hardly need the help of a second-year Initiate. And it seemed like it was *always* Jerinne who got this sort of assignment when she should be running drills.

Not that she voiced such complaints. There was no chance she would let the Grandmaster have any idea that she was anything less than thrilled to go to the docks and wait the entire day away for Heldrin. Miss today's training session? More than happy, Grandmaster, don't think a thing of it. Never mind Second-Year Trials. Never mind that Shield Sequence Eight was still tripping her up. If she could please the Grandmaster with a pointless waste of time, then that would be what she would do.

Madam Tyrell was probably showing all the other second-year Initiates some special maneuver right now. The secret to passing Second-Year Trials. All because Jerinne was missing session. She was doomed to wash out, and Madam Tyrell would make sure of that.

Where the blazes was this Heldrin fellow? Not that Jerinne had any idea what the man looked like. He could have walked right past her and Jerinne would never have known. That would be a laugh. She'd lose the whole day for nothing. All the Grandmaster told her was, "You can't miss him."

The Grandmaster was clearly underestimating Jerinne's ability to miss someone. She still had the worst record at archery amongst the second-years.

The Trelan docks were choked with people. People of all shapes and sizes and hues pressed and pushed their way on and off of ships and barges. Several merchants tried to shove dead fish or live boys at Jerinne. She politely declined all offers. Not that she could purchase such things—even if she wanted them—having no money on her person. Life as a Tarian Initiate wasn't supposed to involve poverty, but in Jerinne's case, that was her only option. Her Initiacy had barely been sponsored, with no further stipend beyond the most meager of living expenses.

What would she do if she washed out? Would Baroness Fortinare even take her back into the household? Probably, out of pity, but she'd surely never rise higher than kitchen maid. Cheese in the rain would have better chances.

She couldn't let that happen. She'd find Heldrin, get him back to the chapterhouse and work Shield Sequence Eight until her arm fell off. She'd go to blazes before she'd wash from Trials.

Jerinne pushed her way over to a pile of crates and climbed on top. Then, at least, she could get a better view, and Heldrin might notice her Initiate jersey and approach her.

Glancing about, she saw a flash of metal in the morning sun. Was that a shield? Who else would even be carrying a shield but a Tarian, even if he was only a Candidate? She put her hand over her brow to cut back the glare. Definitely a shield. And a traveling cloak of Tarian gray.

Also the man in question towered head and shoulders above everyone else around him, traveling case over one shoulder. Blazes, the Grandmaster was right. She couldn't miss this one. Plus, since the man had a shield on his arm and a sword at his belt, the crowd gave him a wide berth that they didn't grant to anyone else. Maybe if Jerinne had come armed as well, she'd have had an easier time with the crowd.

He had looked up and noticed Jerinne. That made it easier.

Jerinne cupped her hands around her mouth. "Mister Heldrin!"

The man gave a sharp wave and crossed through the sea of people to Jerinne's crates.

"You have me at the advantage, Initiate," Heldrin said.

Jerinne climbed down most of the way, standing on the lowest crate so she could approach eye level with the man. Saints, he was absurdly tall. "Jerinne Fendall," she said, extending her hand. "I was sent to escort you to the chapterhouse, Mister Heldrin."

"It's Dayne," he said. He put down his case, which Jerinne realized was a full steamer trunk, and took Jerinne's hand with his massive grip. "I'm sorry they wasted your time on that. I know my way around perfectly well."

Jerinne jumped down to the ground, pointing to the trunk. "I presume you don't need a hand with that, either?"

"Not really," Dayne said. "But the Grandmaster sent someone anyway, right? I imagine it was inevitable." He said this last part to himself, resigned.

"I wasn't told much anything, other than to meet you, and escort you back."

Dayne picked up the trunk with ease and hoisted it back over his shoulder. He gave a gesture toward the main street. "This was the Grandmaster's way of making sure I knew that he knew I was arriving today. I'm familiar with his methods."

"I thought you were from Lacanja," Jerinne said. Dayne spoke like he was familiar with the Grandmaster and the Maradaine Chapterhouse.

Dayne's face fell slightly as he led Jerinne out of the crowd. "I was there for my Candidacy. I did my Initiacy here." He sighed. "Of course, where I'm from is Upper Kisan, about a hundred miles northwest of here."

Jerinne grinned. "Trinital, myself. Small manor house in the same vicinity."

Dayne nodded. "I thought you might be from the Sharain." He narrowed his eyes at Jerinne. "Let me guess. Noble house, you the promising child of a loyal member of the staff?"

"That's right," Jerinne said. "My mother was the baroness's lady's maid, and my father the under butler."

"My father was the horse steward," Dayne said. "You and I, we're special cases in the Order. You've probably noticed."

Jerinne would be lying if she said otherwise. Most of

the other Initiates, if they didn't come from the city, were from the gentry or at least artisan families. There were very few people born to the service class in the Elite Orders.

Such as the Orders were in this day. But for Jerinne, it was the only chance to improve her station.

Dayne looked at her like he understood all that at a glance. "That's probably why Grandmaster Orren sent you to fetch me. Come on, we shouldn't waste any more of your time. I would guess you have Trials coming soon."

"Next week," Jerinne said. "I'm missing a session right now. Even under Grandmaster's orders, I'm sure Madam Tyrell will grind me down for it."

"Madam Tyrell?" Dayne's deep voice cracked. "Would that be Amaya Tyrell?"

"I'm not supposed to call her that," Jerinne said.

"Is she the Initiate Prefect?" he asked. "That's usually a job for a first-year Candidate."

"No, sir, she runs the training drills."

"As a Candidate?"

"No," Jerinne said. What was this guy on about? "She's an Adept, of course."

Dayne stopped dead for an instant, bright face darkening. After a moment, he pursed his lips. "Let's hurry up. You don't want to keep Madam Tyrell waiting."

Chapter 2

THE CHAPTERHOUSE LOOKED EXACTLY as he had remembered it. Dayne immediately chided himself for thinking it would be otherwise. He had only been away for two years, and the house had stood for nearly four hundred. Save for new coats of paint, precious little had been changed over the centuries.

He entered through the iron gates to the outer courtyard, cobblestone pathways through pebble gardens. Almost on instinct, Dayne started along the pathway leading to the Initiate barracks, where he had spent most of his three years when he had been here.

He had gotten around one corner of the building when he saw them—the group of Initiates going through their drills, instructions called out by the Adept in front of them. She had her back to Dayne, but he recognized Amaya easily, her long hair tied back the way she always used to. The only thing different about her was her gray tunic had the blue trim of an Adept.

"I want you to move, Initiates. If it's not hurting, you

aren't pushing hard enough. Sink into that lunge, Gendon. Down, deeper! You control your body, it does not control you!"

Training speech from Master Denbar, word for word.

He was proud of her, but he couldn't understand how she could already hold that rank. Promotion to Adept after only one year of Candidacy was unheard of—technically possible, but unprecedented. How had word of it not reached Lacanja?

And if he hadn't heard about her, how much had she heard about what he had done these past two years? About Master Denbar?

Jerinne tapped on his shoulder. "Mister Hel—Dayne. I think you should report to Grandmaster Orren in his sanctum."

"Right," Dayne said, turning back around the corner before Amaya noticed him. "I know the way. Go join your training."

Jerinne saluted him and ran over. Dayne didn't permit himself another look at Amaya. He'd have to talk to her eventually, but he'd prefer to hold that off for as long as he reasonably could. He silently cursed himself for the cowardice, but this was not the moment. The Grandmaster was waiting for him, and she was teaching. When they spoke, he would want to have the time to do it properly. She deserved to know what happened to Master Denbar.

The Grandmaster's sanctum was the southeast tower of the main house, in as much as a single room built over the top floor could be considered a tower. Dayne was surprised how quiet the chapterhouse was as he made his way up the steps. There should be other Initiates, Candidates, and Adepts going about their business, if not at least the household staff. The Lacanja house always seemed filled with activity during the day, even with only a handful of members in residence. Dayne barely saw a soul, and those he did spot kept a respectful distance.

There was no door at the top of the stairs leading into the sanctum, simply a wide arch, opening out into the bright white stone room. Windows filled every wall, their curtains pulled back, providing a glorious view of the river and the southern part of the city on one side, and the household courtyard and much of the sprawling skyline of northern Maradaine, including the royal palace and the shining white dome of the Parliament. Dayne left his shield and sword at the archway and stepped inside.

Grandmaster Orren sat quietly in one corner of the room, reading a small leather tome. The Grandmaster dressed very simply, with only a gray tunic and trousers, absently flexing his bare feet while he read.

Dayne stood silently, waiting for the Grandmaster to note and address him. The Grandmaster surely knew he was there, and as Dayne recalled, loved giving Initiates and Candidates lessons in patience.

After a moment, Grandmaster Orren closed his book and looked up, a polite smile crossing his white-bearded face. "Dayne. It is most agreeable to see you."

"I'm always happy to be seen," Dayne said.

"Your trip was safely uneventful, I presume? No mischief found its way to you?"

"Nor I to it."

"Excellent." The Grandmaster bounded onto his feet, his body still graceful and lean despite his nearly sixty years. "I think enough troubles have crossed your door for one lifetime."

Dayne shook his head. "A Tarian doesn't back away from the troubles on his door. Or the door of his neighbor."

"Of course not." Grandmaster Orren closed the distance between them, gently touching Dayne on the arm. "But we all must lay down our shield sooner or later."

"With due respect, sir, I would hold my shield for as long as I had strength to hold it."

The Grandmaster chuckled ruefully. "You have such

purity of purpose, Dayne. I've always thought so. That's why it pains me so much to have to tell you this."

"Tell me what, Grandmaster?" Dayne's heart dropped. This destroyed all hope that he had been recalled to Maradaine for good news. Not that Dayne deserved any.

The old man sighed. "Come, sit with me." He did not return to his chair, but sat on the floor, legs in winged-bird position. Dayne sat and mimicked the form.

After a moment of contemplation, the Grandmaster spoke. "At the end of the week, I will advance eighteen Candidates, from chapterhouses all around Druthal, to the rank of Adept."

"Eighteen?" Dayne asked. That was wrong. "Twenty-four is the traditional number of Adepts chosen every year."

"It will be eighteen this year, and for the foreseeable future." Grandmaster Orren's shoulders sagged, as if suddenly heavily burdened. "I shouldn't tell you this now, but I want to be honest with you. You will not be among those eighteen."

That hit Dayne in the stomach, far harder than he thought it would. Of course he couldn't presume to make Adept this year, though he had hoped otherwise. Second-year Candidates receiving the Advancement was uncommon, but far from unheard of. Despite the disappointment, he said, "I understand."

"I don't think you do, Dayne. You see, there are many complex elements involved in Advancement, and it's a more political business than you are aware of." He leaned in closer, lowering his voice. "And that is your great tragedy, dear boy."

"My tragedy, sir?"

Grandmaster Orren sighed. "This is not something any Candidate, or even most Adepts, are aware of, but I believe you deserve to understand the full weight of what will happen to you. You see, my list of Candidates for Advancement needed to be approved by the Parliament."

That was a surprise. "Why does the Parliament have any say? The Charter of the Tarian Order predates—"

The answer was a snap. "Because times change and our Order is not—" Grandmaster Orren stopped himself. "You know your history of the Elite Orders, yes?"

"Of course, sir."

"So you can tell me what happened to the Marenian Order."

"They were folded into the Druth Navy when it was founded."

"And the Hanalian Order?"

"Repurposed into the King's Marshals in the eleventh century."

"Of the twelve Elite Orders, which ones still stand?"

Dayne sighed. "Only the Tarians and the Spathians."

"And why those two?"

"Because we have maintained tradition and discipline—"

That earned Dayne a smack across the head. "That is a lie we tell ourselves, that our Orders persevered due to our purity. The Spathians probably believe it. We shouldn't. Why those two?"

Dayne knew the real answer, as he knew his history very well. "The Spathians because of Oberon Micarum. And us, because of Xandra Romaine."

Romaine's Gift. Her gift to the royal line, and to the Tarian Order. Fifty years ago, a Poasian assassin broke into the royal palace and killed King Maradaine XV, the queen, and the two eldest princes. Xandra Romaine, a Tarian Adept assigned to protect the queen, gave her life to stop the assassin before he murdered his final target: the infant Pomoraine, the king's grandson from his eldest son. After much deliberation, it was decided that Prince Escarel, the youngest of the king's sons, would be crowned King Maradaine XVI. But Escarel was serving as Prince Commander in the Island War against the Poasians. He refused to leave the front, and chose to spend his reign as King Commander of the Druth forces in the islands. He did send his pregnant wife—a Napolic native—back to Maradaine to be queen. Years later his son, despite his mixed heritage, became Maradaine XVII.

But many felt that Pomoraine should have been named king, despite still being in swaddling—the True Line of Maradaine. Many people felt Xandra Romaine gave her life to save the true line, and that gift should be honored. That gave the Tarians political support, allowing their order to survive when so many others had dissolved.

The Grandmaster pulled Dayne out of his reverie. "Those two reasons are already very thin threads, ours almost gone from living memory. So we must play the game with those who see us as relics. We must maintain beneficial relations with the Crown and the Parliament, and thus concessions are made." He waved his hand dismissively. "Most of the time, parliamentary approval is merely a formality. The list is sent to the committee, who accept my decision, and it is of no matter."

"So why is this different? And why tell me?"

"Because the head of that particular committee, Dayne, is Wesley Benedict."

The name was another hammer to the gut. "Lenick's uncle?" That's what this was about.

"One of them. There are actually four Benedicts in Parliament. The family wields considerable power and influence in their archduchy, and with the current government."

"I'm aware," Dayne said. "I'm fairly sure I voted for one last year."

Another chuckle from the Grandmaster. "I wouldn't be surprised."

"I did what I could. I did my best! And Lenick Benedict is still alive thanks to . . ." Dayne trailed off.

"Thanks to who?" the Grandmaster pressed. "Who should that boy, and his very powerful family, thank for the condition he is in?"

"For being alive? Master Denbar," Dayne said. That was the truth.

"And you."

"But the condition he's in, what happened to his body, that falls on the man called Sholiar."

The Grandmaster made an odd noise and nodded. "Sholiar, yes. I have on my desk a collection of news-sheets from Lacanja over the past two years. I fear they paint a poor picture of Master Denbar seeking glory, and you being swept up in that."

"That isn't what happened."

"Well, I don't know what happened, beyond what these reports tell me. I know Master Denbar and you became infamous in Lacanja, to the chagrin of the local Constabulary. Then there was this Sholiar person. I don't know what to make of that. Constabulary says he isn't real, that no one saw—"

"I saw him, sir." Dayne would never forget that face. "He was—"

Grandmaster Orren pushed over him. "And when Lenick Benedict was kidnapped, the two of you—"

Dayne scrambled to his feet, unable to sit still a moment longer. "We did what the Benedicts asked us to do!"

"Peace, Dayne, peace," Orren said, waving him to sit down. "I have these newssheets. I have Constabulary accounts. I don't have your story."

Dayne sighed, taking the floor again. "It did begin with the newssheets praising Master Denbar and me for things we did in the city, helping people."

"Which Master Denbar should have known better than to court. I do not blame you for that. You were the Candidate there."

"Master Denbar felt that while it lauded us personally, it served the good of the Order."

Orren made a very pained face, and nodded solemnly. "Go on."

"So he cooperated with and encouraged the praise, which captured Sholiar's attention. Lenick Benedict may have been his victim, but we were his target . . . "

"Thank you both for coming. Now, we need you to follow these instructions to the letter."

These were the first words said when Dayne and Master Denbar came into the Lacanja Dockside Stationhouse on urgent summons, escorted to a back room where Lieutenant Stenson and Mister Benedict waited for them. Dayne didn't appreciate a Constabulary lieutenant talking down to either him or Master Denbar, but he did his best to hold his tongue and show respect.

Master Denbar clearly didn't feel quite the same way.

"Let me guess, because you already tried doing it your way and failed?"

The lieutenant glowered, but he didn't deny it. "If I had my way, you throwbacks wouldn't be anywhere near this." He gestured at the two of them, dressed in their Tarian tunics, shields on their arms and swords at their belt. Dayne would admit that they looked like something out of an old portrait, especially in the Constabulary House, surrounded by uniformed officers with badges and crossbows. Dayne didn't care. He was proud to be wearing the traditional garb and arms of the Order.

"Let me explain," said Mister Benedict—Ortin Benedict, a minor member of the powerful family, but still a man of influence and position in Lacanja. Despite his calm voice and demeanor, there was something almost wild about his eyes. Like a man who hadn't slept in days. "How long have you two been here?"

"Nearly two years," Master Denbar said.

"Have you heard of the Sholiar Murders?"

"A bit," Dayne said. "Some sort of thing with traps or machines or something?"

"Some sort of thing like that," Benedict said ruefully.

Lieutenant Stenson continued. "For the past few years, we've had waves where people are grabbed off the street—some rich and prominent, some common folk—and then found a few days later, dead in some unholy, elaborate torture device. Sometimes there are demands issued, sometimes not. There are never any witnesses, we have nothing resembling a suspect, but we do have a name. Sholiar. He—whoever he is—always signs his work and sends us taunts."

"And you think this is all the same person."

"The taunts typically include details only the true Sholiar would know. If it is a person. Some of the boys here think it's something else, like actually an immortal Sinner returned to make us suffer."

"So how does this apply now?" Master Denbar asked, giving Dayne a look that told him he should just listen.

"He's taken my son," Benedict said. "Lenick, he's fifteen years old. And this time, he's issued demands. Demands that name the two of you." He held out a letter that Master Denbar grabbed.

"Sixty thousand crowns in goldsmith notes? Seems like a rather mortal request to me."

"Delivered by you two, to this address on the docks," Lieutenant Stenson said. "I will point out this was the second request he sent, and this is the second address."

"You handled the first one on your own, and found it . . . wanting?"

"Empty, save for the traps that killed three of my men," Stenson said. "Now, whatever this place is on the docks? It's surely a trap as well. But it's a trap that Sholiar wants to put the two of you—the Elite Heroes of the Tarian Order—through. So we need you to do this."

Master Denbar nodded. He had been well aware of the high praise the two of them had received in the local newssheets, all for performing what Dayne thought were the basic acts of decency and defense that the Tarian Order was built on. Master Denbar had welcomed that praise. It reminded people that the Tarians were still around, a vital part of Druth life and history. Dayne agreed—that was exactly why he had joined, and hoped to finish his Candidacy to move up to Adept at the end of this cycle in a month. After being so highly lauded in his Initiacy, receiving the honor after only two years as a Candidate was not uncommon. Master Denbar himself had written to Grandmaster Orren advocating it.

"Then give us the crowns," Master Denbar said, "and we'll be about it."

"Sweet saints, man, read the instructions!" Stenson said. "You need to go unarmed. Leave your swords and shields here."

Master Denbar shrugged, and removed his sword and shield, handing them over to the lieutenant. Dayne took his cue from the master, and did the same.

"This is madness," Benedict said. "They'll be defenseless!"

"We're Tarians, Mister Benedict," Master Denbar said. "We may be unarmed, but we are never defenseless."

Chapter 3

*D*AYNE AND MASTER DENBAR approached the docks in question, a nearly abandoned part of the harbor where every warehouse and boathouse was dilapidated and decrepit.

"Perfect place for this Sholiar to set up his traps," Master Denbar said.

As instructed, they were carrying a satchel with sixty thousand crowns in goldsmith exchange notes from reputable houses in northern cities, and they were unarmed.

The only light was from the moons, and those were obscured by the clouds of the evening rains.

A woman holding a tarp over her head approached them. "Are you the Tarians?"

"Are you Sholiar?" Master Denbar asked.

"No!" She looked to be in a panic just from Master Denbar saying the name. "I'm just supposed to give you a message."

"From . . . him?" Dayne asked.

She nodded. "You're to go to that boathouse. The old

man is to bring the money through the east entrance, and the young man go in through the west."

"Why would we do that?"

"He said you would ask. He said if both doors aren't opened at the same time, the boy will be killed."

Dayne nodded. "Did you see him? Or the boy he has?"

"I never saw a face. He wears a mask. A grotesque mask!" She broke into tears. "I'm just telling you what he said, I swear!"

"Ma'am," Master Denbar said gently, "what sway does he hold over you?"

"My husband," she said. "He's holding him somewhere. Said he would die if I didn't do this!"

"It's all right," Master Denbar said. "We will try to help him as well. I swear."

They left her and made their way over to the boathouse.

"Surely it's a trap, sir."

"Of course it's a trap. Not that knowing that will really help us at all."

"Maybe it will," Dayne said. "Let's not quite play his game."

"Dayne, that could be very dangerous. From what we've seen, this Sholiar is quite capable of designing a trap that will fire if both doors are not opened at once."

"Yes," Dayne said, taking the sack of bills. "But what if we switch doors?"

The Master nodded. "I see your thinking. If we presume he's studied us, than each door is a trap he's concocted specifically for us. By subverting that—"

"We might overcome his traps."

"I think it's a capital idea. To your door and call out a count."

Dayne took his position, sack in hand. Despite the master's confidence earlier, he would have preferred some sort of weapon. While waiting for the master to get into position, he noticed a handful of barrels by the door. He *grabbed the lid of one. It wasn't much, but it could serve as a rudimentary shield.*

"Ready, Dayne?" the master called. "One, two, three!"

The boathouse door opened easily enough. As soon as he pushed it open, a series of clicks and pops fired around the frame. Instinctively, Dayne pulled back, but the only things that appeared to have been triggered were a dozen oil lamps, lighting all at once.

If this Sholiar could be counted on for anything, it was showmanship.

There was a short hallway, newly constructed, with a door on the other end. The wood of the walls was completely different from the outside of the boathouse. Dayne took two steps and something clicked in the floor. The outer door swung shut, and then the hallway walls started to move. They slowly started to narrow, squeezing Dayne in.

Dayne immediately braced his back against one wall and pushed at the other. It continued to close in on him for a moment, but soon he could hear the gear work grinding as it fought against his strength. Then there was a hideous snap and the closing stopped.

"That's all you have?" Dayne asked himself. Of course, this meant his idea worked—Master Denbar wasn't anywhere near as strong as he was. He would have been stuck, if not killed, by the trap. Dayne pushed his way through the narrow passage to the door. It was latched, but he kicked his way through it. In a few moments, it was open, and he entered the rest of the boathouse.

The boathouse was sizable, large enough for the great yacht moored inside. It was a handsome craft, though there were far more ropes tied to it than should be necessary to keep it in the boathouse. Dayne glanced about. Ropes and pulleys and gears all around. The whole place was one big trap.

Standing on the dock was a man dressed in what looked like an old-style Kieran theatrical robe. He also wore a grand ceramic mask with a great frowning face on it. At the end of the dock was the yacht, rigged up to sail. The ropes tied to the dock were the only thing keeping it from shooting out into the bay. On the deck of the yacht, a small figure sat, struggling against his bonds, with a sack over his head.

That must be Lenick Benedict.

There were also ropes tied around his feet, which appeared to be fastened to gear-work devices on the dock.

"No step farther, Tarian-to-be," a voice echoed from the masked figure. Northern accent, highly educated, dripping with oil. "Or not-to-be, I would think."

"Are you Sholiar?" Dayne asked.

"Sholiar is speaking to you," he said. He raised a hand, holding two ropes. "You know what happens when I pull these?"

"Something hideous, I'm sure." Dayne held the satchel up high. "You want this, you let him go."

"You want him to go free, you'll do this how I tell you, Tarian-to-be." Every time Sholiar spoke it echoed about. Dayne was wondering why Master Denbar hadn't emerged yet. Was he stuck in a trap? If he was, Dayne knew he would want him to continue on, save the boy.

"What do you want me to do, Sholiar?"

From behind the mast something flew out, running on a pulley line. It came to a stop a few feet in front of Dayne—a simple cloth sack.

"Put the bills in the sack."

Dayne held the satchel open. "Bills are here. Come take a look if you need to. But they don't go anywhere until Lenick is out the door."

"Is that how it is?"

"If you want the money."

"I'd like the money, to be sure. But I don't need it. Not like you need the boy to go free."

"The boy goes free, Sholiar. I'm afraid I must insist." He moved toward the dock.

Two steps forward, Dayne knew he had made a mistake. The floor clicked underneath him, and he felt a spring release, gears spinning beneath him. The ropes tied to Lenick's arms and legs tightened. The walls near the other entrance, where Master Denbar had come in, fell open to reveal a cage, with the Master trapped inside.

"It's started now," Sholiar said. "You put it into motion. This boat is about to launch into the bay. And the ropes will pull him apart unless you do what I say. And the pendulums up there will smash into your Master."

Dayne looked up, now noticing a series of giant curved blades hanging on ropes up on the ceiling. As if on cue, one dropped down, the blade going right between the bars of the Master's cage, barely missing his side.

"Save the boy, Dayne!"

"Bills in the sack, Candidate!" Sholiar shouted.

Dayne surged forward. He grabbed the sack and shoved the bag of bills inside it. "There! I did it!"

"Shame, though. You broke the rules. It was supposed to be you in the cage, and your Master facing the choice." Another blade dropped from the ceiling. Master Denbar had nowhere to go in the cage, and the blade went through his arm, pinning him.

"You have the money, let them go!" Dayne shouted. The sack was now riding along the pulley system over to the boat, and dropped down onto the deck next to the boy.

"Why, when this is more fun?" Sholiar yanked the ropes, and then all the things holding the boat in place released. It surged out into the bay, then stopped briefly when the ropes of the boy's legs went taut. In the same moment, the next blade dropped from the ceiling.

"Save him, Dayne!" the Master shouted.

Dayne wasted no time. Taking hold of the barrel lid, he hurled it with all of his might at Sholiar. It smashed into pieces and sent the man flying. Dayne paid him no mind as he charged down the dock to the end. The boat was straining against the ropes tied to the boy's legs. The child must be in agony, as he continued to strain at his bonds.

Then, just as Dayne was about to dive into the water, the legs suddenly flew off the boy. Dayne stopped in shock. Then, a moment later, the boy stood up, revealing perfectly good legs that were hidden beneath his body. Then his bonds came flying off, as if the ropes that held him were nothing but an elaborate jacket. That came fluttering over to the dock as the figure took it off.

Dayne saw it was still connected to the dock by a series of wires.

Then the man on the boat took off the sack on his head, revealing himself to be a balding man, with wild eyes and mad teeth.

"That was incredible, old top!" he shouted from the boat. "That was more beautiful than I could have hoped!"

Dayne glanced back to the boathouse. The figure in the Kieran robes lay flat on the dock, his mask having fallen off. This was the boy, Lenick Benedict, gagged beneath the mask. Dayne rushed to him, tearing open the robes. His body had been rigged up with an elaborate series of cords and pulleys, making him into a marionette, with a copper pipe of some sort connected to the mask.

The boy was unconscious, his chest covered in massive bruising from where Dayne had hit him with the barrel lid. The puppetry-work had also dug into his flesh, but none of it had done the sort of damage that Dayne had caused.

But still, the boy breathed. That was something. Dayne hadn't completely failed. He needed to get Yellowshields, and quickly, for both the boy and Master Denbar.

Dayne looked up to the cage. All the curved blades had fallen, and Master Denbar had been unable to get clear of them. His body had been pierced by five of the blades.

There was no sign of life in him at all.

Dayne's recounting was interrupted by a strangled cry by the entrance. Both he and the Grandmaster looked to see Amaya—still perfect and crisp in her Adept uniform, despite the tears streaming down her face.

"Master Denbar?" she choked out.

"Amaya, I—" Dayne started. He wasn't sure what else to say. Master Denbar had been a mentor and a friend to both of them in their Initiacy, and it had devastated her when he had chosen Dayne to go with him to Lacanja. The last time they had spoken, she hadn't forgiven Dayne for it. Of course, at that point they were both just starting their first year of Candidacy. Now she was an Adept . . .

"Amaya, this is not a moment for you," Grandmaster Orren said. "I will seek you out to discuss this in short order."

She nodded. "Yes, sir." Before she left, she gave Dayne one last look, a hundred emotions playing out over her face.

Orren waited for a moment, and then turned back to Dayne. "I'm going to insist you leave that to me. I should have told her weeks ago when we first received the news."

"She deserved to know. Master Denbar—"

"We are not here to address my failings, Dayne, as abundant as they might be."

"Yes, sir," Dayne said.

"Now, I know from the Constabulary reports that they never saw this Sholiar character, and they doubted you did, either. And that the only reason you were not charged with a crime was the fact that they had invited you to participate in the rescue of Lenick."

"Ortin Benedict wanted me charged," Dayne said. "Screamed up and down that I had to pay for what happened to his son."

"Which was?"

Dayne knew Master Orren knew the answer to this question, and he wanted Dayne to say it out loud.

"His spine was broken. He'll never walk, father children. He'll need constant care by nurses for the rest of his life. Because of me."

"You were tricked."

"I still did it," Dayne said. "I can't deny that. I may have been tricked, but I should have been more aware. I should have paid closer attention. Thinking back, it was so obvious."

"You made a grave error, but you did so in the sincere belief you were saving lives. I cannot fault that."

Dayne nodded. "I appreciate that, sir."

"However, while I cannot, Ortin Benedict and the rest of his family are a different situation. With his uncle Wesley on the committee, it is out of my hands."

"And the authority falls to them? How?"

"Because it does, Dayne. That is the reality of our Order in the present. We are beholden to the Parliament, and to this committee. Therefore, your name will not get past this committee as it stands. Not this year. Not next year."

"Not next year? Sir, you—you can't be serious. If I don't receive—" He stopped himself from saying what the Grandmaster was perfectly aware of: if he didn't receive Advancement after his third year of Candidacy, he was out. He would no longer be one of the Tarian Order. He paced the floor, forcing the nervous energy in his body to work through his legs so he wouldn't do anything foolish with his hands.

"I am aware of what I'm saying." The Grandmaster rose to his feet as well. "It gives me great pain to say it."

"So I will never be a Tarian Adept?" Dayne couldn't hide the bitterness in his voice. His heart was raw, torn by this news. It was not befitting a Tarian, he knew, but this was too much injustice to bear.

It's not an injustice at all, he thought. Deep in his heart, he knew: he had failed Lenick Benedict, failed his calling. That boy would bear the burden of his failure in his broken body until the end of his days. Losing his station, his right to the Tarian Order, that was only a sliver of the fair price for him to pay.

He hadn't even noticed that he had sunk to his knees,

hot tears pouring down his cheeks, until the Grandmaster had handed him a handkerchief. He wiped his face and composed himself as the Grandmaster meandered over to the window. "I'm terribly sorry, sir. That was unbecoming."

"No apology is needed."

Dayne stood back up. "I presume you'll be wanting my shield, tunic, and amulet."

The Grandmaster turned back to Dayne, raising on eyebrow. "Absolutely not!"

"But you made it quite clear there's no chance—"

The Grandmaster's eyes narrowed, the slightest of grins on his lips. "Even if there is no chance, what will you do?"

Dayne had been asked the question many times as an Initiate. He needed no further coaching. "Stand and hold and fight."

The grin broke out wide. "Exactly! Candidacy lasts three years, and no man named Benedict or Parliament committee can take that from you. At least not yet. The world may change on us again. It may be in another year, the Benedicts will ease their hearts, or at least yield their seat on that committee. Hope is never futile, even if it's the barest of embers."

Dayne nodded. "Hold my shield in front of my chest, for I hold my heart upon it."

The Grandmaster gave a dismissive wave, "Yes, I know you can quote doctrine. No need for more of that."

"As you say, sir."

The Grandmaster came back over, putting a hand on Dayne's shoulder. "And since you have another year of Candidacy, this roof stays over your head for that time. But you should start to consider what other options the future might hold for you."

"This is the only future I ever wanted."

The Grandmaster nodded, patted Dayne's shoulder, and sighed. Dayne knew not to push further, the old man was going to change the subject. "The girl who collected you, where did she go off to?"

"She wanted to get to training with Am—Madam Tyrell."

The Grandmaster's eyebrow went up again. "Yes, I imagine that she would. Her technique is . . . solid, and she has a lot of dedication to her physical skills. But I wonder about her heart. Do me the favor of keeping an eye on her, help her if you can. Find out if her heart is truly that of a Tarian."

"I don't know if I'm your man for that, sir."

"Trust me, Dayne." The old man put his hand on Dayne's chest. "I can't think of anyone whose heart is more true than yours."

Dayne blushed, and stepped away, bowing his head. "I will see what I can do. Will that be my official duty?"

The Grandmaster shrugged. "For the time being. We are right upon Quiet Days and then Initiate Trials, so it will be a bit before we can fit you into anything official. After Trials and Advancement, there will be plenty of movement."

"Should I not expect to stay here in Maradaine?" Dayne asked.

"No, you definitely should," Orren said. "Honestly, I believe I made a mistake in letting Master Denbar choose a Candidate to travel with him to Lacanja. That set up . . . never mind. I will want you here, Dayne. However, for another informal duty, Master Hendron will be leaving for Lacanja shortly after Trials and Advancement."

"Taking Master Denbar's position there," Dayne said.

"The chapterhouse must have a Master. But if you could write up a report—nothing formal, just your impressions—about Lacanja and the chapterhouse there, it would be useful for Master Hendron."

"I can easily do that," Dayne said. He would strive to be fair in his writing. In truth, he did not enjoy living in Lacanja—too warm, too humid, and terrible food—but he wouldn't disparage it with his own opinion. The city had its many good qualities; it was simply not to Dayne's taste.

"Good." The Grandmaster plodded over to a small desk in the corner of the room. "How are you for money?"

"I've a few ticks on me," Dayne said, not sure why the Grandmaster would ask such a question.

"Few ticks," the Grandmaster said derisively. He came back over with a small purse. "Ten crowns here. That should be fine."

"Fine for what, sir?"

"I'm giving you permission to be a bit selfish, son. What was the name of that little brasserie you loved so much when you were here?"

"The Nimble Rabbit?"

"The Nimble Rabbit! Yes, take those ten crowns, and take the evening to enjoy yourself at the Nimble Rabbit. In a day or two we will consider what use you will serve us here."

"Are you sure, sir?"

"Consider it an order." He clapped Dayne on the shoulder. "Dismissed, out of my sight."

"As you say, sir," Dayne said, pocketing the purse. After two years in Lacanja, he needed no further prodding to get a proper Sharain meal.

Chapter 4

JERINNE WOULD LOVE EVENING contemplation exercises if they weren't led by Aldric and Price. The two third-year Candidates had no business being in charge of Initiates, let alone exercises of calming and reflection. Aldric was boorish and crass, and Price was a lout. How these two had made it through Initiacy was beyond Jerinne's comprehension.

"Consider the flame in front of you," Price droned. He said it exactly the same way every night. No sense that he believed in what he said, or even understood it. Jerinne tuned Price out and focused on the candle. "Your thoughts are one with the flame. Leaping, unstructured, chaotic."

Aldric, in the back of the contemplation room, slammed a staff down on the ground. This would be startling, if this wasn't the exact thing Aldric did every night at this exact point in contemplation exercises. For a process that was supposed to be about finding spiritual, restful calm amid chaos, Price and Aldric constructed a painfully ordered and predictable chaos.

None of the Initiates startled. They all sat, still and quiet, in front of their candles.

"Focus on the flame. Focus on controlling those un-structured thoughts. Focus on awareness of every breath, every beat of your heart."

The staff slammed on the floor again.

The moment was coming, and Jerinne was in the "danger" spot for tonight's exercise. That was fine with her. There was no agreed schedule amongst the Initia-tives, but there was an underlying sense of everyone tak-ing a fair turn. Jerinne hadn't been in the spot for a few weeks; she was due.

"Now close your eyes, and keep the flame in your mind. Shrink your image of the flame; focus on making it as small as you can."

Eyes closed. The moment was coming. Aldric's quiet steps approached Jerinne's position.

An idle thought of Dayne crossed Jerinne's mind. Would he have known Aldric and Price in his Initiacy? Did he learn contemplation exercises with them? Would he start running them now that he was in Maradaine? Would he play the same clockwork dumb show that Al-dric and Price did?

She had spent only a few minutes with the man, but her gut told her that Dayne wasn't like that.

Aldric was right next to Jerinne. The swing was coming.

"Do not let the flame vanish. Keep it in your thoughts. Only the flame."

This was how they did it, every night. Price in the front, droning the words of the exercise, and Aldric mak-ing his noises on cue, culminating with Aldric clocking one of the Initiates in the face. Always the Initiate in the same spot on the floor. Without fail.

Jerinne ignored everything about the flame and kept her ears on Aldric. She heard the rustle of Aldric's tunic as the staff came up. The rushing whistle of the staff swinging down toward Jerinne's nose.

There was no set rule about what one *should* do when Aldric swung his staff. Most dodged. Some blocked it. Enther usually let himself get clocked out of some philosophical point regarding the acceptance of pain. Jerinne didn't understand that.

As the staff swung in, Jerinne threw up her left hand, catching the staff. It stung like blazes, but it was worth the pain. At the same moment she dropped back, grabbing the end of the staff with her right hand. She yanked on the end of the staff with all her might, keeping her left hand firm at the center of her lever.

Aldric hadn't properly planted his feet, and he was wrenched over from the force of his own swing. He flew forward and crashed against the wall of the concentration chamber.

"The blazes?" Aldric snapped, pulling himself together. "What was that, Initiate?"

"A Left-hand Wrench Throw," Jerinne said calmly. "It's one of the advocated defenses for a staff attack while unarmed."

Aldric looked like he wanted to snap something, but before he could speak, another voice came from the doorway. "Advocated, but unorthodox in this setting, Initiate." Everyone turned to see Grandmaster Orren.

"My apologies for disturbing you," he said to the group. "I simply came to encourage you all to take the next three days—the Quiet Days, yes—with the utmost seriousness. Rest, focus, and contemplate. The Trials will be coming soon enough." He rested a hand on Jerinne's shoulder specifically. "You will have sufficient opportunity to prove your ability then."

"Thank you, Grandmaster," Price said with a small bow. Aldric bowed as well, but Jerinne noticed the slight side-eye toward her.

Quiet Days were notorious for Candidates playing tricks on Initiates. Apparently they had little better to do.

As far as Jerinne was concerned, Aldric and Price were free to try.

"Good night, then. Candidates, with me." The Grand-master left, Aldric and Price at his heels. All the Initiates extinguished their candles and put them away.

"You're crazy, you know," Raila said to her at the candle nooks. "Aldric is going to wail your skull for Quiet Days."

Jerinne shrugged. "I needed to practice that move under real conditions." Her hand still hurt, but the last thing she wanted was to let Raila know that. Just looking at Raila—with her piercing eyes and enticing smile—was enough to eradicate any sense of calm that Jerinne had achieved in the contemplation exercise. Jerinne often found herself desperate to appear competent and nonchalant in Raila's eyes, even though she was certain Raila saw through this.

"Where were you earlier?" Raila asked. "You showed up to Shield Drills late."

Enther came up behind Jerinne. "She had a special assignment. From the Grandmaster."

"Really?" Raila's dark eyes went wide.

"Nothing all that exciting," Jerinne said. "Just met this guy Dayne at the docks and escorted him to the chapter-house."

"Dayne?" Vien Reston came over. She was a third-year Initiate. "Dayne Heldrin?"

"That's him," Jerinne said. She noticed many eyes were on her now. "Should I have heard of him?"

"I'm shocked you haven't," Vien said.

"He was the top-ranked Initiate in 1213, wasn't he?" Enther asked.

"Exactly," Vien said. "I remember he and Ama—Madam Tyrell—were constantly at it for the top two spots."

Top two spots. Who were the top two amongst the second-year Initiates? Rankings were only given for the third-years, as additional pressure. Jerinne knew enough to know she was not one of the top two. She wasn't even sure if she'd be in the top ten. Enther would be one of the top ten. Raila probably as well. Jerinne watched the various Initiates filing out of the concentration center. There were twenty-seven in the second year. And sixteen slots for third-year Initiacy. In ten days, eleven of them would be leaving the chapterhouse for good.

Vien had kept talking. "Of course, that's when they weren't all over each other."

"Wait." Jerinne wanted to be sure she was understanding correctly. "You mean, like, sparring in the practice room."

Vien almost giggled, even though she wasn't the type of girl who was prone to giggling. "You could call it sparring, I suppose, and I imagine it happened in the practice room on occasion."

"No!" Raila said.

Enther glanced around the concentration chamber. "Somehow every place I've ever been feels dirty."

The idea finally drilled its way into Jerinne's skull. "Really? But . . . I thought we . . . I mean, fellow Initiates weren't supposed to."

Raila leaned close to Jerinne, her warm breath brushing her ear as she spoke. "I believe the official policy is 'strongly discouraged.' Not the same as forbidden."

Any peace or calm that Jerinne had achieved in concentration exercises was now completely gone. As were her chances of falling asleep easily tonight.

"They were both the favorites of Master Denbar," Vien went on. "He didn't care what they were doing, since in drills and trials they were both so focused. Really, when the two of them had their Candidacy Trial, it was like . . . watching poetry. But when Master Denbar went to Lacanja, he chose Dayne to be his specific Candidate Apprentice. Madam Tyrell stayed here, livid at being passed over."

Except she's now an Adept, and Dayne's still a Candidate. Jerinne understood why Dayne was acting so strange when he mentioned Madam Tyrell.

"Enough of this," Raila said, slapping Jerinne on the shoulder. "I'm exhausted. We should probably all stumble back to our bunks."

"Right," Jerinne said. She was almost—but not completely—certain that Raila meant each to their own bunks. As much as she might hope that Raila meant otherwise, she had no real way of finding out. She wouldn't dare ask her directly. She'd far rather fight every Candidate in the chapterhouse than face that particular fear.

The Nimble Rabbit was tucked away in a small alley off Yenley Avenue, two blocks away from the chapterhouse. It was an old house, a tenth-century holdover that had managed to survive the growth and rebuild around it, with a low stone wall surrounding its yard. A canopy hung over the front yard, shading the scattered outside tables from the setting sun. Only one table had patrons, two young men and a striking woman, who talked over empty plates and freshly filled wineglasses.

Dayne took a seat at a table some distance away from the trio, looking around for the chalkboard listing the specials of the day. He had barely had a moment to get a look at the board when one of the trio called out to him.

"Friend," the one with a full beard and muscular arms called out. "I remember you."

Dayne had to admit there was a certain familiarity about that one. "I used to come here a lot about two years ago."

"And you would come to lectures at the Royal College!" the man exclaimed. "You are not the sort of man that I would forget. Do not sit alone. I won't have it."

"You've already eaten," Dayne said. "I can't join you now."

"I do insist," he said. He turned to his companions. "We are having at least another bottle of wine, are we not?"

"Of course," the woman said, her Linjari accent thick and creamy.

"You must join us, we truly insist," the bearded man said.

Dayne crossed over, looking to the quieter man. "If you insist."

"Apparently we do," he said, looking at Dayne over his spectacles.

Dayne sat down with them, extending his hand to the man who initiated the invitation. "Dayne Heldrin."

"Hemmit," he said, taking Dayne's hand lustily. "Hemmit Eyairin. I remember well. I think we had a few discussions about politics and history over a bottle or two of wine here."

There had been a few people, mostly students from RCM, who Dayne had engaged with back in his Initiacy days, when he had the luxury of coming here. There had been one who was especially outspoken, particularly on matters of his own definitions of manliness—which involved truth, adventure, and wine. This Hemmit was definitely him, but something was different. "Did you not have the beard back then?"

"Students are forced to be so cleanly groomed," Hemmit said. "I am my own man, now."

The woman turned to Dayne, her long braid of honey-brown hair whipping behind her, and he noticed her dress—bright and short, the hem well above the knee, and her stockings ended significantly lower, exposing a fair amount of bare flesh on her thighs. The style was typical in Yoleanne, the major city of her native archduchy of Linjar, and it would have been daring in Lacanja. In Maradaine, it was downright shocking. "Lin Shartien."

"And that would be Maresh," Hemmit said, pointing to the bespectacled man.

"Maresh Niol," he said, extending his hand to Dayne.

"You are not a soldier," Lin said, "but you're built like one."

"Use your eyes," Maresh said. "He's a Tarian knight."

"We don't use the word 'knight,'" Dayne said. "Even for full members of the order. It's always our rank, and I'm just a Candidate."

"But a man of experience," Hemmit said. "Oh, you are to be envied, Mister Heldrin." He snapped over to the server to bring another glass.

"I'm not sure about that." A glass was placed in front of Dayne, which Hemmit immediately filled. Dayne sipped at the wine, and then looked to the server. "What's on special?"

"What are you looking for?" the server asked.

"I haven't had lamb with crisp for two years," Dayne said.

"Light or heavy grill?"

"Very light," Dayne said. The server nodded and left.

"A man of simple, hearty tastes," Lin said.

"A man who's been living in Lacanja. You want oysters, or a fish crackle, Lacanja is the city to be in. But you can't get lamb with crisp down there."

"Lacanja!" Hemmit laughed deeply. "There's a city I want to see. Is the bay as spectacular as they say? A shimmering marvel of crystal blue, dotted with sails of every size and color?"

"More clogged than dotted," Dayne said.

Hemmit turned to his other friend, who was scribbling something with a charcoal pencil in a notebook. "I'm telling you, Maresh, we need to go down the coast. Kyst, Lacanja, Yoleanne."

"You two couldn't handle Yoleanne," Lin purred. She gave a leering look over to Dayne. "And this one is so straight, Yoleanne might break him in two."

"Travel is pointless," Maresh muttered. "The nation pours into Maradaine, the whole world does. This is where things are happening. Look at Lin."

"I always am," Hemmit said, giving her an appreciative grin.

"So are you students?" Dayne asked. "RCM?"

"Not anymore," Hemmit said. "I don't need their approval."

"I received my Letters, not that I had a choice." Lin brazenly undid one button of her blouse, revealing a tattoo of stylized letters surrounded in flame.

Dayne recognized its significance. "You're a mage?"

"Not much of one," Lin said.

Maresh snorted in laughter. "Not much of one." He drank down his wine and refilled the glass, emptying the bottle. "She's being ludicrously modest."

"Modesty is hardly one of my virtues." She held her hand out over the table, splashes of light dropping from her fingertips. The light landed on the table as crystals of color and luminescence, until a small spiraling tower formed. "I only use magic for my art."

"Impressive," Dayne said, even though the hairs on the back of his neck stood up. He understood, intellectually, that mages weren't much different from any other folk, but a childhood full of prejudices and midnight stories was a powerful thing to overcome.

"Impressing a Tarian, that's something." She spun her fingers again, and the tower morphed into a new image— a shield over crossed swords. The same symbol as on Dayne's medallion.

"You should see her dance," Hemmit said.

"Hush." She brushed her hand, and the Tarian emblem vanished.

"So, if you aren't students," Dayne said, pointedly changing the conversation, "what do you do?"

"Have you read the *Veracity Press*?" Hemmit asked. He finished his wine, and poured himself another glass from a bottle the server had gracefully slipped onto the table.

"He hasn't," Maresh said, glaring at Dayne.

"I'm afraid he's right," Dayne said. "I literally stepped off the boat today. I haven't had much chance to check any of the city's prints."

Hemmit pulled out a newssheet from the satchel next to him and passed it to Dayne. "We write it, Maresh does the art, I run the pressing."

"Very nice," Dayne said. The *Veracity Press* was little more than a pamphlet, with very small type. There were several sketches in it as well, most of them apparently depicting members of Parliament as large-headed buffoons. That was what Dayne had expected. He had pegged these three as mild political activists, even dissidents, so the fact that they printed a subversive newssheet wasn't a surprise.

A glance at the writing confirmed what he suspected: it was full of Populist rhetoric, calling for members of Parliament to sever their ties to noble families, church and military connections, and moneyed interests. It ignored the fact that almost to the man, every member of Parliament had been elected because of those very things. Five of the six parties—the Loyalists, the Functionalists, the Traditionalists, the Ecclesials, and the Free Commercialists—based their power and platform on those connections. Only the Populists were "of the people"—according to them—and they were the smallest and weakest party in Parliament. Dayne agreed with some of the Populist stances, but the party was one that extremists gravitated to. The type who would never compromise any of their demands—acting as if it was better to get nothing and claim moral superiority.

Dayne didn't see these three as quite that type. No, they were definitely idealists, believing that a salve of truth could heal whatever festering wounds the government might have. In fact, he spotted the phrase "festering wounds" in the text of the main article.

Dayne's plate arrived, just in time to save him from having to actually read the newssheet in front of the three of them. Sizzling lamb chop, dressed in a beer and onion sauce, with a generous mound of crisp—thin sliced potatoes, fried in rendered duck fat. This was a plate of bliss. Dayne stabbed his fork into the crisp and took a glorious bite of the hot, crunchy, salty rapture.

"That is the face of a satisfied man," Hemmit said, topping off Dayne's wineglass.

"It's been too long," Dayne agreed. He focused his attention on his meal, while his companions talked about some outrage the Parliament planned to vote on. Dayne did not engage, though he noted their approval of a handful of the members, namely a pair of Populists named Montrose and Parlin. Dayne wasn't familiar with Parlin, but he knew the name Montrose quite well. Alphonse Montrose was easily the most famous man in Parliament; something of a folk hero, even as a "people's man." Dayne didn't know enough about the man's specific politics to have a very strong opinion, but what he had read about showed Montrose as a man of solid common sense, understanding the reality of getting things done in Parliament. If these new friends approved of him, then their politics couldn't be too radical for Dayne's taste.

"We know they'll be at the opening tomorrow," Hemmit said. "We couldn't ask for a better opportunity."

"Opening?" Dayne asked between bites.

Nervous looks passed among the trio for a moment, until Lin said, "A museum is having an opening ceremony. We mention it here." She pointed to the copy of the *Veracity Press* in front of Dayne. He scanned the tiny print for the appropriate text. When he found it, he felt a flush of excitement.

"An official Royal Museum of Druth History?" he asked, his voice cracking a bit higher than a twenty-year-old man's should. "And it's opening to the public?"

"You like that?" Maresh asked.

"History is my passion," Dayne said. "I learned to read from a cracked and faded copy of *The Lineage of Royalty.*"

"Ha!" Hemmit shouted. "That was one of my firsts as well."

Lin leaned in to Dayne conspiratorially. "Hemmit was pursuing his History Letters before his discharge."

"I withdrew myself in protest before they could discharge me!" Hemmit pounded his fist on the table.

Dayne looked to Maresh. "Is that your story as well?"

"Oh no," Maresh said. "I botched, plain and simple, and was honestly drummed out."

"To have had that luxury." Lin sighed with rich melancholy.

"Tomorrow at eleven bells," Dayne noted from the article. An official Royal Museum of History was exciting news, in and of itself. But with members of Parliament in attendance, that made the event attractive. Maybe having Tarians showing up in full dress uniform would provide a gentle reminder of the role the Tarian Order had played in the centuries of Druth history. It might not make a difference in terms of his own advancement, but it would be for the good of the Order. "I may have to make a point of that."

"And we'd be thrilled to see you," Lin said.

Dayne took another bite of lamb and crisp. His situation may be dire, but at this moment there was good food, wine, and company, and the potential for an intriguing outing. Despite what hung over him, it was good to be back in Maradaine.

First Interlude

JULIAN BARTON HATED the ritual of these meetings, forced to wear the ridiculous mask and cloak and answer to the code name "The Parliamentarian" for the farce of concealing his identity from the rest of this council. These meetings were an absurd bit of theater, where his fellow conspirators all pretended not to know perfectly well that he was Julian Barton, 4th Chair of Maradaine to the Druth Parliament. And he pretended not to know who they were.

Millerson claimed it gave them all deniability. If, somehow, one of them were exposed and questioned, they could answer honestly. Who are you? Who are your collaborators? We are the Grand Ten. We are The Parliamentarian, The Man of the People, The Lord, The Duchess, The Lady, The Priest, The Soldier, The Justice, The Mage, and The Warrior. We will save Druthal from itself, from the corruption that engulfs it.

Barton believed Millerson simply liked the masks and code names.

Barton didn't need the self-aggrandizement. He believed in what they were doing, but they were nothing like the original Grand Ten, the people who saved the Druth throne and rebuilt the shattered nation two centuries ago. Those people fought, they suffered, they lived through the Inquest and the Incursion. That crucible had given them the wisdom to bring about the Reunification, to share in rebuilding a nation.

This conspiracy paled in comparison. There was no denying that they were ten people in comfortable positions of power who were all cooperating to consolidate and expand their influence. To enact the change they needed without a war. Barton considered himself a patriot, just like Geophry Haltom, the great man whose moniker of "The Parliamentarian" he claimed, but he had no delusions about his own name being so lauded.

Better to win from the shadows than lose in the light.

In this dark meeting room hidden under, fittingly enough for the drama of it, a shuttered opera house, he wore his mask with the rest of them so he could be The Parliamentarian, just as Millerson was The Man of the People. Barton thought that was especially silly. Millerson was the 3rd Chair of Sauriya, as much a Parliamentarian as he was. For that matter, couldn't Barton just as well be a Man of the People?

Millerson chose everyone's titles. Millerson brought this conspiracy of ten together, and despite his flair for the dramatic, Barton had to admit that his fundamental ideals were sound. They wanted the same things—a Traditionalist government, a strong hand at the throne, and a prosperous Druthal.

Millerson also wanted the better mask.

The others all took their places, masks donned, identities secreted away. As they all were supposed to, absurd though it was.

"Tomorrow," Millerson intoned, with ominous timbre, as if he were reciting holy words straight from the saints themselves. "Tomorrow we move from intentions to actions, subtle though they may be."

"Hardly subtle," The Justice said. "You intend to have one of your fellow Chairs of the Parliament murdered."

"We," The Soldier said. "That is what *we* intend. Or are you revoking your assent?"

"No, of course not," The Justice said. "I agreed to this, I won't deny it. But it is his plan. And while it is many things, it is not subtle."

"His slow plan," The Duchess growled.

The Mage chuckled, her voice deep and throaty. "I do not understand your urge to rush, Duchess. Our friend here is quite right to craft the opening maneuvers to set the board for a long, arduous game."

"Do we need a long, arduous game?" The Lord asked. "I mean, for two years now we ten have played at being conspirators. How much longer do we just talk and take 'subtle' actions?"

"We agreed, a direct ploy invites counter play. Invites rebellion. The point of our engagement is not to spark a revolution, but to have the changes we desire offered to us."

"I don't know about you, but I can't maintain this charade forever." The Duchess clucked her tongue, the sound muted by her mask. "Just this place alone is starting to make me look the fool."

Barton was sympathetic there. The Duchess owned the opera house, and at public gatherings she was often asked when her renovations would be finished and she would reopen its doors. She constantly had to answer, "Soon, very soon," even though she had no intention of continuing such a project until their private need had concluded. The place was shut down explicitly to give them a location to hold these overtly theatrical meetings. But at the same time, a small amount of public ridicule was the only real risk she was taking at this point.

The Mage nodded, and Barton imagined a condescending smile under her mask. "Believe me, Duchess, every one of our meetings is quite trying on me." Barton didn't pretend to understand it, but he knew she was using her magic to keep the light and sound of their meetings from reaching the rest of the world. If someone stood fifty feet away, they wouldn't see or hear a thing. Barton was deeply disquieted about including her in their confidences—he was never one for trusting mages. Millerson insisted she was a crucial member; they were all "crucial members." Barton half-believed Millerson said so in order to have a complete Grand Ten.

Barton didn't believe in the symbolism anywhere near as much as Millerson did. Millerson sometimes believed symbols were more important than details.

"What more do you need from us?" The Soldier asked. "I can arrange for a small honor guard at the event. To keep it from getting too chaotic."

"A bit of chaos is necessary," Barton said. "Isn't that at least part of the point?"

The Lord nodded. "We want people to believe that things aren't under control. That a change is needed on the highest level."

"Within reason," The Lady said, putting a hand on The Lord's arm.

"Yes, of course, within reason," The Lord said. "After all, some of you will be in the thick of things tomorrow. Your safety is assured, yes?"

Barton glanced over to The Warrior, expecting him to contribute something. As usual, he said nothing. Barton answered on his own. "The people involved in the plan haven't been instructed along those lines. You understand, of course, we cannot tell them who *not* to hurt without giving them names we don't want them to know. They certainly don't know, and we can't have them know, that their actions come from our design."

"Because they're dupes," The Warrior said. "They'd probably be horrified at the idea that we were pulling their strings."

"We must be insulated," Millerson said. "Right now it's The Parliamentarian and me who are at the most risk."

"It is appreciated," The Priest said.

Barton hoped they damn well appreciated it. Millerson's depiction that they were the two at the most risk was self-serving. Not that Millerson wasn't at risk—he was the one who had made many of the arrangements for the pawns they were putting into play tomorrow. If things went poorly, a clever investigator could draw the connections back to him. But Barton's risk was going to be far more visceral. After all, he was the one who was going to be up on the speech platform tomorrow. He was the one presenting at the museum opening.

If something went wrong, it would be his chest that got an arrow in it.

Chapter 5

DAYNE WOKE AROUND DAWN, later than his usual custom. He was still a bit foggy, which was also unusual for him, but drinking half a bottle of wine was definitely not usual. His drinking was nowhere near as prolific as Hemmit or Maresh—for a small man Maresh could drink them all under the table. Dayne hadn't even tried to keep up, but even still, he had reached a rather hazy point. He couldn't quite recall when Lin had left their company, though she definitely must have left before Hemmit suggested moving their gathering to a basement stage performance he was overly fond of. Dayne remembered declining that invitation, though he ended up having to decline multiple times, ultimately right outside the building. Hemmit had extracted several promises from Dayne to meet them again at The Nimble Rabbit, to join them in the basement at a later date, and to tell many stories about life in the Tarian Order.

Dayne wasn't sure why he made the last promise. The last thing he wanted to do was tell Hemmit about Lacanja,

Lenick Benedict, or letting Sholiar get the best of him. He certainly didn't want to talk about Master Denbar.

Dayne put that all out of his mind and went to his trunk. He hadn't yet bothered to unpack it. Despite what the Grandmaster said, he wasn't sure if he wanted to make himself too comfortable here. He knew that they would find some duty for him. Grandmaster Orren would treat him with honor and respect. But that didn't matter much if all he was doing was waiting out the calendar. Other arrangements should be made, sooner rather than later. If nothing else, he needed to have a plan once his Candidacy ended.

He took out a simple cotton pullover and slacks and closed the trunk back up. Dressed enough for the sake of decency, he went down to the practice floor. After two weeks on ships and barges, he hadn't had an opportunity to properly perform his morning exercises.

The practice floor was a wide room, slat floor sanded to a smooth shine. The plain white walls were decorated with wooden training weapons: swords, shields, and staves.

It was not unoccupied.

This normally would not be a problem. The room was large enough for thirty people to run through staff sequences without disturbing each other.

But there weren't thirty people. There was only one.

Amaya.

She was working through quarterstaff sequences, her muscular arms and her weapon all moving in fluid unity. She was immersed, perfection of form. Amaya had been the best at the staff amongst their Initiate cohort. He could edge her out sparring with shield-and-blade, but with the staff she was unstoppable. The past two years hadn't slowed her down.

She hadn't noticed him. Or, at the very least, she hadn't reacted to him. He was certain she was aware someone had come onto the practice floor.

Dayne slipped over to the shelf of Incentives: wooden

balls, wrapped in thin leather padding. Master Denbar would throw them at students, full strength, with no warning. After a few dozen hits, Dayne had learned to dodge, parry, and block them by instinct.

Dayne picked one up and hurled it right at the center of her body.

Amaya didn't break form. She didn't even look. She swung the staff around the right side of her body, executing a perfect ending to Sequence Fourteen while knocking the Incentive back at Dayne with a resounding crack. It shot back at his face. Instead of dodging it, Dayne caught it just before it smashed into his nose.

That hurt.

Dayne was reasonably sure he didn't break any bones in his hand, but it stung like blazes. He wore the pain plainly on his face as Amaya finally turned to him.

"It was stupid of you to leave Lacanja."

Dayne shook out his hand. "After what happened—"

"I heard the story. It wasn't your fault. You did what you were supposed to."

"I had to leave," was all he could say. She was right, but his sins were too grievous. Without Master Denbar there, there was no way he could stay in Lacanja.

"You won't get promoted to Adept if you're here. Not this year."

She didn't know. "That's why there's three years of Candidacy," Dayne said. "For most people."

That came out more bitter than he intended. Dayne put the Incentive back on the shelf.

"One throw is all you have?"

His hand hadn't even left the shelf. He took the Incentive up and hurled it at her, aiming for her knee. Then he grabbed a second Incentive, and rocketed it at the center of her body.

The second one he threw with everything he had in his arm.

The two balls flew true, but Amaya planted her staff

and pulled her legs up, twisting out of the way of them both. She landed running at Dayne, jabbing the staff exactly where his head had been a moment earlier. He rolled out of her way, diving toward the wall of shields.

This wasn't the exercise he had planned for the morning, but by the Saints, it would do quite nicely.

She executed four perfect attacks—attacks that never touched him, since his dodges were just as perfect—before he got a shield. Now he was ready.

"That all you have, *Adept* Tyrell?" Her staff came in close, but he blocked it, pinning her weapon against the wall.

She tried to smash her forehead against his chest—he was far too tall for her to reach his face—but he opened out, forcing her off balance. He pushed her down and away, wrenching the staff out of her grip as she dropped to the floor. She dove into the push, rolling away from him, but now unarmed. Not that she would stay that way long in this room. She went for two handsticks and came back at him.

"Was promotion that easy last year and I missed it?" Dayne asked, dodging her blows.

"Every Candidacy is different," she said with almost as much venom. "We all thought going with Master Denbar would have been the sweetest plum."

"I wish it had been someone else."

"No," she shot back, coming in with a variant of a standard attack sequence. "You do not get to do that."

"Do what?"

"Wallow in your blame and misery," she said. "You were the one he chose, and—"

"And now he's dead, it's my fault!"

"Did you stab him?" They were now in a rhythm of attacks and blocks.

"I may as well have."

"Dayne," she snarled. "Did you kill him, or did you merely fail to save him?"

As if the distinction mattered. "For a Tarian—"

She pounced toward him. "No, not that sewage. No one tried harder to beat that out of your skull than Master Denbar."

Dayne shoved her away, hard. "And now he's gone. My fault."

He hurled the shield at her—normally an incredibly stupid tactic, but with multiple shields on the wall next to him, there was no real loss. Surprisingly, the shield hit her square in the chest, knocking her off her feet. He was certain she'd dodge it. There was no reason why she wouldn't be able to dodge a thrown shield. For a split second, his heart raced up to his throat. He had thrown too hard, too strong. He could have . . .

He hadn't. She flipped back onto her feet, landing in a ready stance.

"Are you all ri—"

"Don't even," she snarled. She was winded, holding one arm close to her body. The hit had hurt her more than she would admit. "Let's go on."

If that was what she wanted. Warily, he picked up her staff and tossed it to her.

"Really, though. No one makes Adept in their first year of Candidacy." He took up another shield. "It doesn't happen."

She launched into a furious offensive. He first thought it was in rage, not worthy of a Tarian Adept, but he quickly saw she was moving perfectly through her sequence patterns. Despite her obvious anger, she was in absolute control of her weapon and her body.

As was he. Not one strike landed.

"You think I don't know that?" she snarled. "You think it isn't whispered by every other Adept and Candidate?" Thrust to his solar plexus, dodged. Swing around across his left side, blocked. "Even the Initiates!"

Despite her excellent form, she was in pure attack mode, leaving herself open on several occasions. Dayne didn't press the advantage, didn't attack. Only dodge, block, retreat. She kept at it, cycling through advanced sequences faster and faster.

Dayne jumped back to avoid a surprise sweep when she broke out of sequence. She threw the staff down on the floor.

"What is wrong with you?" she snapped. Sweat was pouring off her brow, and she held her hand against her side.

"Why is something wrong?" Dayne asked. "I thought we were . . ."

"My left side was open, you didn't strike. My knees were vulnerable, you didn't strike. I all but presented my bare throat to you, and you didn't take one attack."

"I threw the shield," Dayne said. "I think I may have broken your ribs with it."

"You may have," she said.

"And I didn't want to—"

"Blazes, Dayne!" she shouted. "The last thing I need is for you to coddle me."

"I'm not—" Dayne started, but he was interrupted by the sound of more people coming into the training room.

Amaya stormed off to the exit.

"Amaya," he called out. "I don't want—"

She was gone.

Not that he really could have told her, explained why. She wouldn't understand.

He wasn't coddling her. He would have done the same sparring against anyone else. He had only thrown the Incentives and the shield as hard as he had because he was confident she would be able to defend herself.

Once she had been hit, he didn't want to risk anything else. He knew damn well that at his strength, with his skill, he needed to be more vigilant than anyone else.

He was lucky she had only been injured.

Lenick Benedict had only been injured. He was lucky he hadn't killed the boy. It wasn't from a lack of trying.

Master Denbar had been right about that. He had to be more careful.

Dayne hung up the shield, and then picked up the other weapons and Incentives. No need to leave the practice room a mess.

An hour later, after the course of stretches and calisthenics he had originally intended, Dayne went to the dining hall. Tables were mostly filled with Initiates, Candidates, Adepts, and Masters all segregating themselves by their rank. Dayne saw where he ought to sit, with other Candidates. He knew many of them from his Initiacy, but after the ugliness with Amaya, he wasn't sure what to expect from any of them.

But the last thing he needed was to be afraid to sit down and eat. That would not be worthy of a Tarian.

A hand clapped down on his shoulder. Dayne immediately recognized Aldric, a third-year Candidate, and the only Tarian almost as tall as he was. "Good to see you, Heldrin," Aldric said. "You got here just in time for Trials."

"I suspected as much," Dayne said, turning just enough so Aldric's hand would naturally fall off his shoulder, without making it look like he was trying to pull away. Aldric had an oily charm that always troubled Dayne. "I was met by an Initiate who is worried about Second-Year Trials."

"Which one?" Aldric looked over to the table of Initiates, his attention clearly focused on the group of young women there.

"Fendall," Dayne said, nodding at Jerinne. Jerinne, for her part, was not engaging with her fellow Initiates. She ate her breakfast in distraction, nose deep in a book. Dayne was more than a little reminded of himself in his Initiacy.

"Right," Aldric said. "Should be fun to see them sweat through their Quiet Days, hmm?"

"Those start today, right," Dayne confirmed. With no

Initiates in Lacanja, he had forgotten the exact schedule.
Initiates were granted three Quiet Days where they were
given no training or instruction, to rest and prepare for
their Trials. That explained why the practice room was
relatively empty.

"They do," Aldric said. "Price and Richens and I were
planning—"

Dayne didn't bother to listen to the rest—he was sure
it involved a mean-spirited prank, knowing Aldric. He
didn't care. Grandmaster Orren had given him a duty,
even if it was an informal one. He walked over and
crouched next to Jerinne, who almost jumped out of her
chair on Dayne's approach.

"First Quiet Day before your Trials, right?"

"Right." Jerinne spoke with hesitation. She had probably already been on the receiving end of one of Aldric's
games.

"I heard about an event happening later this morning.
Come with me, and I'll help you with your Shield Sequences later."

Jerinne glanced around, as if she was expecting a
prank to reveal itself. "What sort of event?"

"A museum opening. Should be some important people there. And you might learn something."

"Really?"

Dayne nodded. "Meet me in the front hall in dress
uniform after breakfast." He gently clapped Jerinne on
the shoulder and took his own seat at an empty table.

Jerinne was shocked to find Dayne actually in his dress
uniform. She had thought the museum invitation was an
elaborate hazing ritual that Dayne had cooked up with
the other Candidates. Aldric had been whispering to
Dayne right before he approached, and Aldric was by far
the worst of that lot. But there Dayne was, waiting patiently in crisp grays and cap, sword at his belt and shield

gleaming on his arm. Jerinne had never seen a shield that well polished.

Jerinne started to suspect that it was Dayne himself that was being hazed.

At the very least she no longer felt as self-conscious about wearing her own dress uniform. The outfit — bordering on costume — was elaborate and impractical. The coat alone was almost long enough to be a dress.

"Why are we wearing these, Dayne?" she asked.

"I understand there will be some members of Parliament, some nobility. We're representing the Tarian Order, so we should look the part with respectability and honor."

"Did we get orders to do this?" Jerinne asked. Technically, the Masters and Adepts wouldn't give any orders on the Quiet Days, but they would give strong suggestions. And Candidates . . . would be a problem. Jerinne swore to every saint that when *she* was a Candidate, she would never do that.

Looking at Dayne, proudly wearing the dress, there was no way he was the type of Candidate who would do that sort of thing. He looked like the perfect model for the Tarians. This was the guy who bucked convention for a torrid fling with Madam Tyrell? It was almost impossible to believe.

"Not at all," Dayne said. "If there were orders, it wouldn't be just you and me. I was going to suggest to Grand Master Orren to have more of us there, but I couldn't find him. Come along."

Dayne led the way out into the street. Jerinne followed close, feeling less conspicuous about the stares of passersby when she was near Dayne. Dayne nodded and waved and said "Good morning" to most everyone they passed, which seemed to startle people.

"Is that how it is in Lacanja?" Jerinne asked.

"How what is?" Dayne asked.

"Greeting strangers as they pass by. I guess it's a friendlier city than Maradaine."

Dayne chuckled. "No, I don't think so. I'm sure I stood out there as well."

"I think you stand out anywhere," Jerinne said. "Why more of us?"

"It would have been a sight, don't you think?" Dayne said. "Imagine it, a score of Tarians marching down the avenue to the museum in full dress. A whole parade. Wouldn't that be exciting?"

Jerinne could imagine it, but what she saw in her head surely didn't match Dayne's vision. "Or frightening. Twenty armed men and women, in matching uniform? People might get the wrong message."

"Wrong? We're Tarians, Jerinne. We're the Shield of the People. The people know our order has only ever—"

"I don't know if people know that," Jerinne said. "I mean—excuse me, sir?" She approached a man walking by—dockworker steve or shipbuilder by his build and smell. "Could I trouble you for a moment?"

The man looked apprehensive, his eyes darting between Jerinne and Dayne. "What can I do for you, my graces?"

"No, sir," Dayne said, "We're not—"

Jerinne cut him off, holding up one finger. "If you would be so kind, could you tell me who we are?"

The man bit his lip. "Your graces don't know who you are?"

Jerinne shook her head. "I'm sorry, good sir, I wasn't clear. We are in our right minds, of course."

"Of course," the man said, though he didn't seem convinced.

"What I meant to ask was, do you recognize what we are, by our uniform and arms?"

"Oh," the man said, his brow screwing up in thought. "You're not navy men, I know. Or army, I'm pretty sure."

"True," Jerinne said, glancing over at Dayne. The big guy looked out of sorts.

The man snapped his fingers. "You're King's Marshals, aren't you?" He suddenly turned pale. "You're not here for me, are you?"

"No, sir," Jerinne said. "Sorry to have troubled you. Good day." She gave the man a quick salute, and the man scurried off.

"That doesn't—" Dayne started.

"We're a block away from our chapterhouse, Dayne," Jerinne said. "To most people, armed folk in uniform are all the same."

Dayne looked quite cross. Jerinne started to sweat, her throat tightening. She may have gone too far. She was only an Initiate, and Dayne a Candidate.

"This is why we need to be out here, don't you see? This is why we need to excite people. And draw that excitement to the history museum. If the people learn—"

He stopped short, his eyes narrowing, focusing on something far off. Before Jerinne could turn to see, Dayne was running. It took a moment for Jerinne to spot what had Dayne's attention. A block away, there was an overturned cart with a man pinned underneath, and another man running from it.

Dayne was going to the cart, so Jerinne focused on the man running away. He had a wad of crumpled paper in one hand, likely notes of exchange. The other hand held a knife.

Thief.

Jerinne drew her sword and charged. The man was about to dash into a dark alley when Jerinne closed the distance, blocking the man's escape.

Sword and shield in ready stance, Jerinne barked out in her deepest voice, "Hold fast!"

The man jumped in with his knife, quicker than Jerinne expected. She parried the blade, but the thief had moved in too close for Jerinne to do a proper riposte, so she pulled back.

The man barreled onto Jerinne's shield, forcing her to take his weight. Jerinne's attention was still on the knife, which was about to slice her belly.

Jerinne rolled back, dragging the man with her and flipping him over. The man crashed into a brick wall and dropped to the ground, coughing. Jerinne got back on her feet, and with a dismissive swipe, knocked the knife out of the man's hand. The thief wasn't in any condition to fight back. Jerinne sheathed her sword and relieved the thief of the stolen bills.

She turned back to the scene of the crime. Dayne crouched next to the man under the overturned cart. The cart had pinned the victim, surely crushing him.

"Come on," Jerinne yelled to the people around. "Perhaps together we can—"

No one else moved, as the crowd on the street stood transfixed as Dayne grabbed hold of the cart with his massive hands. With barely a sound of effort, he righted the cart and freed the man.

Dayne knelt back down, "It's all right, sir," he said calmly. "How bad is it?"

"Think . . . leg . . ." the man wheezed out.

"Call for Yellowshields," Dayne said to the crowd. Some of them broke from their spell and ran off.

Jerinne knelt down by them. "I got your money back, sir," Jerinne said, holding out the bills.

"Thank you," the man managed. His eyes weren't focused much on Jerinne or Dayne. Dayne took the bills from Jerinne's hands and put them in the man's coat pocket.

"The thief?" Dayne asked.

"Over there," Jerinne said. "I took care of him."

"Does he need the Yellowshields as well?" Dayne asked. At first, Jerinne thought Dayne was making a joke, but he gave the appearance of real concern for the thief's wellbeing.

"Bruised and winded is all," Jerinne said. "I don't think I really hurt him."

"Good," Dayne said, clearly relieved.

Constabulary and Yellowshields both arrived. The constables groused and gave ugly looks to the two of them, and the Yellowshields helped the injured man onto their stretcher. Dayne approached the Yellowshields, spoke warmly with one and shook his hand, and then let them do their work.

"Old friend?" Jerinne asked.

"Caskly," Dayne said. "He was in our Initiacy cohort, but he didn't make it past second year."

"So now he's a Yellowshield?" Was that what Tarian washouts did? Join the city loyalty?

"It's quite fitting, actually," Dayne said. "Not just because Caskly was more of a healer than a warrior. Did you know the Yellowshields actually evolved from the Ascepian Order?"

"No, I didn't." Jerinne could never keep the disbanded Orders straight. Even though they were taught the history of the various warrior orders of Druthal, they weren't expected to memorize them.

At least Jerinne didn't think so. Maybe that was part of the Second-Year Trials.

Dayne nodded, but offered no further comment. After a few minutes, both the thief and his victim were taken away. Dayne watched the wagons roll off, his expression wistful.

"Something wrong?" Jerinne asked.

"I just wish we could have done more to help him," Dayne said.

"I don't really know what else we could do," Jerinne said. "You saved his life, I caught the thief and returned his money. Yellowshields will get him to a hospital ward."

"I don't know if it's enough," Dayne said. His attention was on the cart.

Jerinne didn't know how to respond to that. What more could it be? The man survives, his livelihood maintained. The worst is it may take some time for his body to heal. "He was lucky we were here," Jerinne finally said to Dayne.

"That's something," Dayne answered. He pointed to the faded yellow lettering on the side of the cart. "Casen's Dry Goods. We can return the cart."

"Don't you want to get to—"

Dayne grabbed the cart handles and picked it up. "Should only take a few minutes. And, if memory serves, it's only a few blocks away." He pushed the cart away effortlessly. Jerinne didn't know what else she could do besides follow him.

Chapter 6

ANY CITIZEN OF MARADAINE worth his thumb ought to have taken that cart back to the shop. But it only seemed to have occurred to Dayne. Constabulary, Yellowshields, even Jerinne were all content to walk away and leave it there in the middle of the street. Jerinne, at least, understood the importance of doing the simple task once Dayne started. Jerinne was gracious, and chatted amiably with the shop owners, who were thrilled to have their property returned. They offered a reward, which Dayne and Jerinne rightfully refused.

Of course, they were a bit late to the museum, which meant the opening ceremonies were already underway.

Dayne knew where the museum was—Hemmit had told him the address—but he couldn't think of what used to be there. It was on Fenyon Street, on the stretch between the Parliament House and the Royal College campus—the triangle of city blocks that wasn't quite in any neighborhood. Upon approach, it looked like a large noble house, with wide marble stairs from the street to the giant, open doors.

Jerinne stopped on the front steps. "Who lived here?" she asked absently.

"I don't think anyone," Dayne said. "Most of this block is owned jointly by the College and Parliament. These houses are used as guest lodgings for scholars and other important visitors to Maradaine."

"So the museum usurped one?" Jerinne asked.

"I'm sure that wasn't the language used. The museum, in all likelihood, is a joint project of the Royal College and the Parliament. Not to mention some nobleman holding the purse."

They reached the main doors, where two King's Marshals had guard duty, in their crisp blue and white coats, matching felt caps and tasseled rapiers.

"A pair of Tarians!" one of them said, with more than a little contempt in his voice.

"What brings you two out here all dandied up?" the other asked. Dayne thought this was particularly ironic, given their standard uniform.

"We're here for the opening of the museum," Dayne said. "I was informed it was a public event."

"Public event," the first one said, with a strange nod that was half neck-crack. "But we've got two members of Parliament, quite a few nobility rubbing elbows in there. Care must be taken."

"Meaning you've got to check your swords and shields here, with us," the second said.

Jerinne stepped forward, "Why would we have to—"

"Because we've got to keep people safe," the first marshal said. "You Tarians know about that."

"Exactly, we are members of the Tarian Order and as such we should be given—"

"You're not members," the second marshal said. "You're a Candidate and Initiate. I know blasted well what those marks on your collars mean. Now you can either turn in your arms and enjoy the museum, or you can dust your feet on the walkway." Dayne knew pips and ranks as well, and this marshal was a marshal chief—equivalent to captain in the Constabulary. Regine Toscan, by his brass nameplate. Not worth picking an argument with over no matter what. Surprising that someone of that rank would be working the door at this event.

"It's fine," Dayne said, unhooking his sword. "We're here for culture, Jerinne. Not a fight." He passed it and his shield to the first marshal, and Jerinne did the same.

"Thank you, friends," Chief Toscan said. "You can collect your belongings upon your exit."

As they walked away Jerinne whispered in his ear, "That was complete posturing. They think—"

"That security of this event is their responsibility," Dayne said. "We're not here to use our weapons. It's fine."

Dayne looked around the entry hall, which truly was a grand and impressive lobby. A lot of work had to have been done to transform this building into the museum. Portraits of every king of Druthal for the past twelve centuries filled the walls. Maradaine the First hung just to the left of the door, with a brass plaque identifying him and his reign. It circled the room chronologically, with gaps at the entryways to other exhibits. Intricately woven ropes barred off entry to the other exhibits.

Along the back wall, in front of the disastrous kings of the seventh century, a small stage had been assembled. Several well-dressed people milled about up there, as well as other men in scholastic robes. Dayne didn't recognize anyone up on the stage, but the two men in dark suits with silk cravats were clearly members of Parliament. Flanking the stage were two sweeping stairways, leading to a balcony rounding the entire room, and presumably containing additional exhibits.

Dayne searched through the crowd, looking to see if his new friends from The Nimble Rabbit were around.

The crowd was diverse, though it mostly consisted of minor nobility, mixed with several students from the Royal College. But he was thrilled to see how many people were here, and the attention to detail that was being paid, both to the museum itself and the spectacle of the event.

What thrilled Dayne the most was the servers. Someone had spared no expense on this event, as a dozen servers weaved their way among the crowd with trays of culinary delights and cups of wine. The servers were dressed in authentic eleventh-century outfits, including the red neckerchiefs covering their faces. They looked exactly like the classic depictions of the ad-hoc army that filled the streets in 1009 to help reclaim the city and the throne for Maradaine XI.

Someone put a lot of money and care into making this happen.

"Dayne!" A woman's voice called through the crowd. Warm, refined, and so very familiar. Dayne turned to its source, his heart quickening just at the thought of who it might be.

There she was, the very picture of Druth elegance, her richly embroidered peach dress complimenting her fair skin, though with her white gloves and the lace veil on her hat, very little of her skin was to be seen. Her delicate blonde curls spilled down her back, and her dark blue eyes hinted at wisdom beyond her age. She cut her way across the hallway, one handmaiden at her side.

"Lady Mirianne," he said with a bow. Jerinne, he noticed out of the corner of his eye, followed his lead.

"No bowing," Lady Mirianne said. Her gloved hand touched the side of his face, leading him back to standing. "How is it you are here?"

"I've only just come back to Maradaine, my lady," Dayne said. "If I may, this is Jerinne Fendall, second-year Initiate to the Order."

"Your servant, my lady," Jerinne said, offering her hand.

"I have no need of more, Miss Fendall." Mirianne took her hand gently. "Lady Mirianne Henson, daughter to the Earl of Jaconvale."

"How is your father?" Dayne asked.

She gave a playful slap to his arm. "I've not seen your beautiful face for nearly three years and you ask after my father."

"I'm sorry, my lady," Dayne said. "I only thought it—"

"Proper, as always. Dear, sweet, proper Dayne. He's quite well, happy at the estate in Jaconvale. He's not a fan of traveling to the city anymore, so the household here is effectively mine." She turned to her handmaiden. "Is he not adorable?" Her smile was a treasure. Dayne had almost forgotten how lovely she was.

"I should have asked after you first, my lady."

"No," Lady Mirianne said. "How are you back in Maradaine?"

Dayne glanced over to Jerinne, and at the handmaiden. "It is an involved tale, Lady, and not one for public telling."

She nodded. "Of course. I will hold you to a private counsel later." She gave a light trill of a laugh, and a knowing wink to her handmaiden. Turning back to Dayne, she added, "I know why you are here, of course. A history museum must have been like honey to a fly."

Dayne grinned, despite himself, taking another look around the wide entry hall. "I have to admit, this is incredible. I'm amazed at what they've done."

"Thank you," Lady Mirianne said. "It was quite the undertaking."

"You had a hand in all this?" Dayne asked. Of course, he should have guessed it. If anyone had both the means and the desire to make a monument to Druth history, it would be the Earl of Jaconvale and his daughter. It was through them he had developed his own love for the subject, as well as the sponsorship that led him to the Tarian Order.

"Mostly organizing the funding. Professor Teal and his team were the real champions." She pointed over to the stage, where Teal and other scholars now sat patiently behind the Parliamentarians.

"Will he be speaking?" Dayne asked. During his Initiacy he had had the privilege to sit in on a handful of lectures at the RCM. Professor Teal was a living treasure of Druth history, possibly the most knowledgeable and dynamic speakers on the subject.

"Not until the fools from the Parliament have their chance to babble," Lady Mirianne said. She took his hand. "Let me show you something."

"What?" Dayne asked, surprised at her soft gloved hand staying curled around his.

"There's an exhibit you should see. Please."

"But . . ." They hadn't actually opened the exhibits yet. "The speeches." He said it halfheartedly. He knew the Parliament speeches would be less than thrilling.

"It won't take long," she said. She turned to her handmaiden. "Jessel, keep company with Miss Fendall."

"As you say, Lady." Jessel curtsied.

Lady Mirianne pulled Dayne to the side as he gave one last look over to Jerinne. The Initiate merely smirked at Dayne, and then gave her attention to Jessel.

Dayne followed along after Lady Mirianne, and they slipped under one of the ropes, with Lady Mirianne nodding to one of the servants as they went. They entered a back stairwell, Lady Mirianne giving Dayne the same impish smile she would use back at her father's manor when she snuck into the stables. As they ascended, he wondered if her intentions had anything to do with an exhibit.

"Don't even look at this room," she said when she pulled him off the stairs on the next level.

"But I thought—"

"You're just going to get angry." She went to the opposite end of the gallery.

"Why would I get angry?" Dayne asked, but then he saw the large portrait filling one entire wall. He stopped dead in his tracks and stared at the monstrosity. "The blazes?"

"I knew you'd hate this," she said, coming back to his side.

The portrait was of ten eleventh-century figures, recognizable to even a casual student of history. "The Grand Ten? In a portrait together?"

"I know what you're going to say," Lady Mirianne said.

"They were never all in the same room together!" Dayne said. "Most of them never even met!" And yet, here, in the museum curated and blessed by the Druth Historic Society, the Grand Ten sat and stood together, in one enormous portrait. Of course, each one of the Grand Ten were instrumental in the Reunification of 1009, key figures in history. Dayne wouldn't deny that. But the tendency to rewrite history, to pretend that they had been some sort of united club that organized the Reunification—that set his teeth on edge.

"I know," Lady Mirianne said. "It was the Honorable Mister Barton's idea. His one adamant insistence."

"Mister Barton? Who is that?"

"He's in the Parliament. Traditionalist from our archduchy."

"Why did he insist on this?" Dayne asked.

"He's very passionate about the Grand Ten. He even commissioned the portrait from his own purse."

"Waste of money," Dayne said. "It's just bad history."

"I'm well aware," Lady Mirianne said. "Though if you look at it as an ten individual portraits put together, it is well done."

Dayne nodded. "Individually, yes. All classically done." They all were at their most iconic. Geophry Haltom, The

Parliamentarian, with his red neckerchief, like the servers were wearing downstairs. Baron Kege, The Lord, with broken manacles on his wrists and his head held high. Oberon Micarum, The Warrior, in the full uniform of a Spathian Master. "I was just talking to the Grandmaster about how Oberon is the main reason why the Spathians still stand."

"And Xandra Romaine?" she asked.

"And Xandra Romaine, yes." It hurt his heart that the Order was not only considered a relic, maintained just out of gratitude to two historical figures, but that this narrative was so ingrained that they didn't even have to explain it to each other.

Then he looked over to The Mage—Xaveem Ak'-alassa—an Imach whose magical skills were instrumental in defeating the leader of the Incursion and restoring Maradaine XI to the Druth throne. The depiction of Xaveem was ridiculous: Druth clothing, and a skin tone only slightly darker than the rest of the group. Save the curved blade on his hip, there was nothing in his appearance to identify him as Imach.

"Classically done, indeed," Dayne said. "This sort of history is troubling. It inflates the importance of some people for the sake of narrative, ignoring the important work of people like Lief Frannel or Hanshon Alenick, or—"

"Please don't get too upset," Lady Mirianne said, cutting him off from his rant. That was probably wise, and she knew him well enough to not let him get worked up over these things. "This isn't what I wanted to show you."

"Of course," Dayne said, turning away from the aggravating painting. "Lead on, my lady."

She took his hand. "Enough with the 'my lady,' Dayne Heldrin. Especially when we're alone."

"That's asking quite a lot," Dayne said.

"I have the privilege of asking a lot," she said, flashing another mischievous smile. "I am a Lady, after all. This is it."

The new room opened up into a wide oval, with twelve mannequins on small platforms, forming a semicircle. Each mannequin was faceless, dressed with uniforms, armor, and weapons, some of which were centuries out of style. Only two had modern design, in the center of the semicircle. The one on the left wore the same gray coat and tunic that Dayne was wearing, save the coat bore the epaulets and insignia of a Master. That mannequin stood in classic Position Three, round shield high and short sword held low.

The brass plaque at its feet read "Master of the Tarian Order."

The other mannequins each represented a different Order, almost all of which had long been inactive or disbanded—all but the Tarians and the Spathians, represented by the other central mannequin. The Vanidian—forest guardian with ax and bow. The blue uniformed Hanalian, the antecedent of the King's Marshals downstairs. The fully armored Grennian. The healing master Ascepian. Pike-wielding Braighian. All these mighty and honored Elite Orders that had been abandoned or folded into the army or other new organizations.

"This is . . . incredible," he said, his voice cracking just a bit in his attempt to hold back the tear in his eye.

"I knew you would appreciate it." She came up behind him, placing her arm in the crook of his elbow. "Mister Barton insisted on the Grand Ten. This . . . this is what I insisted on."

A smile found its way to Dayne's lips. "You really were listening to me."

She stepped around and faced him. "Always."

Dayne couldn't resist her any longer, and had no reason to. He bent down to kiss her.

Before he could, screams cut through the air.

Chapter 7

JERINNE WASN'T PLEASED WITH being abandoned in a museum lobby, about to be bored by parliamentary speeches. This was not how she had hoped to spend her first Quiet Day. The one saving grace was the company of Miss Jessel, which was proving to be quite pleasant.

"You haven't known Mister Heldrin long, have you?" she asked.

"I just met him yesterday," Jerinne said. "He's a good sort, but I wouldn't have thought he'd just leave like that."

"The lady and he have quite a history." She gave a suggestive smirk. Jerinne was not opposed to suggestive smirks from this woman.

"That was quite apparent." Jerinne leaned in closer. "But I'm not much of a history student."

A bright, coy smile, and a flash in her eyes. "But you are a student. A young lady like you is usually eager to learn."

This could be a very good Quiet Day indeed, even if she never mastered Shield Maneuver Eight.

One of the eleventh-century-dressed servers bumped his way in between them. Jerinne was about to snap at the man for his rudeness when a few people stepped up on the dais.

"Thank you, thank you," a robed man said, loud enough to hush the crowd and claim their attention. "It's very kind of you all to show such support to this worthy endeavor."

"Professor Teal," Jessel whispered, having moved back toward Jerinne.

"Of course, there are many people without whose kind and generous support we would have been unable to create this wonderful testament to the history of Druthal." Teal coughed and looked to the well-dressed men standing by him. "I would like to take the time to thank, of course, the Earl of Jaconvale and his daughter, Lady Mirianne . . . is she here, I just saw her . . ."

He looked around for a moment. Jerinne and Jessel shared a conspiratorial chuckle at the idea that the Lady was not going to be spotted anytime soon. The crowd kept their attention on the Professor as he glanced about, save the costumed servers. They all were moving to the edge of the crowd.

"But beyond that, there was the tireless work of my students and researchers. To name a few . . ."

One of the well-dressed men behind the Professor coughed strongly.

"Which I will do in due course," the Professor said, looking to the two well-dressed men. "But first, certainly, I must also acknowledge the tireless efforts and cooperation of the Parliament, especially two key members, whom I have the privilege of sharing this stage with today. If I may, the Good Misters Erick Parlin and Julian Barton."

The crowd gave a smattering of polite applause. One of the Parliamentarians stepped forward.

"Thank you, Professor," he said. "The Good Mister Barton and I—"

As soon as he began speaking, two of the servers leaped to the stage, wielding crossbows.

"No one move!" one of the armed servers shouted. The other aimed at Parlin.

More servers pulled out crossbows, all of them in position at doorways.

Jerinne quickly put herself between Jessel and the closest crossbow.

"You!" the server on the stage shouted, pointing at the marshals who had disarmed Jerinne when they came in. "You and your men throw your weapons on the ground." The marshals scowled, but none of them argued. Blades and crossbows clattered on the floor in a matter of seconds.

"Tharek," the one who was obviously the leader said, "gather those up."

One of the servers on the floor level—closest to the exit—came over with a sack and started tossing the weapons in. This man stood out over the rest of the armed servers. A bit taller, broader of shoulder, certainly. But there was an ease to the man, a fluidity of movement as he picked up weapons and bagged them. This man knew what he was doing, even if he wasn't in charge. The man in charge was on stage, holstering his crossbow. He pulled down his neckerchief, revealing his face. He had a manicured beard and narrow chin. He looked far more like a student than a thief or thug.

"I apologize, good people here. Even though you are among the swells and jeets, I presume some of you are good and true sons of Druthal. Please understand that I mean no ill will to you. However, right now, I cannot immediately distinguish you from the enemies of our country."

He walked along the front of the stage, voice like silk and smoke. One of his men shared the stage with him, finger on the trigger of his crossbow. That one seemed almost terrified that he held a deadly weapon in his hand. Jerinne slid herself around Jessel again. If an errant shot killed anyone, it was likely to come from this man. With no shield, no weapon, there was only one way to put herself between that crossbow and an innocent bystander.

Stupid marshals.

"My name is Lannic," the leader said. "Though today I am of the same spirit as Geophry Haltom. And we are Haltom's Patriots."

Blazes. Haltom's Patriots. Ill-considered rebels. Mostly privileged boys who lashed out blindly against the system that gave them that privilege.

"All of you, please, sit on the floor. I'm terribly sorry if it damages your fine clothes." The people on the stage started to sit, as did all the crowd. "Not you two, good sirs," Lannic said, pulling Parlin and Barton to their feet. "You two are the message. Tharek, corral the marshals into the center. We want to keep an eye on them."

Tharek and the others guided the marshals over, and they sat on the floor with everyone else.

"Good," Lannic said. "Now, as you are surely aware, a poison cuts through the heart of this beautiful country, just as surely as the great Maradaine River cuts through the city! This poison, this toxic rancor, taints everything that was fought for in 1009. And as we are here, in this ostentatious and extravagant tribute to the history of all things Druth, we all know what great sacrifices were made in that glorious year to make this nation what it is. But yet, some men—" Lannic bowed with an exaggerated flourish in the direction of Barton and Parlin. "Some men who should be honoring the spirit of these sacrifices—they are the ones most apt to forget it. These men, the very representatives of the common man, the makers of law and policy—these are the great traitors."

"Now just a moment—" Barton earned the butt of a

crossbow across his head from Lannic's associate, drawing a shocked gasp from the crowd. Barton dropped to his knees.

Lannic crouched down. "You do not have the floor, Good Mister Barton. You have not been elected to speak for anyone here. This—" Lannic leaped to his feet and swung his arms out wide. "This is the true Parliament of the common man! We are Haltom's Patriots, and we have formed our own Parliament, and we will people the Court." He knelt back down, his face mere inches away from Barton. "And we shall dispense justice."

Jerinne swore under her breath. Someone was going to get hurt, and there wasn't anything she could do about it. Not yet.

Her gaze darted up to the balcony surrounding the entrance hall. No Patriots standing guard up there. With any luck, Dayne was up there, free to act. Maybe Dayne could do something to give them half a chance.

"We are Haltom's Patriots, and we have formed our own Parliament, and we will people the Court." The man's voice echoed up to the balcony. "And we shall dispense justice."

Dayne stayed crouched out of sight. Surprise was his best advantage. Once they knew he was up here, he would have no chance of rescuing anyone.

Lady Mirianne hid around the corner, completely out of sight to anyone on the floor below. That was as close as he wanted her to be. If nothing else, he would make sure that she remained safe. He owed that to her and her family. He owed that to his pledge to the Order.

"How many?" she whispered.

He crawled back over to her. "At least twelve, all with crossbows."

"Blazes," she said flatly. He must have shown his shock,

as she said, "Really, Dayne, if any moment called for vulgarity, this would be it."

"Of course, Lady Mirianne."

"I told you—"

"As of now, you are nobility under my charge." Dayne went around the corner and rose to his feet. He took her hand and helped her up as well. "And therefore, my lady, out of propriety, I will treat you as such."

Lady Mirianne stifled a laugh, looking back over to the balcony as Dayne pulled her back down the hallway toward the Grand Ten exhibit. "I'm so fortunate to be under the charge of such a capable Tarian."

Dayne knew that, even with her flippant tone, she wasn't mocking his capability. He still felt the sting, his thoughts went to Lenick Benedict; alive but broken.

Lady Mirianne must have sensed his despair, as her small hand squeezed his warmly. "I am," she said.

He smiled back at her. Her eyes were so bright and giving. "I'm glad you think so. I will get you out of here safely. Is there another exit?"

"There are a few," she said. "But I don't think we can get to them."

"Why not?"

She glanced around the exhibit room. "I don't know all the stairwells. But those lead back down to the lobby. And that one leads to the service offices and loading doors."

"Good," Dayne said, leading her toward the stairwell she pointed at, taking them back through the Orders exhibit.

"That won't be safe," she protested. "Think about it, Dayne. The Patriots are disguised as the event servers."

"So they are certainly guarding that exit," Dayne said. "But probably only a couple of them."

"That's only a guess."

"It's a reasonable one," Dayne said, taking a glance

down the stairwell. Unoccupied. "The lobby is where everyone is, including the marshals. Most of their force will be needed to control that situation. At most they'll spare only two or three people to cover anywhere else." He went over to the mannequins of the Orders. A touch of the Tarian's shield told him all he needed to know. Plaster and paint. Nothing he could use. The Spathian weapons were the same. "You couldn't have tried for authenticity?" he asked Lady Mirianne.

"I had no idea it would be worth the expense," she shot back. "What do you think you can do, even if there are 'only' two or three men down there?"

"Stay here," Dayne said, going to the stairs. "I'll call when it's safe."

"Dayne!" she hissed, clearly keeping herself from shouting and drawing attention. "They are going to shoot you!"

"With all due respect, my lady," Dayne said, "they are only going to shoot *at* me."

Dayne slipped down the stairs as quietly as he could. Once he reached the landing, he could hear two men chatting quietly just through the threshold. Not chatting, grousing.

"You're just annoyed because he's Lannic's favorite," one said.

"That ain't it," the other said. "I could roll a badger over what Lannic thinks of him or me. I'm saying he ain't right. I can't figure out why he's with us."

"All that matters is he is," the first said. "He believes in our cause."

"He said he does."

Dayne chanced a glance. Two men, in the historical outfits, both armed with crossbows, paced lazily around the loading floor. Three other bodies were on the ground. Dayne couldn't tell in the brief moment he looked if they were alive or dead. Given that they were tied up, it was more likely they were still alive.

Tied up. The two Patriots didn't want to have the burden of actively guarding those three. So they were lazy.

Dayne constructed the other details from the scene in his head. The loading floor was filled with wooden crates, hand trucks, and rolling platforms. The loading doors were shut, but the doors leading out toward the lobby were open. Loud noises would carry.

The men were likely true believers, based on their speech. He could probably dodge their crossbows all day, since it was highly unlikely they were mercenaries or former soldiers. The people who fell prey to groups like the Patriots tended to come from academia and honest trades. They might be small game hunters, but they'd find Dayne a lot harder to hit than a rabbit or squirrel.

He couldn't just dodge them, though. He needed to subdue them, and it had to be quick, and it had to be quiet.

Dayne swore under his breath. He could see no resolution that didn't involve at least a minimum of violence. His stomach turned at the idea.

His feelings didn't matter. The safety of Lady Mirianne was paramount. That was enough to resolve any qualms he might have regarding harming these two men.

Fast. Quiet. Dayne spun around through the threshold and charged the two men at full speed.

He had covered half the distance before they noticed he was coming, and he was almost on top of them when they got their crossbows up. The one on the left didn't even aim, he just raised up and fired wild. The other at least had the decency to shoot in Dayne's general direction. A slight shift of his body was enough to avoid it.

Both of them were about to shout out when Dayne wrapped his hands around their sweaty heads, and with the minimum strength necessary to accomplish it, cracked their skulls together.

They dropped like sacks of potatoes.

"My apologies, gentlemen," Dayne whispered. They

both were breathing, and not bleeding, so hopefully he had only caused minor injuries. The brief, bemused thought crossed Dayne's mind that perhaps he had knocked some sense into their heads, or at least knocked out the flawed interpretation of the Rights of Man and the Accords of 1009 that plagued the Patriots' philosophy.

He quickly rebuked himself for even thinking that. He could have easily killed them. They might still die, or be permanently injured. He did what needed to be done, but he shouldn't let himself make light of it in any way.

He checked on their victims. The three men—all marshals—were hurt, alive but unconscious. They had been beaten, with ugly bruises across their heads. Not shot with crossbows, though. Blunt trauma. Fists or handsticks, likely. The two Patriots didn't have any weapons besides their crossbows. They would all need Yellowshields, if not proper doctors. Hopefully it wasn't too late.

Dayne checked their crossbows—cheap, two-crown devices that weren't worth blazes if one hoped to shoot with any accuracy.

Dayne untied the men, not that it really mattered, and with the rope tied and gagged the two Patriots.

"My lady," he quietly called up the stairwell. "It's safe to descend."

Lady Mirianne came down, and Dayne immediately noticed that she had removed the extraneous and frilly portions of her gown, leaving her in a practical, stripped-down dress that still fulfilled all the duties of propriety.

"Are you all right?" she asked.

"I'm not injured," Dayne said, which answered her question as honestly as he was willing to at this point. He went to the loading doors and quietly pushed them open. "You'll have to hurry. We'll need Constabulary and Yellowshields as quickly as possible."

"What do you mean I'll have to hurry? You're staying here?"

"Miri—" Dayne felt his voice faltering, despite himself. "There are two members of Parliament, several other nobility, and dozens of innocents in there. I cannot abandon them. Putting your safety above theirs is the most concession to my heart I can allow."

"Your heart?" she asked, touching his face.

"Please, go get help. I'll do what I can."

She leaped up and wrapped her arms around his neck, kissing him strongly. He allowed the indulgence, if only for a moment. She ended the kiss, but held on, her eyes locked onto his.

"Stay alive, Dayne. Don't do anything foolish."

"I'll do my best."

She dropped down to her feet and went to the door. With one wistful look back at him, she dashed out into the alley.

Dayne looked back at the doorway leading to the lobby. Last he saw, they had gathered the hostages into a tight circle in the center of the room. There were about twelve men in all, each of them with crossbows. Crossbows like the ones these two had.

Bad shots, hard to reload.

If he could draw their fire, give them something to shoot at, get enough of them to shoot, then they'd be sufficiently disarmed that he could handle them.

Not that he could handle all twelve, certainly not with civilians in the mix.

Of course, they weren't all civilians. There was Jerinne, and at least four King's Marshals. They might prove of use once the crossbows were taken out of the equation.

The crossbows were still sticky. Even he couldn't dodge twelve shots, presuming that he alone could even draw every Patriot's fire.

He needed to give them more to shoot at.

A wild idea occurred to him. He grabbed two of the rolling platforms and hauled them back up the stairs.

After ten minutes of Lannic's rhetoric against the Parliament, taxes, and legal accountability, Jerinne was almost hoping to take a crossbow bolt to the head. It would be less painful.

"And it is this mandate for the people to defend the very Rights of Man that they take for granted! I will enumerate . . ."

Jerinne turned her head to see if the marshals were doing anything. They were in charge of security, after all. They sat on the floor with everyone else, but without the frightened expression. They were bored. They were waiting.

What were they waiting for?

What was Jerinne waiting for? Dayne? For all she knew, Dayne was waiting for her to give him an opening. Or Dayne had left out the back with the Lady Mirianne.

The point was, who else was going to do something?

" . . . the thwarted will of the common man—"

"Do you have any demands?" Jerinne said, getting to her feet.

Every crossbow was now trained on Jerinne.

Lannic was clearly stunned, unsure how to react. He quickly recovered. "Of course we have demands. The system *must* change. We must expunge Druthal of these hypocrites we call leaders. The sooner people like you, Tarian, who live to prop up the fetid rot—"

"Yeah, I heard all that," Jerinne said. "But right now, what are your demands?"

"Shut it, Tarian!" one of the other ones snapped.

"No, let the Initiate speak," another said. Jerinne glanced back to see it was the one called Tharek—he was masked with his neckerchief like all the others, but in physicality, the grace of his stance, he stood out.

"You're not going to get the whole Parliament to resign from inside this museum," Jerinne said. "You've got sixty or so hostages of varying value. What do you want out of that? And who are you going to ask?"

"You are not hostages, young lady," Lannic said, shaking his head as if he was talking to a child. "You are the people. You are my congress of the people! You are all here to bear witness!"

"So we're free to go?" Jerinne said.

"No one is free, young Tarian, though that is the lie they sweeten the poison with. We call the common man a freeman, don't we? Isn't that the polite term?" He turned to Mister Parlin, still standing on the stage in a cold sweat. "Isn't that what you were called, Good Mister Parlin? Freeman Erick Parlin?"

"Some called me that," Parlin said.

"Populist, aren't you, *Good* Mister Parlin? Man of the people? In touch with the common man?"

"I try." Parlin held his chin high.

"Try, indeed," Lannic said, running his hand on Parlin's coat. "Turjin silk, is it? And the rings? Gold and sapphires, I see? And where do you live, *Good* Mister Parlin?"

"I'm the Fifth Chair of Acora. I live in Porvence."

"Oh, yes, of course you live in your archduchy. I'm sure it's a rustic, simple place. But here, in Maradaine, Mister Chair, where do you reside?"

Parlin said nothing.

"I'm sorry, Mister Chair? I didn't hear an answer."

The other one on the stage shoved his crossbow at Parlin. "Answer!"

"That's quite all right," Lannic said, waving his man off. "I already know, Good Mister Parlin. Your home is in Callon Hills. Quite the Populist, living up there, hmm? Quite the man of the people."

He turned out to the crowd. "And that's the great joke, isn't it? The entire Parliament should be composed of common men, and we cannot manage that. Instead one party—the smallest party in the Parliament—are the common men. And here, Erick Parlin of Callon Hills, is the shining example!"

"And so?" Jerinne snapped back. Again, all eyes and crossbows turned to her. "You don't like him, vote him out."

Lannic stepped forward, shaking a long finger at Jerinne. Giving her his full attention. "If only, young Tarian. If only the voting process wasn't so intrinsically corrupt. What are the alternatives to Good Mister Parlin? A man like Barton, who may as well live in a rich baron's purse?"

That was the opening Jerinne wanted. She took two steps forward, keeping her arms open. Show no threat. Every crossbow stayed trained on her. Including the one that had been on the Parliamentarian's head. No one was in immediate danger, except for her. "So what's next?"

"Girl, cut it out," one of the marshals said. Now they looked engaged. And frightened. Good. Maybe they might do something.

"What's the glorious plan, Lannic?" Jerinne hissed.

Lannic didn't answer, either in word or action, as the other man on the stage shouted and aimed his crossbow at a figure that suddenly appeared on the balcony. Without any hesitation, the man on the stage fired. Three other men shot at the figure up there.

Lannic's gaze trained on the figure as well, and Jerinne rushed in. She grabbed Lannic by the waist and pulled him off the stage. Jerinne sent a knee into the man's groin, and as Lannic dropped, Jerinne wrenched his arm behind his back, pinning him down.

Another figure appeared on the balcony, this one in full Spathian regalia. Four more men shot at him—no, it. A faceless mannequin. That point was clear since one bolt buried right in the thing's head. Jerinne spun around and saw exactly who had fired: Tharek.

Another mannequin—in classic Tarian trappings— came at the top of one of the stairs, drawing two more shots.

Then another at the other stairs. This wasn't a mannequin, though. Dayne, charging down, dodging the last shots sent his way.

By Jerinne's count, that was every crossbow.

Chapter 8

THE SITUATION WAS ESCALATING in the lobby.
More to the point, Jerinne was escalating it. Dayne
left the Hanalian mannequin on its platform behind the
corner and snuck over to look down.

Jerinne was taunting the leader. She was standing, and
she had every eye, every crossbow, trained on her. Good.
That's what a Tarian should do. He had to admire the
girl's instincts. Plus, that would make them easy to distract.

He needed to move quickly, or else there would be no
crossbow fire to draw. Jerinne would be a pincushion.

He hurried back to the Hanalian and shoved it out
onto the balcony. He raced around through two exhibi-
tion rooms to where he had the Tarian and Spathian
staged. He had to hurry. Shots fired. Hopefully they were
all at the mannequin.

Rounding the corner, Dayne slammed into the Spathian mannequin, and it spiraled out onto the balcony.
More shots fired as he reached the Tarian mannequin.

He pushed it onto one stairway as he hurried to the other one. How many were distracted? How many fired? Could Jerinne and marshals help him subdue the Patriots before it was too late?

Thoughts hammered through his head as he leaped down the stairs. How many lives were at stake this time?

Two bolts whizzed past him. Terrible shots. He hit the landing unscathed.

Twelve men, most scrambling to reload their crossbows. Couldn't give them the chance.

Jerinne had the leader down. Good. The girl had the raw skill.

Dayne charged at the closest two, arms wide, giving a mighty roar. It was, on some level, ridiculous, but he wanted the Patriots to panic. They weren't soldiers or mercenaries. Some judicious fear should be enough to instigate a mass surrender.

It was an effective strategy against those two Patriots, as they both yelped and scrambled to get away, crashing into each other. Dayne slammed into them, knocking them both to the floor. Minimum injury, maximum effect.

Dayne turned back to the crowd. The marshals were scrambling to their feet. The Patriot on the stage with the Parliamentarians was reloading. Dayne needed to take him out of the equation. Three quick bounds to the stage. The man almost had a new bolt in his weapon. Dayne grabbed one wrist and twisted the Patriot's arm behind his back.

"Drop your weapons!" Jerinne shouted. She had the leader in a headlock, hauled up off his feet. One hand was pressed against the man's head, as if she meant to break his neck. "Crossbows on the ground!" Dayne's heart raced, leaping into his throat.

The Patriots dropped their weapons, except one.

Easily the tallest of the group, he threw his crossbow directly at Jerinne. As it flew across the room, he drew out two more crossbows.

These were not like anyone else's. These were fine craftsmanship; Dayne could see that clearly.

Two shots sang out across the lobby, as the crossbow clocked Jerinne square in the face. Those shots were coming at the stage. At the Parliament members.

No time. Dayne shoved his prisoner at one member of Parliament, while unceremoniously grabbing the other and pulling him down.

Barely in time. The bolt sliced right past Dayne's face, the fletching shaving the barest of marks across his cheek.

"You all right?" he asked the Parliamentarian.

The man nodded, his face coated in cold sweat. Dayne looked to the other one. Throwing the Patriot at him had been effective: he was knocked out of the way. Unfortunately, the Patriot had taken the bolt instead; a clean shot in the head.

"No!" Dayne shouted, the word clawing its way out of his heart. He had as good as killed that man.

The tall Patriot was on Jerinne, delivering a series of punches with blinding speed and breathtaking skill. Jerinne, dazed from being hit, had no chance to defend herself. In two breaths, the girl was on the floor. The tall Patriot scooped his leader up over his shoulder and ran to the back exit. Several other Patriots followed, though the marshals were now grabbing them and pinning them to the ground.

The crowd panicked and screamed and ran for the doors.

The doors burst open, sunlight streaming into the hallway.

The dead man's blood pooled on the stage.

Two of the Patriots were escaping.

Dayne wanted to run after them. Capture the tall one and the leader. Get them before they could do anything else. They were heading to the alley. Lady Mirianne might still be out there. For her, he had to stop them.

Yet even those thoughts weren't able to spur his legs. He wasn't able to look away from the pool of blood.

He had made a choice, he had taken action, and because of that, this man was dead. He had taken an oath, to the Order and to Master Denbar, and most importantly to himself, to protect all life. He had failed that oath.

Again.

"Enough, Tharek! I'm not hurt!" Lannic struggled to get out of his comrade's grip. He didn't need the man carrying him any farther. They needed to get away from the whole area of the museum, and quickly, but having one man carry another Brigade style, while dragging two more hogtied men was hardly a way to be inconspicuous.

"Fine." Tharek put him down just at the edge of the alley. "Constabulary will start a street crawl soon, if not a full blockade." He dropped Kemmer and Braning, who were struggling in their bonds. "Stop squirming." Tharek pulled out a knife from his coat and sliced their ropes.

"Blazes, Pell," Kemmer said, rubbing at his wrists. Kemmer hadn't been too accepting of Tharek into the brotherhood of the Patriots, so used only his familial name. "Didn't have to drag us like that."

"You're lucky I didn't leave you there," Tharek said. He tore off the neckerchief and coat, effectively removing any obvious sign of where they had just been. Lannic started doing the same.

"Are you two all right?" Lannic asked.

"Some loon in a uniform jumped us," Braning said. "He knocked our skulls before we had a chance to move."

"That loon was a Tarian," Tharek said. "Could have cracked your skulls like eggs if he wanted to."

"That girl was a Tarian as well," Lannic said. That girl with her smart mouth. Not as smart as she liked to think she was. The fool had no idea how corrupt the system was. She had clearly subscribed to being a part of it, entrenched in it. "They're all just part of the problem."

Braning and Kemmer had taken off their disguises as well. "Now what?" Kemmer asked.

"What about Shaw and the others?" Braning asked.

"Shaw is dead," Tharek said.

"What?" Braning asked, almost wailing. Shaw was Braning's brother.

"It was that Tarian," Tharek said. He scowled and glanced out the alley into the street. "I tried to shoot the Parli, but the Tarian used Shaw as a shield." Tharek's voice dripped with contempt. Lannic understood why, if Tharek had seen the Tarian do that. That man—that Tarian—had shown such clear contempt for life, for his fellow man. Anything to maintain the current, rotting order.

"And everyone else?" Kemmer asked.

"Not sure," Tharek said. "They weren't behind me when I got to the door. Killed or arrested."

"We have to get out of here," Lannic said. He had finally taken his own disguise off. He had shown them his face, of course, but now he was dressed like an average student. No one would give him a second glance.

"I have been saying," Tharek said. "Constabulary will be on top of us. Having to kill a few of them would be inconvenient."

"We're going to get killed," Kemmer said. "We're already blazing dead."

"We should split up." Lannic needed to get them all back on track. "Each of you, just walk out of here, calm and easy. Everyone back at the Alassan by three bells. I need to talk to the chief, figure out our next step there."

"What about everyone else?" Braning urged.

Lannic took him by the hand. Good-hearted Braning. Always thinking of others. "We'll figure that out. I promise you, my friend, we will not forget anyone."

Braning nodded, tears forming at his eyes. "And our statement? That was Shaw's job."

"I think I could take care of that," Kemmer said.

"You know someone?" Lannic asked.

"Maybe," Kemmer said. "I have some friends who haven't stepped up to action yet."

"We need them to answer the call, Kemmer," Lannic said. He put an arm around Braning. "We've lost enough for now."

Braning nodded again, wiping his eyes and putting on a brave face. He turned, head down, and walked off. Kemmer did the same. Both were gone into the crowd.

"Should have left them, too," Tharek muttered.

"Don't say that," Lannic said. "We need every true heart right now."

"True hearts sometimes have blind eyes," Tharek said. "Three bells."

"I count on you. Now, more than ever."

"And I will do whatever is necessary," Tharek said. His great hand clapped Lannic on the shoulder, and with that, he was gone.

Lannic glanced back down the alley. No one watching. Good. He didn't have time to worry about being followed, being arrested right now. Enough friends were martyrs today. Kemmer was right, there were more friends in the city. It was time for them to answer the call.

"Dayne?" The voice rose above the din of the crowd, but Dayne couldn't make out a face through the haze of anger and tears. But he knew the voice well enough. Lady Mirianne. The reality of the moment crashed in on him. How long had he been sitting on the stage, shocked by the dead Patriot? Where was Jerinne? Where were the Parliamentarians? He jumped to his feet. Did anyone need his help? Lady Mirianne seemed calm, no sign of danger.

"Why are you back here?" he asked.

She smiled coyly. "I brought the Constabulary." She pointed to the green-and-red jacketed men helping the hostages out the front door. A pair of Yellowshields were tending to Jerinne, who for her part was mostly fending off their ministrations. A Constabulary lieutenant and one of the King's Marshals were arguing in front of the nine Patriots they had bound in irons on the floor. "Of course, by the time I got back, you had more or less saved the day."

"Very much less," he said, turning back to the dead Patriot. The Constabulary bodyman had thrown a tarp over the corpse, but that didn't make any difference to Dayne. "I didn't save a blasted thing."

"This boy is too modest," one of the Parliamentarians said, coming down off the stage. "Though, that's a rare trait which should probably be encouraged more." He extended his hand. "I'd say Good Mister Barton and I might have found ourselves at the wrong end of those crossbow bolts were it not for your quick thinking."

"But someone did find the wrong end of one, good sir," Dayne said.

"And that someone was almost me," the other Parliamentarian said. This one must be Barton, meaning the first was Parlin. "I'm not sure having a ruffian shoved at me was a better option."

"It most certainly was, Julian," Mister Parlin said. "Frankly, my good Tarian, I'm quite grateful you were here. Aren't we?" Mister Barton grunted something in agreement.

"His name is Heldrin," Lady Mirianne said. "Dayne Heldrin. Second-year Candidate."

"Candidate, hmm?" Mister Parlin said. He gave a good-natured laugh, and leaned in to whisper. "I'm afraid I've stepped off the approval committee, son. Perhaps you picked the wrong Parliamentarians to save!"

"Enough, Erick," Mister Barton said, taking his colleague by the arm. "You have our thanks, Mister Heldrin." He dragged Parlin away, heading over to the King's Marshals. Another marshal—Marshal Chief Toscan, specifically—brought Jerinne over. Despite the bruises on her face, Jerinne was smiling.

"You're the ranking Tarian, so she's your problem," the chief said. "Though the two of you better show reason why you shouldn't be ironed up."

With one Patriot dead and at least two at large, Dayne wasn't sure he had one, other than he had no formal responsibility for the security of this place beyond his duty as a Tarian. He considered saying that he only acted where the marshals had failed, but Lady Mirianne spoke before he could say so.

"Because I refuse to let you do such a thing!"

The marshal's face dripped with condescension. "With all due respect, my lady, you have no authority—"

Lady Mirianne put her tiny body between Dayne and Toscan. "With all due respect, Marshal, I suggest you review your Books of Decree. Namely, Royal Decree 172, dated Nalithan the 9th, 1017, which reads—"

"I know what it reads, my lady."

"Then you know that all members of recognized orders—like the Tarians—including members in training, are to be given all courtesies as officers of justice."

"Within limits," the marshal said.

Jerinne snorted. "You're just mad because Dayne and I saved the day while your men sat on their hands."

"You're going to get the courtesy of my fist, child!"

Dayne raised up a hand. "There's no need for that, Chief. Tell me, honestly, do you believe you have a just cause for laying a charge upon us? If so, we will face it."

"Dayne!" Jerinne said.

"We will face it," Dayne reiterated. "Though as the senior member present, I do take full responsibility for Miss Fendall."

The marshal scowled. "Probably nothing. You're both lucky no one got hurt."

"There's a dead man here," Dayne said.

"Not to mention my face," Jerinne added.

The marshal's condescending expression returned. "I meant no one of—consequence." He glanced at Lady Mirianne, as if expecting her to agree with him, but the look on her face was anything but that. He coughed awkwardly. "My lady." He gave a correctly formal bow toward Lady Mirianne and walked off.

"Swine," Lady Mirianne muttered. "Truly, Miss Fendall, are you well? I have an excellent doctor I can call upon. Or perhaps I can instruct Jessel to engage in some healing arts?"

"The doctor and other healers we have in our infirmary are quite skilled," Dayne said. "We'll return home and let them tend to her."

"I'll be fine, my lady," Jerinne said. "It looks worse than it feels."

"It really does look quite horrible," Dayne said.

Jerinne shrugged. "Two of us against twelve. At least it was that Tharek character who dropped me."

"Tharek?" Dayne asked. Was that the tall one's name? "He wasn't like the rest. He had better crossbows. More like a mercenary."

"Even a mercenary can believe in a cause," Lady Mirianne said.

Dayne conceded that point. Even still, it was worth learning more. Especially since Tharek was free.

"What are you going to do, Dayne?" Lady Mirianne asked.

"I don't know. I just . . . I feel like there's more that I could do."

"Not here," she said. "Perhaps you should take Miss Fendall back to the chapterhouse before the marshals decide there is a crime to charge on you."

"Like killing that Patriot?" Dayne asked.

"Hush," she said, lowering her voice. "I know you blame yourself, and you just stop that." She spoke normally again, leading him off the stage. "I'm going to have to spend the rest of my day arranging for the museum to be cleaned and reorganized." She glanced up at the Spathian mannequin, a bolt shot into its face. "That won't be inexpensive, you know."

"I will made reparations," Dayne said.

"Nothing of the sort. Take her home. And I insist that the two of you come to dinner tomorrow. You remember where the city household is?"

"It is burned in my memory, my lady," Dayne said.

"Good," she said. "Now be off."

They had only made it to the door before one of the marshals called to them.

"Your swords and shields," the marshal said, delivering their armaments to them.

"Oh, good," Jerinne said, sheathing her sword. "It was really important these were taken from us. Saints know what might have happened otherwise."

Chapter 9

THE CHAPTERHOUSE WAS far too active for a Quiet Day, with Initiates, Candidates, servants, and even the dogs running about in almost a mad panic.

"The blazes is this?" Jerinne asked. Her bruised face and body were aching. Tharek had gotten the drop on her, but she wouldn't let that happen again.

"Not sure," Dayne said. The big guy was looking like his heart had been torn out of his chest. Jerinne couldn't quite wrap her head around that. They had saved two members of Parliament and who knew how many nobles and civilians, and most of the perpetrators were being carted off for trial. On top of that, a gorgeous noblewoman who was clearly interested in Dayne had invited them for dinner. This morning was a victory, pure and simple. Jerinne didn't understand how Dayne couldn't see that.

Frankly, Jerinne was ready to bask in it.

"Will you look at this face?" Jerinne said to the first batch of Initiates who passed them. "Scars earned in battle!"

"We've heard," Vien said as she passed by. "What do you think's happening?" No one else took much note of them.

"Don't crow," Dayne said. "It's unseemly."

"What is happening?" Jerinne asked. "Is this about what happened at the museum?" Everyone was in a frenzy, and it seemed to be leading most of them into the dining hall. Jerinne realized they hadn't had lunch. What time was it, even?

"Let's find out." Dayne followed the train of people into the dining hall. The room was filled with just about everyone who lived in the chapterhouse. Grandmaster Orren was pacing about, looking distraught. He approached them both as soon as they entered.

"Dayne, dear boy . . . are you . . ."

"I'm fine, sire," Dayne said. "Though Jerinne could probably stand some time in the infirmary."

"Nothing that won't heal, Grandmaster," Jerinne said. She didn't need to be coddled right now.

"I'm sure, but healing is a process, young lady," the Grandmaster said. "It's best done with proper care. No need for hubris to impede that."

Jerinne accepted the rebuke. "As you say, Grandmaster."

"Well, as the two of you have been in the heart of this particular storm, I don't need to get you up to speed." He walked into the center of the room, all eyes on him. "As you've all heard, there has been an incident today, in which two members of Parliament were nearly killed. Fortunately—and truly, this was pure fortune—two of our own were on hand, ready to stand between them and harm. Lives were saved because we were there, even if it was of pure happenstance."

A smattering of applause came from the group of Tarians. Jerinne noticed Madam Tyrell looking over at Dayne, giving him a nod of appreciation.

"With that comes an unintended consequence, which

is why I've called everyone here. It is feared that this was not an isolated incident, and members of Parliament are remembering where to look when they want the best protection possible. As such, I am assigning Adepts and Candidates on escort duty, both at the Hall of Parliament and protecting the men themselves."

There was a murmur of approval amongst everyone.

"Initiates, I know these are your Quiet Days, and we will do our best not to have these incidents disrupt your intended schedule. However, you may consider following Miss Fendall's example, and seize the opportunity to prove what kind of Tarian you might be."

He walked around the room, taking moments to touch his fellow Tarians on the arm, or pat their shoulders. "This is a hard day for Druthal, but we are ready for it. There are those who need defending, and we will stand between them and harm."

A quick, brutish cheer echoed through the room. Jerinne had done it herself, almost unconsciously.

"All right. Initiates, dismissed. I'll speak to the Candidates and Adepts individually."

Dayne patted Jerinne on the shoulder. "To the infirmary, all right?"

"All right," Jerinne agreed. "But, really, I'm fine."

Dayne gave her a bit of a smile. "You did quite well. Good instincts."

"You were pretty clever, too."

Dayne's brow furrowed. "Do you have another dress uniform for tomorrow?"

Jerinne looked down at her uniform, realizing it was a mess of dirt and blood. "I'll see what I can do."

"Good," Dayne said, giving her more of a smile. Jerinne was glad to see whatever melancholy was affecting Dayne had broken. "We're dining with a noble lady. Can't have you embarrassing me." He knocked Jerinne jovially on the shoulder and went over to the Grandmaster.

Jerinne was barely out the door when Raila and Enther were on top of her.

"You just happened to be at the center of one of the biggest crises the city has had this year?" Enther asked.

"Really?" Jerinne asked, trying to maintain her nonchalance. "Was it that big?"

"Huge," Raila said, wrapping one arm around her shoulder. Jerinne felt her heart suddenly leap in her chest. Nonchalance was going to be very hard to maintain. "Two members of Parliament probably would be dead, if not for you and Heldrin."

"At least that's the rumor," Enther added.

"Rumor's pretty close to true," Jerinne said. "At least by what you two are telling me." Jerinne was mostly amazed that rumor had infected the chapterhouse so thoroughly in the time it took for her and Dayne to get back. A running dog couldn't have beat them by more than half a bell.

"So it's true you stood up and dared all the Patriots to shoot at you?" Raila asked.

"That's a bit of an exaggeration," Jerinne said, though it was tempting to let the lie ride out. "I did stand up and draw attention to myself. But I never actually encouraged them to shoot me."

"And you clearly weren't shot," Enther said. "Despite the bruises."

Raila lowered her voice. "We heard you were tackled by four of them, while Heldrin drew their fire."

"Who did you hear these things from?" Jerinne asked. "Because I'm kind of amazed that anyone who was in the room came here so quickly."

"People did come here," Raila said. "Like, lords and members of Parliament. I don't know if they were in there at all, but they certainly were worked up about it."

"Like we said, they are saying it's the biggest crisis this year!" Enther said.

"Oh, come on," Jerinne said. "Just a couple weeks ago

there was the scandal over that south side gambling house. It nearly killed a few high and mighty when it burned down."

"No," Raila said. "That was a freak accident. This was a deliberate attack! And you stopped it!"

"Why don't you two get me to the infirmary?" Jerinne said. "Because this is all making my head hurt."

Dayne worked his way closer to the Grandmaster, who was now going about the room whispering brief messages to various other members. The Grandmaster was nearly at the door by the time Dayne reached him.

"Grandmaster?" Dayne asked. "You're making assignments?"

The Grandmaster nodded, though he looked pained. "Indeed. Dayne, this will be hard to ask of you."

Dayne steeled himself. How hard could it be? Would he be asked to guard Benedicts? He would do so without hesitation. "I will do whatever is required of me."

"I know you would. This situation is going to push our resources, at what is already a challenging and hectic time for us."

"I am here to serve, sir," Dayne said.

"And you will. Right here." He sighed. "You've done your part out there."

Dayne was confused. "What is my assignment?"

"The rest of us will be out there, defending the lords and members of Parliament as we have been asked. But that means that those who would be serving to supervise the Quiet Days, organize the Trials . . . they will be occupied. I need you to take up their duties here."

"You need me to . . . take charge of the Initiates?" He didn't mean to sound put out. He would do whatever task was required of him, including this. But he was expecting a more meaningful assignment, a chance to show his worth. The Grandmaster clearly heard that in his voice.

"Please do not take this as a punishment, Dayne. You have done your share. It's in our—this will sound mercenary and crass, but we have an opportunity to show the city, the whole nation, how much value our Order still brings to Druthal. But that means we need to be seen, as many faces as we have. I fear . . ." He spoke in hushed tones. "I fear the possibility of this becoming more about one man—you—instead of the Order. So I would like you here. At six bells, you will be the ranking member on Watch."

Dayne understood the dangers. Master Denbar had attained fame in Lacanja. Courted it, even. And that had drawn the attention of Sholiar, which led to his death and Dayne's own doom. Repeating that could be disastrous. "Of course, sir. I want you to know that I would not seek glory for myself beyond that of the Order."

"Too late." Amaya's voice pierced from behind. She stalked over to the Grandmaster, handing him a newssheet. "Glory has already been bestowed upon you."

The Grandmaster glanced at the sheet, shaking his head. "It is an excellent likeness, Dayne." He handed Dayne the newssheet and walked off.

"I did nothing to seek this," Dayne said to Amaya. "You know I wouldn't."

"Of course not," Amaya sneered. "It's just that the press loves you. How could they not, with your pretty face?"

She left. Dayne looked at the newssheet. At the center was an excellent sketch—Dayne in his dress uniform with a gleaming shield, standing in front of Barton and Parlin, who were drawn more in caricature. "Tarian Hero Saves Museum" was writ large across the top, under the newssheet's banner, which was the part that stood out the most to Dayne.

The Veracity Press.

The infirmary sent Jerinne on her way with only a foul-smelling poultice wrapped around her head. That was more medical care than she really felt she needed, and she argued that point, loudly, but to no avail. Her bruises would heal, and she felt fine. Now she felt fine with a reeking head.

Raila waited for her outside the infirmary. "So, what does the conquering hero want to do now?" She gave an impish smile that, under any other circumstances, would lead Jerinne to think she might be interested in stealing a private moment away in the bunks. But there was no way anyone could intend that with the poultice plastered to her face.

"Too late for lunch, too early for supper," Jerinne said.

"You're hungry?"

"A bit," Jerinne said. "I did miss lunch in the excitement. But it can wait."

"This was really a crossbow hitting you in the face?" She touched at the poultice gingerly. Brave girl.

"Embarrassingly enough," she said. "Bruises I can handle. Indignity takes longer to heal."

Raila laughed, patting her on the face. "Poor dignity. Next time, duck."

"In my defense, he was clearly a soldier or something. He had moves."

"Of course he did," she said. "You want to hit the training room? Maybe work on some Dodge Sequences?" Now Jerinne knew she was teasing her. But it wasn't a terrible idea.

"Let's get down there," she said.

"We should have it to ourselves," she offered. "Almost everyone is either gone, assigned to protection details, or getting ready for them."

"Then what are we waiting for?"

They had only gotten halfway there when one of the house servants chased them down. "Miss Fendall, miss. You're needed in the lobby!"

"In the lobby?" Jerinne asked. "Why?"

"I'm afraid I don't know, sir. The Grandmaster and the gentleman asked for you."

"Gentleman?" Raila asked. "You are having a busy day, Jerinne."

"Let's go see." Jerinne went off without seeing if she was following or not.

The Grandmaster and a very well-dressed gentleman were speaking in low voices when Jerinne approached. "Can I be of service, Grandmaster?"

The Grandmaster looked up. "Ah, Miss Fendall. How are you feeling?"

"As fit as I can be, sir," Jerinne said. "Ready to serve as needed."

"Excellent," said the gentleman. He was young—barely a few years older than Jerinne—but his suit was impeccably tailored, including a cravat of Turjin silk. That had to have been expensive. "She's the one, indeed."

"Do I know you, sir?" Jerinne asked him.

"I was at the museum this morning, though you probably wouldn't have noted me." He extended his hand. "Mason Ressin, personal attaché to Jackson Seabrook, the 10th Chair from Sauriya."

Jerinne took his hand. She wasn't familiar with Seabrook at all, but if he was the 10th Chair, that was no surprise. Chair rankings were based on seniority in the Parliament, so he was one of its newest members. "How can I serve?"

"As you are aware, the incidents of today have left members of Parliament . . . trepidatious. Many of them have secured the services of your fellow Tarians."

"And what does that have to do with me?"

"I saw your performance at the museum, Miss Fendall. Needless to say, I was impressed, and I conveyed my thoughts to the Good Mister Seabrook. We are in agreement that you would be the ideal candidate for his personal security."

"But she's just an Initiate!" That was Raila, hanging back at the lobby entrance.

The Grandmaster gave her a hard stare. "Miss Gendon, I'm sure you have other places to be."

Raila scurried off.

The Grandmaster turned back to Ressin. "Her interruption may have been unseemly, but her argument was valid. Miss Fendall is only an Initiate. All others assigned to such duties were Adepts or Candidates. It would not be appropriate for an Initiate . . ."

"Are you denying the Good Mister Seabrook protection?"

"Of course not," the Grandmaster said. "This Order will do its utmost to maintain the safety of every member of the Parliament who asks for it."

"Then let me make something clear. Good Mister Seabrook craves the skills of Miss Fendall, regardless of her rank. We know quality when we see it. She is our choice."

"I can do it, Grandmaster," Jerinne offered. Despite the strange feeling she had about the way Ressin phrased the offer, Jerinne wasn't about to let an opportunity like this pass her. Even if it was with a 10th Chair.

"I appreciate your enthusiasm, Miss Fendall. But you must prepare for your Trials."

"We are in Quiet Days, sir," Jerinne said. "What better way to prepare than by serving?"

"And the Good Mister Seabrook—as well as his friends in the party—would not forget this boon, Grandmaster."

The Grandmaster opened his mouth, looking as if he would object, but then he waved it off. "Very well. Miss Fendall is, as she said, in her Quiet Days. She is free to spend them as she sees fit. However, when her Trials begin, she will need to attend to that."

"Of course, Grandmaster," Jerinne said.

"We are ever so grateful, sir," Ressin said.

The Grandmaster clapped Jerinne on the shoulder. "Serve the Order well, Jerinne." He stalked off down the hallway.

"Well then, Miss Fendall," Ressin said. "I will wait here while you prepare yourself. We should be off by five bells. And you should . . . clean yourself, appropriately." His hand went to his own forehead, as if to point out what, exactly, Jerinne should attend to. Jerinne matched the movement, touching the poultice.

"Of course, yes. I will be presentable shortly."

"And a bit of face paint would not be remiss," he said. "But just a hint."

"Of course," Jerinne said. Not that she had any on hand; she never used it. But if that made Ressin and Seabrook happy, fine enough. Someone must have some. Vien Reston probably would.

"Excellent," Ressin said. "We must not waste time. Mister Seabrook is at his home currently, and will need escort to the Talon Club by six bells."

Jerinne nodded and, with a few polite words, went off to the bath chambers. She hoped she had hidden her excitement. No one she knew had ever been inside the Talon Club. That alone made the pain of bathing and face painting worth it. Her entire day was certainly shaping into something very different from what she thought it would have been when she woke up.

She would have to thank Dayne for that.

Chapter 10

THE ALASSAN COFFEEHOUSE was a dark, quiet establishment, nestled in a back alley on the southern edge of the Trelan neighborhood, a few blocks' walk from the shipping docks and the Royal College. A strange, subversive set of city blocks, about the only place in Maradaine where foreigners lived outside of the Little East, certainly the only area on the north side. The coffeehouse was run by a pair of brothers from Imachan, whose cousin was one of the key coffee importers to Maradaine. Coffee drinking was an uncommon pastime in Maradaine, limited to those with cosmopolitan tastes. Wealthy sophisticates would not dare step into a place like the Alassan, so the clientele was composed almost entirely of current and former students, and mostly those whose politics did not fall into the mainstream. Those who knew that none of the Six Parties truly represented the people.

The Alassan offered several isolated tables, and at each one clades of radicals would whisper of revolution and subversion, at least in the abstract.

Until this morning, it had been in the abstract for Lannic and his friends.

None of the customers paid him much mind as he came in. He may have shown his face at the museum, but clearly no one in here now was aware of that. Or if they were, they secretly admired him.

Khalal Alassan gave him a slight nod from behind the counter, sending him to the back room. Khalal was no fool; he was surely aware of what had been plotted under his roof. That said, if the Parliament and the Palace were burned to the ground, Khalal would likely chuckle to himself and get back to work.

Braning and Kemmer were in the back room, as were a handful of others. Lannic knew each of them, men who shared their values, even if they hadn't been at the museum. That had been part of the plan, of course, as the Chief had outlined it. The Chief had made it clear that even if things had gone monstrously wrong at the Museum—and it couldn't have gone much wronger— that there should still be allies ready to take further steps.

They were here, and they were ready.

"Have we seen Tharek?" he asked, sitting down at the table.

"I haven't," Braning said. "Look, Lannic, I know you like him . . ."

"And we agree he is useful," Kemmer added. "Saints know he knows what he's doing."

Braning nodded. "He's not like the rest of us, you know? I'm not sure why—"

"Friends," Lannic said, shaking his head. "I know he's new to you, but I implore you, trust in me. I've spent many long nights talking with him, and I'm convinced his heart is as true as all of ours."

"True and ready," came words from the entrance. Tharek stalked into the room like a cat on the hunt. "And believe me, gents, no one is more upset by the failure of our mission today than me."

"Don't say that, Tharek." Lannic pushed a chair out.

"I missed the shot and Parlin still breathes!"

"Keep your voice down," Kemmer said. "It was the Tarian. We couldn't have planned for that."

"Besides," Braning added, "from what I hear, we did a lot."

"How do you mean?" Lannic asked.

"Well, the plan was for Parlin to be dead and Barton to be soiling his pants, right? Well, they've both soiled their pants, and the whole Parliament is in a state of panic. Good on us."

"Except the Chief was plain in what we were to do," Lannic said. Parlin had to go, for falsely holding up the idea that he was a "people's man." That was what the Chief wanted, and Lannic agreed. That was the message that needed to be heard.

"We have to make it right," Tharek said.

"What about our statement? Kemmer, you had a contact for getting it out?"

"Bastard rabbited," Kemmer growled. "I've got a few other possibilities, but nothing solid."

"We need to get the message out," Lannic said. Everything was pointless without the statement, the manifesto. Else it was all just senseless violence.

"No, we need to lie low," Braning said. "We made some noise, now let it simmer."

"Simmer?" Tharek said. "Hardly. The fear out there is thick and hot, and we must use it while we can."

"Use it?" Lannic asked. This was intriguing.

"The Parliament is scared right now. But not scared enough."

"Right," Lannic said. "None of them are going to change how they vote, or resign. None of them will step aside and truly let the will of the people rule!"

"Not yet," Tharek said. "But we've planted a seed of fear. And now we water that seed with blood."

"How do we do that?" asked one of the radicals in the back. Yand, probably.

"Parlin?" Lannic asked.

Tharek nodded. "And I know how to get to him. Tonight."

"His home?" Lannic asked. "Surely he's protected."

"I can deal with that. And we won't do it in his home. We want the fear to grow, we need it to be public."

"Yes!" Lannic said, unable to control his excitement. "That will make them all scurry, and the people will see this supposed august body for what it really is!"

Murmurs and nods of agreement filled the room. Only Braning looked nervous.

"We can do this," Lannic said, putting a hand on Braning's shoulder. "We need to do this, you know that. For Shaw, and all our friends."

Braning nodded. "For Shaw."

Lannic turned back to Tharek. "So what is your plan?"

Tharek started to tell it, giving each man his part. It was complicated, but brilliant. And it would cut right into the fetid heart of the parliamentary elite.

There was a nervous energy in the air as Dayne worked his way over to The Nimble Rabbit. The news of the museum incident had spread; fear and trepidation radiated off of the citizenry. People walked the streets, with glances over their shoulder, quiet murmurs. Dayne saw more than a few furtive looks his way. Of course, he was still in his Tarian dress uniform, sword strapped to his belt. He hardly looked inconspicuous.

Also, if any of those people read *The Veracity Press*, they had seen *him*, lauded as the hero, put in the center of events. That wasn't right. Beyond the fact that he had failed—he had made a choice that killed one of the Patriots—he had fully learned the dangers of infamy. He could not let the mistakes of Lacanja repeat themselves here. He had to stop Hemmit and the rest of them from writing about him, before it caused more trouble.

Several people sat at the outside tables at The Nimble Rabbit, including familiar faces: Hemmit, Maresh, Lin, sitting in a crowd of almost a dozen. They immediately perked up and recognized Dayne as he approached.

"There he is!" Hemmit stood and raised a wineglass to Dayne. "Good friends, this is a man! This is what we should aspire to! This is what we should celebrate!"

Dayne bit back his temper as best he could, throwing the copy of *The Veracity Press* on the table. "This is how you celebrate me, friends?"

"And a blazing good likeness, if I do say!" Hemmit said. "Well done, Maresh."

"Lin helped," Maresh said.

"The likeness isn't my problem, Hemmit!" Dayne said, more snarl in his voice than he had intended. He leaned hard onto the table, shaking all the plates and cups. "You made the story about me!"

"The story is about you, Dayne." Hemmit snatched the copy off the table. "What do you want it to be about? The Parliamentarians who stood knock-kneed while the Patriots ranted? Or the King's Marshals who did *nothing* while you and your friend saved everyone in that room?"

"Including me," Maresh said.

Dayne stared hard at Maresh. "I didn't see you there." The ugly idea hit Dayne's mind—that he didn't see Maresh because his face was hidden behind a kerchief.

"I think your attention was elsewhere," Maresh said. Dayne nodded. He had to be fair—he had hardly spent any time in the main hall, and in his memory, the crowd was exactly that—just a sea of faces. His own father could have been in there and he might not have noticed.

"And the rest of you?" Dayne asked.

"Stuck outside," Lin said. "We were late, and trouble had already started."

"But we got the word from eyes inside," Hemmit said. "Including Maresh. Oh, we dug for some truth today!"

"Dayne," Maresh said, passing a cup of wine to him. "You saved us all. End story. People need to know that."

"People need to know that a man steps up and does what needs to be done," Hemmit added. "Not a politician yammering on to line his own pocket—a man. With sword and shield."

"Shield and sword," Dayne corrected.

"Sorry?" Lin asked.

"It's the oath," another woman at the table said. "The Tarians swear to stand up, with shield and sword."

"But I'm not a Tarian!" Dayne snapped. "I'm just . . . just a Candidate."

"Just a Candidate," Hemmit said. "Saints, the modesty!"

"I shouldn't be the story," Dayne said. His energy sapped out of him. Deflated, he sat down and drank the wine. "I shouldn't be praised here, for so many reasons . . ."

"You're wrong," Hemmit said. "You are the story. And those two Parliament men are. And the marshals. And even the Patriots. Every man needs to have a voice. The Parliament and the marshals are making official statements, and what are they showing? Cowardice." He poured himself another cup of wine, drank it down, then filled his cup again, followed by topping Dayne's. "The Patriots said that there is a toxin filling this city, and they may be right."

Dayne perked up. That was a troubling thing to hear Hemmit say. "How do you mean?"

"I mean the very men who are supposed to be the spine of the nation, to be men, are unable to face the very people they represent. Even Parlin, who is supposedly a hard-fisted Saltie, had no interest in hearing people speak their grievance."

Lin shook a finger at Hemmit. "Speak their grievance? Is that what the Patriots were rutting well doing?"

Hemmit tapped a finger on the table, hard enough to shake it. "What I'm saying is, beneath their violence, their histrionic display, there rests a legitimate argument, something the people feel."

"What's that argument?" Dayne asked. "I didn't hear one. I only heard ignorant ranting from a group of morons who think quoting from the first chapter of Haltom's *Practices of a Free Man* means they understand the full scope of the founding of the Parliamentary Monarchy!"

Everyone at the table was giving Dayne their full attention now.

"A scholar and a warrior," Lin said. "That, dear Hemmit, is the mark of a true man."

"I couldn't disagree," Hemmit said. He pushed the wineglass closer to Dayne. "All right, Dayne. Tell me what the story needs to be."

Dayne pointed to Maresh. "He's the story."

"I am?"

"You are," Dayne said. "You and every other civilian and peer in the museum."

"You're the one who did something, though," Hemmit insisted.

"Yes, but that's my oath. To the Order, to the people. My choice, to step in harm's way. Same with Jerinne, same with the marshals. And to some degree, the Parliamentarians. They accepted their Chairs, and with that, a certain burden. But Maresh and the other civilians did no such thing. They went to a museum, and for that, the Patriots terrorized them."

Someone at the end of the table started speaking. "They took extreme measures just to get their voice heard!"

"The Patriots claim to speak for the common man, yes?" Dayne said. His mind was spinning a bit. He had come to the Rabbit so angry about being pushed into the center of the story that he hadn't thought about the whys and hows behind the Patriots' attack. "But what were their goals, their demands?"

"They said it, if not clearly," Maresh argued. "They want to increase the voice of the common man. They want to kick out the corruption in the Parliament. And they made Parlin the centerpiece of that argument."

Dayne nodded. "All right. But every common man has a voice, he has a vote. And with that, every man is part of the process to change the Parliament. The ten archduchies each fill ten chairs, and every man gets to stand up and say who is in those chairs."

"I hardly do," Maresh said. "I've voted the past three years and never had a right say."

"Wait, wait," Hemmit said, focusing on Maresh. "Montrose is a Populist. Didn't you vote for him?" Dayne was familiar with the 2nd Chair of Maradaine, a man known to be honorable and sensible.

"He's an old man who's sat in Parliament for over twenty years," Maresh said. "I don't buy his 'common shepherd' act one jot."

"You had your say, even if your choice doesn't win," Dayne said, "and that's the point. Every year, every single year, the body of the Parliament changes. And even if you don't get your way, Maresh, you still get your say." He tapped his finger on the copy of the *Veracity* for emphasis, and paraphrased from the Rights of Man. "Your voice, your opinion, unrestrained."

One man at the end of the table scoffed. "Unless you live in Corvia. Or Monitel. Or one of the Napolic colonies. Filled with Druth citizens who have no voice in the Parliament."

A woman next to Lin added, "Every archduchy is filled with citizens with no voice. They're called women."

A third student shook his head, "Neither suffragism or the Added Chairs movement will address the real problem."

"But we need—"

"I agree, but that doesn't change—"

"I get your point," Dayne said, feeling somewhat shamed. There were many voices silenced, not represented in Parliament. "Our voting system has a long way to go before it is just. But we also can express our dissatisfaction freely and openly."

"Aren't the Patriots exercising their right to expression as well?" offered someone at the table.

"More like the right to carry arms," Lin said.

"Abusing it," Dayne said. "The Patriots, for all their rhetoric, want their vote to count more than anyone else's. Since their right to expression hasn't given them what they want, they've taken up arms to force it."

"The nobility does the same thing, just with money," Maresh said. "You can't tell me that every Disher in the Parliament isn't deep into the pocket of some lord or another."

Dayne wasn't going to concede that. "That's not the same thing. They can be voted out if the people don't like them. Gibbs lost his chair just last year."

"To another Disher!" Maresh shouted. "Nothing changes!"

"Of course, the Traditionalists do not control the august body," Hemmit said. "So that hardly matters."

"The Minties and Crownies can't hold their coalition without the Frikes," Maresh said. "You can't tell me the Frikes wouldn't align with the Dishers to stay in power. No moral center."

"The Functionalists will keep the government running," Dayne said. He never liked calling the Functionalists "Frikes," and he was far more likely to vote for a Functionalist over anyone else. They understood the fundamentals behind making government work day to day, year to year, in a way that supported all Druth citizens. Everyone else at this table was clearly a Populist—if not further on the fringe—and Dayne could see the appeal.

Maresh continued. "What good is running if it doesn't help the people? None of the Six Parties represent the voice of people like us."

Dayne realized something. "Wait, wait. Parlin is from Acora, right?"

"That's right," Hemmit said.

"And Barton. Traditionalist from Maradaine?"

"Of course, he's a Disher," Maresh said.

"What is it?" Lin asked.

"Of the two of them there, wouldn't it make sense for the Patriots to be more angry at Barton? Focus their rage on the member of Parliament who has opposing politics, and represents them here?"

The other woman—the suffragist—offered an answer. "But Parlin should represent them. He should be the one fighting for them, and he doesn't. They may hate Barton, but Parlin specifically failed them."

"But he didn't, because he's not their man," Dayne said. "Not any of ours. In the next election, all of us—"

"Not all of us."

Dayne amended his point. "Those of us who can vote, including the Patriots, vote for the Chairs from Maradaine. Whoever Acora votes to represent them is their business, not ours."

Lin chuckled. "You are all terrible fools," she said, her sweet Linjari accent nearly dripping all over the table. "I would put hard crowns on the fact that they didn't give a saint's damnation about the particular politics of either man. It was a public event with two men from Parliament, thus it was an opportunity. They would have done the same with any two from the august body."

Maresh nodded, "She's right."

"Of course she's right. She's smarter than the rest of us." Hemmit took a charcoal pencil out of his pocket and scribbled a few notes, speaking as he wrote. "They couldn't care less about anyone's politics, anyone's choice. All they care about is using their force of arms here to subvert the true voice of the people *there*. That's what the story is about."

Dayne chuckled. He might not agree on everything with the man, but Hemmit had a sharp mind, and Dayne couldn't fault the man's dedication. He glanced around the courtyard, noting the long shadows on the ground. "What's the hour?"

"Around five bells," Hemmit said.

"I'm sorry," Dayne said. The Grandmaster had assigned him to be ranking member on watch, starting in an hour. He couldn't waste any more time here. He had to get back to the chapterhouse, attend to the Initiates. Make sure Jerinne was doing well, specifically. "I must be off." He got up, putting one hand on Hemmit's shoulder. "Please, if you could, keep my name out of your newssheet."

"I can't withhold the truth, Dayne," Hemmit laughed.

"Then credit the Order, not me."

Before Hemmit could answer, Lin reached out and touched his arm. "They'll keep you off the front page. I'll make sure they do."

"Thank you. Now, duty calls."

With that, he bounded back to the chapterhouse.

"I do appreciate this, Vien." Jerinne tightened up the laces on the vest of her friend's dress uniform. It was hardly a perfect fit—a bit loose around the shoulders—but it would serve.

"I wasn't planning on wearing it tonight," Vien said. "But try not to make a mess of mine."

"Honestly, I think the worst that's going to happen to it may involve food stains."

"Are you actually eating at the Talon?" Vien sat down on her bed. "Or how does it work?"

"I haven't a clue. I just know a handful of the Parliament are dining there tonight—Seabrook included—and they want their assigned Tarians present. Maybe we'll just be put on display in the middle of the dining room."

"They're putting on a big show, you know."

"Commissioning us?"

"No, I think . . ." Vien furrowed her brow in thought. "That, I think, is legitimate. They're afraid of what happened today and want extra protection, and it also makes a good show, what with you and Dayne saving the day. But going to the Talon tonight? That's the show."

"Put on a good face, all is as it should be, nothing bothers us, so night on the town. That sort of thing?"

"Exactly. But don't muss these. Really." Vien patted her on the shoulder. "I'm going to need those in a few days when I make Candidate." She left the room before Jerinne could respond. Jerinne had to admire the open confidence Vien always showed in her skills, in the inevitability of her promotion in the Order. Jerinne wished she could do the same.

Shield strapped on and sword belted, Jerinne made her way down to the courtyard. Mister Ressin was already waiting, patient in closed stance, hands behind his back. A very familiar pose. "Are you ready to depart, Miss Fendall?"

"Of course," Jerinne returned. Ressin held the door for them as they went into the street, where a cab was waiting.

"Top of Kinter, north side of Welling," Ressin told the driver, taking the rear-facing seat automatically.

"So," Jerinne said, "I was raised in the household of Baron Fortinare. Yourself?"

Ressin gave her the slightest smile. "It shows?"

"Undoubtedly."

"The Earl of Grinnal. My father was the underbutler. Your parents?"

"Father was valet to the baron, mother was lady's maid to his daughter, and then head mistress of the staff.

You have the bearing of a man who had a life of service beaten into him."

"Quite true," Ressin said. "Trained to serve at table, to dress, receive guests, every rule of etiquette. I'm sure you know."

"I know how to serve or sit at the table tonight," Jerinne said. "Though I don't think you would call on me to do the former."

"It—" He hesitated. "No, of course not. You'll be dining with the Good Mister Seabrook. He's eager to meet you."

"So how did the son of an underbutler wind up at the right hand of Good Mister Seabrook?"

Ressin paused, his mouth poised to speak for a moment longer than was comfortable for Jerinne. Finally he said, "The earl's household—a sort of story I'm sure you've heard—had no positions available when I came of age."

Jerinne nodded. Stories of noble houses cutting down their staffs, especially in the countryside of the northern archduchies, were exceedingly common.

"So I enlisted in the Navy. Spent three years on the *Pride of Sauriya* under Captain Seabrook, until Hantal Bay."

He said "Hantal Bay" like it was something anyone with any sense was already familiar with. Jerinne didn't know where it was, let alone what of significance might have happened there. She nodded in feigned understanding, not wanting to appear ignorant.

"Since then, at his request, I've stayed at Good Mister Seabrook's side. And I've found my loyalty has been richly rewarded."

"Clearly," Jerinne said. The man was riding in a personal carriage, wearing Turjin silk and about to dine at the Talon. That was impressive for the son of an underbutler.

The carriage pulled up to a walled manor house, staying outside the gate. Ressin politely excused himself and went inside, which implied Jerinne was to wait with the driver. Jerinne left her shield on the rear-facing seat and stepped down.

A quick glance at the household told her that actually securing the place would be a challenge, if that was to be asked of her. There was a wall around the house, and it was high enough, at least ten feet. But even from here, she could see there were several spots where it would be easy to climb. On top of that, as far as Jerinne could tell, there were some tall trees on the property that could easily hide an intruder's ascent. She couldn't see much of the house itself, but she imagined there were several entrances, large bay windows. A nightmare for security. Was that part of what Seabrook expected? Or was this all more about putting on a show, walking about town with Jerinne by his side?

The thought drilled its way into her skull: she had no idea what was expected of her. Or how to accomplish it.

In fact, if this mission involved much more than walking around town and being seen at Seabrook's side, Jerinne was doomed.

Ressin came back out, presumably with Seabrook. He seemed young for a Parliamentarian, hair and neatly trimmed beard a rich brown without even a hint of gray. He was dressed in a rich suit, hints of silk lining and silver hasps, designed to almost resemble a naval officer's uniform, down to the braids on the cuff.

"Miss Fendall, a pleasure," Seabrook said, extending his left hand. Jerinne realized the man's right arm didn't move, instead it was slung to his body. The suit did a good job of hiding this fact.

Jerinne took the man's hand with her own left without missing stride. "It's my pleasure, good sir."

"Ressin here tells me you are the hero of the hour, as it were," he said, taking his place in the carriage. Ressin entered as well, with Jerinne sharing the rear-facing seat. Jerinne moved her shield onto her lap as the carriage started off again.

"Not me, sir," Jerinne said. "Dayne—Mister Heldrin, that is, he's really the one."

"Ah, not how I hear it." He shook his left finger at Ressin. "Though it does you credit to say so. No, from what I hear, your friend Heldrin was blessed with opportunity. He had time to assess the situation, make a plan. All well and good, don't get me wrong, and he's given good name to your Order."

"Indeed he has, sir."

"But you were in a very different situation, young lady. In the very center, and what did you do?"

Jerinne wasn't sure if she was supposed to answer this question.

"You stood your ground against them! Only one who talked back!"

"It wasn't—"

"Do not be modest, dear girl. I won't have it."

"No," Jerinne said holding up her hands. "In all honesty, I just couldn't take any more of that Lannic's speech. I had to say something."

Seabrook burst out laughing. "Excellent! You were right, Ressin, this young pip is a good lady, indeed. Now, we are going to the Talon. You've been?"

"Never, sir," Jerinne said.

"Then I am honored, indeed." Seabrook grinned wildly. "I get to be the one to introduce this fine girl to proper society. Let the others claim the Adepts and the Candidates. I have the real thing right here."

So it was to be about being seen at Seabrook's side. Jerinne could handle that just fine.

The chapterhouse was significantly quieter when Dayne returned. The kitchen staff could be heard, clangs and shouts common to preparing dinner. There was almost no sign of any of the Adepts or Candidates about. The Initiates were surely in the compound; Dayne had seen a few of them on the grounds, going through training steps.

Dayne stopped a passing servant. "The Grandmaster, is he in his study?" He needed to know what, exactly, would be expected of him in the next few days.

"He's gone, sir," the young man said. "I'm told you're to be the ranking member on the Watch. Is there anything else I could do?"

Dayne noticed his hands were filthy, and likely the rest of him was as well. That wouldn't do. "Hot water to the baths."

"There already is, sir," the servant said. "We've been on that for the past few hours, if you pardon. With everyone being commissioned by members of Parliament . . ."

"Of course," Dayne said. Faces to wash, armor to polish. That is, if they were going out in armor. They might all opt for dress uniform, given the situation. He was still wearing his. Stripping off the coat, he handed it to the servant. "So the baths are ready? I'll be about that, then."

"Of course, sir. From what I gather supper will just be you and the Initiates. Is that correct?"

Dayne nodded, not sure how to take that. "If you say so."

"Very good. Half past six bells for that."

The servant excused himself. Dayne made his way to the bathhouse, out past the back garden. The fact that the Tarians had a private bathhouse was something of a luxury, though unlike the various public ones in Maradaine, it wasn't built atop a natural hot spring. Servants had to lug great bins of water out to the bathhouse. Another luxury. One, frankly, that Dayne often thought the Order should do without. At the very least, it could be a task assigned to Initiates.

Dayne entered the warm wooden structure, his eyes

adjusting to the lamplight as he entered. Before he could see, he heard someone in the tubs.

"Close the door, you'll let the chill in," a caustic voice chided him.

Amaya.

He did as he was instructed, now seeing her in the large copper tub in the corner of the room, scrubbing her arms. "Sorry to disturb you," he said.

"I purposely avoided the rush," she said, giving her arms all her attention. Dayne looked to the other three tubs. In each of them, the water was already cold and brackish.

"Is there something you needed?"

"No," Dayne said.

"Then why did you come out here?"

"To take a bath."

She huffed. "Well, you're just standing there, fully dressed, with a stupid look on your face. So it doesn't seem like you're interested in bathing."

Dayne touched the surface of the water of one of the other tubs. Definitely wouldn't get him clean. "I'll have to wait for the water to be changed out."

"Don't be ridiculous, Dayne," she said, shifting her focus to her neck. "This tub is hot and fresh."

"I didn't want to presume." He took off his shirt and slacks. "There was a rush, then? Everyone getting ready for their assignments?"

"They want to look their best to cozy up to the Parliamentarians," Amaya said. She lay back in the water.

Dayne finished undressing and cautiously got into the tub. "You can't tell me you're not doing the same."

"I'm going to be spending my evening at the Talon Club," Amaya said. She sighed, as if in disgust. "I have to look presentable enough not to offend."

"I'm sure you'll manage. But you aren't trying to impress your Parliamentarian?"

Her gaze locked on him, hardening. "Is that what you think of me?"

"I just see what's happening here."

She ground her teeth. "You think you're any different? Why else were you and Master Denbar rescuing the Benedict boy?"

"That's what we're supposed to do, Amaya. Protect people."

"Do you think if it had been, say, a carpenter's daughter you would have been called in? No, you were asked to rescue the son of a prominent *parliamentary* family."

Dayne sank into the water to his chin. "And doing that did me more harm than good."

"What do you mean? You can't hold yourself responsible for what happened to Master Denbar. He needed to be responsible for you."

Dayne sighed. He was responsible for Master Denbar, completely. "There's more that my mistakes that night have cost me."

She gave him a piercing look, completely disarming him. "What cost?"

There was no way he could be dishonest about this, not with Amaya. "The Grandmaster told me that I've made enemies of the Benedict family, including the ones in the Parliament."

"I'm sure you made a few allies today, though."

"But are they on the approval committee?"

She looked up at him sharply. "What do you mean?"

Maybe she didn't know. He didn't know before yesterday. "Apparently the yearly lists of Candidates to be promoted to Adept are sent to a committee in the Parliament for approval. One of the Benedicts is on it."

"Where did you hear this?" He had her full attention now.

"From the Grandmaster. When he told me that I would *never* make Adept."

"You . . . what? No, that can't be right." She moved

closer to him. Dayne became far more aware of her body, the heat of the water.

"That's what he told me."

"That's impossible. You should be getting it this year. Certainly next, at the very least. How can the Parliament—"

"Because they decide!" Dayne snapped. "That's how it works."

Amaya was silent, but clearly more because she was in her own thoughts, rather than cowed by his outburst. "That makes sense," she finally said. "The first month into my Candidacy, I was sent as an honor guard for a delegation to Imachan." She sat up, pointing out an ugly scar over her right breast. "When we were set upon by marauders, I took two arrows, right here, saving the life of a member of Parliament." She sank back into the water, the side of her body now against Dayne's.

"That's how you made Adept in one year."

She nodded. "I thought it was because of *what* I did. But clearly it was because of *who* I did it for."

"What you did matters, Amaya."

"I try to tell myself that," she said. She leaned her head against his shoulder, like it was something she had always done. It was something she used to do, back in their Initiacy. It felt natural to Dayne. "That's who I'm assigned to."

"Who?"

"The Honorable Greydon Hale. I saved his life in Imachan, and he asked for me tonight."

"Lucky you."

"I wish he hadn't." Her words were coated with bitterness. "I never liked how he looked at me."

"How do you like to be looked at?" Dayne asked. She had turned toward him, her body now crouched on top of his in the water.

"Like this," she said, her eyes fiery and alive.

Then they were kissing.

Dayne wasn't sure who had initiated it. His hands

were all over her body, and hers on him. It felt familiar, and in that moment, there was nothing he wanted more than to be there with Amaya.

"You stupid fool," she whispered between kisses. "What am I going to do with you?"

Dayne pushed her away. "What does that mean?"

"You believe you're never going to make Adept?"

Her words cut harshly, despite the passion in her eyes. Her lips pursed, as if she were hungry for more of him. He forced himself to focus and respond to her. "The Grandmaster told me plainly."

"And you just take that? And you'll take orders to cool your boots for another year until finally you're cashiered out?" Despite the fact that she still straddled him, the look on her face made it clear now that the kissing was not about to continue.

"What would you have me do, then?"

"Fight for your placement!" she snapped. "Or walk out that door and be your own man."

Dayne couldn't think of what to say to that. He had no idea what being his own man would even mean. All he wanted was to be a member of the Tarian Order. Without that, what would he do?

His silence had lasted a second too long, as Amaya shoved herself off of him in disgust. Climbing out of the tub, she said, "You need to figure out what you want."

"I know what I want," he said.

She grabbed a towel off the shelf and wrapped herself with it. "And you've already decided that you can't have it."

"I can't."

"So then sit there and wallow in wanting." With that, she left the bathhouse.

Dayne sank back into the water. It was starting to turn cold.

Chapter 11

"WE'RE BEING PUNISHED," Kemmer said. He and Braning were thigh deep in sewer waste, with only a dim oil lamp for light, so he was comfortable with that assessment. "Tharek and Lannic blame us for the museum going badly, and we're being punished."

"They should blame us," Braning said. He trudged through the muck with his head hung down. "We messed up."

Kemmer wasn't going to take that. "No, Braning. First of all, the guy was a Tarian. We're lucky our skulls are in one piece. Second, he may have taken us out first, but he pretty much got everyone. Singlehandedly. That can't be our fault."

"Lannic doesn't blame us," Braning said. "Tharek might."

"That guy has something missing in his head, I'm telling you," Kemmer said. "How did he end up giving us orders?"

"He had the plan." Braning shrugged. "It's a damn sight better plan than the museum one, if you ask me."

"Except we've got the filth job." Something skittered by along the wall, just outside their vision. "What was that?"

"Roach or rat, I figure."

"How far do we have to go?"

"First one's just up here." Braning pointed into the darkness. "Look, it makes sense to give us this."

"Makes sense for you. You and Shaw worked the sewers."

"Well, Shaw is dead," Braning snapped. "So I need you to carry the lamp."

Kemmer kept his mouth shut. Braning was still an open wound about his brother, and Kemmer couldn't blame him. He trudged behind Braning, doing his best not to breathe through his nose.

"All right," Braning said eventually, as they approached a metal wheel. "Hold the lamp up."

Kemmer raised it while Braning took hold of the wheel and turned it. From the distance, a metallic groan echoed through the sewer, until a clanging knock ended it.

"This one's closed now." Braning said. Even though Kemmer had lost track of the details of the plan once he heard he was going into the sewers with Braning, he understood they were sealing flood control doors to back up the sewage where Tharek needed it.

"Is that it?" Kemmer asked. It seemed easy enough.

"Blazes, no," Braning said. "We have to close fifteen more, and fast. Come on, we've got a lot of walking to do."

"You know there's going to be a whole mess of bedlam in the streets."

Braning gave the slightest smile. "Won't there just be?"

"And we're going to miss it."

"So that chuffs you?"

"That's just it," Kemmer said. "After getting skulled at the museum, I am just fine with missing it."

Braning nodded. "Let's hurry up. We've got to get this done by eight bells."

Talon Circle was the central part of the Welling neighborhood, a wide plaza where the two main roads of Fenn and Hege met at the sprawling Fountain of Victory, the largest fountain on the north side of Maradaine. The Talon Club loomed over its namesake circle, a grand stone edifice a story above any other building in the plaza. The only thing matching its height was the center of the fountain, a great pedestal culminating in an empty plinth.

"Why isn't there a statue up there?" Jerinne wondered idly as the carriage pulled in front of the club.

"Well, it's symbolic, of course," the Good Mister Seabrook said. He glanced up at the fountain. "Wouldn't you say, Ressin?"

"Most definitely symbolic, good sir," Ressin offered.

"There you have it," Seabrook concluded. Jerinne let the matter drop as the doorman approached the carriage.

"Good evening, good sir," the doorman said to Seabrook. "It is always a pleasure to have you here."

"It is a pleasure to be had," Seabrook responded. "If you would take note of Miss Jerinne Fendall, Initiate of the Tarian Order and honored guest of the evening."

"You do us the honor, Initiate," the doorman said. He opened the door for them.

Jerinne entered the entry hall, to find herself immediately encountering stairs.

"Up we go," Seabrook said, "Three flights."

"Three, sir?" Ressin asked. "Very well, indeed."

"Stop at one for you, Ressin." Seabrook went on up.

"What's this, now?" Jerinne asked Ressin.

"Right, you've never stepped foot in here," Ressin said, a bitter note clearly heard in his tone. "Ground floor here is where the kitchens are. One flight up is the main dining room, where I'll be dining tonight."

"All right." Jerinne was rather shocked that Ressin wasn't dining with them. Was that how things were usually done?

"The next floor up are various smaller dining rooms. Special reservations and the like."

"And the third floor up?"

"That is the elite hall." Ressin, having reached the top of the first flight, looked wistfully up the spiral staircase. "Invitation by the Talon's Inner Circle only."

Jerinne's heart pounded in sudden panic. "And I'm supposed to—"

"You stay at his side, Miss Fendall," Ressin said, nodding after Seabrook, who continued up. "It's your charge, and your honor."

"I couldn't possibly, Mister Ressin."

"This might be the only chance in your lifetime. Best seize it."

Jerinne steeled her jaw, and took the next flight of stairs, catching up to Seabrook.

"The truth is, Miss Fendall," Seabrook said, speaking as if Jerinne had been by his side this whole time, "I'm a man of simple tastes. Stand on the bow of a ship, salt spray in the air, what else does a man need?"

"Little more, sir," Jerinne offered.

"This is what I'm always saying. Sadly, even men of my stature—blazes, due to my stature—but men of my stature must engage at a level of luxury that is expected of us. Oh, I could putter about like Montrose in his little house in Fenton, of course, but you see the influence *he* holds, for all his—"

Seabrook kept going on about Montrose as they passed they second floor, but once they reached the landing of the top floor, Jerinne was unable to focus on a word the man was saying. The door in front of her had two suited stewards, in full suits, brocaded vests with silver hasps, and white gloves. The anteroom alone was richly appointed—candles in silver sconces, paintings and rugs from far East Tyzania, gilded frames on the door.

Even the country household of Baron Fortinare didn't have this kind of ostentatious display of wealth. That wasn't the baron's style.

"Welcome, Good Mister Seabrook," one of the stewards said. "This would be your escort this evening?"

"She is," Seabrook said. "We are expected, yes?"

"Your arrival is anticipated," the steward said. "Though I must insist . . ." He let the phrase hang, raising an expectant eyebrow at Seabrook.

"Of course," Seabrook said, leaning in to whisper.

"Very good," the steward said after Seabrook pulled away. "Enjoy your evening, sir."

The other steward opened the door, allowing them both entry.

One long table dominated the room, with many people already seated, dressed as finely as Seabrook. Jerinne didn't recognize most of them on sight, but by their dress and adornments she could easily tell that many were Parliamentarians, seated with ladies of station. It was unlikely that the ladies were the wives of the Parliamentarians. By age, daughters were more likely, but Jerinne doubted that. There were also two noblemen—an earl and a baron, if Jerinne were to guess—and an army colonel.

And Madam Tyrell, in her dress uniform, next to one of the Parliamentarians.

She noticed Jerinne right away, giving her an odd regard, raising her glass.

"Good sir, miss," one of the stewards said, pulling out chairs for them both. Jerinne sat down next to Seabrook as the stewards poured wine for both of them.

"Arrived right on time to make an entrance," Seabrook whispered to Jerinne. "Seems almost everyone is here."

"Everyone?" Jerinne asked.

"My dear, you are surrounded by the true power brokers of Druthal." He pointed casually to the various Parliamentarians. "Millerson. Orton. Corvi. Barton, of course, you recognize him." Jerinne did note one of the men from the museum.

"Yes, of course," Jerinne said, giving a respectful nod to the Good Mister Barton as he gave them both note.

"Parlin's not here, though I'm not surprised. He was invited, from what I understand. Courtesy for the events of the day. But he's a Populist, and I suppose he must maintain an image to his voters. Colonel."

He shook hands with the army officer, who had approached them both. "Good to see you, Seabrook. Who is your young friend here?"

"This is the veritable hero of the hour, Colonel. Jerinne Fendall, Initiate of the Tarian Order. The very one who saved Barton and Parlin this morning."

"Fendall, good girl." The colonel offered his hand. "Colonel Estin Neills, vice-commandant at Fort Merritt."

"A pleasure, Colonel," Jerinne said.

"What are the odds you could be put in a proper uniform, hmm?"

"Her uniform is quite proper," Madam Tyrell offered from across the table.

"Of course it is," the colonel huffed out. He leaned in and whispered, "But the Green and Gray would suit you, perhaps in the Irregulars." He patted Jerinne on the shoulder and walked away. That confused Jerinne a bit. There were no women in the army, unless that's what these "irregulars" were. Why would he want her for that, whatever it was?

"Mark me, dear," Seabrook offered, "he'll be the full commandant by next month."

"Is that a fact?" Jerinne asked.

"Not a verifiable one," Seabrook said a slight grin crossing his face. "But I know how things are going to go in committee."

The steward came up behind them and presented a bottle of wine to them both. "Nitaria Province, 1198."

"Perfect," Seabrook said, indicating for the steward to pour. "Fendall, my dear, you will enjoy this. I think you're in for quite a night, indeed."

Washed and dressed in his cottons, Dayne found his way back to the kitchens, where the staff was finishing up their dinner preparations. All of them stopped and came to attention as he entered.

"It's all right," Dayne said, waving them down. The head of staff—Ellist—came over as the rest returned to their work.

"Can I be of aid, sir?" Ellist asked.

"I understand it's only myself and the Initiates to-night?"

Ellist nodded. "Unless I'm mistaken, you are the highest-ranking member on premises, sir. Have you special instructions?"

"Do me a favor and put the tables together. I want to be able to talk to all the Initiates while we eat."

Ellist gave Dayne a look that made him think his re-quest was akin to dancing naked in the light of the moons, but he nodded. "As you wish, sir. You are the ranking member on premises."

"I'll help you move them," Dayne said. As soon as he said this, he knew that Ellist was even more offended by the notion.

"We can manage, sir. Ten minutes, and the bell will be rung."

Dayne took that as a cue to leave Ellist's domain, and he made his way back out to the main foyer. Kevo, the old household dog, was dozing in a corner. Dayne hadn't seen Kevo since his arrival; he had almost forgotten the little beast.

"Hey, Kevo." Dayne scratched the dog behind the ears. It lifted its head and sniffed half-heartedly at Dayne's hand before lying back down.

"He's nearly blind, poor thing" someone said from behind. Dayne turned to see a third-year Initiate coming down the stairs. She was familiar—of course, she'd have been first-year when he was a third, but he couldn't quite place her.

"Vien Reston," she said, as if she noticed his confusion. "Do you have something planned for us, sir? Or do we have our Quiet Days in peace?"

"Dinner and conversation," Dayne said. Her eyebrow went up, so Dayne continued. "Nothing more. No pranks, not from me. I never saw the point. Or the humor."

"Then we're lucky it's you staying with us when everyone else is gone."

Dayne nodded. Maybe that was the purpose behind this assignment. The Grandmaster knew that Dayne would treat the Initiates with dignity, something the likes of Aldric and Price would not understand.

Aldric and Price had a better chance of becoming full Tarians than he did.

"Sorry, sir?" Vien asked. "You mumbled something about a better chance."

"Nothing, Initiate," Dayne said. "Just thinking out loud. But . . . I'm going to flout convention a bit tonight, by having us all eat at one large table."

"That's a bold choice, sir."

"I could hear Ellist's teeth grinding when I suggested it," Dayne said. "But the truth is, I really don't know any of you, and . . . well, I'm just doing what I can to help. In Lacanja, we all ate at one table together."

"How many Tarians were in the Lacanja chapterhouse?"

"Eight at the most," Dayne admitted. "Let's just humor me on this."

The dinner bells rang out. "It seems I'm left with no choice," she said. "Let's go see what you've done."

Ellist and his people had done a fine job pulling the tables together, creating a space for them all to eat as one unit, as he thought it should be. Dayne sat down at the center of the table, so he'd easily be able to talk to everyone. Vien took a seat near him as the rest of the Initiates came in. Most of them looked perplexed, but took their seats.

The servers brought plates of stewed lamb and beets with cups of cider. Simple fare, as traditional and basic as it got.

"Why are we all like this?" one Initiate—a second-year—asked.

"What's your name?" Dayne responded.

"Enther."

"Usually, Enther, we're broken into our various ranks. Initiates in one part of the room, Candidates in another, and so on. Tonight we're all Initiates."

"Except you," a second-year woman said.

"He knows that, Raila," Enther offered.

"Yes, except me," Dayne said. "But I remember being you. I remember Quiet Days, tricks from the Candidates—"

"Which this seems like the makings of, sir," Raila said.

Dayne had to accede that. "That isn't my style. Jerinne can vouch for that. Right, Jerinne?" He looked at the various faces surrounding him, not seeing Jerinne anywhere.

"She's on assignment, sir," Enther said. "One of the Parliamentarians asked for her, so . . . she's off at the Talon Club."

"Ah," Dayne said. Seems many were at the Talon tonight. "Good for her."

"Why aren't you assigned anywhere?" someone else asked.

"Because I've had a full day," Dayne lied. "And I wanted the luxury of a simple dinner with you fine people. The future of the Order."

"Only a handful of us are the future of the Order," someone else said. "Many of us won't be here next week."

"That's true, I'm sorry," Dayne said. "You're all at the point where your work may be for naught. Some of you may—no. Some of you will be leaving. Believe me when I tell you that the line between those who make it and those that do not is narrow."

"How narrow could it be, sir?" Raila asked.

"The Trials will test your martial skills, and from what I've seen of you all, you have them well mastered. Show your discipline, show what's in your heart, and that's the best you can do."

"What do you mean what's in our heart?" Vien asked.

Dayne knew he shouldn't give away too much about what the Trials were about, especially for second- and third-years. The skills with shield and sword and other fighting arts were crucial, of course, and everyone who advanced to Candidate had to master them. But the Trials had far more to do with character. "As in, do you have the heart of a Tarian?"

"They'll push us hard," from one young man at the edge of the table. "See if we break. See if we surrender. That's what matters, right? That we keep on fighting."

This didn't sound promising. He had to give them something more to think about. "All right," Dayne said, pushing his plate to one side. "Are any of you familiar with the Question of the Bridge?"

With one exception, who was sitting at the corner of the table, they all shook their heads.

"You stay quiet," Dayne said, pointing to the one who didn't shake her head. "The rest listen. This story comes from Monitel; any of you ever been there?"

Again, heads shook. The Question of the Bridge had passed down from the Cascian Order—mountain rangers, who were later folded into the Tarians and Spathians. But there was no need to confuse these Initiates further with these details.

"Up in the eastern mountains, mining city. Now, to deliver ore from Monitel down to the river, they've built a series of cart tracks down the mountains to the base towns. The carts are loaded up and roll their way down, and they get going pretty fast. So every cart has a brakeman who rides on it, keeping it from going out of control. Everyone clear on this?"

"Silver mines up north have a similar system," one of the Initiates said. "But they get ox pulls."

"Because they don't have mountains," Dayne said. "So you don't get the carts going anywhere near as fast as in Monitel. Even with the brakemen, accidents happen. In the Question of the Bridge, as one ore cart is approaching the base town, the brakeman has become ill. He's passed out. So the cart is out of control, smashing down the track. Is everyone clear on this?"

Nods again from all the Initiates. None of them looked confused so far, so he had explained it well enough.

"Good. Now, the track leads to a bridge. Crossing the bridge is a family on a wagon. Mother, father, and three children. They're right on the track, middle of the bridge, and there's nowhere they can go. And that ore cart is going to smash into them and kill them."

"Who designed this?" Raila asked. "It's a pretty bad plan if people have to cross a bridge where an ore cart might kill them."

"Ah, but there's a safety switch. Turn the switch, and the ore cart goes on another track into a crash wall. The family will be safe."

There was a noticeable sigh of relief among the Initiates.

"Of course, if the ore cart hits the crash wall, the brakeman will be killed."

Every one of them—save the one in the corner who knew this story—tensed up again.

"So, you—" Dayne pointed to one of the Initiates at random. "You're at the safety switch. What do you do?"

The Initiate—a tall woman with short blonde hair— stammered for a moment before saying, "Throw the switch, of course!"

"You just killed the brakeman!" Enther said.

"Are you saying not to throw the switch?"

"If you do, you're a murderer!" Enther said.

"Wait, wait," another Initiate said. "That's not murder. The brakeman will die anyway!"

"But if you pull a switch, he's dead because you did it! How is that *not* murder?"

"We're training to fight and defend the innocent. Like that family on the bridge. Sometimes that requires killing. Isn't that right, Mister Heldrin?"

Dayne hesitated. For himself, the answer was clear: absolutely not. But he knew that was not the official stance of the Order. That was his own code, and his alone. Something only Master Denbar seemed to understand about him, and even then he would tease him with, "Maybe you should have been an Ascepian." But he knew better than to drill his own choice into these Initiates.

"What you have to understand . . ." was all he managed to say before a loud crack came from the direction of the kitchen. It wasn't a sound like something had been dropped or broken. It was a deep, resonant sound of something bursting, followed by cries and shouts. Dayne was about to run to the kitchen when there was another bursting sound, echoing beneath their feet. Then another in the opposite direction, right where the closest water closets were.

The scent hit the whole room next, rancid and choking.

"Saints, what is that?" one of the Initiates asked.

"Sewer pipe cracked," another said. "Only explanation."

"Is that even possible?" Dayne asked.

"It came from the kitchens," Vien offered. "We should check if everything is all right."

"Right," Dayne said. He moved toward it with her,

then stopped, tracing the sewer line with his finger. "It started under the kitchens, then under us, and continued that way."

Vien raised an eyebrow. "So it moved. And?"

"It moved in a straight line," Dayne said, now pointing in that direction.

"The sewer line, right?"

Something churned in Dayne's gut, and he was certain it wasn't just the repulsive odor. Something was happening, heading in the direction he was pointing. He couldn't dismiss it as coincidence that it was in the exact direction of the Talon Club.

Chapter 12

THERE HAD BEEN A soup course—roasted shallots in braised lamb stock—and some sort of mushroom-stuffed pastry. Both danced across Jerinne's palate like nothing she had ever tasted before. She savored every crumb, which seemed to delight the Good Mister Seabrook to no end. Seabrook made a point of keeping her wineglass filled as well.

"Now," Seabrook said, "you know your etiquette, dear girl, I'm quite impressed. Served in a noble house, yes?"

"I had this talk with Ressin. It seems our breeding is quite obvious, yes?"

"Quite," Seabrook said. He leaned in, conspiratorially, for the seventh time that evening. "I'll tell you, it took me some time to get the knack of these things."

"This is my first time on this side of it, sir. I'd be a champion were I waiting on the table."

"I'm sure you would be, dear. So, what is next?"

"Next would be a selection of cheeses and bread, if memory serves."

"Indeed. And wine to match."

"Good sir," Madam Tyrell called from across the table. "Do recall that Initiate Fendall is here on duty. She must be capable of holding her sword."

"Yes, Seabrook," one of the lords said. "She won't be very useful if she can't handle a sword."

"Hush," Seabrook said. "I don't need you all ruining our fun this evening."

"This was supposed to be fun?" Mister Barton asked. "I may have had my fill for the day."

"Yes, Julian," the lord across the table said. "You had quite the exciting day already. It's quite brave of you to venture out."

"More than Parlin could manage," another Parliamentarian chuckled.

"Be kind." This came from the Parliamentarian Madam Tyrell was sitting with.

Barton scoffed. "Parlin wouldn't come here regardless of what occurred this morning."

"It's his loss," the one next to Madam Tyrell said. "Wouldn't you say, dear?"

"Of course," she said, her lips pursed tightly. From the look on her face, Jerinne knew she did not want to be on the wrong end of Madam Tyrell's sword tonight.

"Absolutely," Seabrook said. "The poor man is truly depriving himself. And the cheese is here!"

The stewards came and delivered plates of assorted cheeses to everyone. While Seabrook's attention was focused on the plate being placed in front of him, Madam Tyrell gave Jerinne a signal. Two quick moves with her fingers made her message clear: drink no more wine. Jerinne nodded to her as the next plate was delivered. As Seabrook had predicted, it was a selection of tiny samples of cheese: hard, soft, crumbly, veiny. And strong in scent, all of them.

"So what do we have here?" Seabrook said, leaning in to his plate. "Looks like quite the variety, hmm?"

"Smells strange," Jerinne said. The scent in the air was rather unpleasant.

"Some of them are quite strong, yes. But that will build character for you, young lady. You must really—"

The odor was suddenly much stronger. It wasn't from the plate in front of her.

"Something's not right," Jerinne said, getting to her feet. Her head spun more than she was prepared for. She had drunk more wine than she had thought.

Madam Tyrell was on her feet as well.

"What, there's nothing," her Parliamentarian was saying.

"No, something is rancid," one of the young women at the table said. Everyone could smell it now.

"We'll look into it," the head steward said, heading to the door. "There's nothing any of you need to worry about."

"Fendall," Madam Tyrell whispered. "Look sharp."

Sharp. Jerinne took deep breaths. Her body wanted to drop back down into the chair, but she couldn't let that happen.

"Sit, please," someone said. Jerinne wasn't even sure who. "Don't let this—"

A crack boomed through the club, shaking the building. Jerinne stumbled and fell to her knees.

Screams and cries came from everywhere, all around Jerinne, as well as the floors below. The stench hit again, like a wave crashing, stronger and more vile than before. Jerinne fought down the bile that wanted to force its way up her throat.

"Child," Seabrook said, clutching Jerinne's shoulder.

"Stay here," Jerinne barked, swallowing back the burning wine in her mouth. She pushed herself back to her feet, getting to the main door as Madam Tyrell did. She held one hand over her face, the other on the hilt of her blade.

"Sewers," she said.

"Burst pipes?" Jerinne asked.

More screams, and people pounding on wood. Before it was fear, now it sounded like panic. They reached the top of the stairwell, only to find a swarm of people from the floor below pressing their way onto the stairs, trying to get to the ground floor. No one was able to progress down the stairs. Jerinne spotted a Candidate, nearly buried in the sea of bodies.

"Oy!" Madam Tyrell called out. "What's word?"

The Candidate yelled back, but there was no hearing him.

"They aren't able to get out," she said to Jerinne. "Something is very wrong. Window."

They both made for the windows in the dining room. Nearly everyone in there was in a state of fright, save the colonel.

"Something is very wrong," he said. "We need to—"

"We're aware of that," Madame Tyrell said, cutting him off. Jerinne was already trying a window, but she quickly realized that it wasn't designed to be opened.

Down in the circle below, people were running in chaos. Carts had smashed into each other, blocking off the entry to the circle from each direction.

"We can't get out this way," she told Madam Tyrell.

"We have to get these people out of here."

"It may be worse out there," Jerinne said.

"That doesn't matter." Madam Tyrell looked out the window. "Before too long—what is that?"

Jerinne saw exactly what she meant. Up on the empty plinth, there were two men. One was on his knees, tied, hood over his head. The other, the one standing proudly, Jerinne recognized him despite the darkness outside.

Lannic.

Lannic was quite impressed with Tharek. This wasn't just a worthy plan, it was masterful. The events in the museum this morning had been a debacle, that was clear, and Lannic wondered why he hadn't given Tharek a more active role in planning things before. For that matter, he was surprised that Tharek had been content to merely follow instructions when his skills would have helped ensure their success. Perhaps that was a mark of his loyalty.

The man clearly was a marvel. In a matter of hours, he had pulled their people together, gathered the handful of carriages and horse carts they would need, and gave everyone their orders. That hadn't even been the most impressive part. Right at sunset, he had guided Lannic through the northern neighborhoods, stopping in a well-appointed district. Tharek hopped off the cart and vanished into the shadows. Moments later he reappeared with a prisoner, bound and unconscious. The Good Mister Parlin himself. Tharek had captured him as easily as Lannic would order a coffee at the Alassan.

"Now what?" Lannic found himself asking over and over as the evening progressed. As they pulled the cart up Hege into Talon Circle, that was the obvious thing to ask. The other men were in their places, each with his eyes toward the cart. Waiting for Tharek to give them the signal.

"Do you have a speech ready?" Tharek asked. "In a moment, this is going to be your show."

"Of course," Lannic said. He wasn't sure what he was going to say, exactly, but he was about to get an audience, and he knew what to do with that. "How's it going to work?"

Tharek glanced around. There were plenty of people in the Circle, traffic going in all directions. He got off the cart, putting his hand on the cobblestone. "Shouldn't be long. Think Braning and Kemmer are right on task."

They were getting a few odd looks from passersby. It wasn't that unusual for a cart to be stopped on the side of the road, even in a busy circle. But they had eight carts, each staged at different parts of the circle with suspicious folk standing around, and one covered in a tarp. That wouldn't stand for long. Constabulary was sure to stick their nose in shortly. "We don't have long."

"No," Tharek said. He looked over at the fountain. "Things are going to move fast when it hits. Long as everyone does what they need to. You've got the hard job, though." He reached under the tarp that covered Parlin, pulling out a leather vest covered in metal clasps. "Put this on. Now."

Lannic did as he was instructed. Tharek went behind him and adjusted a strap, making it a bit uncomfortable. "Does it need to be so tight?"

"Yes," Tharek said. "Stay limber. I'll get you up there, but it's up to you to stick the landing."

"Right." Lannic didn't know what else to say. This was a lot more daunting than the museum. This morning had been dangerous, but it didn't require the raw physicality of what he was about to attempt. Even with Tharek explaining it to him, he didn't fully grasp what was going to happen, just what he needed to do.

Tharek put a hand over Lannic's heart. "This won't be easy, I'm sorry. But it's got to be you. You are our voice."

"I know, Tharek," he said. "Don't worry about me."

Pounds and knocks came from beneath the street. Braning and Kemmer had done their jobs, that was obvious. Very good. The moment was here.

"Ya!" Tharek cried out. That was the cue. Men on their carts at the two alleyways next to the Club all charged out. Some quickly beat the doormen with handsticks, while others went to work slamming huge boards in front of the Club door. At the east entrance on Fenn, the boys shoved barrels of pitch off their cart into the road.

Then there was another boom, and suddenly hot sewage blasted out of every crack in the street around the club.

Lannic was momentarily dazzled by the whole spectacle, he hadn't noticed Tharek had pulled out a device far too large to be a crossbow. It looked more like a harpoon launcher from a naval ship, but it was loaded with some odd pulley contraption, with ropes trailing off it. Lannic was amazed that Tharek could even lift it. He aimed at the top of the club, and fired the contraption across the circle.

It was only at that moment that Lannic realized that the ropes from the contraption were attached to the vest he was wearing.

"What now?" he shouted, as the pulleys hit the roof of the club. Tharek had already dropped the harpoon launcher and hauled Parlin's limp body out of the cart. With astounding agility, he draped the man onto Lannic's back, clipping him to the vest.

"You go!" He pulled a lever on the carriage, and the horses were let loose, stampeding down Hege. The other end of the rope was attached to the horses. Lannic barely had a moment to register that fact before he was launched off the ground, hurling through the air.

The following seconds were a blur, and before he even knew what was happening, he was dropping onto the plinth. He landed chest first, and almost tumbled over the edge before he caught himself. As he got back onto his feet, he glanced back over to Tharek, now alone by the cart. He held the rope in one hand, having cut it loose from the horses with the sword in his other hand. His arm held the rope strong; he wasn't going to let Lannic fall.

This man was a true Patriot, indeed.

Lannic undid the clasps, and Parlin dropped down. Before he could fall off the plinth, Lannic grabbed Parlin by the collar of his coat, hauling him up on his knees. The man was moaning, but hadn't roused yet.

Drawing his knife, Lannic stood tall on the plinth.

Parlin was his now. The crowd was his, as well. The people in the Circle were in a state of panic, and the streets were blocked by crashed carts, flooding sewage, and pitch. Everyone in the Talon Club was blockaded in. They weren't going anywhere, and none of them could help their friend Parlin.

"People of Maradaine!" he yelled out. "The filth of this city has been released, and the decadent swells who have been poisoning you are now swimming in it!"

Dayne ran full bore up Hege Street, outpacing every carriage and pedalcart. People dashed out of his way, staring incredulously. He tried to dodge every person he passed; at his size and speed, if he knocked someone down he might kill them. But he had to get to the Talon, no matter what. He couldn't explain how he knew it, but every instinct told him that something terrible was about to happen, down to his bones.

Panicked screams cut through the air, confirming his fears.

Two blocks away from Talon Circle, he could hear chaos exploding there. A swarm of people scrambled, frightened and confused, running away from the Circle.

Dayne leaped out of the way. Pressed against a shop window, he saw a handful of Constabulary trying to force their way upstream through the crowd. There was no moving, no getting closer to the Talon.

Then horses thundered wildly down the street, crushing people under their hooves. The pair were yoked together, a loose rope trailing behind. He had to stop them before more people got hurt.

Dayne shoved his way through the crowd to the open lane, chasing after the stray rope. The horses kept barreling down the road, oblivious to anyone in their path. They smashed through a pedalcart, which crashed into a group of boys. Dayne pushed his sprint, heart hammering as he grasped for the jerking rope. He stumbled, losing his pace. The rope danced out of his fingers until he was able to get a solid grip. As soon as he had it, he yanked back with every ounce of strength he had, planting his heels onto the road.

The horses, fortunately, were well trained enough to yield once force had been applied. If they hadn't, he might have been dragged off. Even with them stopping, he still slid several feet, his boots gaining no purchase on the cobblestone.

People kept coming from Talon Circle, panic transformed into terror. Sewage and smoke choked the air. The Constabulary on the street had their hands full just trying to maintain order on this block; there was no chance of them getting to the Circle.

Dayne drew the horses over and turned them around. He didn't have time to waste unhooking them from their yoke, and he'd have to make due without a saddle. It was an imperfect solution, but that was all he had right now. Mounting one of the horses, he wrapped the rope around its neck as a makeshift rein, and kicked it forward. The two horses ran in tandem, and Dayne, wearing his Tarian tunic with his shield held high while riding on one of them, found himself the new center of attention amid the chaos. The crowd, despite their agitation, now looked upon him with a bit of calm. There was even a spark of hope in their eyes. If he could give them just that in this moment, he was doing his duty.

"Clear a path!" he called out, and miraculously, they listened. He kicked his horse into action, and the people got out of his way, giving him an open route to Talon Circle.

He drove forward, through a haze of smoke into madness, the nauseating odor of sewage hitting him in waves. Fires burned, blocking the other roads approaching the circle. This road was blocked by a cart turned sideways.

Throughout the Circle a handful of armed, jeering men ran wild. Patriots by the look of them.

One such man stood on top of the blockading cart, an imposing figure of strength and power. Just seeing the man in shadow, silhouetted by the flames across the way, Dayne knew this was the same man from the museum this morning, the one who struck down Jerinne.

Tharek.

With another kick to the horse's flanks, Dayne charged at him. Tharek dropped down into his cart and came up with a crossbow.

The horse barely made three paces before it dropped out from under Dayne. Dayne rolled out of the way as the collapsing horse hit the street—crossbow quarrel between its eyes. The other horse panicked and kicked as it was dragged down by their shared yoke, but Dayne couldn't give it much thought. Another crossbow shot bounced off his shield.

"Tarian!" Tharek shouted with an almost manic glee. "I had no idea I would be blessed with your presence."

Dayne drew his sword and dove in at Tharek, who dropped his crossbow and pulled up two more from the cart. Both shots fired, dead true at Dayne. Dayne let one hit his shield while twisting his body enough for the second to miss him. He allowed himself the barest glance back to make sure there were no innocents behind him who could be hurt by the stray shot. Most of the people were fleeing away from Talon Circle, where sewage creeped and bubbled through the street.

Not losing any stride in the dodge or the glance, Dayne leaped up onto the cart with the intent of ramming Tharek with his shield.

He made contact, but instead of knocking the man down, Tharek grabbed hold of the edges of the shield and twisted as he dropped backward. Dayne's momentum hurled him, and he was in the air, sailing past the cart, the shield wrenched off his arm as he flew.

Surprised, Dayne rolled with the throw and sprang back up to his feet, bringing up his sword in a defensive pose.

Tharek drew his own, a great steel beast of a blade. "Let's give these folks a worthy show, hmm, Tarian?"

Chapter 13

THE STENCH OF SEWAGE and fear thickened, as the various Parliamentarians clawed their way to the stairs.

"There's no way out down there," Jerinne said, pressing her face to the window. "They've barricaded every door."

"They'll tear each other apart before too long," Madam Tyrell said. "Blazes. We need another option." She glanced at the ceiling. "With me, Fendall."

Jerinne stayed at her side as she forced her way to the stewards by the service doors. She glanced back at the dining room. Most of the Parliamentarians were losing all vestiges of control. Two of the ladies were curled up on the floor under the table, grabbing each other in a manic embrace of tears. Only two were calm: Seabrook and Barton. They both stayed in their chairs, Seabrook still enjoying his cheese and wine as if nothing was happening. Barton was only waiting, palms together in a repose of utter patience.

"Can we get to the roof?" Madam Tyrell asked the steward.

"There's no way down from the roof," the steward said. "It won't help you."

"But can we get up there from here?" Madam Tyrell asked.

The two stewards looked at each other. "The dumb-waiter?" one offered.

"It doesn't go any higher."

"But the shaft does."

"Good enough," Madam Tyrell said. "Jerinne!"

She was running, Jerinne at her heels down the hallway, the stewards taking the lead. "Over here!" one of them said, opening up the panel to reveal the dumbwaiter.

Madam Tyrell shoved the box frame down, revealing the bare shaft leading upward into darkness. It was very narrow—possibly too narrow for either of them to fit in.

"Leave the shields," she said, dropping hers. She shoved her head in, then came back up. "You'll have to go first, Jerinne."

"Why?" Jerinne bit her tongue as soon as she said it. Madam Tyrell gave an order, she should just follow it.

"That pulley system is housed in some sort of wooden vestibule, up on the roof it looks like. You're going to have to smash your way out."

"Me?" Her feet still weren't moving forward. Why was she talking instead of doing?

"You're skinnier," she said. "You'll have more space and leverage to knock your way out of that."

"Of course," Jerinne made herself say. Grabbing hold of the edges of the portal, she pulled herself in head first.

Dark. Musty. Her shoulders were pressed against the shaft walls. Barely any room to move.

"Can you climb?"

"I think so," Jerinne lied. She had no idea. She stretched up her arm, scraping it against the wheel track, grabbing hold of the pulley rope. Getting a strong grip, she pulled herself up.

All that did was pull the box frame back up, jamming it into her knees.

"Saints and blazes!" she shouted.

"Use both ropes, Initiate."

Jerinne cursed some more under her breath as she grabbed both ropes and yanked again. This time she pulled herself instead of the frame, squeezing up through the shaft. A cloud of dust and cobwebs hit her in the face, giving her a coughing fit.

"You all right?"

"Fine," Jerinne said. She was not going to tell Madam Tyrell about the thing crawling on her face. She prayed to every saint that, whatever it was, it would not bite her.

She kept climbing, inches at a time. She couldn't see a blasted thing, and she hoped each time she moved her hands that they wouldn't touch something horrible.

There were probably bats living in this thing.

"Initiate?" Madam Tyrell called. "You there?"

"Almost, I think." In fact, she had gotten her hands on the pulley work of the dumbwaiter. Bracing herself with her legs, she tapped at the walls around her. It sounded like open air, a simple wooden housing, hopefully on the roof. She knocked harder, and then formed a fist and struck at the wooden slats.

All it did was hurt her hand.

"Can you get out that way?"

"One . . . moment . . ." Jerinne answered as she grabbed hold of the pulley work and pulled in her legs tight. She slammed both feet against the wall with everything she had. It creaked, but didn't budge.

"Jerinne?"

She kicked again. Dust showered her and dropped down the shaft. The wood gave a little.

"I think I have it." Another kick, and her foot went through the wood with a satisfying crack.

"I'm coming," Madam Tyrell said.

Jerinne kicked away the slat, and then the next. She pushed her feet out the hole, blindly searching for some sort of landing. Her toes brushed something solid as she scraped her body through the hole. Part of her coat caught on the loose wood, which she realized just as she let her weight drop down. The sound of fabric tearing made Jerinne wince.

Vien was going to kill her.

Fires were now burning in the street, blocking access to the circle on two sides. People were clearly trapped in the circle, huddling in the various store fronts, while other men—Patriots, obviously—ran around with truncheons, shouting and laughing.

Two men were fighting full out with swords at another roadway. They were only shadowy figures in the firelight, but even from the rooftop, it was quite clear to Jerinne that one of them was the same man who had pummeled her this morning. The man called Tharek.

And given the size and skill of the man holding him off, there was only one person Jerinne thought it could be.

"Dayne," came the whispered voice of Madam Tyrell at her ear. "What the blazes is he up to?"

Jerinne's attention turned to the plinth, where Lannic was in the middle of a frothing rant, despite the fact that there was little chance anyone could hear him. But he held a knife in his hand, and he looked like he would use it on the man kneeling at his feet at any moment.

Madam Tyrell's eyes were on the ground below them. "We need to get those doors free. Let's get down to the street, and clear those goons out, hear?"

"I hear," Jerinne said. Thoughts on how to get to the street flew through her brain. There was the rope at-

tached to Lannic, which was latched to the harpoon contraption stuck in the side of the building.

Jerinne grinned. This couldn't have been better. She
jumped off the roof and grabbed the rope, swinging it
down with her weight.

Lannic came flying off the plinth.

Dangling halfway off the building, Jerinne quickly
climbed down the rope to the ground, while Lannic lay
in the fountain, moaning.

There wasn't any chance to enjoy it, though. As soon
as Jerinne touched ground, several men with truncheons
set upon her.

Tharek's attacks were relentless and fiendish. Dayne's
skills in defending himself were furiously put to the test,
especially since he didn't have his shield. Every parry
was a hair away from missing. Every step back was met
with Tharek's advance.

It would almost have been fun, except there was plenty
of other trouble all around the Circle. The rest of the
Patriots—not the craftsmen with a weapon that Tharek
was—were running about in pure chaos, wielding their
truncheons with zealous glee on nearly everyone. The
people trapped in Talon Circle were trying to get inside,
get away. The Patriots enjoyed terrorizing them.

Out of the corner of his eye, Dayne saw something
fall, and heard a sudden cry, and then a splash. Someone
fell into the fountain. He didn't dare glance away, but
whatever happened gave Tharek pause, just enough to
give Dayne the advantage. He parried the blade and
stepped in close, grabbing Tharek's wrist. A simple twist
would relieve the man of his weapon.

Twisting his wrist did not prove simple. Tharek managed to turn Dayne's disarming maneuver against him,
spinning his arm in a way so that Dayne found himself
diving headfirst into the ground.

Dayne rolled, using the momentum to get away from Tharek. If he could get to his shield, get some distance, he could rethink his strategy.

Tharek didn't press his advantage, dashing back to the cart. Dayne went for his shield. As he scooped it up, screams drew his attention to a woman taking shelter under the canvas awning of a dress shop. Two of the truncheoners were on her, ready to pummel her senseless. Or worse.

Dayne charged in, shield raised, and crashed into the two Patriots. One of them was floored, the other merely knocked back. He raised his truncheon to strike at Dayne's head—despite it being out of his reach—but Dayne grabbed his arm mid-swing. With one swift motion, Dayne twisted his arm around and pinned it to the ground.

"Help! Help! Sweet saints, please!"

Dayne looked up, pinning the Patriot to the ground with his knee. On the plinth there was the one man—blindfolded and on his knees with his hands tied behind his back—screaming. Dayne prayed he wouldn't try to move. He'd easily plummet to his death.

"Please!"

Dayne realized it was Good Mister Parlin of the Parliament up there.

He leaped up from the ruffian on the ground and ran toward the fountain, but he only got two steps before he heard the familiar twang of crossbow shots. Two bolts suddenly struck true in Parlin's chest. He dropped off the plinth with a dull splash into the fountain, and ribbons of blood flowed out into the water.

Dayne saw Tharek, standing on top of his cart, still pointing his crossbow up at the plinth. Tharek looked to Dayne, making sure that they saw each other.

"The fate of all who betray Druthal!" Tharek shouted directly to Dayne.

Tharek ran toward the fountain—toward Lannic, who

Dayne now saw was floundering in the water, mere feet from Parlin's body. Dayne moved to put himself in between the two of them. If he read the situation right, their goal was accomplished: fear, chaos, and assassination. There was nothing more to do but escape. Dayne would be damned if he let Tharek get to his associate.

Braced and ready, shield on his arm, there was nothing Tharek could throw at him that had a chance of passing through his defenses.

"Dayne!" the desperate cry came from his right. He permitted himself a glance, still not letting Tharek gain an inch of ground. Jerinne was there, in dress uniform, trying to hold off at least five men with truncheons, using only her sword and her wits.

"Girl won't last much longer," Tharek taunted, now doing little more than feinting with his sword. He wasn't pressing at all anymore.

But he was right. Jerinne was lucky to have held them off as well as she had.

Dayne wouldn't give Tharek the satisfaction.

"She's a Tarian," Dayne snarled back, shoving Tharek with his shield. "She will hold."

Something caught Tharek's eye, and the taunting glee on his face washed away. "We'll dance again, Tarian." He stepped back and pulled out a small dagger, which he threw at Jerinne.

Dayne dove out, putting his shield between the blade and the Initiate. In another moment he was in the thick of Jerinne's fight, barreling down on the truncheon-bearing Patriots. Jerinne's spirit was clearly renewed by him entering the fray—it only took a few moments to rout them. Some ran off, the others collapsed in the road.

Dayne looked back to Lannic, and saw the very thing that must have sparked Tharek's retreat: the raven-haired beauty in Tarian uniform, dragging the sputtering form of Lannic out of the fountain. Amaya held him in a headlock, and though he tried to claw at her arm, nothing he did had any chance of breaking her grip. Tharek was in there, but Amaya had her sword ready. She fended off his attacks fearlessly without yielding her hold on Lannic.

"Dayne!" Jerinne shouted. While Dayne stared in a daze at Amaya's glorious technique, Jerinne had run over to the cart that was blocking the entrance to the Talon Club. Her best efforts weren't moving it an inch. Dayne rushed over to help shove it out of the way.

Even with the two of them pushing, it was hard going. The Patriots had gummed the wheels somehow, and their combined strength could only force it to roll the barest amount.

"Never mind pushing," Dayne said, grabbing the handles of the cart.

With every ounce he had left, he flipped the cart over on its side.

As soon as it was clear, the door of the Talon burst open, and a frenzied crowd came pouring out. Dayne was knocked off balance, losing any clear sense of what was happening as well-born and high-class people forced their way out into the street. A hand grabbed hold of his, giving him anchor enough to pull himself out of the stream of bodies to the side of the door.

Jerinne, still grasping Dayne's hand, gave him an incredulous smile. "How the blazes did you even get here?"

"I ran," Dayne said, even though he knew it was a ridiculous answer. He looked back over to the fountain, eager to help Amaya before Tharek got the best of her.

Tharek wasn't to be seen anywhere.

Only Amaya, standing victoriously on the edge of the fountain above the sea of refugees from the Talon. Her quarry still struggled pointlessly in the crook of her elbow.

She was glorious.

At that moment, there was no doubt in Dayne's mind that she was a true Adept of the Tarian Order.

The next moment, three King's Marshals were on top of him, shouting that he was under arrest.

Chapter 14

JERINNE WAS SHOCKED AT what she was seeing. King's Marshals were trying to clap Dayne in irons, even though he had just nearly saved everyone in the Talon singlehandedly.

"You've got it all wrong!" Jerinne shouted, grabbing one of the marshals by the arm. "He wasn't one of them!"

"Don't tell us our job, girl," the marshal said, smacking her hand away. "Go back to playing with the rest of them."

"Oy!" came a shout from Madam Tyrell, who held Lannic in a rather satisfying headlock. "Why don't you arrest the proper man here?"

The lead marshal signaled to the others to push Dayne down to the curb. "We've got plenty to take in tonight, ma'am. Plenty of mess to clean up here."

"I'm sure," Jerinne said.

"You want irons too?" the marshal asked. Constabulary, Fire Brigade, and Yellowshields were all arriving in the Circle. The marshal pointed his men around the place. "Start clapping everyone who seems appropriate. We'll get things sorted, take statements, and then haul off whoever needs it." He gave a stern finger to Dayne, as if that was authority enough to keep the man in place, and then went to organize the rest of the emergency personnel.

Dayne stayed seated on the curb in front of the Talon. Jerinne sat down next to him. "So who were you assigned to?"

"No one," Dayne said. "I just—I had a feeling trouble was going to start at the Talon. And I was right."

That seemed strange to Jerinne, but she let it go. "Thank the saints you did. It could have gone much worse."

"A member of Parliament has been murdered, Jerinne." Dayne's tone was full of resigned finality.

"And many more are safe," Jerinne said. Many still filed out of the Talon, most looking little more than rattled. "It could have gone much, much worse."

"Heldrin." Price and Aldric strode over, their uniforms stained and stinking of sewage, but otherwise unhurt. "What the blazes are you doing in irons?"

"A misunderstanding," Jerinne offered before Dayne could speak. "The marshals are still trying to sort things out here."

"That's rot," Aldric said. "Heard what happened. We'd be stuck in that mess if not for him."

"You seem to have gotten it pretty bad," Jerinne said, though the glare from Price made her regret it.

"We tried to get the back kitchen doors open," Aldric said.

Price added, "When we couldn't do that, we pulled the cooks and stewards out of there before the whole place flooded over."

"Any deaths?" Dayne whispered.

"We stayed to the last," Price said. Both he and Aldric had a strange expression, like they had seen something they couldn't shake out of their heads. Dayne nodded, like he understood everything they weren't saying.

"Let's talk to the marshals," Aldric said, tapping Price on the arm. "Get this nonsense sorted out."

They both walked off, and Jerinne sat silently with Dayne for a while. Finally something struck Jerinne, and she was sure Dayne knew the answer.

"Why the empty plinth?"

Dayne raised an eyebrow, then looked over to the fountain. "You know about the Incursion of the Black Mage, right? When he executed King Maradaine IX, he disintegrated the statue and put the body on display up there. Later, when Oberon Micarum—you know, the Spathian warrior? When he killed the mage's second-in-command, he also put the body up there as a message, announcing—" Dayne paused, a shock of recognition on his face.

"Announcing what?"

Dayne recovered. "Announcing it was the fate of all who betrayed Druthal. That was the event that sparked Geophry Haltom to organize his rebellion that overthrew the mage. Anyhow, in the years that followed the Reunification, there was talk of replacing the statue, but the newly formed Parliament decided that it would be disrespectful. That leaving it empty would serve as a reminder of the tragedy and hope that occurred there."

"Tragedy and hope," Jerinne echoed. "That's about right."

"Where's the hope now?" Dayne asked.

Jerinne pointed at the various men around the Circle who were shackled in irons and being led into Constabulary wagons. "The rest of the Patriots are arrested, including Lannic. They're done. And I think after this, no one is going to be talking about the Patriots like they might actually be heroes."

"Don't be so sure," Dayne said. Lannic had been taken off to a lockwagon, a grin of satisfaction on his face despite his arrest. Madam Tyrell was being questioned by several people now. Not marshals or Constabulary. If Jerinne had to guess, they were representatives from various newssheets.

Price and Aldric returned with a marshal, who removed Dayne's irons with a look of utter resentment. "I've been told to release you to the care of these two as representatives of your Order. No charges will be laid upon you at this time. We reserve the right to seek you out for further questioning regarding these events." He stalked off as soon as Dayne was unlatched.

"Come on, Heldrin," Price said, helping Dayne to his feet. "I think we need to get out of here and let the city's people clean things up."

"We need to get cleaned up," Aldric said. He looked over Jerinne. "Your dress uniform is in a state, Initiate."

"It's not my—" Jerinne started, looking down at herself. The coat was torn and scraped in several places, not to mention blood and grease stains.

Vien really was going to kill her.

At that point Mister Seabrook emerged from the Talon, with Ressin at his heels.

"There you are, dear," Seabrook said. "Quite a bit of excitement we had, yes? And a good show from you, I hear."

"Sir," Jerinne said. "Just doing my duty." Her ears were burning, and she noticed that Price and Aldric seemed to be snickering at her.

"Well done, indeed," Seabrook said. He glanced about at the mess in Talon Circle. "We won't get the carriage out of here in any reasonable time, will we, Ressin?"

"I think not, sir," Ressin offered. "I've been told they're arranging cabs for us a block from here."

"Then let us stroll, Ressin." He turned back to Jerinne, giving a glance at Dayne and the other two, and a bit of a wistful sigh. "Rest up, and we'll see you at nine bells tomorrow. Ressin will send the carriage, provided we manage to rescue it." They walked off.

Both Price and Aldric started laughing once they were out of earshot. "Let us stroll, Initiate," Price said. "I'm afraid we won't have the carriage tonight."

"Let it lie," Dayne told them both. Amazingly, they acceded to him and made no further comment. They started walking toward the chapterhouse, Dayne taking one last moment to glance back at Madam Tyrell. Jerinne noticed her looking back at him, despite answering questions from the press. They seemed locked together, only for a moment, before Dayne broke away and continued to walk.

No one spoke again the whole way home.

Chapter 15

DAYNE AWOKE TO Grandmaster Orren sitting on the edge of his cot. The man was not watching him, but rather sat with his eyes closed in quiet contemplation.

"Sir?" Dayne said, sitting up.

"Ah, Dayne," the Grandmaster said, turning toward him. His face was a mask of neutral serenity, impossible to read. "I wanted you to wake naturally. Yesterday was a very trying day for you."

"It . . . had its challenges." A guarded response seemed best at this point. The Grandmaster did not seem upset, but Dayne considered it highly unlikely that he was in Dayne's quarters at sunrise to express his satisfaction.

"I'm certain it did. It took me the greater part of the night to fully untangle the events that have occurred since yesterday at this time. I must confess, I'm not entirely sure I have been completely successful."

"You haven't slept, sir?"

"Not yet, no. Nor am I likely to for some hours yet." Now there was a hint of irritation in his voice.

"Have you come to get my version of last night's events?"

"Your version, yes." The Grandmaster stood up. "You are familiar with the Question of the Gate?"

Dayne was definitely in trouble.

The Question of the Gate involved a gatekeeper being assigned to a post far away from his compatriots. The gatekeeper sees trouble in the distance, which he believes poses a grave threat to his compatriots. He cannot warn them without leaving his post. The mistake most Initiates make when responding to the Question of the Gate is presuming it is about following orders. Of course, that was part of the lesson learned in the Question of the Gate. The real core of the lesson, though, was trust and pride. A Tarian must trust that his fellows can handle their own fights. A Tarian must not be so proud as to think he is the only one who can take action.

Despite knowing that was where the Grandmaster was leading him, Dayne wasn't interested in being shamed. Not over this. He rose off his cot. "I was not assigned to watch a gate, sir."

The Grandmaster's voice became tight and clipped. "You were given an assignment, though. You were the ranking member on Watch. You abandoned that post."

"With good cause, sir!" Dayne immediately regretted raising his voice, as a single look of recrimination made his heart wither.

"From what I've gathered from the Initiates, some pipes burst, and you took this as a sign to run off into the streets."

"I had a hunch, sir. And you cannot deny that I was right about it."

The Grandmaster sighed and motioned for Dayne to sit back down. "Were you right that something was going wrong in Talon Circle? Yes. You have very good instincts. But you went racing to a place where there already were several Tarians. Which you knew, yes?"

"I knew they were with members of Parliament, and many of them were at the Talon, yes."

"Did you doubt their capabilities? Are you so proud—"

"Even with me there, sir, it wasn't enough. Mister Parlin is dead. If you're going to reprimand me, then it should be for that failure."

"Dayne—"

"I apologize for speaking out of turn, Grandmaster," Dayne said. "But if I know that lives are in danger, I will always run toward it and save every life I can. Are you truly saying that I—that any Tarian—should do otherwise?"

The Grandmaster's jaw went tight. "Humility, Dayne, is also the mark of a Tarian. As is sound judgment. To abandon your charges here—"

"Abandon?"

"Yes, Dayne. Your assignment to stay here with the Initiates may have felt minor compared to the glory of another victory, but—"

"Glory?" Dayne couldn't believe it. "Do you think I am some swell seeking to promote my name about?"

"That is four times you have interrupted me." The Grandmaster did not raise his voice, but his anger was quite clear. "I will point out that you and Master Denbar were the subject of many items in the Lacanja news-sheets, and you have already found that here as well."

Dayne took a moment to be sure that the Grandmaster was done speaking. "Not by my choice, sir. I explicitly went to the writers of the *Veracity* to keep me off their pages."

"You went to them? You are familiar with them?"

"I—" Dayne broke. He couldn't lie to the Grandmaster, not about this, but he was suddenly shamed at the implications of what he had done. "I met them for the first time the other night at The Nimble Rabbit."

"Just coincidence."

"Indeed, sir."

"Hmm." The Grandmaster paced about the room in silence, and his demeanor made it quite clear that he did not want Dayne to interrupt his thoughts. "I am not a man with a devious or suspicious mind, Dayne. Therefore, when you tell me that it is merely a coincidence that you met the writers of this newssheet, I am inclined to believe you. Just as I'm sure it was a coincidence that you attended the event that was first attacked. And another coincidence that your instincts led you to their second attack. I am inclined to believe these things, Dayne. Many others would not be."

Dayne wanted to protest. It was true, meeting Hemmit and the others was just a coincidence. So was being at the museum. It had to be. And it was his instincts that led him to Talon Circle last night.

"Perhaps so," Dayne said. What else could be said? "Will you be wanting my shield and tunic now?"

Dayne had made the same offer two days ago, and the Grandmaster had immediately refused it. Now he looked at Dayne with weariness for several seconds before replying. "I presume that you are deeply troubled by the news I gave you. It is for that reason, Dayne, that I'm allowing you a fair degree of latitude. I will not be officially reprimanding you at this time."

Dayne did not feel relieved. He wasn't sure what he felt. There was a horrible tension in his jaw and chest.

"I do feel compelled, however, to remind you that there is no shame or dishonor in serving three years of Candidacy and moving on to a new career. I am not sure the same could be said of being cashiered out after only two."

Dayne understood and nodded.

The Grandmaster's face lightened, ever so slightly, as he continued. "I am given to understand you are invited to a dinner this evening in the household of Lady Henson. I see no reason why you should be forced to decline. That said, I expect you to fulfill your duties here until that time."

"Of course, sir," Dayne said.

"Very good. We are still in Quiet Days, but many of the Initiates will be seeking some last-minute guidance before their Trials. You shall be available in the practice room to assist anyone who may require it. I think until five bells this afternoon." Dayne was well aware of the Grandmaster's style of punishment from his Initiate days. He needed to go to the practice room immediately and stay there. No meals, no breaks, until the end of shift, twelve hours from now.

Grandmaster Orren bowed his head slightly to Dayne, showing they both understood each other, and left him alone in the room.

Dayne hurried to get his uniform on and make it to the water closet. It was going to be a very long day.

Morning breakfast brought Jerinne many stares. She was wearing only her regular uniform this time, of course. Two ruined dress uniforms were more than enough. Vien didn't stare at her, she glared. Jerinne's many profuse apologies and promises of restitution over the night had done nothing to improve her mood.

"So what's on deck for your second 'quiet' day?" Raila asked, sitting in across from her in the mess hall. "Carriage chase through Trelan Square? Rescuing orphans from a fire?"

Jerinne gave her a warm smile. She was the only one of the Initiates who wasn't staring or glowering or sneering. "I was thinking of sailing out to the Napolic Islands, foiling a pirate attack."

"That's ambitious."

"That is the life of a Tarian," Jerinne returned. Raila's laugh was infectious.

"Let me give you some advice," Raila said. She leaned in close, conspiratorially.

"All right," Jerinne said, mirroring her.

"Corner of Hale and Ross. There's a laundress there—Iala—who works wonders. And she's a gifted seamstress as well."

"Vien's uniform?"

"And your own. Iala will have them both looking fresh and crisp by this afternoon. Mark me on that."

"I'll see if I have enough crowns hidden away to pay for that," Jerinne said.

"None of that," Raila said. "Iala is my cousin. She's got you, hear?"

Jerinne couldn't accept charity from Raila or take her cousin's sweat for nothing. "That isn't right."

Her smile faded only slightly and her eyes became very serious. "Twice in one day you saved many, many people."

"Helped save."

"Saved. So let me save you with this."

Jerinne sighed. "Hale and Ross? I won't be able to bring them until this afternoon."

"No, this afternoon you'll be picking them up," Raila said. "I already grabbed them and brought them over."

"Raila!"

"I don't want to hear it." She lowered her voice and leaned across. "Just don't forget about me when I'm flushed out after Trials."

Forget about Raila? No chance. "You won't be flushed. I'm more likely to."

Raila laughed again. "You really have no idea, do you?"

"About?"

Before Raila could answer, one of the stewards stepped over. "Initiate, there is a carriage here for you, sent by the Good Mister Seabrook of the Parliament."

"Don't keep the man waiting," Raila said, giving a little shake of her head.

Jerinne took one more bite of her breakfast and followed the steward out to the main hall.

The carriage waited out in the street, Mister Seabrook and Ressin reading through newssheets. Seabrook even had a tea tray laid out in front of him, with fine porcelain cups. Jerinne was mostly surprised that Seabrook would even be interested in tea on a day like this. Even for late spring, it was unseasonably hot.

"Dear Jerinne," Seabrook said as Jerinne came up into the carriage. "As you can see we were able to rescue the carriage. Have you read the newssheets today?"

"Not yet," Jerinne said. "I presume last night's activities made the news?"

Ressin passed one of the newssheets—the *News of Throne and House*—showing a front page story about the attacks in Talon Circle. The story was dominated by an image of Madam Tyrell triumphantly holding Lannic in submission. One part of the story was all about Madam Tyrell. Farther down the page were the usual stories about Parliament votes, the dress Princess Carianna wore at an event, and an evolving scandal involving city aldermen.

"I'm afraid you didn't quite seize your moment, dear," Seabrook said. "It seems Adept Tyrell has taken the glory."

"It's quite all right, sir," Jerinne said. "I fear my shoulders are not broad enough to rest so much upon them."

"I love this girl's modesty," Seabrook said to Ressin. "She really is a jewel."

"Indeed, sir," Ressin said. He turned to Jerinne—Mister Seabrook's attention was now entirely on his newssheets and tea—and read from his notebook. "Today we will be in session at the Parliament. Am I correct in presuming you've never attended a session?"

"That's right," Jerinne said.

"The protocol dictates that only the members are allowed on the floor proper. Every member has his box in the gallery, which is where you and I will be seated for the duration of the session."

"How long is the session?"

"As long as it is." Ressin shrugged. "Sorry, that isn't helpful. Typically, it's over by three bells. But it goes until the Prime Speaker accepts the call to end the session."

"Today's session will be quite short," Seabrook offered from behind his newssheet. "We've lost a man. Ending the session early in his honor is the standard response."

"Even in a situation like this?" Jerinne asked.

"There, I couldn't say," Seabrook said curtly.

"I'm fairly certain this is the first time that a member has died . . . quite like this," Ressin said.

"Killed?"

"Executed."

Jerinne kept silent for the rest of the trip to the Parliament House.

Jerinne had walked past the Parliament House several times, so she was familiar with the outside of it: a grand circular building of bright white stone, raised up over the wide plaza, surrounded by ten sets of stairs. The entrances—also ten— were all flanked by tall columns, each one carved from stone unique to each archduchy. The carriage came to a stop in front of the Sauriya entrance.

King's Marshals stood at attention at the bottom of each stairway. Dozens of citizens were gathered around the plaza, many trying to get as close to the approaching Parliamentarians as the marshals would allow. A small group gathered near the base, serenely holding a wooden placard that read: "The True Line Lives."

"Only four of them here today," Ressin said, noting the group. Aside to Jerinne, he added, "They're always here, at least a few."

"At least they're not a nuisance," Seabrook commented, getting out of the carriage. "I may not care for them, but at least they are content to just stand there with their signs."

"Our friends from last night could learn a thing from them," Jerinne said, giving a small smile. "Quiet persistence over violence."

"Bah," Seabrook said. "They're all a waste of flesh, if you ask me. Traitors to the crown wearing the robes of patriotism. But let's not tarry."

Seabrook took the lead up the steps, with Jerinne taking one side, shield slightly raised. If she was going to be here as a Tarian guard, she might as well look the part.

The marshal she passed gave her an ugly sneer.

Inside, several functionaries in gray suits moved about, quickly and quietly. Two came directly to Seabrook, gave him a slight nod, and took his cloak. Jerinne was amazed the man was even wearing a cloak, given how hot it was.

They were then escorted through a door labeled "Sauriyan Chairs" into the main Parliament hall. The hall was a grand circle, and where they entered there were several open cubicles with desks and chairs, and a stairwell down to the Parliament floor itself, where the actual Parliamentary Chairs sat. The one hundred chairs on the floor were works of art, ornate masterpieces of mahogany and velvet and gold inlay. One hundred thrones.

Rounding the floor were ten flagpoles, one for each archduchy, surrounding the tallest flagpole in the center of the floor, above the podium, where the flag of Druthal flew proudly: royal blue with ten colored rings in an interlinked circle.

Seabrook went down to the floor and took his chair there, as many other Parliamentarians were doing as well. They had not yet come to order, so he chatted amiably with the two members closest to him.

The furniture in the cubicles was simple and unadorned, but clearly of high quality, cedar and oak. Dozens of functionaries populated the cubicles, and Ressin led Jerinne over to one, with a plaque indicating it was designated for the 10th Chair of Sauriya. "This is our place."

"Only members of Parliament and the functionaries of the floor, right?" Jerinne confirmed.

"That's correct. Now, of course, if there is an attempt on the Good Mister Seabrook's life, feel free to disregard that custom. But only then."

"Somehow I doubt that would be an issue," Jerinne said, looking up. A level above them, the viewing gallery was filling up, with each aisle and balcony manned by a King's Marshal. The gallery was populated by dozens of common citizens, though Jerinne knew most of them came from the various newssheets. There were a handful of obvious nobility as well—Jerinne spotted Lady Mirianne and her fetching lady-in-waiting, Miss Jessel.

She looked around the gallery and the hall, realizing that something was missing. Not one other person in the Parliament hall was in a Tarian uniform.

She didn't have much time to think about what this might mean, as one old Parliamentarian stepped up from his chair onto the podium of the Parliament floor. He knocked three loud raps on the podium. "Be it heard. Be it heard. Be it heard. Today is the twelfth of Joram, in the year 1215. The Parliament of Druthal has been convoked. A quorum has been achieved. This august body is now in session."

"Welton, the Prime Speaker," Ressin whispered. "Crazy old coot."

"Good Mister Porter," Welton said, turning to a man in the chair closest to the podium. "You may take the floor." He left the podium and went back to his chair, closing his eyes.

Porter, presumably, stood up. "I take the floor. So it is done."

Ressin whispered again. "The position of Prime Speaker is entirely based on seniority. This is Welton's thirty-ninth Convocation. Thirty-nine years here. But he doesn't do a damned—sorry—a thing besides saying the opening words. He puts it all in the hands of the leadership, and the High Chair of the Floor runs the session. At least it does under Welton."

Jerinne pointed to the four chairs behind the podium, where Porter had just come from. "The leadership of the Parliament?"

Ressin nodded. "High Chairs of the Floor—Porter—and the Table, the Call, and the Decree. They're the leaders of the Reform Coalition."

"The Functionalists, Free Commerce, and Loyalist parties," she said.

He acted as if he didn't hear her, pointing to four chairs placed facing the podium, behind most of the other Parliamentarians. "And the leadership of the Opposition, our Values Coalition."

She kept silent this time. Seabrook was a Traditionalist—which she knew, but didn't think too much about. The Traditionalist Party was, in essence, the political arm of the nobility, representing a movement to cede authority claimed by the Parliament and national government back to the minor nobles, letting them control their own taxation, and tend to the needs of their own lands. She knew the Baron and Baroness Fortinare supported those ideas, and so did many of the people Jerinne had grown up with. Her own parents, even, believed in the order of things, and the Traditionalists were the party to make that happen.

Jerinne wasn't sure what she believed, politically, but she was assigned to protect Mister Seabrook, and that was what she would do.

The High Chair of the Floor called out, "We shall proceed with business, if the Good Mister Wrennit agrees that the floor, indeed, has achieved a quorum."

"We are assembled," said Wrennit, who Ressin indicated was the Opposition Chair of the Floor. "We may proceed."

Another man stood up—a thin, spry, white-haired man in a suit that was both charmingly quaint and out of fashion. He was dressed unlike any other man on the Parliament floor. Their suits were all dark shades—deep blues, cold grays, dark browns. His was a fair, bright blue, like the sky in the early morning.

His face did not match the brightness of his suit. "I would be recognized as the Ranking Chair of my party."

"You are so recognized, Good Mister Montrose."

This was Alphonse Montrose, the 2nd Chair of Maradaine. He was a Populist—a Saltie, by the typical epithet—same as Parlin. He was also a hero to many people back in the Sharain. Born a common shepherd, he had gained notoriety—and his Parliamentary Chair—through a unique act of valor in the war, in one of the few moments when Poasian soldiers landed on the Druth mainland. The story had grown into a tall tale of impossible proportions in the past thirty years, but Montrose had proven himself to be a sharp leader of uncommon wisdom.

"Last night," Montrose began, "I lost a dear friend. I would like to say you all did as well. I would very much like to. But you can all say we lost a colleague and fellow. It is only appropriate that we honor him."

"Indeed," said another Parliamentarian. "So I—"

"I have the floor, sir," Montrose said. The other man nodded and kept quiet. Montrose continued, "We should honor him by continuing the work that he would want done. Were Erick Parlin with us, he would be calling for action. We have only two days before this convocation of the Parliament draws to a close. There is much work to be done. Therefore, I put forth the proposal that we proceed with business as usual."

"A proposal is set forth," said a sandy-haired man

with a heavy Monic accent, who Ressin quietly identified as the High Chair of the Table—the member of the majority government who declared when a vote would actually be called.

"We would have it in plain terms," said the Opposition Chair of the Table—Ressin was very quick with his identifications, at least in terms of title. "Upon what, exactly, would we be voting?"

"Plain terms, Good Mister Montrose," Porter said.

"I propose that on this day—and the remaining days of this convocation of the Parliament—that we do not make any motion to close the session earlier than the standard time of six bells in the evening. We still have much we can accomplish."

"Point of order." One member stood, and was acknowledged by Montrose. "Is 'we still have much we can accomplish' part of the proposal upon which we will be voting?"

"Is it, Mister Montrose?" The High Chair of the Table asked.

"No, it is not," Montrose said, his tone clearly showing that he had played this particular game of pedantry before, and was quite tired of it.

"The proposal is stated. Do any support bringing this to vote?"

A very old man—almost as old as Welton—raised his hand, but did not stand up from his chair. "The proposal is sound." Between his age, Acoran drawl, and placement amongst the Chairs, Jerinne presumed he was the 1st Chair of Acora.

Another man—a young one, in this crowd—raised his hand. "This is a matter most grave."

Amongst the Parliamentarians there were several highly audible sighs. Montrose himself seemed to growl as he sat back down. Ressin, however, chuckled. Whatever just happened, it was a small victory for the Opposition.

The High Chair of the Decree spoke. "So it shall be. Place it to a vote."

The High Chair of the Call then called each member, identified by their ranking and archduchy. Functionaries in the cubicles scribbled furiously, including Ressin, but Jerinne couldn't keep track of who voted what. She found her attention mostly on Mister Seabrook, who had been barely engaged with any of the proceedings, alternating between chatting with the Chair next to him and reading his newssheets.

Once all ninety-nine had been tallied, the High Chair of the Decree declared the vote was complete, and looked across to the Opposition Leaders. "Is its authenticity in question?"

On the Opposition side, one member—the Chair of the Question—stood up and smiled coyly. "We question the vote, and would call it ourselves."

"What's happening now?" she asked Ressin.

"The leadership of the Opposition is exercising their right for a second round of voting, to confirm if it matches. It usually does, but it's a safeguard to prevent the governing coalition from boatrolling the opposition."

The Opposition Chair of the Call ran his own vote. It didn't take long before Jerinne was desperate for a cup of tea, desperate to step out of the cubicle, desperate to do anything other than sit there and listen to them go through the exact same vote again. She was shocked that no one else saw this as an exercise in absurdity. The Parliament seemed to run entirely on the process of procedure. She had expected, at least, a bit more grandstanding and speechmaking.

An insufferable period of time later, the second vote concluded. After a bit of deliberation, it was determined that both votes were in concurrence, so the Opposition recognized the validity of the vote.

"So we are agreed, and it has been decided," the High Chair of the Decree said.

"And what is the decision?" Porter asked. More procedure.

"The proposal—which was considered grave—did not meet the requirements to be enacted. The proposal has failed."

Jerinne was surprised. She had lost count, both times, but despite that she thought she had heard more "yes" votes than "no."

"What was the count?" she asked Ressin, who had long since ceased pointing out anything to her.

"Fifty-five to forty-four," Ressin whispered back.

So she had been wrong. She hadn't been paying much attention at any rate. She didn't even know how Seabrook had voted, though she suspected her charge had voted against Montrose's proposal.

"The proposal is defeated," Porter said. He turned to Welton, who appeared to be half dozing at the podium. "In that case, Good Mister Welton, I propose in honor of our fallen colleague, as is our tradition, we close the current session, so that each man may attend to his grief."

"Agreed," Welton said.

"Now wait a minute," Montrose shouted, rising to his feet, but Welton was already knocking on the podium.

"Today's session is ended. We are adjourned. This convocation will resume tomorrow morning at ten bells."

Montrose tried to say more but other members were already on their feet, joining their staff and clearing the Parliament floor.

Mister Seabrook strolled past Jerinne and Ressin. Ressin gathered up documents and raced after his master, signaling Jerinne to follow them. Seabrook walked with brisk purpose until they were outside and at the bottom of the steps.

"What a colossal waste," he finally said when Ressin and Jerinne had caught up with him. "And such a lovely morning."

Jerinne noticed that the noon bells were ringing at the Royal Sainted Cathedral on the other side of the plaza. The whole process of the session had taken nearly two hours, and all they had accomplished was deciding not to do anything.

No wonder the Patriots hated the Parliament.

"It seems, Miss Fendall, that I am behind the fashion today," Seabrook said.

"I'm sorry, sir?" Jerinne asked.

Seabrook glanced around, squinting in the harsh midday sun. "It seems that none of my peers elected to bring their Tarian guards. Dreadful miscalculation on my part. Terribly embarrassing."

"It's no trouble, sir," Jerinne said. "I found the experience . . ." She struggled to think of a word that would neither be insulting nor deceitful. "Illuminating."

"Yes, well," Seabrook said dismissively. "I feel quite foolish now." He walked off toward his carriage.

Ressin stood in front of Jerinne before she could walk with them. "I trust you can make your way back to your chapterhouse, Miss Fendall."

"Well, of course," Jerinne said. "But I thought . . ."

"Very good," Ressin said, turning on his heel and joining Seabrook in the carriage, leaving Jerinne standing in the plaza in bewilderment as they pulled away.

"You wouldn't think a Navy man would turn into such a feathered robin," a cool woman's voice said at her ear. Jerinne turned to find Miss Jessel's lovely face only inches from her own. She wanted to say something, but her voice had deserted her. Miss Jessel continued, "Of course, he's new to all this. He tries too hard to fit in, don't you think?"

Jerinne managed to bring words to her mouth, even though they cracked when she spoke. "I really don't know what is going on."

She smiled, warm and sweet. "You fare much better against madmen with crossbows."

"Crossbows, I understand," Jerinne said. She must have sounded like an idiot.

Jessel sighed, looking off to Seabrook's carriage in the distance. "He really must have been dreadfully embarrassed not to realize no one else would bring Tarian protection."

"I did think it was strange I was the only one being picked up this morning," Jerinne said, finally able to speak like a normal person.

"And now you're left on the walkway." She brushed her hand against Jerinne's cheek, which made her heart race. "I never did get the opportunity to thank you for everything you did in the museum."

Ideas raced through Jerinne's mind as to what possible thanks she could offer. "That's quite all right. I just did what any Tarian would do."

"So humble." She laughed. Then her manner became more sober. "I didn't come out here idly, though. My lady wanted me to remind you that you and Mister Heldrin are invited to dinner at her home this evening. She can send her coach to you at half past five bells, if that will suffice."

Jerinne couldn't help but laugh at that. "Two days ago I had never had a carriage sent for me in my life. Now it's happening all the time."

"Dear Jerinne," she said. "Yesterday you were launched from the catapult. You must expect that will take you to new places."

"I will see you tonight, Miss Jessel?"

"You most certainly will," she said with the slyest of smiles. "Now I can dally no further. My lady awaits." She curtsied and went back up the steps.

Jerinne strolled at an easy pace across the square toward the chapterhouse, finding herself whistling the old country tune her father always used to sing. This had been a very strange couple of days, but she was definitely interested in where it might be taking her.

Chapter 16

KEMMER DIDN'T THINK the clubhouse was much. It had been a basement pub, the sort that any Druth man used to be able to run from his household. But that had been before the Brewers Guild had colluded with the city aldermen, imposing new laws to crush the average man just trying to earn a living through simple trade. The pub had been shut down years ago, since Gillem hadn't greased the right pockets in the Guild. Gillem still owned the house, and thus the pub, where he freely let the Patriots assemble, especially to discuss the sorts of things that couldn't be said in the Alassan. Gillem was a good sort, having seen how the common Druth were being shackled. He was an old man, too old to be in the thick of things, but he was with them in spirit.

Kemmer had come alone, leaving Braning to rest in the back alley boarding room they had rented last night. Braning was still recovering from the blow to his head at the museum, and reeling from the loss of his brother. Kemmer thought it best to let him do that, while he got a scent of the air on his own. It was possible that Constabulary or marshals were looking for them, separately or together, but Kemmer was at less risk than Braning. Kemmer at least had resources he could reach out to, were he arrested. He could demand a lawyer, and someone from his father's agency would come. Braning had no such luck.

Kemmer had come in through the back alley, where no one but a few cats had seen him. He wasn't sure if anyone was specifically watching for him. They must be. With most of the Patriots in shackles, they were surely being beaten for information. Lannic wouldn't talk, of course, but the others might. The Alassan couldn't possibly be safe. Gillem's clubhouse probably wasn't either, but only a few people knew about it. Enough did, though.

Other than Braning, he had no idea who was still free. The newssheet he read that morning only mentioned Lannic by name, though it said "was arrested with others." Who? How many? Was Tharek out and about? The newssheet talked about Tarians helping capture the Patriots. Kemmer hadn't known much about the Tarians before yesterday, other than the old fables, but from what he had seen, it would take a Tarian to bring in Tharek Pell.

"Who's that?" Gillem stood behind the old bar, crossbow aimed at the door.

"Just Kemmer." He held his hands up, so Gillem wouldn't get too nervous.

Gillem put down the weapon. "Been wondering if anyone was still around. Today's newssheets are all about our boys being ironed up."

"Rather," Kemmer said, closing the door behind him. "Only a handful of us free at best. Maybe just me and Braning. No one else came in yet?"

"Not unless they were mouse quiet," Gillem said. "Ever since I got word, I been keeping an eye on the door."

"Mouse quiet, indeed," came a low growl from the

corner of the room. Gillem and Kemmer both startled, Gillem grabbing the crossbow in a scramble. The shot fired uselessly against the wall.

"Tharek, that you?" Kemmer asked. He knew the man was skilled, apparently skilled enough to be hiding in here without Gillem knowing.

Tharek came out of the shadow, silent as a soft breeze. "You're lucky it was me. Anyone else, and you two would be pinched."

"Saints, how long you been there?" Gillem asked.

"Long enough to see you doddering about, thinking you're guarding this place," Tharek said.

"I own this place, so don't you treat me —"

"Gentlemen, please," Kemmer said, intentionally using the calmest voice he could muster. "The last thing we need is to argue amongst ourselves. We must be strong, and we must be focused. Agreed?" Perhaps mustering a little authority would help matters along. He wasn't sure who was in charge now with Lannic gone, but he was reasonably certain it shouldn't be Tharek.

Gillem grumbled. "Agreed." He put the crossbow down on the bar.

"As you say, Kemmer," Tharek said, crossing the room to pull the bolt out of the wall.

"Very well." Kemmer sat down. "Gillem, I could use a glass of whatever you have stashed back there. You, Tharek?"

"I'll stay sharp, thank you."

Gillem poured out two cups from a dusty bottle. Kemmer took a sip — a cheap attempt at Fuergan whisky, very poor. But he wouldn't complain of it, not to Gillem.

"What's the plan?" Gillem asked. "Is there one?"

"I haven't a clue," Kemmer said. He had no bluff to pull, not here, not even in front of Tharek. Lannic had wanted his spectacle at the museum, and then again last night, to draw the people to their cause. Clearly that was not happening. "Do we even know who's still free? And have we heard from the Chief?" This was a bluff. Kemmer had never even met the Chief. For all he knew, the Chief was just something Lannic had made up, to give his orders an authority beyond himself.

"Nothing yet from him," Gillem said.

"Nothing today?" Kemmer pressed.

Gillem shrugged and gave a look at Tharek.

"I've no idea," Tharek said. "But I know how Lannic made contact, received instructions. I've left a message. We'll see what instructions we get."

"When did you do all that?" Tharek had been busy. "But what would he want us to do? We did what we were supposed to, right? You got Parlin. People are scared."

"I don't know if they are," Tharek said. "They got Lannic, they see him as the leader. They may not fear anything more."

"What more can we do?" Kemmer asked. "Most of our people gone. And when the marshals put the screws, they'll talk."

"No, never," Gillem said. He paced behind the bar. "Those are good friends of ours."

Tharek shook his head. "Friends or not, between our men in custody and questions about how we got into the museum, someone will crack."

"They're loyal to the cause!" Gillem snapped.

"Loyalty doesn't matter," Tharek said. "They are men of principle, but they don't have steel in their bones. They're far too soft."

Kemmer considered this. He had to admit, as loyal as he considered his friends to be, he held no illusions about whether or not they would break under pressure from the King's Marshals. He would probably break, himself. Surely the marshals would have no compunction breaking the Rights of Man to get the information they wanted. Humane treatment, indeed. That was a lark.

Gillem kept bickering with Tharek. "They won't betray us!"

"Is there an us? I didn't see you at the museum. Or Talon Circle."

"You know what I meant," Gillem said. "I do my part."

Kemmer stepped up. Nothing would be gained by letting these two get heated. "You do, Gillem, and everyone knows it."

"Point is, they're going to start digging around and they will find this place and the rest of us."

"This place, of course, being your primary concern," Tharek said.

"I live here, Tharek! Where am I going to go when they come pounding? And who will they keep looking for?"

"He's right, Tharek," Kemmer said. "Right now, his risk is greater than ours. We can't count on the safety of the clubhouse, not after last night."

"Agreed," Tharek said. "That's why I have a safe house for us. A contingency in case things did not go as planned."

Kemmer didn't like that. Tharek was taking a lot of liberties. He was taking charge. But who else was going to take charge? Braning? Gillem? Himself? Kemmer was dying to actually meet the Chief, hear a plan from the man's own mouth. "Lannic and the others don't know about it?"

"No," Tharek said, his head hanging low. "I see what you're thinking, Kemmer, and you're right. It wasn't my place to do such a thing. I've stepped over my bounds. But it will be safe. Our friends cannot be forced to betray what they know nothing about. Isn't that what we need right now?"

"It is," Kemmer admitted. Tharek Pell was still a new man with the group, but he had shown himself to be very valuable. Lannic had trusted him. Perhaps Kemmer should trust him as well.

"Very well," Tharek said. "We'll move ourselves to

this new safehouse. And then we need to rally, bring our friends out, whoever is still free."

"Braning is resting in an inn a few blocks away," Kemmer said.

"Anyone else?" Gillem asked.

"I'm not sure," Kemmer said.

"If anyone else is out of irons, I'll find them," Tharek said.

Kemmer looked to Gillem. "Do we have any allies who weren't part of the museum or last night's events?"

"I've might've heard from a few folk," Gillem said. "People who are interested, now that they know this isn't just talk." He poured himself another drink, and looked to Tharek. "So we move to your new place, and wait to hear from the Chief?"

Tharek pulled the cup out of his hand. "First, we stay sharp."

"Right," Kemmer said. He didn't need anything more to drink. Gillem's mash wasn't doing his head any favors, and it was still pounding from that clocking the Tarian had given him. "What about weapons, supplies?"

"Don't worry about that, Kemmer," Tharek said, flashing a wicked grin that looked entirely unnatural on his face. "I've got that taken care of. The thing we need to do next is get our message out."

Kemmer twitched. He wasn't sure that he and Tharek were on the same page in terms of message. "What message is that, exactly?"

"Simple," Tharek said. "Free Lannic."

Dayne launched a series of attacks on Vien Reston, who held her ground admirably. Of course, he wasn't trying to actually hurt her, but was doing his best to score a touch upon her with the practice sword. She was good, she had absorbed the lessons well, although the gnawing distraction of hunger and thirst kept him from giving her his best.

The day had been a blur of Initiates coming in and out, but from what he had seen of the third-years, Vien was the one with the least to worry about in terms of advancing to Candidacy.

"I'm still holding my arm low," she said after she stepped back.

"Not appreciably," Dayne said. "You shouldn't worry about that."

"Right," she said. "Should I be worried about the Question of the Bridge?"

Dayne wasn't sure how he should answer that. "Worried isn't the right way to think about it. You should be thinking along the lines of what the Question of the Bridge is asking you."

"I thought about that all last night. Could hardly sleep."

"And what did you conclude?"

"That there isn't a right answer."

This was on target. "How so?"

"If you do nothing, people will die. So leaving the switch alone is all wrong."

"So therefore?" Dayne prompted.

"But if you pull the switch, you kill the man on the cart. So you can't do that either."

"It's a hard choice, isn't it?"

"It's not a fair choice."

She was almost on it. "No," he admitted. "Were you expecting it to be? More to the point, do you expect being a Tarian involves easy, fair choices?"

A slight gleam lit up in her eye. Then she stepped back and regarded him. "You've been in here all day. Almost ten hours so far."

"That's right."

"You're being punished for last night, for rushing to the Circle."

"I've been given orders for today," Dayne said. "And a stern reminder that I did not follow orders last night."

"Blazes," Vien said. "There isn't an Initiate here who

isn't kicking themselves today, wishing they chased after you."

"You see?" Dayne offered, casually pointing at her with his sword. "Hard, unfair choices. And consequences will fall on you no matter what you do."

"Like spending all day in here?"

"The trick . . ." He paused, not wanting to give away too much to her before her final Trials. "The trick is accepting whatever consequences come your way. Because the choices you make—the important ones—are about doing the things that you have to, or you can't live with yourself."

Of course, that had been the very choice he had made in Lacanja. He had done what he thought he had to, and he was living the consequences now. As much as he wanted to blame that Sholiar for it—and it was Sholiar, there was no denying he had engineered a trick for Dayne to walk into—it still was on Dayne's shoulders that he had fallen for that trick, and it had a cost.

Vien nodded, and she seemed to be absorbing this. "Next time, I'm running out into the night with you."

"If that's the right choice for you," Dayne said. Maybe that was exactly what the Grandmaster was trying to impress on him, that he didn't need to charge in. That he needed to trust, he needed to wait and assess the situation.

But if Dayne had done that last night, more lives might have been lost. And charging in, that was exactly what he had—

He shook himself out of the reverie, seeing that Vien was still looking to him for some words of wisdom. He noticed in the corner of the room a first-year struggling with basic stances, trying to work them into his muscles. "Why don't you give him a spar, and I'll note your style."

Vien went to the first-year, and after a bit they were engaged.

"She's my champion this year, you know," Amaya's voice whispered in Dayne's ear. Cool and detached, no intimacy betrayed in her voice.

Dayne turned to her, standing just a few feet behind him. She must have come into the room like a mouse. "So you're saying she's this cohort's you."

"I should be so lucky to think I was where she is," Amaya said. She produced a cup of water. "I imagine you need this."

Dayne took it gratefully. "This won't get you into trouble?"

"None that I can't handle." She watched him with an odd regard while he greedily drank the water. It did little to ease the gnawing need in his stomach, but it gave him some relief at least. Once he finished, she added, "I need to apologize about yesterday."

"You do?" He was pretty sure she was not apologizing for storming off from the bathhouse. She wouldn't do that, not here. He doubted she would even admit what happened in the bathhouse.

"I accused you of seeking glory in the press," she said.

"I don't think you said that, exactly."

"Maybe not those exact words, but that was my meaning. But it was entirely foolish."

"I'm glad you think so." Dayne paused, watching Vien draw in the first-year, then he turned back to Amaya. "Why, exactly, do you think so now?"

"You've been in here all day, haven't you?"

"Yes."

"So you haven't seen any newssheets from today."

"I've seen nothing but swordplay today," Dayne answered. "Though I recall a certain number of newsmen paying you some mind last night after events calmed down."

"Calmed down," she said with a scoff. "When was that?"

"In the sense that the perpetrators were under irons. That's when Price and Aldric dragged me back here. Was there more trouble?"

"Not trouble, but plenty of work for the Yellow-shields."

"What were the final reports?"

"Depends who you ask. But most of the papers say seven dead in all, including Good Mister Parlin. Two others beaten to death by the Patriots, two drowned in sewage in the Talon, one trampled by a runaway cart, and one killed in a fire. Injuries are in the dozens."

"Blazes," Dayne cursed. "Most brought to Saint Katri's Ward?"

"Saint Katri and Redborne. I spent a good portion of the morning with some of the Adepts down at Redborne, helping with whatever scuttle they needed."

"I should have done the same," Dayne said. That would have been a far more fitting penance, being forced to care for those he hadn't saved.

Amaya must have read his mind. "The Grandmaster knows that the best way to punish you is to keep you from there. Besides, by noon they kicked us out, said we were underfoot."

"I should have stayed last night, helped then."

"There was plenty of help already. You had done enough." She gave him a slight, sly smile. "What I want to know is how you managed to sleep last night."

Dayne parroted one of Master Denbar's favorite aphorisms. "'A rested mind is vital to a Tarian's success.'"

"You make it sound easy."

"Master Denbar made sure I learned how to sleep in any situation. Compared to some nights under him, last night was easy."

"Easy for you, maybe. You got left alone all night."

Dayne almost choked. "Your night . . . wasn't alone?"

She smacked him on the arm. "Not like that. Why do you care?"

"I seem to recall you celebrating victories—"

That earned him another smack. A much harder one.

"I came here to apologize."

"Because you realized how easy it is to be lauded by the press?" Dayne asked. "I imagine they've sketched you in a stunning portrayal on the front of the newssheets. Proudly triumphant with Lannic caught in the crook of your arm." He didn't realize until he actually said it how upset he was, bitterness dripping from every word.

"Yes, that's it exactly," she replied, her voice rising. "In fact, I was thinking of going out tonight to pose for a few artists."

"Really? Portraits, or for your eventual sainting statue?"

"Sainting?" she screeched. "Why would I do that, when *clearly* I should pose as Sinner Jessalyn?"

"I'm *sure* that's exactly what you would do!" he returned, just as loud and indignant.

"Well, I need to do something with my evening," she said, pulling a note out of her jacket and slapping it against Dayne's chest. "Since you already have an engagement, it really shouldn't concern you!"

She stormed out.

Dayne looked at the note—from Lady Mirianne, of course, reminding him that he and Jerinne were to join her for dinner that evening at her home, and that her carriage would come for him at five bells.

Dayne's empty stomach soured. Amaya had that in her hand, yet she had come to apologize.

He wanted to chase after her, apologize himself, say he had been an idiot.

But he couldn't leave the practice hall. Not for another hour. And then it would be time to go to Lady Mirianne's. He'd barely have a chance to get ready.

⚔️—▶

Jerinne had to give credit: Raila's cousin was a miracle worker. Both dress uniforms were impeccable. Vien grunted in approval when Jerinne returned her uniform, clean and repaired. When Jerinne put her own on, she imagined that it even fit better than it had yesterday. Though perhaps she was remembering wearing Vien's.

The carriage from Lady Mirianne was waiting when she came down to the lobby, as were several Initiates.

"Two nights in a row!"

"Think you're a big star, Fendall?"

"Going to skip the rest of Initiacy, and go right to Adept?"

"Hey, hey," Jerinne yelled at the lot of them. "It's not my fault people think I'm incredible."

Someone landed a playful punch on Jerinne's shoulder. "You're taking the hot spot in evening contemplation for a week, Fendall."

"If she's even an Initiate after next week."

"Enough!" The voice boomed through the lobby—Madam Tyrell coming in from up the stairs. "Since it is Quiet Days, I suggest you all find someplace else to *be quiet*."

The rest of the Initiates scattered. Madam Tyrell came over to her, brushing off her dress uniform, as if it wasn't perfectly crisp and clean.

"I'm sorry about all that," Jerinne said. "I didn't mean to . . . get so much attention."

"Believe me, Initiate, I understand completely." She sighed. "This sort of thing happens every year. Everyone is nervous that they won't be here in a week. So they gang up on the person they know will be."

That threw Jerinne. She was the one they knew would be? "No, this is just about the carriages and the action."

"Jerinne," Madam Tyrell said, bracing her hands on her shoulders. "They're training to be Tarians. But you're doing it. Do you understand?"

"I think so," Jerinne said, though she was more confused than ever. Partly by Madam Tyrell talking to her like she was her peer.

Any response Madam Tyrell was about to give was interrupted by Dayne rushing into the lobby, adjusting the hasps of his coat as he came in. "Are we ready to go? No need to wait, right? Carriage is here?"

Madam Tyrell left the lobby with only a quick, heated glance at Dayne. What was it Vien Reston had said about the two of them during their Initiacy? There was something happening between them, but Jerinne felt far happier not even thinking about it. Too much in her head already.

"This way, Mister Heldrin," the carriage driver said. Jerinne hadn't even really noticed him, but Dayne smiled brightly when he approached.

"Kaysen! Saints, man, it's been ages! You're driving the carriage, now?"

The driver helped them into the carriage, grinning back at Dayne broadly. "I serve the needs her ladyship requires."

"Jerinne, this is Kaysen Ford," Dayne said warmly. "He and I served in Lady Mirianne's father's household together."

"Listen to this one," Kaysen said, mounting the driver's seat. "Be clear here, girl. I served the earl's household. As did Dayne's father. Dayne didn't serve one blasted day. They pegged him as a boy with talent early on, and put him on a path to be sitting right where he is now."

Dayne laughed. "I had no idea, Kaysen, that the earl had planned so long ago for you to be driving me around."

"Hush now," Kaysen said. "Point is, young Miss Jerinne, this one was raised to be a Tarian. Best not let me down there, Dayne."

Dayne's warm demeanor dropped suddenly. "Right. Absolutely, Kaysen."

As the carriage moved down the street, Dayne stayed in quiet contemplation.

"Quite a crazy bit of business, wouldn't you say?" Kaysen asked, though not to either of them in particular.

"What do you mean?" Jerinne asked, once it was clear that Dayne wasn't responding. "The two attacks from the Patriots?"

"Patriots, right," Kaysen said. "That's right. But they're taken care of. Thanks to you two in no small part, I'm given to understand."

"We just did our duty."

"Of course, of course," Kaysen offered. "Shame, though."

"What's that?"

"They still got away with what they planned."

"Pardon?" Dayne asked, suddenly very engaged.

Kaysen looked back at Dayne, his attention only partially on the road. "Well, they still managed to kill that man, right? That's what I'm talking about."

"I suppose," Jerinne said.

"What they planned," Dayne whispered. Then he leaned in close to Kaysen. "Listen, I need . . . I'm going to ask you a favor, old friend."

"Is this the kind of favor that would get me in trouble?"

"Probably not," Dayne said. "But I need to take a side trip. Can we swing by The Nimble Rabbit for a few clicks?"

"If you're worried about the dinner, I was in the kitchens earlier, and . . ."

"No, nothing like that, Kaysen," Dayne said. "Though I am beyond famished. I need to talk to some people there. It won't take long."

"All right," Kaysen said. "But it really can be only a few minutes. I presume you don't want to mention this side trip to her ladyship."

"I don't think it would be strictly necessary. Would it?"

"Don't sell me too hard, hmm?" Kaysen took another

corner, and in a few minutes they were in front of a small, charming house—an old Sharain village brasserie, tucked into the alleyway.

"Just a few minutes," Kaysen said.

"Come with me, Jerinne. I want to hear your thoughts on this as well."

"My thoughts on what?" Jerinne asked. "What is this place, and why are we here?"

"It's The Nimble Rabbit," Dayne responded as if that answered everything. He went through the ivied archway, eyes searching.

"Yes, but why—" Rich smells of lamb and onions and wine hit Jerinne's nose. "Is the food good?"

"Excellent, but we're not here to eat," Dayne said. "Well . . . maybe a crisper. But . . . ah, there they are."

"Who?"

Dayne was already leading her to a table in a far corner of the courtyard, where two men were sitting in quiet conference over a bottle of wine.

"Gentlemen, I trust you're having a good evening," Dayne said as they approached.

"Indeed, Dayne," the taller, hairier of the two men said. "Unless you're here to yell at us again."

"Nothing of the sort," Dayne said. "In fact, I need your counsel."

"Of course," he said. "And this is the young Jerinne Fendall, the other hero of the day."

"That might be pushing things," Jerinne said, taking the man's extended hand.

"Jerinne, this is Hemmit Eyairin." Dayne introduced them. "And his friend with charcoal pencil and sketch pad is Maresh Niol."

"Artist?" Jerinne asked, shaking the spectacled man's hand.

"In part," Maresh said. "But only for the purpose of the truth."

"They're newsmen," Dayne offered.

"We pretty much are *The Veracity Press*," Hemmit said. "Sit, sit."

"Newsmen?" Jerinne asked. "So were you in the Parliament this morning?"

"No need for that," Hemmit said. "I can imagine what happened: a few minutes of posturing and then closing today's session in honor of Parlin."

Jerinne nodded. "That's about right."

Dayne took a seat. "So what is the news today, now that the Patriots' crisis is supposedly over?"

"Is it over, though?" Jerinne asked.

"You tell us," Maresh said. "Most of the Patriots are arrested. Lannic will stand trial before High Justice Feller Pin. That's interesting news."

"Why?" Jerinne asked.

Dayne answered, though he looked distracted. "High Justices don't typically sit before criminal cases, unless the criminal was a nobleman or in the Parliament."

"Even Alderman Strephen is up in front of the city justices, and that's corruption that fills the whole city," Hemmit said.

"I thought that was just a mistress scandal," Jerinne said. It had been the salacious news before the Patriots business started up.

"Listen to her. 'Just a mistress scandal.' As if it were that simple. You know that said mistress has now vanished, no trace? Something foul is going on there. You see . . ." Hemmit got no further before Dayne interrupted.

"I don't have much time here," Dayne said, though he flagged over the server and demanded a crisper. "But something has been gnawing at me all day, and I can't make sense of it."

"Say your piece, friend," Hemmit said. He offered to pour wine into Dayne's cup, but Dayne begged off.

"Yesterday when we talked—"

"We kept your name out of last night's debacle," Maresh said quickly.

"You did, yes, thank you," Dayne said. "But more to the point, we talked about why the Patriots might target Parlin and Barton, two men of different politics."

Hemmit nodded, sipping at his wine. "I recall. Lin chastised us that we were overthinking it."

"I don't think we were, though. Last night they made a point of going after Parlin. Not just killing him, but dragging him into a public place and making a spectacle of him. Parlin was clearly their target."

Hemmit considered. "Possibly so. But if you'll allow me to whisper in the sinner's ear: they were enraged at Parlin and Barton slipping through their grasp. They had a target of opportunity, which they missed. So they needed to re-create that. This time it was personal regarding Parlin *because* of what had happened in the museum."

Jerinne thought that sounded reasonable. Dayne seemed uncertain. He was about to respond when the server brought his crisper, which he grabbed out of the man's hands and bit into greedily.

"All right, let's accept that," Jerinne said, looking at the whole group of men, who seemed to be surprised she was speaking. "They went to a lot of trouble for their show, and the main thing they gained was one dead Parliamentarian."

"And a lot of fear and chaos," Maresh added.

"Right, but what does one dead Parliamentarian actually give them? Who gains from that?"

Maresh tapped his fingers in thought. Hemmit screwed his brow up and took another swig of his wine. Dayne continued to eat his crisper.

"This is something to consider," Hemmit said finally. "The Parliament is constantly dancing on a knife edge. The current coalition of the Frikes, Crownies, and Minties has a strong majority—"

"Not strong enough," scoffed Maresh. "Only fifty-three seats."

"No, but strong," Hemmit continued. "The Salties aren't in the Coalition with them, but they usually vote with them. So that brings their nose count to fifty-nine."

Jerinne leaned in. "Wait, how strong does it have to be? If they have the majority, why does it matter? A win by one vote is still a win."

"You would think, except you have Dishers like Perry or Scott abusing gravity."

That sounded familiar somehow. Jerinne didn't know how gravity could be abused by any member of Parliament. This morning had made it clear she didn't understand all the intricacies of the Parliament, which was clearly something she needed to rectify.

Dayne looked puzzled as well. "I had heard complaints in Lacanja about procedural nonsense causing trouble. But the newssheets weren't much help in sorting out what was going on. Frankly, most of them were squarely Traditionalist, standing up Perry as a hero."

Jerinne waved her hands in frustration. "Procedure? Abusing gravity? Help me out."

Maresh sighed, looking as if the act of explanation he was about to make gave him physical pain. "A majority—fifty-one if all the seats are full at the voting call—is typically enough. Unless someone declares the matter being voted on is grave. A vote on an issue of gravity requires six-tenths of the quorum."

"Grave, yes!" Jerinne said. "Today during the session, they were arguing about cutting it short as an observance for Parlin. Someone stood up and said, 'This is a grave matter.'"

Hemmit nodded. "That's it. And out of courtesy, since the august body is made of gentlemen, any member can attach gravity to any vote. It isn't questioned or even challenged."

"Wait a minute," Jerinne said, remembering the interminable voting session earlier this morning. "So Montrose's proposal this morning, to stay in session, should have passed. Except that one fellow made it grave." She had heard more yes votes, like she thought. But fifty-five wouldn't have been enough to pass a "grave matter."

Hemmit laughed. "I'm not surprised. Perry has declared almost every single vote, on even the most trivial of matters, to be grave."

"How trivial?" Dayne asked.

"I believe in yesterday's session he declared a vote regarding the allotment of lamp oil to Parliament offices to have gravity."

Maresh added, "Fortunately, enough Books voted for that one to allow the offices to have light. But most of the time they all stand in arms with the Dishers to grind everything to a standstill."

"The Functionalists must hate that," Dayne said. Jerinne knew well enough to know that the Frikes were moderate in their views, mostly wanting the government to work. Jerinne didn't care for them—too willing to compromise principle for the sake of moving things along.

"Like how," Hemmit said. "I have some sources, speaking privately, who say that some of the Frikes are considering breaking the Coalition and giving the Dishers the Ruling Chairs, just to put an end to these games."

"It won't work, though!" Maresh shouted. After a glare from Hemmit, he grumbled and poured himself a fresh glass of wine.

"I think we've lost your point," Dayne said, finishing his food. "How does this tie to Parlin's death?"

"Right, Parlin's death," Hemmit said. "Now, he was a Saltie, and the coalition holds the majority without him—fifty-eight to forty-one. But what concerns me is the election."

"I presume Parlin's Chair wasn't up this year," Dayne said.

"Not even close. He was reelected in 'thirteen, so he had three more years. The two Chairs open this year are Callun and Batts. Callun is a Disher, but he's practically an institution in Acora. He'll win back his seat without even trying. But Batts, he isn't putting his name in."

"What's his party?"

"Frike. Been in for two terms, says he's done."

A typical habit of the Functionalists. They believed that Parliamentarians shouldn't hold their Chairs overlong, usually choosing to step down. Jerinne could respect that part of their ideology. "So how's it going to go?"

Hemmit shrugged. "Who can say what they do up there? But I know that two of Callun's top aides resigned and went back Acora. I hear they are both getting their names whispered around as contenders for Batts's Chair."

Dayne's eyes went wide. "With a third Chair to fill, they wouldn't have to fight each other. If there's a strong enough Traditionalist sentiment in the voting . . ."

"Which there surely would be, with Callun being balloted," Maresh said.

"They win those, it doesn't take much more for the coalition to lose the majority and the Ruling Chairs."

"That's crazy," Jerinne said. "Look, whatever the Patriots wanted, it was simpler than that. Minor shifts in parliamentary majorities is too subtle."

"It may not have been their goal, but it's what they may have caused."

Dayne nodded. "True. I doubt the Patriots had any such agenda, but Lannic and his associates have created consequences that we must live with."

"This all makes my head hurt," Jerinne said.

"Then drink more wine," Hemmit said, pouring a fresh glass. "That is what I must do every time I think about what is going on in the Parliament."

"Not too much," Dayne said.

"Please, the girl is one of the heroes of the hour," Hemmit said. "Relish that, young lady." Jerinne couldn't argue with that, and reached for the glass. Saints knew she had had enough happen in the past two days to harry her nerves. A taste of wine was just what she needed.

"Moderation, Jerinne." Dayne gave her a slight smile. "We have still a long night at Lady Mirianne's."

"My, Lady Mirianne. The bright jewel of Jaconvale herself." Maresh spat on the ground, as if his dismissive tone hadn't made his opinion clear enough.

"She is an old and dear friend," Dayne said, with a hint of anger burning under his words. "Do not disrespect her."

"Fine." Maresh shook his head and focused on his own wine.

"Speaking of, Dayne," Jerinne said. "We've probably gone past the few minutes we had to spend here."

"Indeed," Dayne said. "Look, we must be off, but . . . my gut is telling me we're not touching on something in all this. Some point, some goal, some long plan."

Hemmit nodded. "You think that this business with the Patriots isn't over?"

"They're all arrested," Maresh said.

"Not all," Dayne said. "There's Tharek."

Jerinne perked up at that. "Right. He got away last night, didn't he? And he's the most dangerous of all of them."

Hemmit put down his wineglass. "Are you serious? The most dangerous of the Patriots is still free?"

Dayne answered with a nod.

"This is news," Hemmit said. "Go to your dinner. Maresh and I have work to do."

Maresh gathered his supplies. "We do?"

"Indeed, and we should find Lin."

"Are you sure?" Dayne asked. "We could . . ."

"No, no," Hemmit said, his tone now far more sober than it had been during the whole conversation. "You've done what you need to do, friends. Now truth needs to be ferreted out, and that is my job. Trust me to mine as I do you to yours."

He offered his hand to both of them and shook it vigorously.

"I do appreciate your help, Hemmit," Dayne said. Jerinne glanced at the archway and spotted Kaysen tapping his finger against the wood frame.

"Dayne, we really must go."

"Yes, right," Dayne said, and giving Hemmit and Maresh one last salute, he went to the archway with Jerinne.

"I thought we weren't going to eat anything here," Jerinne teased Dayne.

"And I haven't eaten all day. I thought I was going to faint," Dayne said. "Trust me, my appetite for Lady Mirianne's feast will not be diminished in the slightest."

Second Interlude

THE GRAND TEN were not gathered. Only half of them had bothered to respond to Barton's summons, which he found quite vexing. Things were not going to plan, and the risks to his own life were unacceptable.

"Twice!" he shouted, his voice muffled by his mask. "Twice yesterday *my* life was in grave danger by our little operation."

"And yet you live," Millerson said, clearly quite comfortable in his "Man of the People" mask. "And I'll point out I was in danger last night. As were several of our . . . absent companions." In addition to Millerson, there was only the Lord, the Priest, and the Justice in attendance.

"Absent companions," Barton sneered. "They couldn't be bothered to attend when we called."

The Lord spoke. "This meeting was . . . unplanned."

"So was the attack on the Talon!" Barton shouted. "We need to get a rein on this! When I call for a meeting, everyone should respond!"

The Lord snorted. He probably didn't appreciate having a member of Parliament speak to him like that. "We must be forgiving of those who do not have quite the same . . . freedom of scrutiny that some of us enjoy. Even our hostess could not be here." They stood around in the audience seats of the shuttered opera house, not even engaging in the usual ritual. Barton wondered why they were even bothering with the masks. Of course, the Mage wasn't there to shield them. If someone came across them, this time they would be seen.

"Well said, my lord," the Priest said. "I myself was barely able to make adequate excuses."

"Who do you need to make excuses to?" Barton asked. He knew damn well that Bishop Onell wasn't answerable to anyone in this city. As his parish was in Abernar he was formally visiting Maradaine on a study sabbatical. Unless the Archbishop of Sauriya or the king himself called on Onell, no one would mark his comings and goings.

"You would be amazed, dear Parliamentarian," the Priest said. "Although I may not have to answer to many souls in this city, many still question me when I step foot anywhere. The Bishop of Maradaine is very intent on imposing himself on my time. I may not answer to him, but I must be politic."

"Why was this meeting called?" the Justice asked. "Were you two bored after voting yourself the afternoon off?"

"Do you understand what happened last night?" Barton asked. "We need to get a handle on this situation before it floods our ability to control it."

"It seems like the natural consequence of what we put into motion," the Justice said. "I was working on the presumption that it was part of that 'bit of chaos' we were crafting."

"A 'bit of chaos,' not sewage in the streets!" Millerson was incensed. "The Parliamentarian and I could have—"

"We're cleansing the humors of this nation. That sort of thing is to be expected."

"We have to get control of things—" Millerson said.

"And yet we designed this plan to minimize our direct control. Layers of insulation, you said. Deniability."

"Don't forget yourself, Justice," Millerson said. "We all played our roles in these past few days. The Parliamentarian and I are currently the most at risk for exposure."

"How are you at risk?" the Lord asked. "Poor Barton was the victim in all this."

"Names, Lord!" Millerson snapped. He was far too invested in the roles they were supposed to play. Barton didn't really understand it, especially now. They all knew he was Barton. They all knew that The Lord was Archduke Holm Windall of Oblune, and he was at risk as well. Money had been used to forge alliances, ensure key deliveries, move people into place. A clever accountant could trace that the money had come from the archduke, if the right questions were asked. If enough was revealed.

And furthermore, he was someone who theoretically had a personal motive in their goals. He was officially in the line of succession for the throne—twenty-third, if Barton remembered correctly. Not that anyone in this council was interested in putting Windall on the throne, or the bloodbath of royalty that would require.

That would hardly save Druthal. And the next in line was the nation's best chance.

"The ... Man of the People"—Barton almost choked on Millerson's alias—"is the one who could, potentially, be identified should certain people amongst the arrested operatives decide to become talkative."

"I thought you took precautions," the Lord said.

"There are layers between me and any of the Patriots who were arrested," Millerson said.

The Justice sneered. "Really, my Lord, it's almost as if you don't actually listen."

"Don't you—"

Millerson got up, putting himself between the Lord and the Justice. "I was as hands off as possible, considering how specifically we were trying to steer them."

"This was steered?" the Lord asked. "It seemed like pure chaos, from what I read."

"What you read?" Barton asked.

"I wasn't there. Can you imagine, me in Talon Circle? That would have been the story, my friends." The archduke had quite an opinion of his public profile. Of course, he was right.

"It doesn't matter," the Priest said. "The point is, danger to one is danger to ten. How vulnerable are you?"

"As I said, there's no direct connection between me and any of the arrested Patriots. But some of them can draw a line to someone who can draw a line to me. I'm especially concerned with their ringleader."

"Lannic Falson," the Justice said. "He's the one you're worried about."

"Rather."

The Justice sighed. "You think I didn't realize that? Why do you think I stepped in and claimed jurisdiction over his trial?"

"I had presumed your intent was to control the situation," Barton said. A High Justice of the Royal Court like Feller Pin stepping in to preside over a criminal case was unusual. Even one involving the murder of a Parliamentarian. That Pin did so would draw the attention of the newssheets. Hopefully not so much that it would seem suspicious.

"Indeed. And I will make sure that Mister Falson receives humane treatment. No one will get any names out of him by coercive means."

"And you will look fair and just in the process," Millerson said.

"I must give every appearance of that, but carefully. Actual fairness will not happen, since we have to make sure the boy rots away in a cell," Pin said.

"Is there more?" the Lord asked, sighing heavily. "Or are we just going to prattle on for awhile longer?"

"What is wrong with you?" Barton snapped. "Things are spiraling wildly out of control, and maybe we ought to be concerned."

"I'm very concerned," Archduke Windall said. "The last thing I need is you cracking up."

"Enough," Justice Pin said. "The last thing we need is for us to snipe at each other. Things went badly, but we have the Patriots arrested and going to trial. Parlin is dead, as we planned, and we've gotten back on track. There is nothing to panic over."

He was glaring at Barton. It seemed he wanted Barton to concede the point and move on.

"Fine," Barton said. Pin was right about that. No need to belabor it and make himself look weak.

"Very good, then," Bishop Onell said. "Then I suggest no more 'emergency' meetings. The next one as planned. Agreed?"

"Agreed," Archduke Windall said, taking off his Lord mask. "Now let's be off and on our separate ways. I really cannot be seen in this neighborhood at this time of day. What would people think?"

Chapter 17

THE CALLON HILLS NEIGHBORHOOD was surrounded by a fifteen-foot stone wall, with the only entrances iron gates with private guards. It could withstand a siege if it had to—the neighborhood was protected almost as well as the Royal Palace itself. It was no trouble passing the checkpoint—the guards recognized Kaysen and Lady Mirianne's coach, but they still gave his papers a cursory glance.

"Sweet saints," Jerinne whispered as they entered. Dayne had been in here before, but he wasn't desensitized to it. The neighborhood was pure opulence.

Callon Hills had no shops, no public squares. There were parks and statues, and wide, tree-lined walkways, but almost no souls were walking there this evening. The only people Dayne noticed were a few lamplighters, who were clearly attached to the households rather than city employees.

The households were incredible gated mansions on

sprawling acres-wide plots. They were manor houses, tucked away in the middle of the city. Gold and brass gleamed from the individual gates, each one with their own set of guards.

Most of the houses here were owned by nobility or Parliament members. There were a few rich merchants who made their home in the neighborhood, but they were few and far between. Dayne had recalled Mirianne talking about her father's intention to make such people feel unwelcome there, a sentiment most of the residents surely felt as well.

Lady Mirianne's house—the earl's house, more correctly—was one of the more modest dwellings in the area. It didn't have its own brick walls surrounding the property, rather trimmed hedges formed the perimeter, giving a clear view of the house from the street. It had a simple, classic elegance: white stone, smooth pillars, a vibrant plot of colorful flowers bordering the doors.

Two pikemen—actual pikemen wearing the Jaconvale crest— stood at attention at the driveway. Dayne wondered where they came from: mercenaries, former soldiers, or just servants dressed up like the earl's Bannermen from centuries ago. There was no telling from their behavior, as the only reaction they gave as the carriage approached was to salute Kaysen.

The carriage approached the main doors, where Bostler stood waiting. The old man had been the butler of the Hensons' Maradaine household for as long as Dayne had known, as long as Lady Mirianne had lived. Bostler may even have been part of the household when the earl was born.

"Mister Heldrin," he said with a slight bow of his head. "It is always pleasing to see you."

"And you, Bostler," Dayne said, offering his hand. Bostler hesitated briefly, clearly balking at the breach in protocol, and then accepted the offered hand.

"You are later than expected, sir," Bostler said. "I suggest we move with some haste. The rest of the guests for this evening are anxiously awaiting us."

"Of course," Dayne said.

"And this would be Miss Fendall," Bostler said. "You are very welcome here, young lady."

"Graciously accepted," Jerinne said, bowing her head to Bostler in return.

Bostler led them down the main hall, as Jerinne matched pace with Dayne behind the old man.

"What exactly did you do in the earl's household?" Jerinne whispered.

"As a boy, mostly helped in the stables, entertained Lady Mirianne."

"Entertained?" Jerinne's eyebrow was raised at him.

"Shut it," Dayne said. "She usually wanted someone with her when she was riding, and we'd go out to Jaconvale Creek."

"The creek, of course," Jerinne said, her voice dripping with innuendo.

"Remember I outrank you, Jerinne."

"Are you going to punish me, Mister Heldrin?" Jerinne asked, giving Dayne the widest grin.

"Don't push me." The memory of those days came flooding, summers in Jaconvale, riding across the meadow. Dozing under the oak trees while Mirianne read to him from her history books.

"I was teaching him to read," Lady Mirianne said from the archway to the sitting room. She was glorious in a velvet gown, a lush verdant green that made her eyes shine, with a neckline cut scandalously low. It had his full attention. "The only thing that wasn't innocent were some of the pennyhearts I had him read."

"Pennyhearts, my lady?" Jerinne said, bowing with a flourish. "I'm shocked."

She came over and took each of them by the arm, leading them into the sitting room. "You would think reading such things would fill a young man's mind with unseemly thoughts. Our friend here was only interested in the histories, though."

"I'm not too surprised," Jerinne said.

"Are we only going to revisit my childhood?" Dayne asked.

"Dear Dayne," Lady Mirianne said, giving an infectious peal of laughter. "You've had quite a bit of honor and accolade. I think it is only fitting that we keep you humble."

"Of course, my lady," Dayne said, though he had had quite enough humility for one day.

"Do not, Dayne," she said. "Or you either, Miss Fendall. There will be no 'my lady' from either of you tonight."

"Then why am I 'Miss Fendall'?" Jerinne asked. She seemed oddly at ease with this situation.

"Jerinne, then," Mirianne said.

A handful of vaguely familiar faces mingled in the sitting room. Dayne knew he had met them before: young men and women of noble birth but far removed from actual title, the kind who would often visit Jaconvale, or teem about Maradaine to gather favor or attention.

"These are the heroes?" asked one man, who wore a bright purple vest and cravat, as well as having hints of the same color painted around his eyes. "Quite impressive."

"Aren't they?" Mirianne asked.

"Indeed, Miri," the nobleman asked. "Can we move to the meal now before I faint?"

Mirianne made introductions, which were all names Dayne had heard before, though they left his memory almost as quickly as they were said.

"Now let's come along," Mirianne said. "I have something very special planned, which my father would declare wicked and inappropriate."

"It is highly unusual, my lady," Bostler said from the archway, showing that someone was registering disapproval of whatever Lady Mirianne was going to do.

"But he isn't here," she said with a note of defiance at the old butler. "So maybe our indecent behavior will start a new fashion."

"One can only hope," said the purple man. "Can we get on with it?"

"Yes, yes," Mirianne said. "Bostler, is everything in readiness?"

"It has been for some time, my lady. As we have noted, Mister Heldrin and Miss Fendall were not as timely as we had hoped . . ."

"I am deeply sorry for that," Dayne started.

Lady Mirianne waved him off. "Nonsense. You two are our guests of honor. The least we can grant you is patience. Correct, Bostler?"

"As my lady says. Good gentles, if you would follow me?"

Bostler led the way as Lady Mirianne took Dayne's arm again. Her lady-in-waiting came up from some hidden niche and took Jerinne's arm, and the rest of the guests followed behind.

"So what is this impropriety you have arranged?" Dayne asked.

"It's a surprise, Dayne. Can't you wait a few moments?"

"I've had a few too many surprises these past few days," Dayne said. "You'll forgive me if it makes me jumpy."

"Forgiven," she said. "However, I'm not sure if I can forgive you for stopping for a crisper before coming here. Did you not trust my chef?"

"Not at all, my lady. It was improper of me to do, though I can ensure you my appetite is in no way diminished." Dayne couldn't bring himself to lie, though he was amazed she had been able to call him out. There was no way Kaysen had been able to tell her. The two of them hadn't even been in the same room. "How did you know?"

"Your breath reeks of lamb and onion, and I know you far too well, Mister Heldrin."

"We're not going to your dining room, my lady," Dayne said, noticing that they were going to a different wing of the house.

"Indeed we aren't."

They were going to the ballroom.

"I am concerned, my lady," Dayne said, trying to keep his voice level, "that I am not wearing the proper shoes should dancing be required. I would have been better prepared."

"Why, my dear Tarian," Mirianne said, "I do believe you are pale with fear."

"Let me be clear, Mirianne," Dayne said. "I really should not be expected to dance. The results would be quite dire."

"I am quite aware," she said. "I recall trying to teach you the Erien waltz."

Bostler opened the doors to the ballroom, which, much to Dayne's relief, was not arranged for a ball of any sort. Instead, there was a banquet table on one side of the room, filled up with a variety of Sharain regional delicacies.

The other side of the room was what truly captured Dayne's attention, however. Several blankets were laid out in a circle, surrounding a low platform, upon which four men and four women stood at the ready. These eight people were all dressed identically, but not in uniform or servant attire. Rather, they all wore simple gray pull-overs and slacks, not dissimilar to what Dayne would wear for a session in the practice room.

"What is this, Miri?" the purple man asked.

"Indeed, indeed?" Mirianne asked, with a flair of drama. "What is this, good sirs and ladies? Could you introduce yourselves?"

One of the men stepped forward and bowed with a

flourish. "Greetings, gentle friends. We are the Base Street Players, and we have the distinct privilege of giving a command performance for you fine people this evening."

"Command performance?" Dayne asked. "What is this?"

"A play, my large friend," the leader answered.

"Base Street?" the purple man said. "That is scandalous, dear Miri. I've heard stories about them."

"The Base Street Players are a groundbreaking troupe, it is true, good sir," the leader said. He gestured to his fellow players. "We are not content to conform to standard traditions of the Druth stage. Our company is well traveled, and diverse beyond measure."

Dayne took some issue with that claim. There were eight of them, that was easy enough to measure. But there was some truth, the group did have a unique mix of heritages. Two of them were probably Racquin, or pure Kellirac. Another was Kieran, a fourth Fuergan. One woman appeared to be Imach, or possible Xonacan. For one man, Dayne couldn't even place his heritage.

Mirianne was clearly enjoying herself, smile as wide as her face. "Tell us, good players, what makes you so groundbreaking?" She sounded like she was reading her own lines from a script.

"We integrate theatrical traditions from all over the world. The Masqueries of the Kieran Empire! The Morality Spectacles of Acseria!" He indicated the more mysterious woman. "Tlachen-tza dance from Xonoca! The Tsouljan Koh-Jan-Rev!"

"Yes, but will we understand it?" the purple man asked.

"That depends, good sir. Are you actually an intelligent creature?"

The purple man laughed. "That depends, good sir. How much wine have I drunk?"

Now just about everyone laughed, and Dayne decided to move things along. "Since we now have an idea how you will perform, could you let us know what?"

"Is this the man?" the theater leader asked, jumping off the platform to approach Dayne. "Is this the great Dayne Heldrin, twice the hero?"

"That is my name," Dayne said. "But I wouldn't be so presumptuous . . ."

"Of course you wouldn't," he said. "But we have been informed that you are the guest of honor. Our performance tonight is a gift from the most estimable Lady Mirianne of Jaconvale." He spun on his heel to Jerinne. "Do not think you are forgotten, young lady. We are aware that you are as much to be lauded as Mister Heldrin."

"Tarians do not seek laudation," Jerinne replied.

"They are as you said, my lady," the theater leader said with a bow to Lady Mirianne. "Honor to the core."

"The very souls of the Tarian Order," Mirianne said.

"You asked me a question, good Dayne Heldrin," the man continued. "To which the answer is complex. We have been told that you are a student of history, are you not?"

"I am," Dayne said.

"Indeed you are. So we have taken three of Darren Whit's history plays: *Shalcer the Idiot King*, *Cedidore the Mad*, and *Maradaine VII*, as well as a translation of a curious Tsouljan play called *Reng-kav-pyan, 'Ten Broken Shards.'* We have melded these texts together into a new work, which we call *The Shattering of a Kingdom*."

This sounded fascinating, even though Dayne had never seen either *Shalcer* or *Cedidore*, and had never even heard of this Tsouljan work. There was also the matter that Maradaine VII's reign was nearly two hundred years after Shalcer and Cedidore, but that intrigued Dayne even more. How could these works be integrated into a cohesive performance?

"We will prepare ourselves," the theater leader said. "And you all do the same." He went back to his troupe.

"How do we prepare ourselves?" Jerinne asked.

"With our dinner for the evening," Mirianne said, indicating the banquet table. "If you were expecting a staid, traditional event at a table where we are brought our courses in the proper order, as I'm sure they are doing in every other house in Callon Hills, then I will have to disappoint you."

"I don't think I'm disappointed," Jerinne said.

"So this is how it's done, my friends," Mirianne said with a flourish matching the actors. "Plates and silver are here. A variety of dishes all along here. Bostler is on hand over there with the wine."

"We serve ourselves?" One of the ladies gasped in a mock display of horror. "My mother would die of the indignity."

"Serve yourselves, indeed," Mirianne said. "It gets even more wicked. Once you've loaded your plates as decadently as you choose, take it to one of the blankets. Lie down, gorge yourselves, and enjoy the show!"

The purple man rubbed his hands together. "Miri, you are a sinner. The very best sinner in all of Maradaine."

Everyone went to the banquet table, which had several glorious delicacies, though every dish had its roots in simple Sharain country cooking. Roast lamb seasoned with rosemary and mustard. Crisped potatoes, cooked in duck fat. Duck and lamb sausages in a white bean cassoulet. Rich creamed onions. Dayne could have eaten it all until he burst.

"Hurry up and fill your plate," Lady Mirianne whispered in his ear. "I've already chosen which blanket we'll share."

Kemmer's pounding head was getting worse. In the last day and a half he had had his head cracked, trudged through a sewer, and drunk a cup of Gillem's rough mash. But none of those made his head spin like the sight of Tharek Pell's "safehouse."

It was not a house, but an abandoned chemist shop far out on the west side of Trelan. It had been boarded up, but the back door was open, disguised to look nailed over. The actual "safe" part, according to Tharek, was not the shop itself, but the basement. The way into the basement was obscured by one of the shelves of chemicals. Kemmer had to admit, it certainly seemed safe, as there was no way that anyone could possibly find their way down to the basement without Tharek to guide them.

"And Lannic really doesn't know about this?" Kemmer asked as they went down the steps: he and Tharek, Braning and Gillem, and three others. Yand, who had also escaped arrest the night before, and his friend Wissen, an angry young man, and Wissen's sister Jala. Those last two were, as far as Kemmer knew, completely new to the Patriots, but they spoke with passion, and Yand vouched for them. Tharek had pressed them with many questions before leading them to this place, and if they were not honest and loyal, then they held up to his scrutiny very well.

Kemmer wasn't even sure he would hold up if Tharek doubted him.

"No, Kemmer," Tharek said. "No one does, except us."

They continued into the basement, completely enshrouded in darkness until Tharek lit a lamp. The light immediately flickered over the gleam of metal. An absurd amount of metal.

It wasn't a basement, it was a bunker.

Every inch of the walls was covered in weapons. Swords of every size and description. Druth swords, Waish and Kieran swords. Swords from every country in the world, as far as Kemmer knew. Pikes and spears. Bows and crossbows. Maces and axes and hammers. Devices of pain that Kemmer couldn't even put name to.

Kemmer wasn't sure if it was glorious or insane.

"What is this?" he asked, pointing to one particularly strange blade.

"Aeedjhak," Tharek said. "Turjin sword. Don't touch it."

Kemmer pulled his hand away.

"Do we have a plan?" Yand asked. His fingers twitched. "We're gonna stick them good, right?"

Kemmer didn't really know Yand very well, other than occasionally seeing him at the Alassan. He wasn't someone who Kemmer ever had a good feeling about. He wasn't a believer in the cause. If Kemmer had to guess, Yand was just angry, raging without focus, so doing damage of any kind was good to him. He might as well be in one of those south side street gangs.

Blazes, between him and his two friends, they looked like a south side street gang. Wissen and Jala weren't Druth, not by heritage. Coloring was a bit too dark. Racquin or Acserian, perhaps. Jala had long black hair, tied in a single braid down her back, and Wissen had a full beard. Both wore shirtsleeves and canvas vests, like dockworker steves, and they had arms to match.

Of course Braning and Shaw were like that at one time. Just two angry sewer workers who needed a cause. Lannic found them and gave them focus, gave them the cause.

Kemmer missed the early days, sometimes, when it was just him and Lannic in the Alassan, talking about the flaws of the government. Talking about revolution.

"We have goals," Tharek said, sitting at a small desk with some elaborate sketches on it. Kemmer took a glance: maps of the city, detailed layouts of buildings. "Prioritizing our goals will make how we proceed clear."

"Righteous," Jala said.

"What are our goals right now?" Braning asked. "I would think the main one would be staying out of Quarrygate."

"Quarrygate ain't that bad," Wissen said, talking like he knew from experience.

"I'd prefer not to know," Braning said.

"Are you saying you're out?" Tharek asked.

"No, just ... what are we in for? And ... are you in charge now, Tharek?"

"I'm not, not really," Tharek said. "When it comes down to it, the Chief tells us what to do."

"If he's actually real," Braning said.

"He is," Kemmer asserted, even though he felt doubt gnawing at his gut. "I can't think Lannic would go that far to pretend he answered to someone else."

"No, he is," Gillem said. "I ain't met him, but I know that's part of the plan. He talks to Lannic, Lannic talks to us. That way we can't turn him in, he can't turn us in, and we don't know about any other groups he's got."

"There's other groups?" Yand asked. "First I heard."

"No, there are. Or, at least, the Chief has influence," Tharek said. "That's how we got into the museum. The Chief's other people arranged it."

"So we get in touch with him, somehow, right?" Braning asked. "Ask him what to do next. Someone has to know how Lannic stayed in touch."

"I do, and I've tried," Tharek said. "But he hasn't responded. Maybe he'll talk only to Lannic. That's why our top goal is to free Lannic."

"So you said." Kemmer needed things to move ahead, but also keep a hand on the reins. Braning was the only one here he trusted not to be a runaway carriage. "What else?"

"Rekindle the fear they had yesterday."

"Yes!" Yand said, far too enthusiastically for Kemmer's taste.

"Right," Kemmer said. "So: Free Lannic, reclaim fear, don't get arrested."

"That's not my preferred order," Braning said.

"And we need to do it decisively," Tharek said. "We don't have any other choice. I want every swell in the Parliament to wake up tomorrow morning and see the safety they've imagined withered like a dead flower."

"If I may suggest," Kemmer said, "the last two times we put on a big show. And that didn't go too well."

"You weren't really there for the show," Yand sneered.

"And you weren't there for the first," Braning snapped back. "He and I nearly got our heads caved in."

"Point is," Kemmer said, aiming his argument at Tharek. If he took control, and got Tharek on his side, the rest would fall in line. "We did a big, public thing that drew attention immediately. So we had to tangle with marshals and Constabulary and Tarians."

"It made them afraid," Tharek said.

"Yeah, but it put us in danger as well," Kemmer said. "That's why most of our friends are in irons right now."

"So what do you think we should do?" Tharek asked. There was an edge to his voice—Kemmer wasn't sure if Tharek was mocking him or just pushing to get a strong idea out of him.

"A display. Something that the people—including the Parliament and the newssheets—can see, make them be afraid, hear our message, but we don't need to be standing around to get our heads bashed when they do."

"Lannic would want to give a speech," Gillem said.

"And Lannic is in irons," Braning said.

"It's good," Tharek said quietly. "We hit one or more of those swells somewhere private. Somewhere personal. And let them be found there."

"Right, right," Yand said, almost panting like a puppy. "Then the rest will know, they'll know, there ain't no place safe. We can get you wherever!"

"Most of them got houses up in Callon Hills," Wissen said. "How we gonna get in there? Especially Jala and me?"

"Every road in there has gates and private guards,"

Gillem added. "Ain't that the way to spend the people's money?"

"The roads have gates, but what about underground?" Tharek asked, looking at Braning.

"There's gates in the sewers, too," Braning said. "But a lot of them are old and rusted. Chap like you can crack them down."

"Sewers will be patrolled after last night, though," Kemmer said. "They know we sabotaged it."

"But everyone thinks the crisis is over," Tharek said. "They might patrol a bit, but they won't send too many Constabulary down into the stink when everything is fine."

"So do we have an idea what we're going to do?" Kemmer asked. "Do we know who?"

"Yeah," Wissen asked. "Who's it going to be?"

"Oh, my friends," Tharek said, picking up a scrawled note from his desk. "Don't you worry about who. I've got a list of the most deserving souls of all of them."

For the first time since he had met the man, Kemmer saw glee in Tharek's eyes. And glorious insanity.

Chapter 18

DAYNE'S PLATE WAS LOADED with roast lamb, sausages, crisped potatoes, creamed onions, white beans, and grilled asparagus. He would almost feel guilty, but he could see that everyone else was being similarly voracious. The scents all mingled together, intoxicating him.

True to her word, Lady Mirianne had selected a blanket on the side of the stage closest to the banquet table. She reclined on the blanket, resting her blonde head on one hand, while nibbling on a bit of hard cheese. The rest of the guests were finding their own places around the stage—Jerinne was sharing a blanket with Miss Jessel—as Dayne joined Lady Mirianne.

"You know you can always get more food," she teased.

"And get up during the performance?" Dayne asked. "Terribly rude."

"And yet it will happen," she said, signaling to Bostler. "You did get the mustard?"

"Of course," Dayne said, showing her the small dish

of spicy, creamy mustard, her family's signature commodity. To many across the Sharain, across the entire archduchy of Maradaine, Jaconvale was synonymous with mustard. She reached over and dipped her cheese into it. She bit it, allowing a dollop of the mustard to stay on her lip until she licked it away.

"You had your own," Dayne said.

"I wanted yours."

Bostler came over with a decanter of red wine and two glasses.

"As you requested, my lady," he said, pouring their glasses and leaving the decanter.

"We shouldn't be getting up and disrupting the performance to refill our glasses," she said. "That would be far too tragic." She held out a glass to him while raising up her own.

"To long absent friends coming home," she said.

"To home being a peaceful place," Dayne toasted back, a sincere wish that yesterday's troubles were an isolated incident.

"Peace and tranquility," she returned, and they both drank together.

In short order everyone had settled on their respective blankets with their plates, and the troupe took that as their cue to begin.

They stomped their feet, simulating a marching army as their pounding echoed under the platform. This continued for just long enough to feel awkward, until one of the women stepped forward.

"Indifference breeding incompetence, a failed line of false kings. Fools named Bintral, through plague and famine, lose their grip on a people, a land, a kingdom. Bring forth the final son, the grandest failure, the imbecile with a crown, the simpleton on the throne, the dullard who brings doom. Step forth, Shalcer, Idiot King of Druthal!"

One of the men came out of the marching line, putting on a mask he removed from a niche on the edge of the stage. The mask was simple, but effectively portrayed an iconic image of Shalcer: confused face with a tilted crown.

"What word from Rinaser? What of Duke Malcor? I did expect news of my dear friend."

Another man came forward, augmenting his costume with a helmet. He knelt before Shalcer. "My king, great tragedy in Rinaser. The duke, deeply in debt from the mishandling of his affairs, has enacted harsh and unsupportable taxes that would have broken the backs of the people under his care."

"This sounds most sensible."

"Nay, my lord. For it did spur the wrath of the common man. They have rebelled against the duke, under the banner of Ian Acorin!"

The Xonacan woman stepped forward, putting on a blue tabard. "No more! My friends, dear friends, these men are no leaders, and their birth gives them no rights over you! Take up arms! Take up fire! Be held down no more!" The stomping intensified, as the actors still on the back lines screamed and shouted.

"Most disagreeable!" Shalcer said, and then the actor removed his mask and rejoined the line.

The play continued along these lines, with the eight actors briefly taking on roles and abandoning them again, using only a mask or a prop to indicate the shift. The technique was effective, and the actors gave it every bit of commitment it needed to work. Dayne had to give them that credit, even if he found the whole affair strangely stilted.

It wasn't a traditional production, for certain, but that was what they were promised.

The food was exquisite, a testament to the skill of Lady Mirianne's chefs. Dayne had not had its like in years, since he had last visited this household. Even The

Nimble Rabbit, which was a fine example of Sharain country cooking, had nothing on this glorious feast. He had his plate cleared by the time the troupe had reached the point in history where Druthal had shattered into many kingdoms, and Shalcer was forced to attend a peace conference and acknowledge these newly crowned kings. Shalcer had counted on the Orders of the day— Tarians, Spathians, Braighians, Vanidians, and others—to maintain their fealty to him and Druthal Proper. Dayne was about to get up to refill his plate when one actor came forth, having put on a coat of the Tarian Order.

"In these dark years ahead, we shall be the ties that bind these kingdoms together. The Orders must place themselves in the light of the greater good, and we must place ourselves above any nation, any king, any lord, and even any God who strives against the light. Each member of the Orders shall decide for themselves which fight they lend their arm to, as their honor decrees, but our pledges are to the Orders first."

This was Grandmaster Alamarkin, one of the giants in Tarian lore. In history, Shalcer had decried him a traitor, and he was forced into hiding in Oblune, but his words proved prophetic: the Orders had been a source of light in those dark centuries. The honor and trust placed in them allowed them to travel relatively freely between the kingdoms, and they were instrumental in keeping the idea of Druth unity alive.

"Traitor! Traitor!" shouted Shalcer, the actor playing him sounding much like a spoiled child.

"No such thing, false king, for I am loyal to what matters most: the ideals of Druthal, and that it may one day have a king worthy of its throne."

That was new. Every historical account showed that Alamarkin had always been very respectful of Shalcer. Dayne wasn't sure if this line was part of Whit's text, or something this troupe had added.

Lady Mirianne refilled his wineglass, and casually caressed his leg, giving him meaningful looks. Dayne decided this was a good time to refill his plate.

As Dayne refilled his plate, the play moved on at a rapid pace, transitioning to the *Cedidore the Mad* portion. He found Jerinne by his side as he got more sausages.

"Wild stuff, isn't it?" Jerinne whispered.

"It's . . . different," Dayne said. That was a politic answer.

On the stage they had finished a scene where Cedidore called for walling off what remained of Druthal, calling for the Quarantine.

"Is that what happened?" Jerinne whispered.

"Roughly," Dayne said. "The script is taking a few liberties with the history."

"I suppose they'd have to," Jerinne offered. She had refilled her own plate. "Time to rejoin Miss Jessel. Good luck."

Dayne mused to himself as he returned to the blanket and Lady Mirianne's doe eyes. Luck wasn't something he was particularly worried about.

Jobs had been assigned separately. Tharek had done that intentionally, made sure no one knew more than their part of the plan. Tharek had also made sure to pair Wissen with Braning, and Jala with Kemmer, so that his two most trusted lieutenants could keep an eye on the new people he didn't know.

As frustrating as it was, Hemmit had to admit he saw the wisdom of it, especially since "Wissen" and "Jala" were complete fictions, ready to betray Tharek and his Patriots once the opportunity availed itself.

When Hemmit first conceived of "Wissen" over a year ago, it had been a lark, a game to play while bored with school. He'd go to the seedier taverns by the docks, pretend to be a streetwise tough. Over time it became more than that: it had become a source of truth. "Wissen" could meet people, get close and find out the real story in ways he never could as Hemmit. When Lin found out, she was eager to take her own role as Jala, Wissen's sister. She was truly amazing when she did it. While turning into Wissen involved little more than a change of clothes and putting up an attitude, becoming Jala was a complete transformation. Lin used magic for part of it, an illusion to darken her hair, skin, and eyes, as well as give herself elaborate tattoos, but her whole performance was something to behold. Her Linjari accent was gone, turned into a flawless west dock accent, as she became Jala completely.

Even though Hemmit knew it was her, he could almost be fooled.

Now he didn't know where she was, other than she was with Kemmer on whatever mission Tharek had assigned them.

It had been something of a stroke of focused luck that the two of them had found the Patriots so quickly. Yand was a fellow Hemmit had met months ago, and from how he had spoken, Hemmit suspected he was connected to the Patriots. At best, Hemmit had hoped Yand would know someone involved, give him something he could use to write a story, get word to Dayne.

Instead he found Yand on the run. He had been part of the chaos the night before, and was looking for help. It wasn't hard to play the role that Yand so desperately wanted Hemmit to fill.

And that brought him to Tharek Pell.

Saints, that was a man, all right. Easily the most intimidating man he had ever met. He had grilled both Hemmit and Lin, and had Hemmit been alone, he might not have held up to the scrutiny. Lin had been amazing, and that had won Tharek's approval, at least provisionally. Like Yand, Tharek had needed allies. That made all the difference.

Now he was in a carriage with Braning, bringing some contraption to a location that Braning hadn't told him. All he could figure out was that they were heading east, in the direction of the Parliament and RCM. On the off chance he could slip away from Braning and not ruin his cover, what could he do? Go to the Constabulary? Tell them *something* was happening, but he had no idea what? He suspected that Tharek was going to go into Callon Hills to find whatever victim he had intentions on, but Hemmit had no idea who that might be. Or what Tharek intended to do. Or even if Callon Hills was his destination.

Hemmit was deeper in the river than he had expected when he left The Nimble Rabbit.

"So where are we taking this thing?" he asked Braning.

"This way," Braning said, pointing in the direction he was driving the carriage. "Look, you helped me put the thing in the carriage, and when we get there, you'll stick with me. That's all you need to know."

"Yeah, but—"

"Look—Wissen, was it?"

"Yeah."

"Look, I know you're all heavy hammer about what we're doing tonight, and that's good. I like that. But believe me, friend, sometimes it's better just not knowing what's going on."

"How can you say that?" Hemmit asked, maintaining the fevered passion he'd been playing as Wissen. "I mean, you were in it yesterday, weren't you? You helped show them good!"

"Yesterday morning, I kept watch on the back door," Braning said. "That got my head cracked by that Tarian bastard."

"Right, but that was the thing in the morning. In the night, you guys really hit them!"

"And Kemmer and I were well out of the action, down in the sewers. And that suited me just fine."

"But now, we're all in it, right?"

Braning turned away from the reins. "Please, for the love of every saint, calm down. We ... we have a job, and the ideal is we all do our job well, and no one else ends up arrested."

"Yeah, sure," Hemmit said. "I know I don't need to get ironed."

"Good." Braning focused on the road again.

"So, if things turn left, I should run?"

"Blazes, I'm gonna ... I'm going to tell you something. Right now I've got a lot of mates who are locked up because of what went wrong yesterday. I can't do them a damn bit of good if I'm in there with them."

"So that's what you want, eh? Get them out?"

Braning mused. "Tharek says we need to send a message. 'Free Lannic.' I'm not sure how that will really help."

"You don't agree with him?" Even in the danger here, there was a story. Who was Braning? Why was he a Patriot? What had brought him to Lannic and the rest?

"It's not that, just ... don't take this the wrong way, but a week ago, Tharek was you."

"How's that?"

"None of us knew him. Lannic was the one who brought him in, so—and again, don't take this wrong—trust wasn't an issue at all. Lannic vouched, and Lannic was the Patriots, save the Chief."

"Right, the Chief. You've never met this guy?"

"Sounds crazy, yeah? But the museum only worked at all was because of the Chief. Least, that's how Lannic said it."

"Bit crazy." He needed to bring it back to Tharek, without breaking character. "Yeah, but Tharek's the boss right now, right? With Lannic gone?"

"He's acting like it. I don't like it, and I'm pretty sure Kemmer doesn't either. But you have to admit, the man is capable."

"That's the truth." They were definitely approaching the Parliament. And whatever was in the back of the wagon was a large contraption of wood and rope.

"So what's your stake? You're not following Tharek just to follow him, and you don't think we're breaking out Lannic here. So what do you want?"

"You ask a lot of questions."

"I want to know what I'm in for."

"And what do *you* want, Wissen?"

"I know, you probably think I'm just some dock-working steve, who just wants to crack skulls . . ."

"Hey, hey, don't pull that on me. My brother and I were just sewer steves, we didn't go to university or nothing."

"So you get it. You don't need education to know things stink in this town for guys working with their hands and arms. And that's on the Parliament, don't you think? Cause that story has to be the same in every city. I mean, we could hit on the Council of Aldermen, but that doesn't help the country."

"No, it doesn't." He was nodding vigorously. "That was the thing that mattered to us. I mean, guys like you and me, here in Maradaine, we get trampled on. What do you think it's like, say, down in Scaloi? You think it's any better for them?"

"Oh, it ain't. On the docks, you meet folks from every part of Druthal. Ain't one of them thinks this Parliament works for them." Hemmit was a little surprised at how easily the words came. How close to the truth it was. This Parliament did not represent the people. They were a bunch of cosseted children, bought with the money of the nobility, or buying influence with their own money.

But that didn't make the Patriots right.

"That's certainly right," Braning said. "Here we are."

They were pulling the cart up by Parliament Plaza.

"So now?"

"Now we wait," Braning said. "But us sitting in the cart would look suspicious, and we don't want that." He pulled up to a group of other parked carts—several shop-carts were locked down and kept in the plaza overnight.

"Suspicious is right," Hemmit said. "Constabulary stroll through here all night on patrol. And there's five whistleboxes I can see from here."

"That there are," Braning said. "But we're gonna get out and leave the cart with the others here for now. See that teashop? We're gonna sit at one of the street tables, drink some tea, and wait for Kemmer and your sister."

"What are they doing?"

"I haven't a clue," Braning said. "And like I told you, I'm happier that way."

The play finished to a smattering of applause. Several of the dinner guests had dozed off, having stuffed themselves into lethargy. Dayne felt the same way, but the play, flawed as it might have been, kept his attention. It played loose with history and time, jumping forward a hundred and fifty years to when Maradaine VII took the throne. The performance made it seem like the Druth throne had gone straight from the Cedidores to him, skipping over the Mishrals, Halitars, Ferricks, and Kelliths, let alone Queen Mara. This was fine for a piece of theater, but Dayne hoped none of the other guests were considering this a serious history lesson.

Of course, given they were half asleep, Dayne doubted they were taking anything too seriously.

The actors stepped down off the stage and accepted accolades and wine, shaking hands and chatting with the guests.

Lady Mirianne was bright and alert, of course. She

went to each member of the troupe individually and greeted them by name. She made a point of recollecting a key role they played in the show and praising each of them personally.

The crowd in the ballroom was thinning out, and Dayne got a definite sense of the event being over. Perhaps it would be best to find Jerinne and make a polite exit. Quiet Days or no, the girl should get her rest, and Dayne was responsible for her. The last thing Dayne needed was for the Grandmaster to be angrier with him.

Jerinne was nowhere to be seen. She must have wandered off somewhere with Miss Jessel. Dayne couldn't begrudge her that, but even still, a certain degree of propriety should be observed.

Mirianne thanked the leader of the troupe profusely and told all of them to make themselves welcome to the house. Then she took Dayne by the arm and looked at him with an odd regard as they walked.

"Something troubles you?" she asked.

"I think the night grows late, my — Miri. I should collect Jerinne and return to the chapterhouse."

"Nonsense," she said. "It's hardly late at all. And you'd have to take my carriage."

"We could very well walk, my lady."

She stopped walking. "I don't want you to leave yet." Her eyes, deep blue like the ocean, were pleading.

"As my lady commands," Dayne replied.

She playfully swatted his arm. "Don't you start with that sort of thing. It won't win you any favor."

"I wasn't aware that favor was something I had to win."

"Come with me to the garden," she said. Dayne allowed himself to be led down the hallway and outside.

The garden was walled in, separate from the rest of the grounds. The stone walls were painted bright oranges and yellows, and every surface was rounded out with soft curves, giving it a warm, cozy feeling even before going inside it. Mirianne led him through the flowerbeds, vivid blooms of purple and blue, other plants vining along the inside walls, to the small fountain at the center of the structure.

Mirianne sat down on the edge of the fountain and invited Dayne to do the same. She sat quietly for a time, only the gentle gurgling of the fountain breaking the silence of the night. She was lit only by the few flickering candles ensconced near the entrances. The open sky above them was splendid with starlight—both moons out of sight.

"Did you enjoy the play?" she finally asked.

"Enjoy . . . might not be the right word. I found it engaging."

"Engaging? How so?" she asked.

"Well, I was frustrated by the inaccuracies. Those are probably from their source texts, of course, and I can forgive that."

"But what about their style? You have to admit it was unique."

"Yes, unique is right." She narrowed her eyes at him. "That may have sounded more critical than I intended. No, I liked *how* they did things, in terms of performance. They did a good job making it clear when they switched characters. I'm impressed they did as much as they did with only eight people on the stage."

"But?" she prompted.

"I started to be troubled by the underlying message, which first hit me during the Alamarkin speech. But the more I think about it, the more I see it throughout the piece." The choice of three core plays made more sense once that message became clear in his head.

"And what was that?" she asked. "Tell me."

"All three plays—Shalcer, Cedidore, and Maradaine VII, have the same structure, to a degree. I haven't read them, but from what I saw here, in each play there is a king on the throne who is doing a horrible job: incompe-

tence in the case of Shalcer, insanity in the case of Cedidore."

"And Kellith II's warmongering in *Maradaine VII*,"
she offered.

"Right," Dayne said. "But there was no Kellith in this
production."

"They merged him into Cedidore."

"Anyway, in all three plays the sitting king is the vil-
lain of the piece. The heroes, in as much as there are any,
are the conspirators who eventually install Maradaine
on the throne. The same set of conspirators is used
throughout this production, even though they were completely different people."

"So what was that message?"

"Well, I felt it was trying for one of loyalty to an ideal
over the person on a throne."

"And you find that troubling?"

"I find it, at least as presented here, mercurial. Because the conspirators were the same, they came off as
fickle instead of principled. They hated Shalcer, so they
worked to get rid of his line and replace it with Cedidore.
But then Cedidore was horrible, and so they worked to
get rid of him."

"That is how it was, of course," she offered.

"Well, the ones who sought to remove Cedidore
failed. He ruled successfully—if brutally—for decades.
Most of his enemies faced the gibbet."

"Let's face it, royal politics—all politics—back then
were much more . . . volatile." She shuddered slightly.
"We now live in a civilized age, with fair trials and no
executions, even for the most vile of criminals."

"You're right," Dayne said, though there was something else to it, an idea that had been brewing for the
past few days. "It's good that now we just have protestors
with placards. The True Line Lives, and all. Foolishness."

"You don't care for them." It wasn't a question.

"I could possibly see the point if, say, Prince Escaraine

was in exile, yearning to claim a throne he felt was rightfully his. But he's in the palace, at the right hand of the king. He's given no sign that he wants to dethrone his cousin."

"That's an interesting point," Mirianne said.

"It also made me think of the Patriots."

"Oh, please, let's not have that ugliness here."

"Hear me out. The Patriots, they aren't that different from the conspirators. They see themselves as the heroes of their play. They're seeking to oust a Parliament that isn't suiting their ideals."

"Dayne," she said, dropping her voice to a sultry whisper. "You've stopped them, and they're facing trial. And you are in a gorgeous, romantic garden with a beautiful woman who wants you to kiss her."

"I didn't stop them," Dayne said. "And my attempts may have hurt me more than I realized."

"Hurt you how?"

"I've turned the Grandmaster against me, and he had already said my chances of making Adept were almost nonexistent."

"Foolish," she said. Placing her hand over his heart, she added, "You are a Tarian. You are my Tarian. There is no man alive who is more of one than you."

"I'm glad you think so," Dayne said.

"And no matter what happens, Adept or no, there will always be a place for you in this house. Wherever I am, I want to have you near me."

She climbed into his lap and kissed him, warm and strong, as if she couldn't breathe unless she was kissing him. She broke off, resting her forehead against his.

"Wherever I am," she whispered again. "I don't want you to go anywhere tonight."

"I—" Dayne lamely offered as his only protest.

"Stay," she said, and began kissing him again.

Hemmit kept one eye out on the street, looking for Constabulary, looking for Lin, looking for any way he could figure out what was about to happen, and how he could stop it. The rest of his senses were on Braning.

Sitting at the teashop had loosened Braning's tongue more than any bottle of wine might have. He didn't reveal any secrets of the Patriots, but he talked plenty about himself, as well his brother, Shaw. Shaw, the Patriot who had been killed yesterday.

"See, Pop had never done a damn thing wrong," Braning went on, having been telling the story of the injustices done to his father. "The materials were shoddy, so it didn't matter how good his work was. All the bosses and merchants were in it with the magistrates, though. Somebody had to take the fall."

"Guy at the bottom gets the boot," Hemmit said.

"That's it exactly. So he's on the outs, Mom's working in the chicken houses, but we're still going hungry. So Shaw needed to go to work."

"How old was he?"

"Nine, but he was a big kid, so he said he was thirteen, and down in the sewers, they didn't ask many questions, you know?"

"When did you go?"

"Three years later, when I was ten. Shaw wanted to keep me out, keep me in school, but we couldn't do it. By then, Pop's hands were shot. So we were both working sewers."

"And they didn't care? Nobody stopped it?"

"Stop it? Like who?" Braning took another swig of tea. "You see, they wanted kids down there. Smaller the better, that's the thing. So nobody was making a fuss. Even when kids got lost in the tunnels."

"So how did you and Shaw find—" Hemmit's question was cut off by Kemmer and "Jala" approaching.

"How did it go?" Braning asked as they sat down.

"Go?" Lin asked, taking Hemmit's tea and finishing

it. "Real exciting. We bought canvas. And paint. And made a sign."

"A sign?" Hemmit asked, trying to give her a signal with his eyes without either of the others noticing.

"Painted it real nice," she said. She rolled her eyes in disgust, and then gave Hemmit the slightest shaking of her head. "This guy really knows how to show a girl a good time."

"Shut it," Kemmer said. "We did our bit, now we wait it out."

"We're supposed to wait here, then?" Braning asked.

"That's what Tharek told me. Get here, put the thing in your cart, and join you at the teashop."

Lin looked around. "You don't think this Tharek is having a lark with us? We sit here in the teashop with our little banner while he does the real deal?"

"What even is the real deal?" Hemmit asked. Maybe Kemmer would prove more talkative.

Kemmer signaled to the server to bring two more teas. "The real deal is sit and shut it."

The wait wasn't long; the waiter hadn't even brought the tea before they spotted another cart coming into the plaza, with Tharek at the reins. Yand and Gillem were in the back. Tharek pulled his cart next to the one Hemmit had come over in, and then stalked over to the teashop.

"Kemmer, Braning, come with me. You two, sit here, keep watch."

"Watch for what?" Hemmit asked. It wasn't a ridiculous question. The plaza was hardly unoccupied. There were at least a dozen other people just in the teashop. Constabulary horsepatrol had been through at least twice since he had been sitting there.

"Won't take long," Tharek said. "Just keep an eye for anyone coming to us."

Tharek and the other two went back to the carts. Finally, Hemmit leaned over Lin.

"You just made a sign?" he asked.

"Yeah. 'Free Lannic.'" She didn't drop character. "You?"

"We loaded a big wooden contraption into the cart and drove it here."

"From where?"

"Some storehouse, down by the docks farthest west."

"Tharek isn't really the leader," she said. "Kemmer doesn't want to listen to him."

"I got the same from Braning. They're biding their time until Lannic is free or this 'Chief' takes charge."

"Something is off about Tharek," she said. "These guys, they're all students and steves."

"Right."

"And he's got resources," she added. "All those weapons? Storehouses and safehouses and gadgets and carts and horses. Where is he getting it all?"

"The Chief?"

"I don't know." She glanced about. "We need to get word to Constabulary. Or Dayne."

"I'm listening. How do we do that?" He leaned in close to her. "Magic?"

She scoffed. "If there was someone we could get word to within line of sight, I could make an image that only he could see. But there's no one. Don't even see a constable. Where's Maresh?"

"At the press, prepping the issue. He'll leave space if we have anything worth printing."

"I don't know what's going to happen," she whispered. "But I bet it'll be worth printing."

Whatever the others were doing, they finished; they all were walking back to the teashop. Behind them, clearly seen in the moonlight, the horses on Braning's cart were slowly trotting toward the Parliament, the heavy tarp still covering its contents.

"Let's go," Tharek said as they approached, throwing a few coins on the table. "Come on."

Hemmit and Lin got up and started walking with them. "What's going to happen?"

"A show," Tharek said.

They walked until they reached an alleyway at the edge of the plaza. Tharek signaled for everyone to stop and watch.

The cart had reached the Parliament steps. A pair of horseback Constabulary had approached it, whistling at the dray horses to halt.

"Perfect," Tharek whispered.

As the constables dismounted and went to the cart itself, there was a loud crack, and then a pop from the cart.

Suddenly the device under the tarp came to life, springing up like a watchdog. As it did this, two barrels burst into brightly colored flames.

The constables scattered back, drawing out their crossbows.

The device reached its full height—a gibbet, with Lin's banner of "Free Lannic" affixed to the top.

A man—clearly already dead—hung from the noose of the gibbet, fully dressed in the regalia of the Parliament.

"Who?" Hemmit asked despite himself. He didn't recognize the man on sight, certainly not at this distance.

"Good Mister Pollock Yessinwood, 8th Chair of Oblune," Tharek said with a tone of smug satisfaction.

Hemmit ran through the names of the Parliament in his head. Yessinwood? An absolute minor player. Not part of the leadership of the Majority or the Opposition. A Crownie, for sure, but little more than a cog in the machine. Why Yessinwood?

"Let's move," Tharek said, grabbing Lin by her arm. "We're done for the night. No need to get ironed for gaping."

They all went off down the alleys. Hemmit stayed

right with them—there was no slipping away yet, nor would he abandon Lin. And he was right in the heart of a story. Words and sentences started to pound together in his head. And questions.

Maresh was going to need to clear a lot of space on the front page.

Chapter 19

𝔥EAVY CURTAINS WERE OPENED LOUDLY, letting sunlight smash Dayne into consciousness. He had a disoriented moment before remembering where he was: Lady Mirianne's bedchamber. Or, at the very least, a bedchamber in her household. She was nowhere to be seen; only one of the house staff was present, opening curtains.

"I am terribly sorry, sir," the servant said, noting Dayne sitting up. "But the lady of the house felt you needed to be roused presently. Breakfast is being served in the sunroom, and it is recommended you find your way there with all due haste."

Dayne thanked the servant, and scrambled about to find his clothes. Fortunately, they had been laid out on a chair neatly—which was most definitely not how Dayne had left them. Dayne dressed and made his way to the water closet in short order.

The sunroom was over on the east side of the house, and turned out to be far more populated than Dayne had expected it would be. It seemed almost everyone who had attended the dinner was still present. A steward led Dayne to his place at the breakfast table—this was all being done in a far more traditional manner—where he was seated next to Jerinne.

Lady Mirianne was not to be seen.

"And good morning to you," Jerinne said, her eyes red and sleepy. "How much trouble are we in at the chapterhouse?"

"I'm not sure yet. I hope you had a good enough evening to make it worth the trouble."

"I'll be honest . . . maybe?" Jerinne shrugged in confusion.

"Weren't you paying attention?" Dayne asked. A steward brought over hot tea, which Dayne accepted thankfully.

"All right, after the play, Miss Jessel led me to Lady Mirianne's library, where I was treated to her personal supply of Fuergan aged whiskeys. Details after that point are . . . blurry."

"Let's agree that each other's details remain blurry," Dayne said. There was no need for either of them to delve into anything particularly personal with the other. He owed Lady Mirianne far more discretion than that.

"I agree," Jerinne said.

Plates of eggs and biscuits, served with apple preserves and honeyed butter, were placed in front of them. Dayne happily dug in, while Jerinne approached her breakfast a little more gingerly. She wasn't expressing it, but it was likely the young lady was suffering more than she cared to admit from her foray into Fuergan whiskey. Dayne's few experiences with the substance were enough for him to know it could be quite cruel indeed.

Lady Mirianne entered the room in a manner that conveyed both grace and gloom, if such a thing was possible, with several newssheets tucked under her arm. She took her seat at the head of the table, which put her at some distance from Dayne. She didn't even look directly at him as she bid good morning to the rest of the room. She barely noted the tea placed in front of her as she put on her reading spectacles and combed through the newssheets.

"Is something vexing, my lady?" Dayne asked, as no one else was marking her dark manner.

"Something indeed," she said absently. "It appears we were very mistaken. Gravely." She passed one newssheet to her steward, indicating for him to deliver it to Dayne.

The front of the *Maradaine Grand Times* was splashed with a gruesome etching to match its headline. "Second Parliamentarian Murdered!" The image of a man hanging on a gibbet with a sign that read "Free Lannic" above it told Dayne all he needed to know.

"Tharek," he said, passing the sheet to Jerinne. Taking a last sip of tea, he got to his feet. "My lady, we must take leave of your generous hospitality."

She nodded, getting to her feet. "Yes, I know you must. Have the carriage brought around." She gave the order to no one in particular.

Walking around the table, she took Dayne by the arm again and led him away. Jerinne hurried with a few final bites and walked behind.

"You're going to think I'm horrible," she whispered. "When I read this, the first thing I thought of was that you would want to leave right away."

"I would never think you horrible, Miri," Dayne said.

"All I wanted was to keep you a little longer," she said. They reached the main doors. "I was telling you the truth last night. There will always be a place for you in this household."

"As what, exactly?" Dayne lowered his voice a little more, giving the slightest glance back at Jerinne. The girl, bless her, was doing her best to walk a fair distance behind, and pay more attention to the wall fixtures and floor tiling.

"I would figure something out," she said. "I would have you as my husband if such a thing could be allowed."

"Your father is probably too much a traditionalist."

"I'm well aware. But I would make sure to find a way to have you here, in a way that would honor everything that you are."

"You always honor me, my lady," Dayne said.

She gave him a playful smile. "Which is why I'm letting you go right now. I know it would kill you to stay, knowing what's happening out there."

"It kills me to leave as well, my lady."

She kissed him once more, lightly, as the carriage pulled up the drive, then cupped his face. "I know where your heart calls you. Go."

He got into the carriage, Jerinne at his right arm, as if the Initiate hadn't been hanging back at a respectful distance.

"So another Parliamentarian is dead, and it's definitely the Patriots," Jerinne said, scanning the newssheet. The carriage pulled out of Lady Mirianne's drive into the Callon Hills streets.

"That's Tharek's handiwork, wouldn't you say?" Dayne said. "Disgusting and sadistic." Dayne looked over the article. The murdered man was Yessinwood, which was surprising. Certainly at least confusing. Even the article, while respectful, spoke of Yessinwood as a minor player in the Parliament, and speculated madly why he was killed. Dayne was at a loss himself.

"I suppose," Jerinne said. "I hadn't gotten much of a read on him, other than capable."

"You fought him, didn't you?"

"I think it's safe to say I got beat by him."

"He's . . ." Dayne tried to put it into words. "There's something special about him."

"Yeah. He can wipe the floor with me and give you and Madam Tyrell a fair fight."

"Exactly." That clicked. "Who could do that? Not just some mercenary."

"Druth Intelligence? King's Marshals?"

"No," Dayne said. "Kaysen! Change of plans."

"Not back to the chapterhouse?" Kaysen asked.

"Not back to our chapterhouse."

Hemmit was trapped. Tharek hadn't let anyone but Gillem and Braning leave all night. Those two were sent for supplies and news.

"Everyone stays together, especially you two," Tharek had said, meaning Hemmit and Lin. Hemmit grumbled, but mostly to stay in character. He had no urge to actually pick a fight with the man. There had been no way to get word to Maresh, let alone Dayne or the Constabulary. He and Lin had ended up taking turns dozing in the corner once it had been clear they weren't going anywhere.

Tharek may have slept, but Hemmit couldn't be sure. He seemed to spend the whole night inspecting and sharpening the massive arsenal they were locked in with.

Yand, that crazy boy, slept like a stone.

Kemmer slept fitfully, spending part of the night curled by an oil lamp, reading a journal.

"What is that?" Hemmit eventually asked.

"It was our manifesto," Kemmer said.

"Was?" Hemmit asked.

"We were supposed to get pamphlets made, you know? Get the word out to the people, get them on our side."

Hemmit reached out for the journal. "Supposed to?"

"Doesn't matter now," Tharek grumbled from his workbench. "We've got a new message."

Kemmer passed it over. "Course it still matters. That's the core, Tharek. That's what everything is all about."

"If I remember, you're the one who didn't get it done."

"That wasn't—" Kemmer snapped. A glare from Tharek backed him down. He turned back to Hemmit. "It's not that. It was supposed to be Shaw's job . . ."

Kemmer went on, but Hemmit was reading. It was a screed, of course, against the Parliament, against the methodology of elections, against the nobility and for the voice of the common man, and fighting back to reclaim Druthal. It was passionate, and while Hemmit didn't agree with all of it, he couldn't deny that it was effectively written. There was a truth deep in there that deserved a voice, and probably had an audience that wanted to hear it.

The real tragedy was, had this been published before the Patriots had turned to violence, it might have had a real impact. They might even have had an ally in him and Maresh.

And maybe that was the way to cool things down: let ink run instead of blood.

"Listen," Hemmit said, "if you still want this out there, I may know a way."

"You know someone with a press?" Kemmer asked.

"I . . . I know of a guy." That was a safe answer. Or as safe as anything could be, as up to his neck as he was in this mess.

"That guy can't help," Lin said, still astoundingly in character as Jala.

"You know him, too?"

"Course I do. But he couldn't get it done." She gave Hemmit a hard glare. "Ain't worth the trouble to drag him into this."

"She's probably right," Tharek said, as Gillem and Braning returned with bread and newssheets.

"Looks like we made the papers," Braning said. "Everyone's talking about it." Food was passed about.

"But what are they doing?" Hemmit asked.

"Soiling their fancy britches," Yand snickered.

"The question is, what are *we* doing?" Hemmit asked. "Next step?"

"Good question," Tharek said. He pocketed a handful of knives. "Maybe we should see. You're with me, Wissen."

Hemmit got to his feet. "Where are we going?"

"To see if we have any new orders," Tharek said. "Rest of you, stay here."

"Fine," Kemmer said. Clearly taking orders from Tharek was starting to grind on Kemmer. Braning and Gillem didn't seem to mind as much. Yand could not care less where the orders came from.

"We'll be back soon." Tharek tapped Braning on the shoulder. "Eyes on her, hear?"

"On it," Braning said.

Tharek led Hemmit out of his bunker, through a back alley, and onto the street. The sun was higher than Hemmit was expecting, brighter than he was ready for. "About nine bells already?"

"Not even eight," Tharek said, glancing at the sun. "This way."

There was hardly anyone about, which was odd, given the hour. Streets should have been heavy with traffic and bustle.

"You'd think it was a holiday," Hemmit said.

"Holiday of fear," Tharek said.

"So what are you, army?" This was his first time alone with the man, possibly the only chance Hemmit would have to figure out who Tharek Pell really was.

"Hush," was all Tharek replied, said with a finality that made Hemmit decide to ask nothing else.

Silence stayed with them until they reached a tiny alley. They were still in Trelan, a few blocks away from the river, but also not far from the Parliament or The Nimble Rabbit.

"Go to the end," Tharek instructed. "There's an abandoned backhouse. Check behind it for anything."

"What'll you do?"

"Keep watch," Tharek said.

Hemmit worked his way cautiously down the alley.

What was Tharek keeping watch for? Was this a trap? Was he already in Tharek's trap? He had no doubt Tharek could kill him with barely a spare thought if that was his intention. Would he even bother taking Hemmit away from the rest of the group to do it?

There was a backhouse, that was true, and it had clearly been all but forgotten about. Tenements and shops in this part of town had water closets now. Hemmit inched around it.

There was a satchel—a clean leather satchel—wedged in the gap between the backhouse and the brick wall the alley dead-ended in. Undoubtedly a recent arrival. The rest of the space behind the backhouse was filled with dust, cobwebs, and mold. There was no way it could have ended up back there by accident.

He pulled it out. It was heavy but soft. Densely packed with something, but not weapons or books. Cloth or rope, most likely.

There was a brief flash of an idea. He could take the satchel and run. Get to Constabulary. At the very least get to a whistlebox. Warn someone.

But there was nowhere to run to. There was no way out of the alley except through Tharek. No chance to surprise him and make a break for it. And even if he did run, even if he did manage to get away, there was Lin. Even with her magic, there was no way she could hold off Tharek and the others. She'd be dead.

He came out of the alley and gave the satchel to Tharek. "This what you expected?"

Tharek actually looked surprised. "Quite a bit more than I expected. The Chief came through."

"You had your doubts?"

"I doubt everything except myself."

Whatever reservations Hemmit had about the man, he had to respect that.

The return to the safehouse was uneventful, even though they did pass several Constabulary on foot patrol. The sticks didn't look at them twice. Hemmit could understand why "Wissen" wasn't being looked for, but he would have thought there would at least be an All-Eyes out for Tharek. It wasn't like the man didn't stand out in a crowd. Not as much in appearance—a little tall, but not excessively, and his well-groomed beard was uncommon but not unusual. What Tharek had was presence; he had a walk that made people instinctively clear a path for him.

"Well?" Kemmer asked when they returned.

"The Chief had something for us," Tharek said, holding up the satchel.

"What is it?"

"I don't know yet," Tharek said. "I didn't think I should go through it in the middle of the street." He opened up the satchel and took out the letter on the top.

"What's he say?" Braning asked, as Tharek kept the letter and the satchel to himself.

"Interesting." Tharek finished reading and passed the letter to Braning. "In brief, he's pleased with our initiative. Both in the Talon Circle and last night."

"Damn well better be," Yand muttered.

"So much so, he's putting the other cells into action. But the center of it is up to us. There's going to be a fire in this city, and we're the spark."

"More fear?" Kemmer asked.

"We've supplied plenty of fear to be the kindling," Tharek said. He reached into the satchel and pulled out what was so tightly packed in there. "For the spark, we need something else: injustice."

In his hand, crisp, clean, and freshly pressed, was a King's Marshal uniform.

The Spathian Chapterhouse was far on the east side of North Maradaine, almost at the edge of the city limits. It was a small fortress of gray stone, lacking any decoration or adornment. Dayne knew where it was only because Master Denbar had brought him there once. The place wasn't secret, but the Spathians did not make any attempt to entice people to their door.

Dayne and Jerinne entered the archway into the chapterhouse, to be immediately met by a stone courtyard full of at least two dozen Spathian Initiates, swords drawn. They moved in crisp unison, each Initiate's blade missing their neighbor by hairs as they went through their motions. Training, but with real, razor-sharp blades.

"Hold!" a powerful voice called out. Each Initiate froze in place, swords aloft mid-swing. One woman came around to the front of the group, a Spathian Master of some years, her gray hair shorn to almost an inch. "We have some soft cousins in our midst."

"We don't mean to intrude," Dayne said. "We were wondering if there was someone we could speak to . . ."

"Tarians have come to speak!" the Master snapped. "Initiate Greya, where were we?"

"Three-seven-four!" a third-year Initiate at the front of the formation called back. Still not a muscle moved, not on her, not on any of them. Dayne watched them in their petrification. He could probably hold position as well as any of them, should he need to. But he couldn't figure out why he would need to.

"All but Greya, two steps clear!"

They moved like a wave pulling away from the shore, only using their legs to step back, their blades held completely still. Greya stood alone.

"This is your Initiate, Tarian?" The Master pointed to Jerinne.

"She is, but I'm afraid you don't—"

"Initiate Greya!" the Master ordered. "Engage the Tarian Initiate, starting at three-seven-five. All others, Greya is the light, you are the shadow."

"Now wait—" Dayne started.

"Engage!"

Greya completed the frozen motion she had been holding, but now in a furious attack launched on Jerinne. Jerinne, in her rumpled dress uniform, had no shield, and her sword was still sheathed. She ably dodged the first swipe, as well as the next two, before she had her own blade out to parry the attacks.

The formation mimicked Greya's moves, now responsive in her attacks to Jerinne's defense. Their own maneuvers were a flurry of steel, almost impossible to keep track of. It was a miracle they were able to follow Greya's movements so well without slicing each other up.

"Master Spathian, this isn't why we came," Dayne said.

"And yet you were here, and it gave us an opportunity. Is she drunk?"

Dayne looked back at Jerinne, who was barely holding her own against Greya. Greya's attacks were savage and lightning quick, but she seemed to barely be expending effort. This was morning exercise. Jerinne's parries were desperate and wild—successfully defending herself, but always a fraction of a second away from getting sliced.

Greya was sparring. Jerinne was fighting for her life.

"Hung over," Dayne admitted.

"That explains why she moves like a pregnant ewe. Talk, Tarian."

Clearly this was his moment. "I don't know if you've been following the news, but . . ."

"You waste my time. Greya, formation. Reskin is the light."

Greya stepped back and rejoined, but Jerinne had only a moment to compose herself before another Spathian Initiate was on her.

"There is an outlaw killing the Parliament members," Dayne said. "Gifted fighter. He may be a Spathian."

"No Spathian would be an outlaw, nor would they kill a member of Parliament," the Master said.

"True," Dayne allowed. "No Spathian would. But you have a three-year limit on Candidacy as we do, yes?"

"If a Candidate is not accepted in three years, they are no Spathian. Reskin, formation. Hathor, light." The Spathian Initiates rotated again with their onslaught on Jerinne, who now was angry enough to give back hard.

"Exactly. But they would—"

"Name."

"Oh, yes, I'm Dayne Heldrin—"

"The name of the outlaw."

"I believe it's Tharek."

The Master's face twitched. "Hold!"

Hathor had his blade almost ready to chop Jerinne's ear off, but he froze in position. Jerinne didn't freeze, instead knocking him across the skull with her fist, sending him to the ground.

"Initiates, leave us. To the course."

The Initiates all jogged off, maintaining their formation. Hathor seemed to give Jerinne the slightest of winks before taking his place with the others. Once they were alone, the Master spoke again.

"Tharek Pell. Finished Initiacy in 1211. Three years of Candidacy. Cashiered out in 1214."

"So he wasn't accepted as an Adept."

The Master paused, clearly choosing her words carefully. "He did not advance, no."

"Was it because of politics?"

She shook her head. "If Tharek had politics, he kept them to himself."

"What about someone else?"

"Are you talking about romantic entanglements? Spathians prefer not to engage in such things."

"No, I mean . . ." Dayne decided he couldn't be coy about this. "Did the decision not to advance him come from somewhere else? Someone else?"

The Master's face grew harsh, which was quite a feat given how it was hardly soft to begin with. "We do not discuss our advancement decisions with others. Especially Tarian Candidates. Go hide behind your shield."

Dayne wasn't deterred. "From the Parliament? Did someone from the Parliament block his advancement?"

Her anger melted, ever so slightly. "I am not privy to the details. But his failure to achieve Adept was . . . unjust. In my opinion. And it would be in the opinion of anyone with the right to have such an opinion. Now, you have intruded enough, and I must attend to my Initiates. Be gone now."

Dayne went back to the carriage, where he noticed Jerinne was already back in the seat, still catching her breath.

"Blazes of a spar," Jerinne said. "I really think I almost had that first one."

"I think we managed not to embarrass ourselves," Dayne said. "But barely."

"Don't blame me," Jerinne said. "If I had known that I was going to have to hold off multiple Spathians, I would have stayed in the carriage. Did you learn anything useful?"

"I don't know how long you stayed in there—"

"Thank you for not noticing my near collapse."

"Tharek was a Spathian Candidate."

"He didn't make Adept? Did they drop him for being a Patriot loon?"

"No. I think the Parliament blocked his advancement. And that sent him to the Patriots."

"Lovely," Jerinne said. "Can we get back to our chapterhouse now? After that drumming, I'm actually looking forward to having Madam Tyrell scream at us for being gone all night."

While most of the city was eerily calm, the Tarian Chapterhouse was even more hectic than ever when Dayne and Jerinne arrived. Amaya and two Initiates—Vien and one Dayne didn't recognize—were stationed at the main door while Adepts, Candidates, and Initiates were all being checked out by them, given orders of where to go.

"What's going on?" Dayne asked as soon as they came in, but the look Amaya gave him made him immediately regret even opening his mouth.

"Oh, look who's here," Amaya snarled. "I'm so glad the two of you bothered to stumble home from whatever cathouse you curled up in last night."

"I'm terribly sorry—" Jerinne started, but Dayne cut her off.

"Don't you even, Amaya."

"Even what? Call the household of her grace, the grand Lady Mirianne of wherever a cathouse?"

"You show some blazing respect!"

"You show respect! I outrank you!"

"Just because we were guests in a noble house—"

"Initiates have a curfew, and you were responsible—"

"Silence!" The Grandmaster's voice echoed throughout the main hall from the stairs above. Dayne kept his tongue, as did Amaya. The Grandmaster slowly descended the stairs.

"I understand that in trying times, tempers are bound to become . . . heated." His voice was little more than a whisper, but it carried enough power to hold everyone's attention. "However, we must keep our heads about us, especially today."

"Of course, sir," Dayne said. "I'm very sorry I've not been available, but we, Jerinne and I, were investigating the man behind the attacks—"

"That's very good, Dayne," the Grandmaster said, holding up one hand to quiet him. "However, let me explain our current situation. You are surely aware that a second member of Parliament was killed."

"Yes, and—"

"And today is the final session of this convocation of the Parliament. Given the situation, you can imagine there is a fair degree of anxiety regarding safety, and therefore we have been called upon again."

"Protection details for the members?" Dayne asked.

"Indeed. Amaya is taking charge of the coordination of these efforts."

"Of course, sir," Dayne said. "I'm glad to serve in any way I can."

"Good." The Grandmaster looked about, as if troubled. "However, where I will need you is the armory. Many of the Initiates do not have their own shields or swords in usable condition. Please be so kind as to take an inventory of what is on hand, inspecting each item for its quality and usability."

Amaya was too dignified to actually snicker at him, but her face said all that needed saying.

"As I am commanded," Dayne said, "I will gladly do. But you should know—"

"Miss Fendall," the Grandmaster added, cutting Dayne off, "you might do well to hurry to your quarters and dress yourself properly for engagement. You can most likely guess your assignment, and your charge is already eagerly awaiting you."

The Grandmaster glanced about the room, where everyone was still standing expectantly. He snapped his fingers at everyone. "Be about your duties. I have my own matters to attend to."

Dayne nodded and headed toward the armory. He stopped one last time to glance back at Amaya, but she was completely engaged in her own tasks, and didn't even bother to give him a parting sneer.

Chapter 20

JERINNE'S WHOLE BODY was sore. Whatever had happened the night before was unclear, but she had woken up on the floor of the water closet, her neck having been cricked in an unnatural position for who knows how long. Followed by the pounding she had taken from those Spathian Initiates, all she wanted was to crawl out to the bathhouse and soak for the rest of the day.

It was clear that the Good Mister Seabrook had decided differently. Ressin was waiting in Jerinne's chamber, laying out Jerinne's uniform and mail shirt.

"I'm afraid today will be more than just a show of color, Miss Fendall," Ressin said as he smoothed out the wrinkles on the jersey. "And I do apologize for my presumption here. However, time is pressing, and I must take liberties."

Acting like he was a valet, Ressin promptly began undressing Jerinne. "Mister Ressin!"

"I assure you this is purely for expedience. It is already

just after nine bells. The session of the Parliament is to convene at ten. Mister Seabrook intends to be there, but he refuses to leave his domicile without a guardian. So today, full armor, sword, and shield."

Jerinne accepted the help, even though it felt incredibly inappropriate. It gave her some small comfort that Ressin didn't seem to have an ounce of prurient intent. Never in her life did she imagine she would ever be someone in this position—at one point her highest ambition might have been to be on the other side, serving Lady Fortinare directly. Even as a Tarian, she'd be in service, in her own manner. Certainly she was being put to service to Good Mister Seabrook. Ressin dressing her like a child's doll didn't diminish that feeling.

Ressin had her in uniform and armor in no time. "You've had practice with that."

"It's not too different from the Navy uniform. I did the same for Mister Seabrook when he was a captain."

"We need to go to the armory," Jerinne said. "Apparently my Initiate sword isn't good enough for today."

"I'll take you at your word for that, but we really must make haste if we're to get Mister Seabrook in place by the calling of the quorum."

Jerinne led the way, noting for the first time that Ressin was also armed. He carried a gentleman's sword, a thin and light rapier, more suited for swordplay as sport rather than proper fighting.

The armory was outside the main house, a low structure through the back garden near the bathhouses. Jerinne was quite familiar with it, as was every Initiate. Initiates were responsible for the maintenance and care of the weapons and shields housed there, including keeping inventory and security. A full inspection of the armory was one of the most traditional forms of discipline put upon an Initiate. Jerinne had only had it dropped on her head once, and that was after being part of a prank she pulled with a few other first-years in the beginning of her Initiacy. The rest of that group had all washed out by First-Year Trials.

That made it all the stranger seeing Dayne working in the armory like a punishment detail. She had never seen such a Candidate doing such a thing before. Nonetheless, Dayne was in the armory, diligent and attentive as he inspected the weapons.

"Dayne," Jerinne announced herself. "I'm going to need sword and shield."

"Shield and sword," Dayne responded, almost as if by instinct. He took a long moment, looking at all the shields on the rack, before finding one and giving it to Jerinne. "This was the one I used for my Third-Year Trials. It's one of the True Tarian shields."

"How can you know?" Jerinne asked. "True" Tarian shields were a thing Initiates whispered about, but no one knew exactly what that meant, and no one above them ever gave a straight answer. Each shield had some minor variation in design, but on the whole they were painted with a series of concentric circles, with the Tarian emblem in the center. Jerinne didn't notice anything different about it as she put her arm through the straps.

"I just know," Dayne said. "How's the weight?"

"Good," Jerinne answered. It did feel right on her arm, solid and comfortable. "And sword? Do you have a special one picked out there?"

"No. A sword's a sword." Dayne said, taking one off the wall. He passed it over to Jerinne. "So you're ready?"

"I guess so," Jerinne said.

Dayne gave her an odd regard, pausing uncomfortably before he spoke. "Did I tell you the Question of the Bridge?"

"No," Jerinne said. "What's that?"

"Miss Fendall," Ressin pressed.

"Ask me later," Dayne said. "Just . . . don't forget what you are out there."

"What's that supposed to mean?" Jerinne asked. "I know I'm just an Initiate."

"Your rank is Initiate, but when you go out there, with that shield and that tunic . . . you're a Tarian. Full stop."

"Miss Fendall," Ressin pressed.

"I need to go," Jerinne said.

Dayne smiled. "You need to say it."

"I don't have time, Dayne."

"Jerinne," Dayne said, dropping the smile and turning very serious. "You really do need to say it."

Jerinne sighed, and gave an apologetic glance to Ressin, who at least seemed to understand. She cleared her throat and gave the oath.

"With Shield on arm and sword in hand
I will not yield, but hold and stand,
As I draw breath, I'll allow no harm,
And fight back death, with shield on arm."

Dayne nodded in approval. "Now get out there, Tarian."

Ressin led Jerinne off, past the main corridor, where Madam Tyrell and her assistant Initiates gave her a slight nod of approval. Good Mister Seabrook's carriage was waiting across the street, and Ressin wasted no time loading Jerinne in and having it set off.

"Fortunately the traffic here is light," Ressin said, scanning down the road as the driver pressed the horses far faster than was typical. The carriage jolted and creaked. Jerinne wasn't sure if the wheels could take it. The carriage proved to be solid enough to make it to Mister Seabrook's home in quick order, though this time it pulled up the drive to the door. Ressin hopped out.

"I will fetch Good Mister Seabrook. For the next leg, please take a place on the right-hand running board. I'll be on the left."

Ressin was in and out of the house in moments, as Seabrook must have been waiting in the foyer. Seabrook was in full naval dress uniform with armor and belted sword. For his part, he had a bright grin, but Jerinne thought it was quite clear from the man's eyes that it was a feigned buoyancy. "Quite the excitement, eh? I didn't think I'd see another day like this since I stepped off the *Heart of Glory*!"

"Indeed, sir," Ressin said, loading his master into the carriage. Jerinne took her place on the runner, and Ressin took the other side and pounded the side to tell the driver to be off.

The driver took the route to the Parliament with the same racing glee he had used to reach Seabrook's home. It had been bad inside the carriage; standing on the runner, it was awful. Jerinne almost lost her grip several times. She saw no point to riding this way. The streets were mostly empty, and she wasn't going to be any good protecting Seabrook if she fell off the carriage.

The corner was turned to approach the Parliament. Suddenly it was clear why the streets were relatively empty.

Parliament Plaza was mobbed.

In the armory Dayne was removed from most of the madness that was filling the chapterhouse. Occasionally someone would come in need of shield or sword— usually an Initiate. According to strict tradition, he wasn't supposed to allow anyone to leave with their shield and sword without first giving the Oath of the Order, but he had only made Jerinne actually indulge him with that.

She was too young, too inexperienced to be put in this position, and Dayne was worried. He realized now that too much had been put on his own head as a Candidate— which may be what led to the disaster in Lacanja. For the Order to put high expectations on a second-year Initiate . . . it was troubling. Especially letting a member of Parliament dictate such a thing, demanding Jerinne when she should be on Quiet Days. In all his studies of the history of the Order—of all twelve Orders—he had never heard of such a thing.

"So is this your final service?" Amaya's voice came from the doorway, piercing him through the heart.

"I have another year of Candidacy," Dayne said. "Did you think I would ignore that?"

"I don't know what to think, Dayne. All I know is three days ago the Grandmaster was almost weeping to have you back here. Today he can barely look at you."

"Clearly I haven't pleased him," Dayne said. "If he asks for my tunic and medallion, I'll accept that."

"I don't accept that!" She charged into the armory and grabbed him by the tunic. "There is no one else in the world I would say is more deserving of Adepthood than me. But you are. And you know why."

"There's nothing I can do! It's not about what's in my heart or what's on my arm! It's about who's on a committee!"

"Dayne—"

"Wait," he said, holding up his hand. Thoughts raced through his head, smashing together at odd angles. "Who is on that committee?"

"You aren't making any sense."

"Is the Grandmaster still here?"

"No, he left," she said. "Probably to attend directly on . . ."

"Excuse me, gentles," one of the servants said, not stepping through the threshold, "but there is someone in the foyer who wishes audience with Mister Heldrin."

"Mister Heldrin is assigned to the armory," Amaya said. There was a hint of a dare in her voice. "You can tell her that he cannot attend her."

The servant coughed. "The gentleman in the foyer did give a card." He held it out, and Amaya snatched it.

"Maresh Niol of *The Veracity Press*? Are you giving interviews?"

"No, he's a friend," Dayne said. He started for the

door, but Amaya blocked him. "If you have even a drop of affection for me, Amaya, let me go."

Her pose faltered. "That's why it's so hard."

"Then come with me. Let's see what he wants."

Maresh paced the floor of the foyer, his fingers twitching like they needed to be wrapped around a glass.

"Dayne!" he shouted when they entered. "And . . . my lady." He gave a slight bow to Amaya.

"He has style," Amaya said.

"What's going on?" Dayne asked. "Did you all discover something?"

"No," Maresh said. "I have no idea, and that's the problem."

"What do you mean?"

"After you left us last night—"

"Left them?" Amaya asked. "I thought you were at Lady Mirianne's household."

"I—I stopped to ask my friends here some questions."

"Oh, questions," Amaya said. "Are you the ones who huddle in The Nimble Rabbit?"

"We frequent there, yes, but, good miss, you are distracting me from my point, which is this: once you left us, Hemmit decided to try discovering for himself where the Patriots were hidden. He has, over the past year, built up quite a few sources in unsavory places, which he often uses for the stories we write, and Lin usually assists him. Now, he goes in disguise, in an established character. As does Lin. And so—"

"Your point, Maresh."

"My point is, he went to do just that, in hope of finding something about the Patriots. I expected them back around midnight."

"And?"

"And, midnight came and went, with no sign. Dawn as well. And . . . you can see what happened last night. Something is building this morning as well, and I fear that Hemmit and Lin are deep in the middle of it."

"Why?" Amaya asked. "I mean, forgive me, I don't know your friends, but couldn't they have just, I don't know, slipped off into some inn chamber for the night and lost track of time?"

"You do not know them, good miss," Maresh said. "Hemmit has many vices, including ones of debauchery, but he is not one to abandon a story or the truth. If he didn't return to print an issue, it's because he couldn't."

"And if he couldn't, you think it's because he's in trouble. Likely with the Patriots."

"Or worse," Maresh said. "Hemmit will go too far for a story."

Amaya gave him a piercing look. "What is it you're afraid of?"

Maresh looked to the floor. "Hemmit would let himself get drawn in. Work with them. Not out of passion or belief, but to get the full truth of their story. And Lin . . . when Lin is in there with him, she goes completely into her persona."

Dayne wasn't sure what to think. The truth was, he didn't know any of them that well. Hemmit and Maresh, and Lin for that matter, were hot-blooded and filled with revolutionary ideals, placing their "truth" over cooler logic. They could easily sympathize with the Patriots, if not get turned completely. "So . . . you think they might have helped kill Yessinwood?"

"No, I . . . I don't think they would. But I don't know where they are or what could happen, and I didn't know who else to go to."

"And I don't know what to do," Dayne said. "Even if we had any sense of where they might be, what they were going to do, what can I . . . I'm already . . ." He stumbled on his words. As much bravado as he had had saying he'd turn in his tunic and medallion if asked, he couldn't bear it. What could he do without further incurring the Grandmaster's wrath? "Amaya, can you . . ."

"I have my own assignment, and I'm already late."

"But . . ."

"Dayne," Amaya said. "The cart is on the track. Do you pull the switch, or let it crash?"

Dayne smiled. He knew exactly how to answer that question.

"Let's go find our friends, Maresh."

Third Interlude

ALL THE GRAND TEN were assembled. This time no one gave any excuses or trouble, or made any fuss about wearing their masks. Everyone followed protocol to the letter.

No one wanted things to go wrong.

And as far as Barton was concerned, he was more at risk than anyone else in the room, save for Millerson.

"You've lost control of everything here, Barton!" The Duchess barked at him.

"I've lost control?" She had just swept protocol out the door. "How much control could I have? Millerson was the one who was supposed to guide these 'Patriots' through his supposed 'layers of separations.'"

"Names!" Millerson insisted. "Those layers are working, I've made sure of that."

The Duchess was having none of it. "Are they? Or are they going to lead back to you, and then from you to here? Because if this place is discovered to be the heart of our council . . ."

"Yes, we are well aware. You own the property."

"I don't think you understand, dear Barton. I've tolerated being a public laughingstock. Oh, yes, Duchess Leighton is throwing her money away restoring the opera house. When will it open? Is she going broke?"

"We appreciate your sacrifices, Duchess," Millerson said.

The Soldier coughed. "The question is, do we take steps, or do we let these things play out?"

"I am tempted to let it play out," Millerson said far too casually for Barton's taste. "It may be out of control, but it isn't hurting our better interests. I've made contact, and we're taking control over these Patriots."

"Yessinwood is dead," Barton said, hoping to shame his colleague a little. "That wasn't part of the plan."

"Yessinwood," Millerson scoffed. "Had you ever spoken to him, beyond pleasantries? I never did. And it is a shame, but on the other hand, he was a Loyalist. That's another Chair that could be filled with a Traditionalist."

"That's a bit much," The Mage said.

"Perhaps, but if our coalition can retake the floor, I certainly wouldn't object. Nor should you."

"Of course I wouldn't," she said. "I know that with your friends in the Leadership Chairs, my programs in Druth Intelligence will get the funding and approval they need."

"That we need you to have," The Soldier added.

These two were pragmatic, of course. Their primary concern was for the greater security of Druthal. And since Colonel Neills was vice-commandant of Fort Merritt, and would be made general and placed in command of the facility shortly—that promotion had already been greased through the parliamentary subcommittees and didn't need full votes for approval. He was about to be in a position to shape the Druth Army in a very real way. He had plans to work closely with Major Silla Altarn, a mage in Druth Intelligence, whose goals involved greater militarized application of magic. They could have an amazing impact on Druthal's security. Especially if the major was able to implement her Altarn Initiatives.

When Barton was being honest with himself, he'd admit that he did not care for Major Altarn one bit. She used magic with an almost casual disregard, like she was brushing dust off her coat. He knew, intellectually, that mages were just like anyone else and he shouldn't judge her for that. But though being encased in her cocoon of magic shielded them from sight and sound, it made the hairs on his arm stand up. He imagined she could kill them all without her breath even quickening, if that was what she wanted.

Despite that, he didn't doubt her loyalty to the council or its cause, or to Druthal itself. The Loyalists and the Minties had been draining Altarn's coffers dry, giving her no resources to fund her projects, which she believed were critical to improving Druthal's overall strength. Barton had heard that some of her people had gone underground to continue their research. Literally. She had her own battles in Intelligence, and she was in the process of quietly maneuvering her people into key positions while undercutting the operatives who had been her adversaries all these years.

Barton wanted a more secure nation—and giving more latitude to people like Neills and Altarn was the way to do it. A strong Druthal, with a strong king on the throne. He knew Prince Escaraine's own views supported projects like the Altarn Initiatives. With him on the throne as Maradaine XIX, the True Line would be restored, and many of their goals would be realized.

"Steps should be taken," The Warrior said quietly. "Before the cost of lives is too high."

There were some halfhearted nods of assent.

"I don't disagree," Barton said. "Though we must not put ourselves too much at risk. These few rogue Patriots are focused on the Parliament. After today the convocation is ended, and their fire will quietly extinguish itself."

"And don't you two need to be there?" The Lord asked.

"Not especially," Barton said. "Nothing of consequence will be voted on. It's just a procedural matter to end the convocation. A few absences are fine."

The Lady shook her head. "From what I've seen, hardly anyone is showing up. You may have a problem, Parliamentarian."

The Justice added, "If hardly anyone shows up, there's no quorum."

"You think there's a risk—" Barton started. What they were saying was suddenly clear. "If there's no quorum, there's no session, and if there's no session, then the convocation cannot be disbanded."

The Justice continued. "And until it's disbanded, there can't be elections, thus no new convocation . . ."

Barton got to his feet. "Millerson, we have to get to the Parliament right now."

For once, Millerson didn't argue about Barton using his name in the council.

Chapter 21

"CLEAR! CLEAR!" Jerinne shouted as the carriage pressed through the crowd. People only scrambled away to avoid being crushed by the carriage, and even then they were smashed by the crowd around them.

"What is going on?" Ressin shouted back to Jerinne.

"You weren't expecting this?" The look of disbelief on Ressin's face told her everything she needed to know.

Jerinne jumped off the runner and pushed her way in front of the carriage. "Stand aside!" she boomed out in her best imitation of Dayne. Between the voice, the shield, and the uniform, it was enough to get some reaction and clear the road for the carriage.

"Let them through!" Marshals shouted and forced their own hole through the crowd, probably a bit rougher than they needed to. "Let the Parliamentarian through!"

The carriage reached the bottom of the stairs, and Jerinne came back to the door to help Seabrook out.

"This isn't my entrance," Seabrook said.

"Sir, I think we should make do," Ressin offered, and Seabrook seemed to accept this.

They took to the stairs, marshals taking flanking positions with Jerinne and Ressin to block Seabrook from the crowd. There were shouts—angry, incoherent—but Jerinne couldn't make out what the crowd was angry about or why they were mobbing the Parliament. They all made their way inside, and slammed the doors behind them.

"What the blazes was that about?" Jerinne asked.

"Language," Ressin muttered, but Seabrook didn't seem fazed.

"I'm quite puzzled. You would think we were the wronging party in the recent events, instead of the victims."

"Good sir, you should get to the floor," one of the marshals said, though he looked as spooked as anyone.

"Are we going to be able to get out of here?" Jerinne asked. The marshal just shrugged.

"Matter for later," Seabrook said, marching around the outer ring of the Parliament hall to reach the Sauriya entrance.

The Parliament floor was half deserted, though the gallery was not. That was packed to capacity, and not with yesterday's pressmen and nobility. Today's crowd was working class: steves and shanas, dockmen and washing women. Of course, every citizen had the right to be in the gallery. Jerinne didn't think too many people exercised that right, certainly not to this degree.

"Is this typical for the last day of convocation?" Jerinne asked Ressin as they took their places in the box.

"There is nothing typical about this," Ressin said in a haunted voice.

Welton, one of only about two score of Parliamentarians on the floor, rapped three times. "Be it heard. Be it heard. Be it heard. Today is the thirteenth of Joram, in the year 1215. The Parliament of Druthal has been convoked. It is now ten bells in the morning."

"We stand without quorum!" another man shouted. "We cannot be convoked."

"Count the numbers, and call the ranks," Welton said, unfazed by the shout.

"Are you nutters?" someone yelled from the gallery. "You've barely got a tetch squad!"

"I can count, and you've only got forty-two!"

"Silence!" Welton tried to boom out with authority, but the aged man's voice was not up to the challenge. "We must engage in procedure."

"Procedure?"

"Wasting time!"

"Wasting crowns!"

"We must call the ranks," Welton said again.

Another Parliamentarian stood up. "This is a matter most grave."

"Goddamn it, Perry, I'm going to make your head most grave!" The Parliamentarian who said this dove for Perry, ready to pummel him with his walking stick.

In seconds there were several members of Parliament in a scrum, and the gallery screamed and cheered.

Jerinne was out of the box and down on the floor before Ressin had a chance to object. She leaped in front of Seabrook, shield high, as someone from the gallery threw down a bottle. Jerinne blocked it and pushed Seabrook up the steps toward the exit.

"This is ... I've never ..." Seabrook sputtered.

"Nor have I, sir," Jerinne said.

Ressin joined them back in the hallway. "Sir, I think it might be best, for all our sakes, if we made a hasty retreat."

"That is absurd!" Seabrook said. "We must have a quorum for the session, or else we cannot disband this convocation."

"You're nearly two dozen short of a quorum, sir," Ressin said. "Your commitment is laudable ..."

"My commitment is my goddamned duty, Ressin! My

fellows may have abandoned it, but I will do nothing of the sort."

Then the screams outside matched the ones inside.

The uniforms had been perfect. Only five of them, so neither Lin nor Gillem wore them. Hemmit found himself dressed as a King's Marshal next to Tharek, Yand, Braning, and Kemmer. They looked like a perfect squad of marshals, with Tharek as the First Marshal.

That meant the Chief, whoever he was, had access either to astounding forgers or authentic material. Either one made a chill run up Hemmit's spine.

They had gone to Parliament Plaza, as they had been instructed, with Lin and Gillem in "custody." The entire walk over Hemmit had done his best to be next to Lin without looking conspicuous about it. Since Yand was leading her, this proved completely impossible.

"Take up the rear," she whispered. At least it was right in his ear, even though he wasn't close to her. He glanced over, and with the slightest nod of her head, she sent him to the back.

"Just whisper," he heard as he took his place. "I can draw the sound from your lips, and send sound to your ears."

"Really?" Hemmit whispered. "That's amazing . . ."

"And it's hard, so no small talk."

"You have a plan?"

"Besides being 'arrested' so you all are let into the Parliament? No. But we need help."

"And we can't trust anyone else in there," Hemmit offered.

Yand glanced back at Hemmit from his place in the procession. "What are you on about?"

"Just talking to myself," Hemmit said.

"Right," Yand said. "And you're right, we can't trust anyone in that place. Gotta be on toes."

"Stay quiet," Lin's voice hit his ears. "Right, we can't trust anyone. Marshals. Or Constabulary."

"Who, then?" Hemmit dared to whisper.

"I can only think of one person. So when the moment comes, I'm going to take my chance. Just be ready."

They reached the plaza—teeming with an angry crowd—taking formation around their "prisoners." It struck Hemmit that they might match marshals in uniform, but they still looked like a bunch of fools when it came to precision or discipline. Except for Tharek, who took the lead like a champion.

However, no one reacted like they were frauds. Half the crowd cheered them, half howled and sneered. Hemmit couldn't figure out where they came from or what they wanted. Maybe the crowd didn't know what they wanted, either. It wasn't like they had been given the truth. They were probably angry for the same reasons the Patriots were, but didn't like the Patriots either. So they raged here, raw and unfocused. Afraid.

They were the kindling Tharek was going to spark.

Somehow, the Chief had made this crowd happen here at the Parliament, just a nudge away from violence.

Tharek shoved himself a path through the crowd, just about reaching the bottom of the steps. Other marshals—legitimate marshals as far as Hemmit could tell—were holding a line at the Parliament steps, keeping the crowd from getting any closer. Two waved over at Tharek, and pushed their way closer.

"What the blazes are you doing?" one asked.

"Got two of those Patriots," Tharek said. "Told to bring them in for questioning."

"Are you daft?" the marshal asked. "Bringing them up through here?" He leaned in close to Tharek and whispered something, pointing off to the church at the edge of the plaza, away from the crowd.

Tharek nodded. "To the church, lads."

They had all started to work their way back through

the crowds when Tharek raised his voice. "You going to give me a problem?"

Tharek was shoving Gillem, pushing the old man into Lin.

"And you, brat? You gonna get what's coming?" He shoved her as well.

Some poor fool in the crowd must have decided to be chivalrous, or at least had taken a fancy to Lin, because he tried to grab Tharek's hand before he could strike Lin again.

The smile on Tharek's face was one of pure victory. With a swift swing of his arm, Lin's would-be rescuer was flat on the ground. A few more people shouted and moved on Tharek.

Lin must have decided this was her moment. Her body began to tremble, and Kemmer caught hold of her, thinking she was about to faint.

She didn't faint, and she was keenly focused, eyes to the sky. Her trembling body glowed, bright white.

"What the blazes?" Kemmer asked. He let go of her, but she stayed on her feet, despite the fact that her body leaned back at a nearly impossible angle. She hovered, held up like a marionette.

The light engulfed her body, too bright to see anything but white, and then blasted high into the sky. Lin dropped like a sack, but for that moment, only Hemmit noted her at all. Every other eye was on the sky, where the light burst into a vivid image.

The Tarian shield emblem.

"Mage!" The cry howled through the plaza, and people ran, some toward Lin and the rest of them, some away. Madness and screams took over. Hemmit scrambled through the rampage of flesh that surrounded him and picked Lin's body up. He wasn't alone, Braning was right there with him, trying to pull her up to her feet before she was trampled.

The whole crowd was clawing and attacking—going

for Hemmit and Lin, going for each other, and especially going for the marshals trying to hold the Parliament steps.

Tharek was not held back. Like a wild dog finally let off a leash, he tore through the crowd with vicious blows, carving his way to the Parliament steps.

Braning grabbed Hemmit by the collar.

"We should—"

That was all Hemmit heard before something cracked across his head.

The Tarian emblem blazed over the sky.

"That's Lin," Dayne said. It had to be; it was exactly like the one she had made when they met at The Nimble Rabbit, except much bigger. He and Maresh had barely gone a block away from the chapterhouse when it suddenly appeared in the air.

"Where is that?" Maresh asked.

"Parliament," Dayne said, but he was already running full bore in that direction. He could hear Maresh trying to keep up—by the time he made it to the plaza, the artist was far behind.

The plaza was pure mayhem, people screaming and fighting. The entire Parliament building was surrounded as people attempted to storm the steps. Marshals did their best to hold their ground, but it wasn't going to be very long until they would be forced to retreat. The Parliament doors were closing. Those doors could be barred and reinforced. The Parliament was built to withstand a siege if it had to.

Today was the day to test that.

"You ... have to ... get in there." Maresh wheezed, fighting for each gasp. He must have just arrived.

"There's no way I can get through that," Dayne said. He realized he'd left the chapterhouse with Maresh in a rush. He didn't have a shield or even a sword. The marshals were retreating, dragging their wounded inside as the last doors were closing.

One of the marshals, up on the highest steps, stood out like a lighthouse, even from this distance. He was no marshal.

Tharek.

He went inside—one of the last ones in— as the doors slammed shut.

Tharek was now locked inside the Parliament, as it was under siege. A wolf in the sheep pen.

"So are they trapped in there?" Maresh asked, still holding his chest.

"No, the Parliament is built over the old—" Dayne was about to launch into a history lecture, but then the actual meaning of what he was about to say hit him full force. "Saint Fenson's!"

Dayne tore over to Saint Fenson's Church, on the far side of the plaza, away from the riots.

Saint Fenson's was one of the largest churches in Maradaine, rivaled only by the High Royal Cathedral. The building predated the Reunification, the Church of Druthal, and of course the Parliament. What it didn't predate was the Parliament building itself, as both buildings had long ago been part of the same compound. In the tenth century it was the Inquest Mission. Underneath the plaza were corridors and cells where political enemies of the powerful were tortured and left to rot.

Those structures had long since been appropriated and put to better use, including housing the offices of the King's Marshals. Even the cells were still in use.

As were the connecting tunnels.

Several priests were clustered in the vestibule when Dayne came in, all of them focused on the riot outside.

"What is going on?" one of them demanded.

"I don't know how it started, reverend, but I need your help."

"We should go out there, minister to the wounded."

"Call the Constabulary, you mean."

"Yes, please," Dayne said. "Yellowshields as well. But I need to get inside the Parliament House as quickly as possible."

"You're going to have a hard time with that," a young priest said, pointing to the riot.

"There's no way to get in there," said another. They all gave each other guilty glances.

Dayne scanned the group of them until he locked eyes with the eldest one there. He pulled his medallion out from under his tunic. "I am Dayne Heldrin of the Tarian Order, and I am a loyal servant of crown, throne, and the saints. I beg your aid."

"Come with me, son."

People came rushing inside the outer ring hallway of the Parliament House—marshals from outside. As they rushed through, they slammed the doors shut behind them and threw crash bars down. No one was coming in.

"What's going on?" Jerinne asked, raising her shield a little higher.

"A blazing riot!" one of them snapped. "Get back in the main hall!"

"There's a riot in there as well," Jerinne said.

"Sir," Ressin offered, pulling Seabrook closer to the wall, "perhaps we should retire to safer chambers of some sort, just for a short time The lower levels, perhaps?"

"Yes, perhaps so," Seabrook agreed. "But only for a moment. The work of the Parliament must continue."

The marshals continued to barricade themselves in, and there were shouts among them to quell the upper balconies.

"You!" Ressin snapped at the closest marshal. "We need to get to the lower levels."

"Right, right," that marshal said. Jerinne imagined he wasn't much older than she was, and looked scared out of his mind.

"We've got injured!" another marshal yelled, carrying someone whose head had been cracked open. "We need to get him to the medics below!"

The young marshal stammered for a moment, eyes darting in every direction. He couldn't possibly be ready to make any decisions.

"Just point the way," Jerinne said. "We're all together here."

"Right, right," he muttered. "You, big guy, help carry the wounded. And lead the Parli down below."

A large marshal walked past them, heaving one of the unconscious ones over his shoulder. Two more went ahead, helping a third limp his way.

"Let's go, sir," Ressin said. "When things calm down, we'll return to the floor."

Seabrook nodded. "Lead on. Jerinne, with us."

Jerinne took position leading Seabrook, behind the group of marshals. They made their way around the curve of the outer ring until they reached a spiral stairway. Going up, of course, would lead to the galleries. They followed the procession down, through three full spirals of the stairs, to a candlelit hallway, cold white stone, leading off to distant shadows.

"I have never liked coming this far down," Seabrook said as they went down the hall. "It reminds me far too much of catacombs."

"How fitting," the tall marshal said, as he unceremoniously dropped his charge to the floor. "Since this is where you're going to die."

Jerinne recognized the voice, and cursed herself for not spotting the rest sooner.

Tharek.

He spun around, blades flying out of his hand. Three of them hit true, killing the other marshals instantly. A fourth would have gone right into Mister Seabrook's neck, were it not for Jerinne's shield.

"How dare you!" Seabrook shouted. "Do you know who I am?"

"Oh, I know, Mister Seabrook. But do you know who I am?"

"I do," Jerinne growled, drawing out her sword. "Run, sir."

"Poor Tarian pup," Tharek said, taking his out as well. "You have no idea what you're facing."

"I know you, failed Spathian," Jerinne spat back. She took stance—High Position One—in the center of the hallway, body turned to the side, sword held over shield.

"You think me failed?" Tharek barked, blasting a fury of sword strikes at Jerinne's upper body. Even with both shield and sword, Jerinne had to race to block and parry each blow. "They failed me. He failed me!" His blade pointed accusingly at Seabrook.

Ressin leaped in with his own sword, but before Jerinne could even react, Tharek effortlessly knocked the blade out of the way and ran the man through.

"Ressin!" Jerinne slammed her shield into Tharek, attempting to pin him to the wall.

"Now for Seabrook," Tharek said.

"Not while I live," Jerinne returned.

"As you wish."

Tharek's foot smashed down on Jerinne's knee, snapping the leg. Jerinne screamed in pain as she collapsed, despite herself. Before she hit the ground, Tharek's foot connected with her skull, sending her into the opposite wall in a dazed heap.

"You were told to run," Tharek said.

Jerinne struggled to keep her eyes open, keep her thoughts focused on the room, on Tharek, on Seabrook. Seabrook had his own sword out. "I fought Poasians at Hantal Bay, vandal."

"And so you judge me?" Tharek said. He knocked Seabrook's blade away. "A soft man like you."

Jerinne's leg was on fire, hanging at an unnatural angle, but she forced herself back up on her good foot, removing the shield from her arm. Using her sword to balance herself, she threw the shield as hard as she could at Tharek.

It smashed into Tharek's head.

Tharek turned back to Jerinne.

"With shield on arm and sword in hand!" Jerinne shouted, raising her blade up. "I will not yield but hold and stand!"

"You're a credit to your Order," Tharek growled.

Jerinne pushed herself forward, one agonizing step closer. "As I draw breath, I'll allow no harm!" Keep Tharek's attention. Give Seabrook a chance to run.

Tharek smirked, and without even looking he struck backward, sending his blade through Seabrook's heart.

"Hold back that, Tarian whelp."

Jerinne struck ineffectually at Tharek, who was so unconcerned he knocked the blade away with his bare hand. He pulled his bloody blade out of Seabrook's chest.

Jerinne's heart pounded, terrified, knowing she had seconds to live. She could barely stay standing another moment. But she wasn't going to show Tharek that. She'd lost her charge, lost the fight, but she would hold that small bit of honor.

Tharek didn't take the killing blow.

Instead, as racing footsteps came down the hallway, Tharek got on his knees and put his hands behind his head.

The last thing Jerinne heard before she lost consciousness was the last thing she expected Tharek to say.

"I surrender."

Chapter 22

DAYNE EXPECTED ANCIENT INTRIGUE. He expected cobwebs, dust. He expected an entrance involving twisting a candle sconce or pushing a sequence of tiles in the fireplace. Instead the priest led him down the steps to an ordinary door, which revealed a clean hallway, lit with rows of candles.

The disappointment froze him in his place for several seconds.

"Wasn't it pressing, Tarian?" the old priest asked.

"Yes, thank you, reverend," Dayne said. With a quick benediction on his head and heart, he left the priest and went down the hallway. He didn't run this time, but he did move with urgency. He was amazed to find Maresh still at his side.

"This is going to be dangerous, Maresh."

"Perhaps, but it's the story."

Dayne stopped. "I don't know what is going to happen, and I'm responsible for your safety."

"No, you aren't," Maresh said. "Yes, you're a Tarian,

sworn to defend. And I'm . . . terrified. But I'm not yours. I'm my own man."

"At least stay behind me," Dayne said.

"Where are we going, exactly?"

"We're going through the marshals' headquarters to reach the Parliament."

"And what are the marshals going to think of that?"

"Identify yourselves!"

Two figures were ahead, marshals by their uniforms, if that could be trusted.

Dayne put his hands up. "I'm a Tarian."

The two marshals came closer. One squinted at Dayne. "Yeah, you are. I know you."

"Is he the one?" the other one asked.

"Yeah, that's him all right. Who's your friend?"

Maresh held his head high. "Maresh Niol, *Veracity Press*."

"Oh, *Veracity Press*," the first marshal mocked. "I keep that in the water closet."

"Real useful there," the other said.

"You have an intruder in the Parliament," Dayne said. "We need to—"

"I know we have an intruder," the first marshal said. He drew his crossbow and leveled it at Dayne's chest. "So how are you going to come?"

"We're here to help."

"You're trespassing in marshal headquarters. That's a Royal offense, Tarian."

The other followed suit with his crossbow. "So choose how you're coming. You've embarrassed my fellows, and I'm itching to put you in your place."

Dayne put up his hands.

Lannic's cell in the marshals' root-cellar facility was un-assuming enough. It could even be considered humane, which surprised him. He wasn't locked off in some lightless hole, chained to the wall. The cells were iron cages, lined up next to each other in a wide chamber. It was airy and well lit. Lannic had certainly slept in worse places.

There was something pleasing, even proper, about being imprisoned in the very same cells where political prisoners of corrupt regimes had languished. Even Haltom himself had been down here. Possibly in this very spot, when he organized the Yenley Rebellion.

Perhaps Lannic would have a similar impact.

His friends had been with him at first, but most of them had been taken elsewhere, probably for quick sham trials, and then shipped off to Quarrygate. Lannic suspected that his fate wouldn't be as simple. He would be the center of his own circus.

Several marshals came in, the first ones carrying injured people. One of them was in marshal uniform, the other was a Tarian.

No, it was that Tarian child who taunted him in the museum. Someone had given the girl a proper thrashing. Her leg was broken, and the child was no longer mocking her betters. They dropped the two injured people in one cage and left them alone. Lannic wondered how these two had earned such disdain from the marshals to be left there, their injuries untended. Of course, these were the marshals; it wouldn't take much for them to ignore the needs of their fellow man.

Then they led in Tharek, in chains. Tharek's head was proud, even smug, as they took him to another cage across the chamber from Lannic.

"Tharek!" Lannic cried out. "Are you all right?"

"I'm fine," Tharek said. "It's good to see you."

They locked Tharek in his cell and backed off from him. All the marshals looked as if they were expecting a bobcat to jump out of Tharek's mouth.

Tharek stood peacefully in the middle of his cell until they left.

"What's happening, Tharek?" Lannic asked. "Are we lost?"

"Not at all," Tharek said. "Right now . . ."

The door opened again, and two more people were led in. A small man in spectacles and another Tarian.

That Tarian.

He locked eyes with Tharek, whose face was unreadable. They were about to put him in his own cell, but when the Tarian saw his young friend on the ground, he rushed into that cell.

"Jerinne, what —"

The girl mumbled something, far too faint for Lannic to hear. While the Tarian attended to the girl, the spectacled man looked at the injured marshal. He tried to hide it, but there was a spark of recognition on his face. The marshals locked them in that cell and left.

"You did this, Tharek?" the Tarian asked.

"The girl fought decently, a credit to your Order," Tharek said. "Allowing for the fact that she is merely an Initiate, she was not a complete dissatisfaction as an opponent." Tharek chuckled. "Of course, how rude of me. I didn't know we were using familiar names. It is Dayne, yes? Second-year Candidate?"

"You killed Seabrook?" Dayne asked.

"It was most fortunate. He was practically handed to me."

Dayne grabbed at the bars of his cell, as if he wanted to rip them open and pummel Tharek with them. "Parlin, Yessinwood, Seabrook. Why?"

Lannic was surprised by that. "You've killed three members of Parliament?"

"I did what was needed," Tharek said. "As I will continue to do."

The girl started screaming. Lannic had to feel for her, as she must be in agony. Even she didn't deserve to suffer on the floor of some cell.

"Do something for her, Tarian," Lannic commanded.

Dayne glared at Lannic, but he knelt back down next to the girl just the same. He examined the girl's leg quickly. "Maresh, I'll need you."

The spectacled man came closer. "What do you need?"

"We're going to set her leg. Fortunately, it seems to be a clean break."

"Of course it is," Tharek said.

"Dayne, Dayne," the girl said, reaching up and grabbing Dayne's tunic. "Just get me on my feet. I can keep fighting."

The girl was clearly delirious with pain.

"I'll hold her down, and you put her leg back in place."

"Dayne, I've never done anything like that," Maresh argued.

The Tarian touched his shoulder. "Then today's your first. You have a good eye. I believe in you."

While the two men got in position over the girl, Lannic's heart went out to them. It was a shame that they were enemies, because the Tarian was a decent soul. He cared about his people. Lannic imagined under different circumstances, they might have argued as friends.

"This is going to hurt a lot, Jerinne," Dayne said.

"Fine, fine," the girl said. "Talk to me. Tell me about the bridge."

"Of course. Do you know about the mine carts in the Briyonic Mountains? They ride on tracks, loaded with ore, from the mountain towns down to the cities at the base. Every cart has a brakeman to keep it from going too fast. Do you understand?"

The girl nodded. Lannic noted that Tharek was paying this story some mind as well.

"Good, now imagine that there is a cart coming down the track, but the brakeman has become too ill to operate it. It's out of control and coming to a bridge, where a family is crossing on a mulecart. Mother, father, and three children. They're right on the track, middle of the bridge, and there's nowhere they can go. That ore cart will smash into them and kill them."

"I'm ready, Dayne," Maresh whispered.

Dayne nodded. "You're at a safety switch. Turn the switch and the ore cart goes on another track into a crash wall. The family will be safe. But the brakeman will be killed. So, Tarian Initiate, what do you do?"

He gave a nod to Maresh, who pulled the girl's leg. The scream was unbearable. Lannic had never heard anything like it. And then it stopped. The girl was out cold. Dayne took the girl's coat off and used it to splint the leg.

Lannic's mind was on the bridge. It seemed clear to him, the switch must be pulled. The family were the common people. Pulling the switch was a sacrifice, but a necessary one. The good of the people was paramount.

"I will tell you how a Spathian would answer," Tharek said. "You do nothing. The brakeman is soft and the family is soft, and if none of them can save themselves, they deserve their fate."

"They deserve it?" Dayne asked.

"I'm sure you have a better answer, Tarian."

Dayne was too worked up to respond to that. "Did the people you murdered deserve it? The ones you maimed? The ones caught in the riot outside?"

"There's a riot?" Lannic wasn't sure if he was excited or afraid. Many things had happened since his incarceration, but if innocent people—people who might be part of the cause—had been hurt, that was the last thing he wanted. The Parliamentarians, though, they deserved it, every one of them, for failing the people. Even if the ones Tharek had chosen were certainly . . . odd choices.

"It's fine, it's part of the plan," Tharek said. "We will burn out the corruption. We will show them that the soft cannot make choices for the strong!"

A flash of understanding crossed Dayne's face, but before he spoke his thoughts, the door to the holding chamber opened, and someone clapped slowly as he entered. "Well said. So well said. Like a true believer."

It was the Chief.

Dayne didn't recognize the marshal who came in at first, until Lannic spoke.

"Chief!" Lannic came over to the bars of his cell. "What are you . . . how?"

Then the face was clear. Marshal Chief Regine Toscan. The same man in charge of security at the museum. He would have arrested Dayne that day. He gave only the barest of glances into Dayne's cell, not even noting Jerinne, Maresh, or even Hemmit. How and why Hemmit was there, unconscious in a marshal's uniform, was the least of Dayne's concerns at the moment.

"The Tarian," Toscan said. "This is a pleasant surprise. A loose end that shows up to resolve itself."

"What is that supposed to mean?" Dayne asked. Was Toscan involved with these Patriots?

"He's the Chief?" Tharek asked.

"You really didn't know, Mister Pell? Oh, that is rich. I should say, though, well done on your part. At this time yesterday I wasn't sure if my grand scheme was going to work, but then you left a sign at the drop spot, like a gift from the saints. You followed orders blindly and did a wonderful job. Even surrendering down here, just as ordered. Perfect."

That confirmed it. Dayne had questions, but Tharek did as well.

"What?" Tharek shouted.

"Now, mind you, I wasn't pleased with the deaths of Yessinwood and Seabrook, but I can make that work. Actually, they might help things work just fine. I can make it work."

"Make what work?" Tharek asked.

"You planned this?" Dayne asked. "Why?"

"I've won. Does the why really matter?"

"The why always matters," Maresh said. "The truth always matters."

"Well said," Lannic returned.

"Shut it." Maresh wasn't going to take compliments from Lannic, it seemed.

Toscan burst out laughing. "The truth. This is fabulous. You're all such idealists. Which made you perfect. Even you, Tarian, in a strange way. Why else would you even be here, unless you thought you could make a difference?"

Dayne didn't have a response. Toscan was right about that: being in this cell, and all the mistakes that were going to get him cashiered from the Order, came from thinking he was the only one who could make a difference. Again he had failed the Question of the Gate. Again he had fallen prey to his own pride.

"He has made a difference," Jerinne said groggily. Dayne didn't know how long she'd been awake. "Was *this* really your master plan?"

"This, exactly?" Toscan mused. "Honestly, no. But it works for me. Because right now, between my men and Constabulary, the riot is being quelled, so the immediate problem is solved. And I've more or less eliminated or arrested a huge swath of subversives and radicals. I will be praised. I will be promoted. The Parliament and the Crown will thank me for it. And since so much damage was caused by the atrocities of a failed Spathian and the ineptitude of a rogue Tarian, both your antiquated Orders will fall into further disgrace. The lingering funds and attention which give your Orders their final wheezing breaths will be cut off, and the King's Marshals will be able to do their jobs without distraction!"

The speech had started lightly, even amused, but when he finished he was nearly in a red-faced rage. It was clear this monologue had been stewing in him for some time, now finally released.

"So that's why," Dayne said. Jerinne had drifted back out while Toscan had ranted.

"Indeed." Toscan reclaimed his composure. "And now, the only people who can name me as the one pulling the strings are here in this room. I could concoct an elaborate story, but I think I can simply kill you all and claim you did it to each other."

"Chief," Lannic pleaded, grabbing onto the bars of his cage. "I don't understand. You're the one who pushed me to lead our movement to action."

"Of course I did," Toscan said, approaching Lannic's cage. "On your own, you might have fermented into a legitimate movement. You might have caused real trouble then. Now you're all felons and fools. Completely impotent."

The Chief drew a knife from his belt and shoved it into Lannic's belly.

Chapter 23

NOTHING COULD HAVE prepared Dayne for Tharek's reaction to Lannic's death. The man howled as if his very soul had been torn from him.

"I'll kill you! I will split you like a rabbit and feed your own heart to you!"

"I hardly think so," Toscan said. Pulling the knife from Lannic's body, he turned to Tharek. "You're already locked in a cell, unarmed."

Tharek's voice turned into an icy growl. "I am a Spathian. I'm never unarmed."

His fingers darted to the front of his uniform and tore one of the brass buttons off the coat. Before Toscan could even blink, Tharek threw the button and buried it in the man's eye.

Toscan screamed, his free hand going to his eye. He stumbled in the direction of Tharek's cage. As the man wailed, Tharek removed his belt in a single fluid motion and whipped it around Toscan's knife hand. A moment later Toscan's arm was yanked through the bars, and Tharek took the knife from him.

"Tharek!" Dayne shouted, pounding on his own bars. "Don't!"

Each movement precise, Tharek snapped Toscan's arm, sliced a line down the side of his body, and then removed the keys hanging at his hip. He let the man drop as he unlocked the irons on his wrists, which had been utterly ineffective at slowing him down.

Toscan wasn't dead, but he was no longer screaming. Instead he whimpered as he attempted to crawl away.

Tharek opened his own cage.

"Tharek, listen to me," Dayne said. "It isn't too late for you to do the right thing. The just thing."

Tharek ignored Dayne, instead opening Lannic's cell. He dropped to his knees and picked up the dead man, cradling his head in his arms. "I'm so sorry," Tharek said quietly. "I didn't see it in time. I couldn't save us."

Toscan reached up at Dayne. "Please ... please ..."

"No more," Tharek said in a low whisper. "Pawn to the Parliament. Pawn to the marshals. No more!"

He rose to his feet and walked out of the cage.

"Tharek," Dayne said, hoping for anything that might reach the man. "You are a Spathian. True to crown and country and God."

Tharek walked almost casually over to Toscan, who struggled to take another breath and crawl to the doorway. Tharek spat on Toscan's face, then raised his boot and brought it down on the marshal's head.

And then again.

And again.

He bent down and relieved the body of its sword.

Then he smiled at Dayne with dead eyes.

"Don't worry, my soft brother," Tharek said. "I'll free us all."

He walked out of the chamber. Then the hallway outside was filled with screams.

Colonel Neills brought out an army squadron, and Barton and Millerson dragged some of their fellow Parliamentarians out of their homes, gathering an impressive parade to march to the plaza. The group they had pulled together were mostly Traditionalists, but they grabbed a few Functionalists and one Mintie—Greydon Hale, with his comely Tarian escort. This wasn't out of any attempt to bring about multi-partisan unity, not for Barton. They brought anyone they could get, as quickly as they could. Barton was pleased he had managed almost twenty-five. Many had chosen to stay locked in their homes with their Tarian guards.

They found Parliament Plaza in a state of wreckage, but controlled. Constabulary and marshals had dozens in irons, while Yellowshields and priests tended to the injured. With their military escort it was relatively easy to cross the plaza to the Parliament stairs, though given the situation they chose not to bother with the formality of each man entering by his archduchy stairs. They went up the closest set of stairs and pounded on the door.

Slowly it creaked open, with a young marshal revealed behind it. "Good sirs." He nodded to all the Parliamentarians in Barton's train. "I presume you want entry to the floor."

"That is our purpose," Barton offered. Strictly speaking, Millerson was the ranking member in the group, as the 3rd Chair of Sauriya, but he was deferring to Barton in the whole enterprise. Barton mused that Millerson was taking their respective roles in the Grand Ten literally. If they needed to speak to the people, he would have stepped up. Since this involved the Parliament, Barton as the Parliamentarian needed to take charge.

That was exactly the sort of sewage that Millerson

would spout as part of his Grand Ten rhetoric. He believed in the trappings, not the history.

"All right," the marshal said. "But just you all. We can't have those army boys coming in here. You understand, sir."

"Fair enough," Barton said. "Thank you, gentlemen. You may wait out here. Assist the Constabulary and the rest in any way that you can."

They all started to file in the one door.

"That means you as well, madam," the marshal said, nodding to the Tarian woman.

"I have a charge, and I will not leave him," she said.

"She's fine, really," Barton said. "She's a Tarian after all, pledged to our safety."

"I understand that, sir, but I can't have any more . . . at the very least she has to leave her weapons behind."

She wordlessly unbuckled her belt and let her sword drop to the ground.

"Shield as well, madam. I know about you Tarians." At this, she balked.

"Go ahead," Hale said, as if his encouragement would be the thing to push her over the edge. Her face said otherwise, but despite that, she surrendered her shield.

The last of them in the building, the marshal closed and barred the door again. "Might I suggest you take the floor right away," he said. "We're still in the process of clearing out the gallery."

"The gallery is closed? And empty?" That could be troublesome. A session of the Parliament required a quorum of members to be legitimate, but it also had to be open to the public.

"The people must be allowed to observe," Millerson offered. "It is crucial."

"The people were pretty blazing unruly," someone said from the stairwell to the floor. Montrose, that hardened Saltie, came up the steps, limping without his signature walking stick.

"How bad was it?" someone asked him.

"Pretty blazing bad," he offered. "Brawling in the gallery and on the floor."

"On the floor?" Barton noticed a decent bruise on the side of Montrose's face.

"Come, quickly," Montrose said, taking in the size of the group. "We have much we can do with you here."

Montrose led them all down to the floor, where an assorted gathering of Parliamentarians paced about listlessly, most of them with a few scrapes and bruises. The gallery was all but empty, save a few regulars from the press. Good enough to fulfill that requirement. The boxes were mostly empty as well, supporting staff absent. That hardly mattered, in terms of procedure. The Tarian woman took her place up in Hale's box.

"I call for a count!" Montrose said. "We have not yet had the count, and I'm calling for it!"

"A count is called for! We will call those assembled for this session of the convocation!"

Perry, that delightful obstructionist bastard, stood up. "This is a—" He stopped at a glare from Montrose. Barton noticed more than a few bruises on Perry's face. "An excellent suggestion."

They called the count as everyone took their chairs and after a few minutes the assembled number had been identified and placed.

Wells took his place at the podium, rapping three times on it. "We stand now at sixty-two present. We have a quorum assembled. Be it heard, today is the thirteenth of Joram, in the year 1215. The Parliament of Druthal has been convoked. A quorum has been achieved. This august body is now in session."

Cheston Porter stood up, and though usually the very sound of his voice would drive Barton mad, he was thrilled to hear what he said now. "Be it heard and be it known, today is our one hundred fiftieth and final session of this convocation. We are to close and settle, and retire to our respective archduchies at the end of session. Some will return, and some will not. Men will stand for election, and the voice of the people will continue to be heard."

Barton breathed a sigh of relief. Seventeen times he had heard that speech by various High Chairs of the Floor, but never before had it meant as much to him. Now it was official. Once the session was closed, the convocation would officially end.

He had done it.

Wrennit stood up. "I understand we are under a great deal of duress at this juncture. Despite that, we must endure. We must be strong. And we must, as my esteemed colleague said, close and settle." He held up a sheaf of papers. What was Wrennit up to? "This is the expenditure and taxation plan put together by Misters Mills, Pike, and LeDois. It has been made available for all for several weeks. I propose that it be put to vote."

Porter blanched. "The . . . the proposal is stated. Do any support bringing this to vote?"

A few hands went up.

Barton was about to boil in his chair. What was Wrennit trying to do? That proposal would never pass, as the Crownies and Minties hated it with a passion, and the Frikes would vote against it in solidarity. Even with Populist support it would—

Barton noticed the numbers in the room.

It would pass right now.

The current session had a clear majority of Dishers and Books. As long as no one played games with the gravity, it would pass just fine.

Barton hadn't planned on this. He had intended the session to open and close without incident. It was an exciting prospect. If they could get their plan passed during this convocation, then the whole agenda would be steps ahead.

Montrose stood up, looking like he was about to pass

a stone. "It must be said, because in this case it is true. This is, indeed, a matter most grave."

Wrennit scowled. Barton didn't bother to do the math. It was possible some of the Frikes would break ranks, and that could get it over. But in the end, it didn't matter. Two minutes ago he hadn't even considered it a possibility to pass that plan, so nothing had changed. As long as no one called for the votes he didn't want called at all — and with this session, these people, he didn't see that happening — this vote could be called and fail. All that mattered was the convocation closing. Everything else was sauce for the meat.

One of the other Crownie Chairs stood up — Torest, the High Chair of the Call, was among the absent. "So it shall be. Place it to a vote."

Suddenly a loud crack came from the boxes. A man in a marshal's uniform — but no marshal Barton had ever seen. In fact, he recognized the man as one of the Patriots from the museum. With sword in hand, irons hanging from his belt, and covered in blood, he stood over the inert body of the Tarian woman. She lay on the ground, still breathing, but with her forehead bleeding, and the desk she had been sitting at nearly split in two.

"Hold, good gentles," the false marshal said. "For the people would speak now."

Chapter 24

HEMMIT'S HEAD WAS POUNDING, like nothing he had ever felt before. It was a regular, relentless bang. Like metal hitting metal.

That wasn't in his head. That was a real sound.

He slowly opened his eyes.

"Maresh?" His dear friend was hovering over him. Where was he? How was Maresh even here? Where was Lin? What was happening?

"Ssh, Hemmit, careful," Maresh said. "I was beginning to think you'd never wake up. What happened to you?"

"I don't even . . ." Bang. Bang. Hemmit turned, let his eyes focus. A young woman lying on the ground next to him, in Tarian uniform, pale and covered in a layer of sweat. Cold hard stone beneath him. He could see bars beyond that. Iron bars.

Bang again.

Hemmit tried to sit up.

"Slowly," Maresh said, helping him. "Tell me what happened."

Hemmit was finally able to see what the banging was, where he was. He was in some sort of cage, and Dayne was there as well, kicking the door of the cage with all his might, again and again.

"I was outside, when a riot—Lin!"

"Lin was with you?" Maresh asked. "She was all right?"

"No, I don't . . . I was trying to get her up, get her out. She blew herself out, like a candle. Trying . . . to bring you."

Dayne paused in his assault on the cage door to look down at Hemmit. "And I came."

"What were you doing?"

"Foolishness," Hemmit said. "She and I managed to infiltrate the Patriots, to get close to Tharek. Get the story."

"Did you get a story?" Dayne asked, kicking again.

"I got roped in, is what happened. Lin and I both."

Dayne stopped kicking again. "Were you part of what happened to Yessinwood?"

Shame burned in Hemmit's chest. "Indirectly."

Dayne glowered and kicked at the door again. It wasn't budging.

"I didn't know what was happening exactly, and I couldn't do anything without ruining our cover!"

"I'm sure that's a comfort to his family."

"Easy, Dayne," Maresh said. "We've made plenty of mistakes, all. Look where we are."

"Where are we, exactly?" Hemmit asked.

Maresh answered while Dayne kept kicking. "In the marshals' holding cells. That dead man there was the Chief Marshal. He was also the secret leader of the Patriots. The public leader was that dead man over there."

"Who killed them?" Hemmit feared he knew the answer.

"The Chief killed Lannic," Dayne said. "And then Tharek killed the Chief. And probably everyone else who got in his way." Another kick.

Hemmit rubbed his head. "Dayne, please stop that. You aren't doing any damn good."

"We've tried everything else," Dayne said. He kicked again. "Tharek took the keys, no one responded to our calls."

"It's an iron door!" Hemmit said. "You can't—"

"Maybe I can't," Dayne said. "But I have to do something."

"There's nothing you can do," Maresh said. "Just like that Bridge thing."

Dayne stopped his kicking, and laughed. "That's not the lesson from the Question of the Bridge, Maresh. The coward does nothing, doesn't turn the switch, because he doesn't want to get involved."

This sounded familiar. The Question of the Bridge was something Hemmit had read in his philosophy classes before he dropped out of the Royal College.

"So that's the answer?" Maresh asked. "You pull the switch?"

"The logician pulls the switch," Dayne said. "He calculates that one life lost is better than five, and accepts that."

Dayne stepped back and slammed his whole body against the door.

"A Tarian doesn't accept that."

He slammed his body into the door again.

"A Tarian doesn't accept one choice or the other, that someone *has* to die."

Another slam that made the whole cell vibrate.

"The only answer is you run like blazes, you jump on that track, you do everything in your power to stop that cart and save every life."

Dayne threw himself at the cell door, and with a horrible crack, it flew open.

"Because you're a goddamned Tarian, and that's what we do."

Dayne wanted to do more for Lannic and Marshal Chief Toscan. Even if this entire mess was their fault, it was unseemly to just leave their bodies unattended and festering in this cell.

"How is Jerinne?" he asked. Maresh checked the girl while Hemmit stumbled to his feet.

With Maresh's prodding, Jerinne mumbled incoherently, and she seemed to be approaching consciousness.

"Where are we going?" Hemmit asked.

"For now, just out." Dayne indicated out of the holding chamber. "You two help carry Jerinne. And stay back."

He didn't want to look at Hemmit. He knew that the man hadn't betrayed him, that he had meant well trying to find out more about the Patriots. But that didn't change the fact that he failed, and people died.

Like you failed Lenick Benedict, a voice drove through his head. *Like you failed Master Denbar.*

Dayne drove those thoughts to the back of his skull as he went into the next room, fearing the horror he was about to see.

It was even worse.

The floor was littered with dead marshals. At least eight, but the bodies were in such a state that there may have been more. Dayne was shocked that Tharek—that any Spathian—was capable of slaughter on this level. He had read some of the stories about Oberon Micarum, The Warrior of the Grand Ten, that he had always presumed were legend and exaggeration. Seeing this, so many marshals—not common folk, but trained peacekeeping officers—killed with such precision, such mastery, Dayne started to believe those legends were true.

Tharek was clearly a Master Spathian in skill, even though he never advanced beyond Candidate. Dayne wasn't sure if he could possibly match that skill. Sholiar had tested his patience, his judgment, and even his wits, but never pure fighting arts. He had defeated Dayne with trickery. Tharek, on the other hand, was an open book. He was pure righteous anger and martial skill.

Dayne knew perfectly well how a Candidate who had failed as much as he had might never make Adept. But this man?

Dayne looked back to the door, where Maresh and Hemmit had just brought Jerinne through. Both of them looked like they were about to throw up.

"This is my fault," Hemmit said. "I could have done more. Been a man, like you are."

"Don't hold me up as some paragon, Hemmit. I've made more than my share of mistakes."

"Well, I'm not making any more," Hemmit said.

"Can we please move on?" Maresh asked. "I can't be in here any longer."

They left the chamber and were in a hallway, presumably leading to the Parliament, definitely the path taken by Tharek. The trail of dead made that clear. The hallway branched off the other way, which led back to the church.

"You two get Jerinne out of here. Get her to a hospital ward, get the Tarians. Get her safe."

"You're going after Tharek?" Hemmit asked. "You shouldn't go alone."

"I should, I have to." Dayne put his hands on the two newsmen's shoulders. "If you come, Tharek will try to kill you to distract me. I cannot fight him while having someone there to protect. My only chance against him is to be committed to the fight."

"All right," Hemmit said. "I just feel we should do something else . . ."

"Just get the truth out there, Hemmit. That's what you do."

Dayne approached Jerinne's limp form and cradled the girl's head in his hands. Jerinne opened her eyes, but it didn't seem as if she was really looking at Dayne.

"If you see anyone from my Order, Hemmit, tell them . . . tell them I said she has the heart of a Tarian."

"Get after him," Maresh said. "And may the saints walk with you."

"And with you," Dayne called, charging down the hallway.

Around two more corners there was another scene of carnage, but not a fresh one. These bodies had been there for almost an hour. No one had gotten a chance to take care of them yet. Things were even worse than Dayne thought. One of the dead was a Parliamentarian, that was clear from the clothes. Seabrook, Jerinne's charge. Were there more dead Parliamentarians upstairs now? Was Tharek cutting through them like a whirlwind of death?

Jerinne's shield and sword were on the ground by the bodies. Dayne took them up and strapped on the shield. It was his Trials shield, he knew it by the weight, by the balance. This shield was an old friend.

Another pair of bodies were marshals, and they both wore belts with sets of irons and keys. He would need those irons. Tharek would not come easily or quietly. Dayne undid the belts from the bodies, giving a brief prayer to Saint Julian as he did so. Individually, the belts were too small to get around his waist, but he connected them to each other and wore it like a bandolier.

Dayne made his way up the spiral stairs to the Parliament level, terrified of what he'd find.

"You have no right to step down here!"

The voice echoed through Amaya's ears, her head hot and wet. Blood. The memory of a hand on the back of her head, being smashed onto the desk, all came flooding back.

She reached for her head, to see how bad the injury was. Her hand didn't come, caught on the chair she was sitting in. Not caught. She craned her neck, and saw the truth. She was ironed to the seat at the wrists and ankles.

She looked up to the Parliament floor. The Parliamentarians were all in their chairs, save the old man at the podium. But there was one more man, in a bloody marshal's uniform.

"No right?" the man said. "What is a free Druth man, but for his rights? They are enshrined, the Rights of Man. Can you recite them, Mister Cotton?" He pointed to one of the men.

"I . . . I'm not Cotton," the Parliamentarian stammered. He pointed to one of his neighbors. "That's Cotton."

The bloody marshal drew a knife and threw it into Cotton's chest faster than anyone could blink.

Amaya attempted to jump to her feet, but the chair didn't budge, and she only pulled at her chains with the few inches of movement she was given.

On the floor no one moved, save nervous shifting. Amaya couldn't believe it. There were more than fifty of them, and some had served in the military. They could stop him, if they only tried.

The man walked in a circle, another knife drawn. Now Amaya saw his face. The same one she squared against briefly when she caught Lannic.

"I know you," she called.

"And I you," he replied. "But now is not your time. I considered rare punishments for you. But I should not blame the hammer for the will of the carpenter."

He walked to the podium, and with a glare made the old man vacate his position.

"This session is still in order, is it not? The convocation has not yet disbanded?"

"No," one member offered.

"Can someone answer me this, whoever is the expert on the rules: there must be a call to end the session, by whoever holds the podium. Am I correct?"

"You are," the same Parliamentarian said.

"And if I hold it, no one can end the session. These are the rules. The floor is frozen."

"Not for you, you aren't a Parliamentarian—"

"Unless I claim the Right of Voice! Do you hear that, you ardent onlookers up there? A *common* man is claiming Right of Voice, and taking the podium! Is that how it works? Can anyone tell me?"

The member who had been answering his questions stood from his chair, but made no threatening moves toward the bloody marshal, the mad Patriot. "It's unorthodox, especially after murdering one of the august body."

"But allowed, yes?" The Patriot tapped the knife on the podium. "It's all so very civilized. Rules and order and the civility of tradition."

He had at least four more knives on his belt, as well as a sword. No one else on the floor was armed. Even if they tried to take him, he could kill several before he was subdued. Clearly none of them were willing to take that chance.

Brute force would not get her out of these irons, not without more noise than she could afford. So she had to use determination instead. She pulled her left thumb in as tight as she could. If she could force her hand small enough, she might squeeze out.

"Now, I will not apologize for Mister Cotton, the Good Man of Scaloi. Nor will I for Misters Parlin, Yessinwood, or Seabrook."

"That was you?" another asked.

"I have the podium, and you have not been recognized, sir. Name!"

The man gasped, and shut his mouth.

"I asked you for your name, good sir. It would be rude not to give it."

"Tellerson. Renwick Tellerson, 6th Chair of Patyma."

"Sixth Chair. Very impressive. You must have been elected, what, twice?"

"Three times," Tellerson said, his face turning paler and paler. "I stand for election again this year."

"And you will probably win, won't you, Mister Tellerson? It's a safe bet?"

"I'm not . . ." Tellerson started quickly, but then his throat caught. "I'm not worried about it," he finally managed.

Amaya twisted her wrist back and forth. Her hand had slipped partly through the iron. Not enough to be free, but a start. Her skin was rubbing raw; she could feel the blood oozing. Pain didn't matter, in her wrists or her head. Only freedom, stopping this man.

The mad Patriot chuckled. "Someone with more patience than I will have to look into how often a Chair is truly unseated in election. Our very fair and considerable system, where the voice of the people is truly heard."

"Do you have a point, young man?" one said, rising from his chair. Amaya knew him by reputation: Montrose. He limped forward toward the mad Patriot. "If you're just here for the murder, I'd appreciate you getting to it."

The mad Patriot chuckled. "This one may be worth more than the other ninety-nine. Sorry, ninety-five. I don't need a point, good sir. I have the podium, and I'm using my voice. This is my right. I am going to voice my opinion. This is my right. I will not be incarcerated without trial or counsel. This is my right." He flipped the knife in his hand. "And I am armed, to ensure that my rights are not easily neglected. This is my right as well."

Amaya had a few choice words in reply, but the last thing she needed right now was to draw his attention to her. Another minute or two, she could be out, and then she could take action. She had held him off before, with Lannic in the crook of her arm. She could take him now.

"Does any member of this august body challenge these rights of mine?" the Patriot asked. After no response, he shouted, "Do you?"

The Parliament gave him silence. Even Montrose only nodded in assent.

"Your silence fascinates me, good sirs. This tells me you think you believe in those words, these rights. But you do not, and this lesson must be imprinted on your very flesh."

The irons dug into Amaya's hand. She kept twisting, flesh be damned.

Each step was a shot, and pain became a familiar companion, knocking Jerinne into her senses. She had been vaguely aware of being in the cell, of Dayne being there, of shouting and blood.

Tharek. Shouting. Blood.

"Where?" she asked, glancing around. She was in a hallway not unlike the one she had fought Tharek in, her arms draped over the shoulders of two men. Dayne's newsmen friends from that Nimble Rabbit place.

"It's all right, Jerinne," one of them said. Hemmit, the vivacious one. "We're getting you out of here."

"Out of where? I don't . . . Where is Dayne?"

"Dayne . . . Dayne went after Tharek."

"Alone?"

The quiet one, Maresh, answered. "He said it was best."

"No, no," Jerinne said. "We have to go with him."

"He didn't want that. He wanted you out of here."

"Blazes to that!" Jerinne wrenched herself away from the two of them, forcing herself to turn around and walk back. She couldn't put her foot on the ground.

"Jerinne, you can't even walk!"

"Then get me a crutch and a shield!"

She dropped to her good knee, and started to crawl. She was a Tarian, and she'd be damned if she let herself be carried out while there was still trouble.

"Dayne's going to kill us," Hemmit said, picking Jerinne up. They helped her onto her foot and limped her back toward the Parliament.

"Never," Jerinne said. "That's the one thing he'd never do."

That's why she had to go back, because no matter what, Dayne wouldn't kill Tharek.

So Jerinne was going to have to.

Chapter 25

THE TRAIL OF DEAD led through the outer ring of
the Parliament halls. Tharek was thorough, not a
marshal or other functionary was left alive. There was no
one for Dayne to save.

Had Tharek left the building, or gone to the Parliament floor? That was the next question. Outside there
might still be a riot, but there might be order and help.
Help that Dayne could trust? Or just more people he'd
put in danger?

Enough marshals were dead. Enough people had
died, and Dayne wouldn't allow another person to die
because he failed.

"Do you?" The voice reverberated from the Parliament floor. Unmistakable. Tharek.

Dayne resisted the urge to charge in. Care had to be
taken. Assess the situation, then act.

He pushed open one door, quiet as possible. Thank
the saints the facilities had been designed to allow functionaries to slip in and out without disturbing procedure.

The Parliamentarians, those who were present, were mostly seated in their chairs. One was dead, under the Scallic flag. Another—Montrose, the trenchant Populist—was on his feet, staring down Tharek, who desecrated the parliamentary podium with his presence.

The gallery was nearly empty, save a few terrified on-lookers. Pressmen, given how they were scribbling notes.

One other presence was noteworthy: Amaya was among the functionary desks, her head wet with blood, arms bound behind her. She struggled with her binds, but her eyes were locked onto Tharek. She hadn't spotted Dayne.

She strained again. Dayne could see that she was ironed, with the same marshal's irons Dayne was carrying. Irons that were likely unlocked with the same key.

Amaya was help Dayne could trust, if he could get her free.

Tharek spoke again. "Your silence fascinates me, good sirs. This tells me you think you believe in those words, these rights. But you do not, and this lesson must be imprinted on your very flesh." He glanced toward the Lacanja flag, which was fortunately on the opposite side of the circle from Dayne. "I have had quite enough of you imposing yourselves upon me. Which one of you is Benedict?"

The Lacanjans—there were only three present—looked perplexed, but one of them raised his hand. A young man. Dayne didn't know which Benedict he was.

Suddenly everything Tharek wanted, and why he wanted it, became clear to Dayne. The illumination of it was almost blinding.

Tharek's hand went to a knife at his belt. Dayne had no time to waste. He leaped down the stairs, while throwing out his shield out in front of the Benedict. With his other hand, he grabbed one of the sets of keys from the bandolier and threw it at Amaya. He prayed he threw true, with both hands.

Tharek's knife flew true, right toward Benedict's heart, and would have killed him. The blade collided into the shield and both skittered to the ground.

Tharek spun on his heel to Dayne, sword drawn. "I thought it would be the girl."

Dayne's own sword was out. "That's not the Benedict you want, Tharek."

Tharek's eyes narrowed. "What do you mean?"

"Four Benedicts sit in the Parliament. I believe that one is Jude."

"Samuel!" the Parliamentarian offered, his voice cracking as he said it.

From the corner of his eye, Dayne could see the keys had landed on Amaya's desk. She picked them up with her mouth. Dayne had to keep Tharek's eyes on him.

"How do you know which Benedict I want dead?" Tharek asked. "Maybe I want them all dead."

"You want Wesley Benedict because he heads the committee that approves advancement to Adept. For both Tarians and Spathians." Tharek's face twitched just enough to tell Dayne he was right. "Parlin, Yessinwood, Seabrook, and him right there, I would imagine." Dayne pointed to the dead man on the floor.

"Cotton," Tharek said, almost haunted.

"They were the committee? The five of them decided that you were not to be a Spathian."

"And now I decide that they are not Parliamentarians!" Tharek drew another knife with his left hand, still holding out the sword with his right. "Is my choice any less just?"

"They didn't kill you."

"Please, Tarian," Tharek said. "You're a Candidate. If one of these . . . fools decided for whatever useless reason that you were not fit to be an Adept, wouldn't it kill you? It would rip your heart right out of your chest."

The truth surely played over Dayne's face. "It has."

Samuel Benedict perked up. "You're the one who—"

He was cut off by a glare from Tharek.

"Did you fail, Tarian?" The sword stayed pointed at Dayne, casually, while his eyes glanced around the room. "Did you fail to save someone important, and they're punishing you for it?"

"I failed," Dayne said. He took a step closer. "But the importance of the person doesn't matter. I failed just the same."

"At least you have a reason!"

"You might have one as well," Dayne said. "Did you ask any of the dead men?"

"There is no reason for me, Tarian. I was the top man each year of my Initiacy. My skills are without parallel."

Dayne stepped closer. "So you're sure that's it? The committee blocked you for . . . nothing?"

One of the younger members of Parliament—possibly one of the former army officers—chose this moment to make a move, jumping for the podium to tackle Tharek. It was utterly fruitless. Tharek's left arm struck like a snake, locking around the man's head in a second. The rest of his body barely moved, sword still pointed at Dayne. With a slight twist of the hand, the knife was now pressing right below the man's eye.

"Without. Parallel."

"I don't question that," Dayne said.

"No closer, Dayne," Tharek said. "Do you want to fail again? In front of this assembled august body?"

Dayne shook his head. A thin red line formed on the Parliamentarian's cheek, blood oozing down the blade.

"Then drop your sword, or this good sir loses an eye. To start."

Dayne put the sword on the ground.

"You fool!" Benedict shouted. "Is that what you did when Lenick's life was on the line?"

"Quiet!" Dayne snapped. He didn't need anyone here second-guessing him. He needed to keep Tharek focused on him.

"And the irons," Tharek said. "Drop the belt."

Dayne removed that and put it on the floor as well.

"You there. Good sir from Monim. Pick up those irons, and be so kind as to use them on our Tarian friend."

"Me?" the Parliamentarian asked. Tharek winked at him. Cautiously he got out of his chair and picked up the irons. Dayne held out his hands.

"It's fine," Dayne told him.

The Parliamentarian mouthed something. "Should I fake it?" was what Dayne understood.

"No tricks, my good man," Tharek said. "Latch them on."

The Parliamentarian did so, well-latched and tight.

"Back to your comfortable chair, my good man. Back to it."

The man skittered off.

"Now, the podium recognizes Dayne, of the Tarian Order. Please, step forward."

Dayne paused for a moment. The floor was only for members of Parliament. Tharek was desecrating that, of course, but Dayne still believed that propriety ought to be held. The floor was sacrosanct for a reason. Elected men made decisions from here. They represented the people.

"Step forward now, Dayne. None of your reverence for the office or the floor."

Dayne stepped down to the floor, but only because there was a life at stake. That allowed it. Certainly none of the Parliamentarians were objecting to his presence.

"Come closer and kneel before the podium."

Dayne followed the orders. He didn't dare glance over at Amaya, to see if she had managed to free herself. Even a turn of his eye might make Tharek look in her direction. He was counting on her to stop Tharek when the moment came. He just had to give her time and opportunity.

"Is this what it means to be a Tarian?" Tharek asked.

"You give up everything: arms, principles, pride, just to save the eye of an 'important' man?"

"You're wrong, Tharek," Dayne said. "I would do it for any man. Even you."

"Ludicrous." Tharek flicked his wrist, and blood gushed from the man's face as he dropped to the ground, screaming.

"The first person who moves to help him gets this knife in his chest!" Tharek shouted. "Do not doubt me!"

"No one here doubts you," Dayne said. He needed to buy more time still, since Amaya hadn't made her move yet. Keep him talking. "So now I'm kneeling before the great Tharek Pell, unjustly ousted from the Spathians, unarmed and bound. What more could you want?"

"Pell?" It was Samuel Benedict who asked. "As in Lord Gilbert Pell, Duke of Oriem?"

The twitch on Tharek's face spoke multitudes. "We will not say that name here, good sir."

"Suits me fine," Benedict said. "Man's a right bastard."

The knife flew from Tharek's hand, but he didn't throw to kill. Instead it sliced the side of Benedict's face, tearing through his left ear. Tharek laughed. "That explains how easily he could recognize me, bastard son of his youngest daughter."

"There's your reason, Tharek," Dayne said. "Benedicts hate your family."

Tharek turned back to Dayne. "You know, ever so briefly, I saw you as a kindred spirit. But seeing you debase yourself before me, as you said, bound and defenseless . . . well, now you just disgust me."

"I said I'm unarmed, Tharek," Dayne said, smiling at him. "But I'm a Tarian."

Tharek's sword shot forth to run Dayne through. Almost any other man would have been killed. Dayne had popped onto his feet and stepped to one side. With the chain of his irons, he parried the blade and pushed it away from his body.

"I'm never defenseless."

Tharek twisted the blade, but Dayne kept the irons between it and his flesh. He slid the chain down the blade and hooked it onto the hilt. With a sharp pull, he jerked the sword from Tharek's hands.

Dayne took an elbow in the face in response. Tharek came up with another knife. He brought it in close to Dayne's belly, but Dayne was able to pull away, grabbing Tharek's wrist. He tried to pull Tharek and twist him around, but he was hampered by the shackles. Tharek used Dayne's maneuver, flipping over and kicking Dayne in the face.

Dayne fell back, taking Tharek with him. Tharek's knife found purchase in Dayne's arm. Dayne let himself scream, and pushed Tharek off of him before he could do further damage.

Dayne hopped onto his feet as Tharek did the same.

"Imagine how good you'd be if you weren't bound," Tharek said.

Dayne pulled at the chains of his irons. That alone gave Tharek pause. Straining his powerful arms, Dayne put everything he had into that moment. For the Order, for Master Denbar, for the four dead members of Parliament. He would not be defeated again, not today. Not by Tharek and not by a few links of metal.

The chain snapped.

"Imagine," Dayne replied. "Gentlemen, the podium is clear."

Tharek's face fell, and he charged back to the podium. Dayne tackled him and the two of them went barreling into the flagpole, knocking it down.

One member ran to the podium, and in a racing voice shouted, "If there are no objections from the august body, the session is ended, we are adjourned, this convocation of the Parliament has ended. We are in recess until after the next elections."

Men leaped from their seats like arrows from a bow

and ran up the stairs in every direction. Tharek howled and drew his last two knives, going after the closest ones. Before he could throw them Dayne was on his feet with the Druth flagpole in hand. Spinning it over his head, he brought the head of the pole into Tharek's chest, the flag fluttering over the man's face. Tharek was knocked off his feet. Before he hit the ground, Dayne whipped the pole around and brought it down from above, forcing Tharek to land flat on his back. The knives clattered on the floor, and the flag draped across Tharek's chest while he wheezed for air.

Despite worrying about dishonoring the flag, Dayne leaped onto it and Tharek, pinning him under it.

Tharek strained at the flag, but with Dayne keeping the cloth tight against his body, he couldn't move at all.

"And now you kill me, Tarian?"

"Never," Dayne said. "You have the right to be tried, remember?"

A boot came crashing into Tharek's head, knocking him senseless. Dayne looked up to see Amaya standing over them, holding up three sets of irons.

"What did you do that for?" Dayne asked.

"I owed him. Besides, how else are we going to get him into these? I doubt he'd go quietly."

Chapter 26

AMAYA WAS FAR TOO overzealous in chaining
Tharek. His arms were wrapped across his body and
then chained from behind, so he had no way to move
them at all. She took off his stockings and put them over
his hands so he couldn't use his fingers. They double-
chained his legs, so he wouldn't be able to do anything
but shuffle. She even removed his belt and strapped it
around his mouth.

"You're enjoying this far too much," Dayne said as
she added that final touch. He collected his shield and
sword. The rest of the Parliament floor was a mess, including blood and the dead man. This space should be
the heart, the intellectual spirit of Druthal. Instead it was
a slaughterhouse.

"I saw him fight you," Amaya said. "I'm not taking
any chances."

Tharek roused as they were taking him out of the
chamber, and tried to thrash his way out of his bindings.

All this resulted in was falling over. Dayne hauled him back up to his feet.

"That's enough," came a voice from the top of the stairs. Jerinne, holding herself up with a makeshift crutch. She had a crossbow in hand, aimed at Tharek.

"Jerinne," Dayne said. "We've got him. It's fine."

"It's not fine," Jerinne said, her voice and hand trembling. "He's a monster. You think Quarrygate is going to hold him?"

"I don't know," Dayne said. "But that isn't for me to decide."

"You don't have to," Jerinne said. "Just get out of the way."

"Initiate," Amaya said. "That isn't our way."

"So we let him live? The man murdered members of Parliament, countless marshals? Does he need a trial?"

"It doesn't matter if he needs one, Jerinne," Dayne said. He moved in between Jerinne and Tharek. "He gets one. Fair and just."

"You'd shield him? Die for him?"

"Anyone, Jerinne."

Jerinne's hand wavered.

The doors burst open, and the Parliament hall was suddenly flooded with Constabulary and marshals. Yellowshields followed directly after, two going to Jerinne, another to Amaya.

Then two men. One was Grandmaster Orren. The other Dayne didn't know, but he bore himself with composure and dignity, and his uniform marked him as a Spathian. Dayne glanced back at Tharek for the confirmation he was looking for, plain on his adversary's face. This was the Spathian Grandmaster.

The Spathian Grandmaster spoke, a quiet gnarled whisper. "You once asked me, Mister Pell, how it was possible that you had not advanced to the rank of Spathian Adept. Seeing you now, the answer is quite clear."

Tharek's whole body went limp, and Dayne grabbed at his arm. For a moment, Dayne expected it to be some sort of ruse, that Tharek would thrash out in an attempt to escape. But he truly hung low, broken.

Dayne almost regretted gagging him.

Grandmaster Orren stepped forward, coughing uncomfortably, as if he was afraid to interrupt his Spathian counterpart. The Spathian Grandmaster yielded to him.

"Mister Heldrin, I still have much to understand about what has occurred here, and what, exactly, was your role in it. I am deeply troubled, however, that you have had a role at all, as my last recollection was assigning you to the armory. Were you abducted from there?"

"No, sir. I was—"

"And you, Miss Tyrell. When I left, you were the ranking member present."

"I had my own assignment, sir, as you are well aware," Amaya said.

"So Dayne was present when you left? Or were you aware that he had abandoned his duties?"

"I was aware," she said. "In fact, I encouraged it."

"I have much that I must contemplate," he said. "Please, return to the chapterhouse, and . . ." He turned and saw Jerinne, still with the crossbow in hand. Her face was pallid and clammy. "Miss Fendall. You do not look well."

"No, sir," Jerinne said. "I'm in quite a lot of pain."

"Yes," the Grandmaster said lightly, glancing down at Jerinne's leg. "I suspect Mister Heldrin was your field medic. It was always his weak area."

"Is this the moment for humor?" the Spathian Grandmaster asked. He grabbed Tharek by the front of his tunic, and despite his age, pulled the man to him with one hand. "This man has crimes to answer to, and I will attend to it."

"A trial," Dayne said, stepping up to the Grandmaster. He suspected the Spathians would practice swift injustice. "A true, fair trial for him."

The Grandmaster raised an eyebrow to Dayne. "Do you take me for a savage, Tarian? Please do not color my Order by the behavior of this man. He will be treated by all the rights he is due. He is not a Spathian, but he is Druth." He whistled to two of the Constabulary to follow him, and took Tharek out.

"As I said, Mister Heldrin," Grandmaster Orren said, all lightness gone from his voice. "You and Miss Tyrell, return to the chapterhouse. Bring Miss Fendall with you, and have her injuries properly attended. Then the two of you place yourselves in confinement until I attend to you."

"As you have said, sir," Dayne said. He put one arm under Jerinne's shoulder, and Amaya did the same. The Grandmaster was no longer noting them, instead walking around the shattered, desecrated Parliament.

Despite the emergent chaos of Constabulary, marshals, and Yellowshields running around the outer hall of the Parliament, Hemmit had stayed pressed up against the wall, watching the entrance he had led Jerinne to, waiting to see who would emerge. He had shed the ersatz marshal coat, so no one would mistake him for someone who could help out. Maresh had stayed right at his side. Hemmit was still groggy from his head injury, and truly needed time to regain his wits. He didn't know why Maresh stayed there. Perhaps he was afraid to leave Hemmit alone again.

At this time yesterday, Hemmit had been sitting in The Nimble Rabbit, nursing a bottle of wine and contemplating the nature of being a proper man. A romantic notion that involved drinking well, romancing a good woman, and diving into the thick of danger. Now he had had his fill of the thick of danger. It was for men like Dayne. Not that his courage had failed him, but . . .

No, his courage had failed him. He had let himself get

wrapped into the depths of Tharek's madness, of the Patriot's whole plan, because he was afraid to step forth when he needed to. Even Lin had been braver.

Lin! He had no idea what had happened to her. If she had been badly injured, he'd never be able to forgive himself. He was about to go look for her, when four people came out the door. Tharek, being led off by a mighty man, a Spathian Master by his uniform. Two Constabulary followed behind. Tharek caught Hemmit's eye, just for a moment, but his face was unreadable. Did he still see Hemmit as Wissen, his ally, who was still free? Or did he see a traitor, someone who he would have his revenge on?

Hemmit couldn't tell. And that terrified him.

Before he could move, Tharek was gone, presumably to his incarceration. He had been taken alive. That simple fact resonated. Dayne had managed to take Tharek alive. How was that even possible?

Then Dayne came out, half carrying Jerinne, while another Tarian—a dark-haired woman the same age as Dayne—was helping Jerinne on the other side. Hemmit guessed, based on the sketches from yesterday's newssheets, that this was Amaya Tyrell, the Tarian who caught Lannic.

"You're still here," Dayne said. "I thought I told you to get her out of here."

"She was persistent," Maresh said.

"You should have let me kill him," Jerinne said, bitterness dripping from her voice.

"Who, Tharek?" Hemmit asked.

"It's not like he didn't deserve to die," Jerinne said, aiming her invective straight at Dayne.

"Maybe he did," Dayne said. "But that isn't for me to decide, or you. And it certainly isn't ours to act upon."

"Why? Because it would have ruined me? I don't know if you've noticed, but I'm already ruined."

"That isn't true," Amaya said. "That could heal just fine."

"I thought we were warriors!" she shouted. "Just like soldiers in war, we kill the enemy."

"Not if we can help it," Dayne said. "We aren't warriors, Jerinne. Or knights, no matter how often people try to call us that. We're Tarians. That means we save lives. Every life."

Amaya added, "And if we do take a life, it's only if there is no other choice."

Dayne's face showed he didn't agree with her, but he didn't speak on that. "In there, with Tharek already bound and captured, you had all the choices. And that choice would have made you a murderer."

"And a thief," Maresh added.

Everyone was confused by that, Hemmit included.

"Care to explain that?" Jerinne asked.

Maresh pointed to the door Tharek was taken out of. "They've arrested him, right? He'll get tried and sent to Quarrygate, I presume?"

"That's right," Dayne said.

Maresh nodded and looked hard at Jerinne, his thin finger pointing accusatorially at the girl's chest. "If you had killed him, it probably would have felt pretty good. For you. But what about the rest of the city, the rest of the country? After all this, they'll need something to grasp onto, to heal. A trial, that man getting his punishment in public, *by* the public. And a fair punishment, not the barbarous executions of centuries past. That will give people what they need. But you would take it for yourself, selfishly."

Jerinne looked at the lot of them, and then to Dayne. "Can we go back home now? I'm ready to get out of here."

"Come on," Dayne said, and led them all out. Parliament Plaza was in devastation. Many of the people had been cleared out, but there were still remnants of the riot: blood on the stones, shredded banners, torn clothes, and burned carts. There were still small clusters of people, mostly Constabulary and Yellowshields, but also the Parliamentarians, sequestered apart from the rest by a group of marshals, as carriages came to pick them up and shuttle them off to safety.

"There he is!"

A score of people came running over. Hemmit recognized many of them—newsmen from the larger publications. *High Maradaine Gazette. First News Maradaine. Throne and Chairs.*

"You, sir! Tarian! You're the one who stopped the madman who held the Parliament hostage!"

"You seemed to know him. Were the two of you close?"

"How did you know him? How long has he been plotting against the Parliament?"

"Is he responsible for all the horror of the last three days?"

"Are you the same one who fought them in the museum?"

"Please, please!" Dayne shouted. "We have injured people here! This isn't the time!"

"She's the girl from the museum!"

"And that's the one who captured Lannic!"

"Why are the three of you at the center of all of this?"

"Enough!" A woman's voice cut through the din of newsmen from below the stairs, shouted with authority and clarity. It was enough to get them all to be silent, which was quite an impressive feat.

The woman, a blonde beauty, clearly of noble bearing, ascended the stairs with both grace and speed, going directly to Dayne. Looking as if no power in the world could stop her, she leaped up to him, grabbed his face, and kissed him with a passion Hemmit had never seen a woman of noble birth exhibit in public.

The newsmen were all too stunned to react.

She broke from Dayne and turned back to the newsmen, utterly in control, utterly a lady, holding on to

Dayne's hand warmly. "People of the press, I am Lady Mirianne Henson, and I will, for the time being, act as liaison for Mister Heldrin and these other fine people. Mister Heldrin and the others here have been through an immensely traumatic experience, and I ask in the name of dignity that you refrain from pouncing upon them all like a pack of wild dogs. If you require questions answered immediately, I suggest you direct them to the Grandmaster of the Tarian Order, who is inside the Parliament House right now. Further harassment of Mister Heldrin and his associates at this time will result in legal action taken by my estate upon your respective news-sheets. Am I clear?"

"You can't do that!" one of the newsmen—Harns, from *Throne and Chairs*. "We have rights!"

"As does Mister Heldrin." The warmest honey smile emerged. "I'm asking you for patience, nothing more. Isn't a bit of time worth the trouble for the proper story?"

There was a grumbling of agreement.

"Now be off," Lady Mirianne said. "You can contact my valet if you have need for further comment from me."

They all shuffled off, Harns giving Hemmit an ugly scowl as they walked away.

"Thank you, my lady," Amaya said coldly, though the bow of her head was perfectly polite. "If you will excuse us, we must get young Miss Fendall to proper medical care."

"My carriage," Lady Mirianne said, with a snap of her fingers. "That will be the fastest way along."

"As my lady desires," Amaya said. Her tone conveyed the opposite feeling, though Lady Mirianne ignored that.

Dayne hadn't spoken since she arrived, nor had he pulled his hand away from hers. "Thank you," he said quietly as they led Jerinne down the stairs.

"Of course," she said. "I had to do something for you, what little I can."

"It means a lot," he added. "I . . . may be in some trouble with the Order. It may take some time to straighten out."

They arrived at her carriage, waiting near the edge of the plaza. Amaya and Dayne loaded Jerinne in, and she got on the outer runner on the other side without even looking at the rest of them.

Lady Mirianne touched Dayne's face, "However long it takes you, I'll be here." She got in the carriage with Jerinne. Dayne turned to Hemmit and Maresh.

"Are you coming with us?"

"We better not," Hemmit said. "I . . . I still need to find Lin, make sure she's all right. And . . ."

"I understand," Dayne said. He took Hemmit's arm with friendship. "When I can, I'll come to the Rabbit. We'll . . . we'll talk things over, all right?"

"Good," Hemmit said.

Dayne got on the runner and the carriage drove off.

"Are you all right?" Maresh asked once they were alone.

"Nothing two days of sleep and a bottle of wine won't cure," Hemmit said. "As long as Lin is well. Oy, Harns!"

Harns had stayed lurking about within earshot, which didn't surprise Hemmit in the slightest. "Well, well, looks like the little *Veracity* has an inside line. Good friends with Tarians, are we?"

"Leave it be," Hemmit said. "Look, the injured from the riot, where are they? Where'd they get taken?"

Harns shrugged. "Depends on quite a few things. The dead—"

"There's dead?" Maresh asked.

Harns nodded. "A few, they got brought to the church until they can be sorted out, identified. Yellowshields took off the ones who were really bad. Hartfort Ward, I would think. Maybe the RCM Ward. The ones who could walk and weren't ironed up went off on their merry way."

Hemmit went through that list. They'd check the

church for Lin, then Hartfort, and RCM. He silently prayed to a few choice saints that she wouldn't be at the first place.

"So, really, you're in tight with this Tarian?" Harns asked. "Because there's something not right with him, I can tell you that."

"How so?" Maresh asked.

"Just what I saw from up in the galleries. That big guy, Tharek, he's killed one Parliamentarian, threatening the rest, and what does your Tarian friend do? Goes in and talks all nice. Acts like his friend. Puts his weapons down. I'm telling you, something's not right, like a wolf in the barn."

"Dayne's not a wolf in the barn," Hemmit said. "He's—"

"Well, that's for me to find out, hmm? What a real newsman does. I'll be off."

Once he was gone, Hemmit and Maresh walked over to the church. An idea started to gel in Hemmit's head. Sentences were crashing together into arguments, truths he had to tell. He knew what they were going to have to do.

"Once we find Lin, we need to get to our press," he told Maresh. "We've got a lot of work to do."

"Saints know we've got plenty to write for the next issue," Maresh said.

"Not an issue," Hemmit said. His fingers itched with the desire to write down what was percolating in his brain. "I've got something bigger in mind."

Chapter 27

N̲O ONE SPOKE on the ride in Lady Mirianne's carriage to the chapterhouse. Very few people were around when they arrived, save members of the staff and a handful of Initiates. Jerinne was quickly swept up by a few of the staff and brought to the infirmary ward.

Dayne wanted to linger with Lady Mirianne, but Amaya spoke before he could. "We've been ordered to confinement. Given our prior difficulties with following orders, we should comply. Immediately."

"Yes, of course," Dayne said. "Thank you, my lady."

"I am but your servant, noble friend," Mirianne said, bowing with a flourish. She then came up and gave him one more kiss, this one genteel and chaste, as Amaya stared at the two of them. Lady Mirianne then bowed to Amaya. "Madam, I am at your disposal as well."

Amaya nodded back, grim-faced. Mirianne took that with grace and returned to her carriage.

Dayne followed Amaya through the lobby and up the stairs to quarters, Amaya dropping her belt, boots, and tunic along the way. Once he caught up to her, she was in just shirtsleeves and slacks.

"Quite the lady she is. And she is but your servant," Amaya said.

"She has been my friend for a very long time," Dayne replied. As much as he respected Amaya, he didn't feel he should have to justify his relationship with Lady Mirianne to her.

"I'm glad she's there for you, because you're going to need her." Amaya reached her own quarters, and turned on him. "I think we can say with near certainty that you will not be promoted to Adept."

"You're probably right," Dayne said. It had occurred to him that the one man still alive on the Parliament committee was the one who hated him. He looked at her, blood still on her face, stitching and bandage on her forehead. "Shouldn't you go to the infirmary?"

"Yellowshield patched me fine, gave me a dose of something, said to rest. And we were given orders."

"Even still—"

"I'll be getting plenty of rest in confinement. This isn't my first head injury." She held herself in the doorframe. "You know, Master Denbar would have been very proud of you out there today."

"Proud of me breaking orders, letting members of Parliament and who knows how many marshals get killed? I remember a very different man."

"No, I let a member of Parliament get killed," she said. "I was sloppy, got ironed, and was in no position to save anyone. Cotton died right in front of me, and I couldn't do anything."

"I got there as soon as I could," Dayne said. Though he wondered if he had spent too much time talking to Maresh and Hemmit, and not enough time chasing after Tharek.

"And as soon as you got there, no one else died. You arrived, and put down your weapons, and still stopped him. And once you had him, you made sure he stayed alive. If that . . . if that's not a Tarian, I don't know what is."

"I appreciate that you think so." Then he found himself saying something that he didn't know he felt with all his heart until he was saying it. "It doesn't matter, though. Because no matter what a Parliament committee or the Grandmaster decides, they don't change me or who I am. Tharek kept ranting that they had no right to define him, but . . . he let them."

"So you don't want to be an Adept?"

"No, of course I do," Dayne said. "But no matter what happens, I am the man that I am, with the skills that I have, and I'll do whatever I can to help whoever I can." He pointed to her tunic, lying on the ground by her feet. "I don't need them to approve me to be worthy. But the fact that you do . . . that means a lot to me." He started for his quarters, then turned back to her. "Everything I did in there, disarming myself, talking Tharek down . . . I was able to do because I knew you were there. I knew you would free yourself and have my shield."

She looked down at her tunic, and picked it up off the floor. "No matter what either of us is wearing, Dayne . . . I'll always have your shield."

"And I yours."

She smiled one more time—a melancholy, halfhearted smile, and went into her quarters.

Dayne did the same. He could live with not becoming an Adept. However, he wasn't going to tempt fate any further by not going into confinement.

Amaya sat down on her bunk, every part of her body hurting. Dayne was probably right, she should check in with the infirmary. The Yellowshield had treated her head and wrists, and that was probably enough. The sew-ups in the infirmary weren't going to tell her anything new.

Confined to quarters for saving the Parliament. That
was definitely a sign of trouble. She had been feeling that
for a while, but now she was certain. Things were wrong
in the Tarian chapterhouse. Wrong in the Order.

The package had been the tipping point. It had arrived the same day as Dayne, probably on the same boat,
but Dayne clearly knew nothing about it. Perhaps that
was for the best. Presumably, Master Denbar arranged
for it to be sent to her in the event of his death.

She reached under her bunk and pulled out the box,
needing to look at it all again. The box itself was
nothing—an innocuous keepsake box, decorated with
Lacanjan seashells. Chosen because it looked frivolous,
no doubt. It was a lovely box, but what mattered were
the three things inside.

First, the locket. That was there to authenticate everything else. She pulled it out of the box. Simple chain, the
whole thing painted tin and copper. Not remotely valuable. Except she knew it on sight.

Her mother's.

Her mother. Master Denbar's cousin. Their secret.
She insisted that no one in the Order know their relation
to each other, not even Dayne, lest she be considered
favored for reasons that had nothing to do with her skills.

She was already fighting enough battles on that front.

Second, the letter. That had confused her at first. It
started with random nonsense, about the beauty of Lacanja, how much Master Denbar missed her and hoped
for the best in her career. If anyone else read it, they
would find it a testament to how much Master Denbar
cared about her, at least as a student.

Sentimental fluff. Master Denbar would never write
things like that to her. She had seen through that quickly,
and decoded the message he had embedded within it,
hidden in the first letter of every sentence.

*Lacanja is an exile. Be wary. Find them. Stop them.
Save Druthal.*

"Them," she could only presume, was part of the third thing in the box. This, she still hadn't fully understood — it was decidedly odd — but she presumed Master Denbar felt even in this posthumous gift, he had to be careful.

Ten cards from a playing deck. Only the ten high-trump cards. The Grand Ten: The Parliamentarian, The Man of the People, the Lord, The Duchess, The Lady, The Priest, The Soldier, The Justice, The Mage, and The Warrior.

There was a Grand Ten out there, he was saying. Ten people who needed to be found, needed to be stopped.

If he knew more than that, if there was some other clue, she hadn't figured it out yet.

She looked at the cards one more time. They were from an unusual deck, certainly. Rather than the Grand Ten depicted as the explicit Ten from history, they were symbolic icons. Not *The* Parliamentarian, Geophry Haltom, but more the idea of a Parliamentarian. Same for all of them.

Which stood out especially with The Warrior. Not Oberon Micarum. Not a Spathian Master. No specific tunic at all, marking him of any Order. Just a warrior with a sword and shield.

Or shield and sword, she mused.

She put it all away and slid it under her bed. She needed to rest, close her eyes, and think about this when her head was clear.

But for now, share this with no one. Especially not Dayne. Not yet.

There had been medicine for the pain. Jerinne didn't know what it was, but it was certainly glorious. A few minutes after drinking it she no longer felt any pain in her leg. A few after that she no longer felt her legs at all, and she had to force herself to look down and see that they were still there.

"Don't you dare cut it off," she mumbled to the physician.

"That isn't my plan," the physician said. "But plans do sometimes get away from us."

He then took his blade and cut into Jerinne's leg right by the break. Jerinne didn't feel a thing, but it was still a blade cutting her leg. Somehow seeing it but not feeling it was far worse than any pain Tharek had caused her. Jerinne's stomach churned and threatened to leap out her throat until she lay back down.

"Happens every time," the physician chuckled.

Jerinne closed her eyes, and opened them a moment later, but clearly more than a moment had passed, as Raila and Enther were hovering over her.

"When the blazes did you get here?" she asked.

"Been here for a bit," Enther said. "Can't you manage to keep a uniform clean?"

"That wouldn't be any fun."

Raila looked her over with a critical eye. "Your leg is set, and the physician seemed pleased with the work he did. I think you will get to walk again."

"Walk, or fight?"

"I think it's one and the same for you," she snorted. "I doubt I can convince my cousin to work her magic a second time for you."

"It's not a dress uniform," Jerinne mumbled.

"And it's not mine," Vien said. When did she get here? And where did Enther go?

Jerinne laughed, and then looked again, but Vien was gone, as well as Enther. Now her leg was a dull ache, but in a strange way it still wasn't there. Raila had sat next to her. Jerinne was losing time between the moments.

"Clearly I'm not passing Trials," Jerinne said. She wasn't sure why she said it, but with Raila there, it seemed like the thing to say.

"I didn't see you until this morning," Raila said. "You came back in with Heldrin. And I barely saw you then.

Was it a marvelous evening at Lady Henson's household?"

Words poured out of Jerinne, as if she had no idea how not to say them. "The lady's household is amazing. Understated, in its own way, but she has a style that . . . the food was unlike anything, and so much. And the play!"

"There was a play?"

"Strangest thing I ever saw. Some sort of Tsouljan or Kieran version of Whit's history plays, with masks and something else. And then I ended up in the water closet which is where I woke up."

"You slept in the water closet?"

"On the floor."

"Sounds uncomfortable." Jerinne thought she sounded amused about this. Or pleased.

"I think it was. Not quite as uncomfortable as I was a bit ago, though. I mean . . ." She looked down at her leg, now heavily bound and splinted. "That was quite horrible."

"You're going to be fine."

"Fine but out on the street." Raila opened her mouth to protest, but Jerinne interrupted her. Her head was clearing, and her leg throbbed with ache. She liked feeling it, knowing it was real. "Can I pass Trials? I don't think I can, not like this."

"But—"

"But I let a member of Parliament die on my watch?"

"You're just an Initiate! You shouldn't have been put in that position!"

"But I was in that position, Raila! I was given a shield and told to be the one who kept . . . to keep . . . they all . . . five men murdered in front of me. And I was useless!"

"You're still alive."

"Five dead men, and I'm still alive," Jerinne said. "Which makes me the worst Tarian on record."

"I think we might want to check the records," she said.

She smiled, clearly thinking she was joking. Normally, Jerinne would find that charming, even disarming, but at the moment it just annoyed her

"I need to rest," Jerinne said. "You better do the same. You have Trials in the morning."

Chapter 28

FOR THREE DAYS Kemmer had stayed holed up in a dingy dockside inn, sharing a room with Braning and Gillem. Yand had been killed in the riot, Kemmer wasn't even sure how. Wissen and Jala, those two... Kemmer and Braning had managed to get them out of harm's way when the riot first started, but then lost track of them both. And Jala, especially, was more than she let on. A mage. Probably a spy from Druth Intelligence. Which meant so was Wissen. Unless he was as much of a dupe as everyone else. Could Druth Intelligence do that? Make a man believe he had a sister? Kemmer had heard stories of things like that. Maybe it was true. He wanted to believe Wissen was a good sort. But last he had seen, the man's skull had been cracked, and he was taken below when Tharek went down there.

Tharek. Kemmer wasn't sure what to think of that man. The newssheets had made him the story, like he was the voice of the Patriots. Perhaps because he was the one who held the Parliament hostage with nothing but a blade and his own force of personality. Kemmer was amazed he had been taken alive.

Lannic was dead. The newssheets made that much clear, but there was still a lot of mystery as to what exactly happened. "Investigation" was a key word used. "Inquiry." "The full details are still being explored." It stank of cover-up, which it surely was. Four members of Parliament were dead, by Tharek's hand, but the rest was unclear. And even though the Parliament was the victim of Tharek's crimes, the public's distrust of the whole august body was at a new high.

To that degree, Lannic's goal was achieved. He might have even considered that martyring himself for that was worth it. Kemmer didn't think so. He'd far rather return to the life he had a few weeks ago, sharing coffee and ideas with his friend.

If Tharek was naming names or giving secrets away, there had been no sign of it. They had spent the three days convinced that Constabulary or marshals or Intelligence was going to kick down the door at any moment. Gillem had ventured out from time to time, picking up newssheets and checking out other things. The inn was their last resort, after they attempted to return to Tharek's safehouse. Tharek had locked the blasted thing down when they left, and none of them could figure out how to open up the secret doors.

But three days came and went, and they remained unmolested.

"I'm going back home," Gillem said on the evening of the third day. "If they even had a clue about us still being out and about—or cared—they'd have swarmed the place by now. Ain't anyone even sniffing around it."

"You're sure?" Kemmer asked.

"I got neighbors I trust. If sticks were looking, they'd tell me. And keep their traps shut. And I'm sick of smelling the two of you."

"That's the truth," Kemmer said, looking over to

Braning. Braning had been pretty quiet the whole time. Kemmer hadn't heard a word out of him all day.

"But what are we going to do next?" Gillem asked. "Lie low some more, or start something else up?"

"I'm not starting anything," Braning said. "I've had my fill of this mess."

"After everything we've already been through?" Gillem asked.

"Especially," Braning said. "I've lost friends. I've lost a brother. I'm lucky to be alive and not in Quarrygate. That's enough."

"But—"

"What were we fighting for, Gillem? Freedom? So respect mine. I'm out."

"What about you, Kemmer?"

Kemmer wasn't sure what to say, but he was leaning toward Braning's idea. For the past three days he thought he was looking down a stint at Quarrygate as well. Freedom, that might just be the thing. "I'd hate to think Lannic died for nothing. That all of what we did was for nothing."

Braning shrugged. "I'm wondering if we accomplished anything at all, besides putting the city on edge and starting a riot."

"That was something!" Gillem argued.

"Something that nearly got us all killed. Blazes, it got poor Yand killed."

Braning shook his head. "You know what Yand was? He was a fool spoiling for a brawl, and nothing else. Blast, Tharek wasn't much more, except he knew how to give a good brawl."

"What that man did wasn't a brawl." Just as Kemmer had expected the authorities to break their door down, he had expected Tharek to suddenly burst in and drop them in seconds. He imagined that no matter how long he lived, he would always be looking over his shoulder for Tharek to show up.

"We need a plan," Gillem said.

"My plan is go back to my life before I got into all this," Braning said. "I don't need much more. You go back to your nonexistent pub, I'll go back to working the tunnels, and Kemmer, you'll . . . do whatever you did."

What he had done, what he had been doing, was spend the months after getting his Letters of Mastery arguing philosophy with Lannic and spending family money on coffee and books. He hadn't been cut off only because he wasn't being a drunken lout. His father had no idea how radical his politics had become.

He picked up the pile of newssheets that they had collected over the past few days. "I think we had the right idea before the museum and the rest of the business Tharek got us into. Wissen—if he was Wissen and not a spy or what have you—he asked why we didn't get our manifesto published. I think we let ourselves get mad at the people for not doing what we thought they should. But they didn't understand what our message was. We failed to deliver it, and maybe that's the thing I've got to do."

"So you're still in?"

"I'm not sure what 'in' means to you, Gillem," Kemmer said. "If you mean attacks, murder, disruption . . . no, I'm not in. But spreading a message, talking to people, changing minds . . . I think that's what I need to be doing."

"What about the Chief?"

"We don't even know who the Chief is. Or was. Or what his goals even were. If there are more Patriots out there, waiting to hear from him, I want no part of that. The violence came from him, or maybe Tharek, and that poisoned Lannic's ideas. That's not what I want. I don't want to hide. I want to stand in the public square and convince people of what they need. What Druthal needs."

"Bah," Gillem said. "Sounds like you're going to run for Parliament."

"There are worse ideas," Braning said. "I'd vote for you."

There were worse ideas. But for the time being, he didn't want to be a Parliamentarian. Or a Warrior or a Soldier. He wanted to be a Man of the People.

"One thing at a time," Kemmer said, getting up off the bed. "And first thing is to get to a barber and a bathhouse, and clean myself up. And from there, I'll figure the rest out."

Gillem shrugged, and offered his hand. "All right. But if you need a place to hide, or just something to drink, you know where I am."

"I appreciate that," Kemmer said.

Gillem nodded to Braning and left the room. Kemmer gathered up his few things—mostly papers—and put them in a satchel, as Braning put his boots and vest on. Kemmer waited for Braning to be ready, and they left together.

"Listen, Kemmer," Braning said as they headed down to the inn's taproom. "I know I'm just a tunnel steve, not much learning, but . . ."

"But nothing," Kemmer said. "You're one of the brightest folks I know."

"I appreciate that. What I'm saying, if this is the path you're taking, talking and changing minds, well . . . that's something I can believe in. If you need help once you figure out what you're doing . . . look for me."

"Always," Kemmer said, and embraced his one real friend left in the world. They walked out of the inn, and with a final nod, they walked their separate ways.

"Get it good, get it good!" a newsboy shouted at the corner Kemmer approached. "No newssheet, no pamphlet, but a full accounting! The full true story! Three ticks for it all!"

"What's the truth you've got, boy?" Kemmer asked, pulling some coins from his pocket. The boy held up what he was hawking. Indeed, it wasn't a newssheet, but a small book, simply bound. Not unlike a chiller or a pennyheart. When he saw the cover, Kemmer wordlessly handed the coins over and took the book from the boy.

The cover was a sketch, simple but well-rendered, of a man. Plain, but noble at the same time. It was a face Kemmer recognized very well, even if he had only seen it for a moment before the owner had smacked Kemmer's head against Braning's.

The book was titled *Dayne, of the Tarian Order.*

Trials were spread over three days, but Jerinne had spent them in the infirmary. She had tried to get up, to force herself to the practice room where the Trials were occurring, but she was thwarted. First the infirmary staff kept her in bed, under the threat of being sent over to Hashrow Ward if she didn't comply. When that didn't work, a few of the Candidates—Price and Aldric, mainly—would come in and impress upon her the importance of rest, and made it quite clear that she should not arrive for Trials until called upon.

"You don't just stroll in there and declare you're doing your Trials," Aldric said on the second day. "When they want you, they'll call for you." Other than one quick, strongly worded warning from a Master who Jerinne had never seen before, those two were about the only ones she saw once Trials began. None of the other Initiates. What really surprised her was that Dayne hadn't come. Probably because he was ashamed of Jerinne.

"They're going to call for me, though, right?"

"I don't know what's going on, kid," Price said. Jerinne had to admit, it was a bit odd the way these two were talking to her. Last week, they barely had said a word to her that wasn't an order or an insult. That had changed—really it had changed the night at the Talon. Something had changed in them both that night, definitely, but also in how they looked at her. Now they talked to her, if not as a peer, at least with some respect. "This year is the strangest set of Trials and Advancement I've ever seen. A whole lot of whispering and secrecy. And lockdown."

"Lockdown?" Jerinne asked. "What's that?"

"The Grandmaster is forbidding anyone under the rank of Master—in other words, just about everyone—from leaving the compound."

"Why?"

"Because he's the Grandmaster, and that's what he wants," Aldric offered. "I think it's because of everything crazy that's happened, he wants to remind us all that he gives the orders and we follow. Blazes, there's the whole thing with Heldrin and Tyrell."

"What happened to Dayne?" Jerinne asked.

"The two of them have both been in confinement this whole time."

"Still?" That was surprising. Perhaps they were in worse trouble than Jerinne suspected. She couldn't imagine that Dayne was receiving anything but praise for what he did.

"Meals brought to their quarters. Not that it's much different for the rest of us."

On the third day, when they came to see her, something had changed. It took a moment for Jerinne to realize it, but the pips on Aldric's uniform had changed. He was now an Adept.

"I see congratulations are in order," Jerinne said. By this time the pain in her leg was mostly an annoying ache, and the infirmary staff had let her crutch her way to the water closet on her own. She had been refusing the pain-dulling medicines for the past two days, as she didn't want her thoughts any cloudier.

"This guy," Price said, pointing to Aldric. "He was convinced he wouldn't get it."

"I thought it would be you," Aldric said. Jerinne noticed that Price's pips were gone, no rank at all. He hadn't advanced, and his three years of Candidacy were at an end. His face didn't betray any bitterness toward Aldric; he just smiled and shrugged. Despite all the hardship Price had put her through for the past two years, Jerinne empathized with Price. The two of them might both be leaving the chapterhouse by the end of the day.

"Who else?" Jerinne asked. Aldric shrugged and deferred to Price, who rattled off names, none of which were familiar. When pressed, Price admitted most of the rest were from chapterhouses elsewhere in Druthal.

"But not Dayne?" Jerinne asked once the list was given.

"No," Price said.

"Between us and the walls, I was convinced he'd have gotten it this year," Aldric said, rubbing at the Adept pip on his collar. "Having this before him just feels strange, given how he dominated during Initiacy."

"Some folks peak early," Price said darkly. "But we didn't come here for this, kid."

"Come with us," Aldric said. "You've been called to Trials."

Aldric and Price let her dress, even if she could get only one boot on. They didn't try to help her, which Jerinne took as a sign of respect. It was the last thing she wanted. Jerinne had hoped to walk with just a cane, but she couldn't manage it. The two of them waited while she got her crutch—only one, though. She refused to use two crutches. She was going to go into the Trials with some degree of dignity.

Jerinne made it to the practice room, where Price and Aldric left her at the door. Jerinne worked her way across the floor, ignoring the growing pain in her hindered leg. On the far side of the room was a table where five Tarians sat: the Grandmaster, two Masters, and two

Adepts. All of them Jerinne vaguely recognized, as they had all handled some aspect of training over the past year, but none of them had been fixtures at the chapterhouse.

"Miss Fendall," the Grandmaster said. "I trust your recuperation has been proceeding at an acceptable pace."

"I'm eager to continue and serve, sir," Jerinne said.

"Yes, I'm sure. Typically over the course of Trials, we do engage you in testing your martial skills. However, given your unique circumstances, we shall not be doing as such."

"Sir, I am willing to—"

"I am certain you are, Miss Fendall. But there is a difference between testing an Initiate and torturing them. We shall forgo." His voice was gentle, but filled with finality.

"Of course, sir," Jerinne said.

"Now, your circumstances are unique, as you have been placed in a position most unusual for a second-year Initiate. This was not fair to you, but it has served a useful purpose. We have some sense of the sort of Tarian you would make."

Jerinne tensed up. The sort of Tarian she would make, based on her performance, is the sort that got her charges killed.

Grandmaster Orren was digging through some papers. "We have, of course, some eyewitness reports of your activities in the events of the past week. Some from newssheets, some from Madam Tyrell and others. But the most interesting one is this, delivered to me from Grandmaster Kothrian of the Spathian Order."

Jerinne didn't know what to say to this.

"He has several things to say. Did you actually visit the Spathian Chapterhouse the other day?"

"I did, sir. Mister Heldrin and I were looking into a hunch that he had regarding . . ."

"Yes, yes," the Grandmaster said. "Apparently one of the Masters used you for sparring practice for her Initiates. Is this accurate?"

"Yes, sir." Jerinne had a distinct sense she shouldn't offer more than yes or no answers unless asked to elaborate.

"It says here that, and I quote, 'While Miss Fendall was clearly unprepared to defend herself from an onslaught of Spathian Initiates, she handled this impromptu lesson with grace and good humor, ably showing skill and aptitude worthy of your order.'"

That was surprising. "I'm glad to hear that, sir."

"There is more. Apparently there was also some form of interrogation of Tharek Pell, which my Spathian counterpart was present for. He is loath to share salient details of this testimony, but he did pass this small morsel along." The Grandmaster held up the sheet of paper and cleared his throat. "'The girl fought on, refusing to accept her failure.'"

Jerinne wasn't sure if that was a compliment or not. Filtered through the Spathian Grandmaster, though, it sounded like one.

"In light of service and sacrifice given, Miss Fendall, and your extraordinary—"

Suddenly Masters and Adepts hurled Incentives at Jerinne at full force. Before she even fully realized what was happening, Jerinne reacted. Leaping to one side with her good leg, she brought up her crutch and spun it in front of her body. It was no quarterstaff, but it served to knock two of the Incentives away, while the other two flew past her, barely dodged by her jump.

"Well done, Miss Fendall," the Grandmaster said. "As I said, in light of service, sacrifice, and dedication, I think it's quite clear that you should continue your Initiacy into the third year."

"Sir?" Jerinne asked, still not believing what she was hearing.

The Grandmaster got to his feet, as did the other four at the table. They all gave her a crisp salute. "Initiate Jerinne Fendall, third-year!"

"Third-year!" the rest shouted. One Adept came over to Jerinne and added a new pip to her collar.

"Dismissed, Miss Fendall," the Grandmaster said.

Jerinne crutched her way back out, to find Price and Aldric, as well as several Initiates and Candidates, all huddled around.

"Hoorah!" Aldric grunted out. "Initiate Jerinne Fendall, third-year!"

Several people grabbed Jerinne in embraces, including Enther and Raila. Both of them also had their third-year pips.

"Trials have concluded!" Grandmaster Orren called from the table. "Be so kind as to take your gallivanting elsewhere."

"Does that mean lockdown is over, sir?" Aldric asked.

"Yes, indeed. Please, vacate the premises."

The crowd dispersed, and Jerinne hobbled her way along until she found himself with just Enther and Raila.

"We should celebrate properly," Enther said. "Something befitting people of our success and stature."

"You know," Jerinne said as they headed toward the lobby, "I think I know just the place."

Three days in confinement were maddening. Dayne bore it as best he could, attempting to meditate or work through as much of his calisthenics as he could within the confines of his quarters.

No one came, save the servants who brought meals on a regular basis. Trials for Initiates were going on. Candidates were being promoted to Adept. Eighteen of them, all around Druthal.

Dayne was at peace with the fact that he was not among those eighteen. He was troubled, though, by the number itself. Twenty-four new Adepts had been the tradition for as far back as Dayne had studied. Twenty-four, blessed by the king to go forth and protect Druthal.

Blessed by the king seemed more appropriate than cleared by a parliamentary committee. Though Dayne wondered if throughout history there had been Candidates like himself, who had gained the king's displeasure, and thus had not advanced. That sort of thing probably wasn't included in the records.

Six bells rang out from Saint Harcourt's Church, meaning supper should be arriving shortly. Dayne wondered how much longer it would continue, or even why. If the Grandmaster was going to cashier him from the Order, he might as well do it.

The knock came on his door, just as he expected, but it wasn't a servant with supper. Instead, it was Vien Reston. Dayne noticed right away the change on her collar: no longer an Initiate, she was now a first-year Candidate.

"Congratulations," Dayne said. "From what I've seen, it's well earned."

"Thank you," she said. "I've been sent to bring you to the Grandmaster."

"Of course," Dayne said. He let her lead the way to the Grandmaster's sanctum. As he approached the steps, Amaya was descending, her face stone and unreadable. There was no change on her collar, so her punishment did not involve being demoted from Adept. Such a thing was unthinkable, almost unprecedented. It would have been too harsh given whatever wrongs she had done. And what had she done? Encouraged Dayne to break orders? Was that enough to earn the Grandmaster's ire?

She gave no sign, no regard to Dayne as they passed. Not even a second glance.

"Amaya—"

She kept walking, and Vien took Dayne's arm and urged him up the steps.

344 Marshall Ryan Maresca

"Not now, Dayne," Vien said.

Amaya went down the hall, and turned out of view.

With another prod from Vien, Dayne entered the sanctum.

The Grandmaster was much as Dayne had found him when he first returned to Maradaine: looking at a book, dressed in simple tunic and trousers, with no shoes. As Dayne entered, the Grandmaster gave a slight nod and invited him to sit by his desk. Grandmaster Orren took his own seat.

"I wish to apologize for making you wait so long, Dayne," the Grandmaster said. "You understand that many things were occurring, and I needed to take time to contemplate. I recognized that originally I was going to make decisions based on anger. Those are decisions that we almost always regret."

"I agree, sir," Dayne said.

"So I considered my anger. You had defied me, but you had done it out of the belief that you had to act to save lives. You had, in essence, made the same choice of the Bridge that you gave during your Trials." The Grandmaster mused. "Many people give that answer, mind you, though few ever phrase it with the same vehemence."

He reached into his desk and pulled something out. "Fewer still demonstrate that it is more to them than a mere answer to an ethical query. That it is how they will truly live their lives as a Tarian."

The Grandmaster placed the object in his hand on the desk. A third-year Candidate pip.

"So I am to remain?" Dayne asked.

"You are," the Grandmaster said. "However, I have been troubled with what role you would fill as a third-year Candidate, or if you should serve your third year here in Maradaine. And then an answer was, quite literally, given to me from on high."

He tapped a paper on his desk, which Dayne noticed had a royal seal upon it.

"It would seem the events of the past few days have attracted a certain degree of attention in the Royal Palace. And all over the city, as you might well imagine."

"It did affect the highest level of government," Dayne said, trying his best to keep his voice from breaking. "I'm just happy to have been able to save lives."

The Grandmaster picked up the paper. "I'm certain. This, in fact, does not name you specifically, so you can relax. Rather, his Royal Highness notes that, and I quote, 'In light of certain truths, far too much agency had been given to my royal marshals without oversight,' while also speaking at length of 'remembering our grand legacy where Tarians and Spathians and numerous other Orders and Circles defended our nation out of loyalty and determination, and we should not let that slip away so lightly.'"

"The king is quite wise," Dayne said.

"Yes, well, liking us is good politics right now," the Grandmaster said. It was, perhaps, the most cynical thing he had ever heard the Grandmaster say. "Anyhow, by the royal authority of the throne, His Highness King Maradaine XVIII, an appointed post will be commissioned for a qualified individual to serve in a capacity of oversight and liaison between the members of Parliament, the marshals, and the Tarian and Spathian Orders. On the sage advice of certain members of Parliament, the king has given me the authority to name this individual. Those same members of Parliament have indicated who they would wish to fill the post."

"Me?"

"You've been paying attention, dear boy." He sighed. "However, I can think of few others who would serve the post as willingly and ably. I could not make you an Adept this year, and I most likely will not be able to next year either. But this I can give you. This commission could extend beyond your Candidacy. Do you understand what I'm telling you?"

"That even if I'm not to be a Tarian, I can still serve the Order."

"And that's what I want for you, my boy," the Grandmaster said.

Dayne contemplated this. Of course it was enticing. He ran the words over in his mind. Something sounded strange. "Certain truths?" he asked the Grandmaster.

"I believe his majesty is referring, however circuitously, to the traitorous acts of Chief Marshal Toscan. I understand you were aware of them." There was a bit of edge to the Grandmaster's voice.

"I haven't been given any opportunity to fully debrief you or anyone else regarding Chief Toscan," Dayne said. "I would not hide such a thing. I will gladly—"

"It's fine, Dayne. We know everything we need to know regarding Toscan, the Patriots, and the events in and beneath the Parliament."

"But how?"

The Grandmaster chuckled, and picked up the book he had been reading. "Truth, apparently, cannot be contained. At least, your friends seem to think so."

He tossed the book onto the desk. Dayne's own face stared back at him, under the title *Dayne, of the Tarian Order*. Credit to Hemmit Eyairin and Maresh Niol.

"Sir, I had no idea—"

"Of that I'm certain." He chuckled. "It's quite all right. I'm glad to have some full disclosure. This city has ... enough secrets." He nudged the third-year pip closer to Dayne. "You better take that."

Dayne didn't waste any time affixing it to his collar.

"Now, Dayne, I imagine you are quite famished. And you probably have some questions for your associates. Why don't you go find your way over to that place you like so much. What's it called? The Nimble Rabbit?"

"If those are my orders, sir."

Final Interlude

THE GRAND TEN were assembled once more: The Parliamentarian, The Man of the People, The Lord, The Lady, The Priest, The Duchess, The Soldier, The Justice, The Mage, and The Warrior. It had taken them several days to all again be in the opera house, under The Mage's protective weavings of light and sound. They again all wore their masks, all filling their roles. Everything was how it should be.

As if their plans hadn't almost gone completely wrong.

"Things didn't go completely wrong," Millerson said. Barton imagined his smug face beneath his Man of the People mask. Millerson had been far too self-satisfied with how the whole affair panned out.

Barton wanted to smack his colleague. "The only reason they didn't is because Toscan had the good sense to get murdered before he could reveal where his marching orders were coming from."

"Toscan was out of control, in his own way," Archduke Windall said from The Lord's seat. "Though that made him seem like the originator of the events. Even that stupid book said he was the 'chief' of these Patriots."

"I found that quite suiting," said the Duchess Leighton, wearing the mask that matched her title. "There is nothing quite as satisfying as seeing a small man hanged by his own overreach. Especially when his guilt obfuscates our own."

"That's a very mercenary approach," offered Major Altarn, the Mage of Druth Intelligence. "I'm quite proud of you."

"Well, we all have to do what we can," said The Duchess.

"And we all have." Feller Pin, The Justice.

"I don't recall much from you at all, sir," Colonel Neills, The Soldier said. He was right, of course, not that Neills had been particularly involved in the events himself. Well, that wasn't entirely true. He did help get the group to the Parliament that gave them a quorum. That had been quite critical, even if it had been in an emergency. Perhaps that was of even greater value to the cause: being able to take action when things went wrong.

"He was not needed," said Bishop Onell, in the position of The Priest. "Let us not forget why some of us are here: solely for our symbolic value. You need a Justice and a Priest, thus we are here."

"It isn't symbolic at all," Millerson said. "We all believe in the cause, we are committed to making it happen."

There was a scoff from The Warrior. "The symbolism is the main thing that matters to you."

Millerson turned to him. "And it doesn't to you? And if anyone here is not committed to our cause, it is you. But yet you are here."

The Warrior shifted in his seat. "I do question the

value of what we've done. Many lives were lost, and for what?"

"For what?" Barton asked. "Let's look what you've gained. A week ago your Tarian Order was a joke. The Parliament had pulled all of your authority, dictating who would be promoted, how many could be promoted. No one cared about them. Now, thanks to these events, once again the Tarians are respected, honored. You are being taken seriously again, Grandmaster."

"That was hardly the intention of the plan," Grandmaster Orren said.

"But thanks to your man Heldrin, things worked quite well for you," Barton said. "Well for all of us, so we should be grateful for his intervention. Thanks to him, no lives were lost in the Parliament that, frankly, didn't suit our needs."

"And more important," The Lady said, sitting coolly in her chair, "you were able to close the convocation of this Parliament without the Marriage Obligation Act being called to a vote. The result we wanted, without anyone we like in the Parliament losing political capital by voting against it. And without the act to compel him, our failed king will be content to wallow in his grief, heirless. Keeping the door open for the True Line to take the throne upon his death."

She then turned to The Priest. "And, yes, your role is symbolic, but the symbolism is crucial to the rightness of what we are doing. Just as the original Grand Ten protected the Druth throne in the eleventh century, we do the same today. Just as loyal servants of Druthal always have."

"You are the history expert, my lady," Grandmaster Orren said coldly.

"I am, indeed, Warrior," she said. Lady Mirianne Henson was renowned for her passion for Druth history. That was why she had worked so hard to open the museum. "As I tried to remind our dear friend, there have always been those who shield this nation from the fools and madmen who find themselves on the throne. Even if Dayne didn't understand at the time, he will see soon enough. We are all loyal sons and daughters of Druthal."

Epilogue

THE NIMBLE RABBIT was busier than Dayne had ever seen it, with every table in the garden filled with customers, and even more standing around with wine in hand, talking and laughing. Two singers with fiddle and guitar were a focus of attention at one end of the garden, and at the other end there was the table Dayne was looking for.

It turned out to be more populated with recognizable faces than he expected.

Hemmit and Maresh were there, as was Lin. She was in good spirits, despite the thin scar across her forehead. She was even wearing her blouse half unlaced, proudly displaying her Circle tattoo. Today she was letting everyone there know she was a mage. Among the other members of Hemmit's larger entourage were very familiar faces: Jerinne and a few other second-year Initiates. Dayne corrected himself: all three were third-year.

"Finally, the man arrives!" Hemmit shouted when he

looked up and saw Dayne. He leaped up from the table and took Dayne in a great embrace.

"Hemmit —" Dayne started, but allowed the moment of jubilation.

"You have three pips," Jerinne said from her seat.

"As do you," Dayne returned. A glass of wine was suddenly in his hand, and one of Jerinne's friends was on the table. A shrill whistle — louder than a human being could possibly make, which made Dayne suspect Lin was involved — quieted the establishment.

"Ladies and gentlemen," the Initiate said, raising her glass. "The hero of the Parliament and the Tarian Order, Candidate Dayne Heldrin, third-year!"

"Hoorah, third-year!" Jerinne and her friend responded.

"Hoorah, third-year!" the entire crowd mimicked.

All wineglasses went up, all drank.

"I'm pretty sure that was out of protocol," Dayne said, taking a seat between Jerinne and Maresh.

"My apologies," the Initiate said, offering her hand. "Raila Gendon."

"And this is Enther," Jerinne introduced the other.

"I wasn't expecting ... this," Dayne said. "Really I came because —"

"Because you are owed apologies," Hemmit said. "Mostly by me."

"I'm not owed anything." Dayne took the book out of his pocket, "But I do have some ... concerns."

"I thought you might." Hemmit snapped to the server to come over.

"It's a very good likeness," Lin offered.

"I know what your concerns are, Dayne. You wanted to be out of the news. But that wasn't possible. You have to understand that."

"But to go this far?" Dayne asked. He remembered all too well the initial laudations from the Lacanja press, reversed when Master Denbar was killed.

"This was how far it had to go, my friend. The newssheets were about to paint you in the same colors as Tharek and the Patriots. I could smell it in the air. So we had to get the truth out there. Big and hard. The truth about you. About Tharek, Chief Toscan, and Lannic. All of it."

"It was the best choice," Maresh said. "And it was the truth."

Dayne sipped at his wine. Perhaps they were right. He couldn't avoid infamy, not with what he had done.

"You protected us, fought for us," Hemmit said. "Being your shield was the least we could do."

"Isn't that our way?" Jerinne asked.

Dayne looked to Jerinne, sitting with one crutch resting next to her, a good-humored smile hiding the guilt in her eyes. "It is, indeed. How's your leg?"

"They tell me it'll heal," Jerinne said. "I'll walk, even run."

"And hold and stand?" Dayne asked.

"With shield on arm."

"Good," Dayne said. "I'd be proud to have you by my side."

A server came and put a plate of lamb and crisp in front of Dayne. He hadn't even ordered it.

"Compliments of the chef," the server said.

"Could you get used to that?" Jerinne asked him.

"I better not," Dayne said. "We don't do what we do for the adulation."

"But it's nice," Jerinne said.

"The man dines with noble ladies," Enther said. "A free meal here is hardly spectacular."

Dayne turned to Hemmit, holding up the book again. "I haven't read this yet. You ... you didn't include Lady Mirianne in here at all, did you?"

"I included the truth, Dayne. I wrote what mattered. And if you ask me, the private matters between the two of you only matter to the two of you."

"Thank you," Dayne said. He had no idea what was

going to happen between him and Lady Mirianne, in the next few days or over the following year, but he didn't need the gossip and newssheets putting further pressure on it.

"No, thank you, Dayne," Hemmit said. He raised his glass to Dayne, and the rest of the table did as well. "To Dayne, of the Tarian Order."

Dayne raised his own glass once more and accepted the toast.

No matter what the future brought, this moment was all the acknowledgment he needed.

Jacey Bedford
The Rowankind Series

"A finely crafted and well-researched plunge into swashbuckling, sorcery, shape-shifting, and the Fae!"
—Elizabeth Ann Scarborough,
author of *The Healer's War*

"Bedford crafts emotionally complex relationships and interesting secondary characters while carefully building an innovative yet familiar world."
—*RT Reviews*

"Swashbuckling adventure collides with mystical mayhem on land and at sea in this rousing historical fantasy series...set in a magic-infused England in 1800." —*Publishers Weekly*

Winterwood
978-0-7564-1015-5

Silverwolf
978-0-7564-1191-6

To Order Call: 1-800-788-6262
www.dawbooks.com

Kari Sperring

Living with Ghosts

978-0-7564-0675-2

Finalist for the Crawford Award for First Novel

A Tiptree Award Honor Book

Locus Recommended First Novel

"This is an enthralling fantasy that contains horror elements interwoven into the story line. This reviewer predicts Kari Sperring will have quite a future as a renowned fantasist."
—*Midwest Book Review*

"A satisfying blend of well-developed characters and intriguing worldbuilding. The richly realized Renaissance style city is a perfect backdrop for the blend of ghostly magic and intrigue. The characters are wonderfully flawed, complex and multi-dimensional. Highly recommended!"
—*Patricia Bray, author of The Sword of Change Trilogy*

And now available:

The Grass King's Concubine

978-0-7564-0755-1

To Order Call: 1-800-788-6262
www.dawbooks.com

DAW 206

Patrick Rothfuss

THE NAME OF THE WIND
The Kingkiller Chronicle: Day One

"It is a rare and great pleasure to come on somebody writing not only with the kind of accuracy of language that seems to me absolutely essential to fantasy-making, but with real music in the words as well.... Oh, joy!"
—Ursula K. Le Guin

"Patrick Rothfuss has real talent, and his tale of Kvothe is deep and intricate and wondrous." —Terry Brooks

"One of the best stories told in any medium in a decade. Shelve it beside *The Lord of the Rings*...and look forward to the day when it's mentioned in the same breath, perhaps as first among equals."
—The Onion AV Club

"[Rothfuss is] the great new fantasy writer we've been waiting for, and this is an astonishing book."
—Orson Scott Card

ISBN: 978-0-7564-0474-1

To Order Call: 1-800-788-6262
www.dawbooks.com

DAW 111